THE STONE WAR

A TOM DOHERTY ASSOCIATES BOOK
NEW YORK

MADELEINE E. ROBINS

THE STONE WAR

THE STONE WAR

Copyright © 1999 by Madeleine E. Robins

Edited by Patrick Nielsen Hayden

A Tor Book
Published by Tom Doherty Associates, LLC
175 Fifth Avenue
New York, NY 10010

www.tor.com

Tor® is a registered trademark of Tom Doherty Associates, LLC

Designed by Lisa Pifher

Library of Congress Cataloging-in-Publication Data

Robins, Madeleine,
    The stone war / Madeleine E. Robins.—1st ed.
      p. cm.
    "A Tom Doherty Associates book."
    ISBN 0-312-85486-2 (alk. paper)
    I. Title.
  PS3568.O2774S75   1999
  813'.54—dc21   99-26075
                               CIP

First Edition: August 1999

Printed in the United States of America

0 9 8 7 6 5 4 3 2 1

For Juliana and Rebecca,
my very own citykids

PART ONE

1

THE air was soft and warm; a light breeze belled out at the corners of the block and whisked bits of paper, dust, and cellophane from the trash cans. Down the block, framed against the late dazzle of the sunset, Stevie Prokop was waving to him: *Come on, come on.* Whatever the game was was less important than the getting there, being part of it. For a moment John just stood, poised to run, feeling the June warmth, the breeze, the sights and smells and sounds of the block run through him like fuel. Every building on the street—the low, dignified brownstones, the blockish granite apartment buildings, even the dark stone church on the corner—was familiar and loved. Each doorway was filled with possibilities. He felt like he was perched on a special moment.

"Johnny, hey, John!" Stevie called again.

John waved back, grinning. Another minute and he'd run after, join whatever the game was. Another minute. He breathed in deeply, feeling the air stir the inside of his nose and fill his lungs. It tasted of a thousand things: the dank, swampy smell of steam vents; the warm smell of sun on the black locust tree in front of his house; the perfume of the woman who'd just walked past; sun on brick and sun on asphalt; the river smell of the Hudson, and rain not far off. The air tasted like everything, forever.

He was ten years old, and he didn't have the words to describe it. But for a moment, he knew, "It will always be just like this, and I will live forever, just like this."

Down this street a woman laughed; a horn blared on Sixth Avenue; heels clattered in jazz syncopation; and kids were yelling to each other. The coiled spring loosed. John launched off up the street toward Seventh Avenue, where Stevie was waiting for him.

•   •   •

Tietjen woke slowly and easily from the dream, enjoying the wakening, savoring the lingering sense of joy and lightness that seemed to infuse his muscles. Eyes closed, he concentrated on the feeling of the sheet against his skin, the way his head sank into his old down pillow. What had he been dreaming? Something about being a kid again, on the street he'd grown up on.

Four floors down someone on the street was praying. The wail of Arabic was one voice, joined by another, then a third. He lived on an open block, and two Muslim families had settled, one in a garden across the street, another in the doorway of a house three doors down from his. Tietjen had found them to be friendly enough, although he'd overheard hard words between them and members of the synagogue half a dozen doors down. For a few minutes he listened to the devotions with his eyes closed, trying to sink back into the dream. Useless. He would not get back to sleep that morning. Anyway, it was Saturday, the day he had the kids.

The sun between the blinds made sparkling strips on the bed and wall, patterned by the shifting shadows of leaves from the tree outside his window. When he drew the blinds the light dazzled him for a moment. Scents from someone's cooking on the street filtered up, making him feel pleasantly hungry. He went off to shower and shave, thinking of breakfast.

The water was cold again. He persuaded himself this was a blessing on a day that promised to be hot, and stepped into the tub to shower. It was an old cast-iron tub with claws for feet, and when he had first moved into the apartment he'd let his sons paint the claws, red and blue with gold trim and generous splashes of paint on the molding and linoleum. By the time he finished his shower the water was almost warm enough to shave in. As he shaved he made plans, improbable and impossible plans for the day ahead, plans made for the city he had grown up in, not the New York Chris and Davy lived in now.

Tietjen combed his wet hair back from his face; the water made it look dark, almost black. For a moment he hardly recognized himself, looking for the ten-year-old from his dream. They shared the light brown eyes and the same lanky body. What they didn't share,

Tietjen thought ruefully, was faith that everyone loved to poke around the city the way he did. His sons didn't, certainly.

Okay. What then? As he dressed he made other plans, *real* plans. Which meant plans Irene couldn't disapprove of; he resisted the thought that anything he wanted to do, she would disapprove of.

He made coffee and pried a couple of pastries out of their sticky bag. While he ate he pulled the day's *Times* up on the screen and tabbed briskly through the headlines before he saved the whole thing to be looked over more carefully later. He had almost sixteen gigabytes of unread *Times*es saved, all collected in the hope that tomorrow he'd have time to do more than scan. He'd keep saving *Times* files until his creaky old drive was glutted with them, then delete them all, mostly unread, in an irritable passion. It was nearly time to purge the *Times,* he thought. Then he remembered that there was an event that had caught his eye, something in the *Times*'s MetroList that he'd thought might make a suitable Father's Day Out activity. Some time in the last three or four days, he thought, and called up the MetroList. It was in Wednesday's edition: a Transit Authority exhibition and film about the history of the subways, a fund-raiser of some sort. Maybe the boys would like that; he'd have liked it at their age. Bad housekeeping is rewarded, he thought, and smiled.

There was no need to tidy up the apartment; Irene almost never let the boys come over to the West Side, which she thought was less secure than their block in the East Nineties. Tietjen was used to the status quo and rarely fought against it. He jotted down the information about the TA program and jammed it into a pocket, grabbed a windbreaker, and was almost out the door when he remembered, and turned back to grab the two remaining pastries, pour hot coffee in a paper cup, and take a juicebox from the refrigerator. Down three flights of stairs, not at a run but a gravity-induced canter, and out of the building. Maia, who slept in the six-foot-square basement garden in the front of his building, was awake, sitting by one of the trash cans and combing out her sparse hair with a broken comb.

"Morning, John." Her voice was melodious. Maia was tall and rail thin; her hair was short and tight-curling gray; her face was ageless, so dark the brown was almost purplish; her smile was beautiful.

"Maia. Brought you breakfast." He offered the pastries, coffee, and juicebox. She smiled as she took them.

"Thanks, honey. Next one's my treat." She said it every morning. "Where you off to today?"

"My Saturday with the boys."

Maia's smile broadened. She rubbed absently at her cheek with one of the two remaining fingers on her left hand. She'd never told him how she lost them; there was something in her past she called My Accident, from which the amputation, and her homelessness, apparently dated. "What you going to do with those lambs?" she asked now.

"I'm going to try to take them to Brooklyn." Tietjen shrugged as if it didn't matter if they got there or not.

"Brooklyn's got itself some bad neighborhoods, John. You take care of those little lambs. And thanks for breakfast."

His apartment was halfway down on a shady open block. East, toward Columbus, there was a white-brick public school, guarded even on weekends, lest the street families try to stake a claim to part of the heavily fenced yard. In the other direction, a synagogue, a funeral home, neat brownstones and small apartment buildings, and living trees guarded and tended by some of the street families. Even with the shade of the trees, sunlight danced in patches on the pavement. He nodded at a couple of the resident street people he knew, stopped to answer a question; somehow, without meaning to, he had become the block's liaison between the housed residents and the people who homesteaded on their stoops and in their gardens. At the end of the block the guards at the schoolyard glared at him blankly, as if they hadn't seen him walk past the yard every day for almost four years. He turned the corner onto Columbus, heading for the Seventy-ninth Street crosstown bus.

The bus stop guard nodded curtly and raised an eyebrow, as though smiling would lessen his scarecrow effectiveness. As far as Tietjen could see, the sum of the guard's effectiveness was in the semiautomatic that hung loosely from his shoulder. Smiling wouldn't have hurt. Five or six other people were crowded inside the bus shelter, although the day was clear. Safety by association, Tietjen thought, and made a point of waiting outside the shelter.

•   •   •

The bus took him across Central Park and at Third he got off to walk uptown. In this part of town only the avenues and the big crosstown arteries—Seventy-ninth, Eighty-sixth, Ninety-sixth— were ungated. At each corner guards stood waiting to ID residents and visitors and ward away undesirables. *What does that make me?* Tietjen wondered. Three times as he went he was stopped and carded by blockcops. Each time he waited as they checked his ID, matched his fingerprints; stood and watched their faces, ruddy and young above the high stock collars of their uniforms. These uniforms were a reflective metallic gray, the color of storm skies over Manhattan, a color he had always thought was a reflection of Manhattan's body heat. On the guards, the color was cold and stern. There were too many uniforms in this city, Tietjen thought; it was hard to keep up when every private security force had its own insignia and dress code. Subway guards wore dull gray serge over full body armor. *That must be hot as hell on a June day,* Tietjen thought.

Irene lived in one of a nest of brick towers that reached upward, away from a brick plaza from which the homeless were endlessly swept away. In Irene's building the security men recognized him at once and made only a cursory scan of his ID. Riding up to the fourteenth floor in the tiny elevator, Tietjen felt a familiar itch, the urge to run. He'd hated this building when he lived here. He hated that his sons were being raised here now, in four square anonymous rooms in this ugly brick tower clustered with the other towers in the development, pulling away from the people and buildings that surrounded them. Architect-speak, Irene called that. She was probably right.

The elevator slowed, wobbled, and stopped. Before he rang the bell to Irene's apartment, Tietjen took one minute at the hall window, staring out at the mosaic of streets below. A little serenity returned. He pressed the bell.

"Who is it?"

"Come on, Reen. They called you from downstairs. It's John." He heard the rusty click of the peepscreen before she began to turn the bristle of locks on her door. When the door finally opened Irene stood there urging him into her apartment as if she were afraid that he had been followed.

"Hello," she said suspiciously. They filed down the narrow hallway to the living room, past the closed door of the boys' room. Irene sat on the edge of a chair, one trousered leg tucked under her, and looked at him with her odd, flat mixture of curiosity, apprehension, and hostility. "The boys are getting their shoes on," she said. "What are you going to do with them today?"

He relaxed against the wall. "I thought I'd wait to see what they were thinking," he hedged, suspecting Irene would not like what he was planning. "I wish you didn't make it sound like I was going to boil them for soup," he added.

"I never know *what*—" Irene began. Then Davy bounced into the room and wrapped his arms around his father's leg. Chris followed a moment after, two years older and trying for a little dignity; he hung back and waved a cool hand at his father. "Hey."

"Hey." Tietjen swung Davy up for a hug, and his younger son wriggled like a puppy. Tietjen wished that Chris had not already reached the age where he was embarrassed to hug his father. "So, shall we go?"

Irene followed them to the door, her expression uneasy. She vented her apprehension in small touches, tugging gently at Chris's collar, briskly reminding Tietjen not to let Davy get overtired. "He had a cold last week." Then she let them out. Behind them Tietjen heard the locks snapping into place, one after another. "Shall we go?" he asked again, and let Chris press the elevator button.

Chris and Davy grew in the city untouched by it. On his days with them Tietjen tried to give them a little piece of it. Today the boys pranced around him in the lobby of Irene's building, full of stories, full of suggestions, ultimately wary of another of their father's weird ideas. They didn't like the Transit exhibit idea.

"*Slipskating,*" Chris demanded.

"I'll tell you," Tietjen countered, man to men. "We try my idea and if you don't like it, we'll go slipskating. We've got time for both. Okay? Davy, okay?" They went through almost the same routine every Saturday. Tietjen knew his role, the boys theirs.

"Okay."

He took them west to catch a downtown Fifth Avenue bus, nodding at the armed bus guard (gray serge, body armor, patent leather hat pulled low over his eyes), smiling at the bus driver. The boys chattered one over the other about school, friends, games, uninterested in the changing ribbon of street, building and person that rippled in the windows. Tietjen watched, listening and answering as best he could. As they passed Sixty-fifth Street he said, not meaning it seriously, of course, "I wonder how the old Zoo is doing?"

Chris broke off his story. "In *Central Park?* Mommy'd never let us." He spoke too fast, and his tone was too old, the sound of someone forestalling disaster.

Tietjen hadn't meant to propose it seriously: you couldn't take a seven- and a five-year-old kid into Central Park. But the exasperated refusal in his son's voice hardened Tietjen's sentimental curiosity. All he wanted was for the boys *not* to dismiss the idea out of hand. "It's just a park, Chris. People used to play ball there and bike and sail— well, when I was a kid they still sailed miniature boats in the ponds. They used to do all those things. Davy, you remember *Stuart Little,* don't you?" They had read it together in the fall. "The boat race happened in Central Park."

"You said it was just a story," Davy said. He tucked in his chin and watched his father cautiously.

He couldn't stop. "Did you know there's a bronze statue of a sled dog in the park? And one of Alice and everyone in Wonderland, and—from the inside of the Park you can hardly see the tops of the buildings, you can pretend you're somewhere—" Confronted by two small, unblinking faces, "Look," he wanted to say. "I love this place. I give it to you."

"My teacher says Central Park should have been torn up for subsidy housing a long time ago," Chris said.

"Your teacher—" Tietjen began.

"Mamma said we shoun't ever go in here. Mamma says people get killed here. All the time. With *knives.*" Davy's eyes widened at the thought of knives. "I want to go slipskating."

The knot of failure in Tietjen's gut tightened. "What about Brooklyn," he said. "I thought we had a deal."

"I don' wanna, Daddy. People in Brooklyn got knives, too."

What was he going to do, argue with a five-year-old about who in Brooklyn did or didn't carry a knife, an automatic, a shotgun? "You too, Chris?"

Chris took refuge in superiority. "Really, Dad. I don't wanna go look at some old trains." He sounded like Irene.

"Okay." Tietjen swallowed and sat back. "Okay. Slipskating. We can stay on this bus to Thirty-fourth Street." He settled into his seat, looking out the window again. What if I dragged them to the exhibit or into the Park? he thought. It wouldn't make them love it.

By the time the bus reached Thirty-fourth Street he had forgotten the idea and was listening to his sons with gentle, conquered affection.

They went slipskating, ate lunch, saw a movie. The boys enjoyed themselves, and Tietjen enjoyed their pleasure. Still, he felt distant and unsatisfied. He had never learned the knack of compromise between what he wanted and they wanted. He loved everything about his sons, loved watching them unfold a little bit each week, a new layer of baby peeling back to reveal the sturdy enthusiasm and sweetness of boy; loved the peachy glow of their skin in the sunlight, the flinty blue of Davy's eyes, and Chris's gap-toothed smile. He looked at them and loved them, and couldn't say no or force the issue of teaching them what he loved about New York. Each Saturday Tietjen wound up feeling a little cowardly, afraid to see dimming light in his boys' eyes.

They were back at Irene's by 5:30, the brassy light of afternoon lighting the upper stories of the red brick towers. As usual when he brought the boys back, Irene invited him in for coffee, and as usual he accepted, wondering if this would be the night when they broke the pattern and he left before a fight started. In the kitchen Tietjen and Irene chatted idly, about the boys mostly. School, friends, dentist appointments, affectionate minutiae. Where he had taken the boys that afternoon. Just as he thought he had handled the question, Davy padded into the room. Tietjen watched as Irene slowly twined her hand through Davy's thick dark hair, reached down a glass for him, and let the boy pour his own juice. Davy's face was a study in concentration; Irene's above him was soft, gentle.

"Daddy was going to take us to the Park, too," Davy said when he had successfully filled the glass. "Can I get some for Chris?"

Irene, reaching for another glass, fixed Tietjen with a familiar look. She waited until Davy had both glasses carefully balanced in his hands and had made a cautious way back down the hall again. Then she summoned a smile strung tight as wire.

"*Central* Park? Jesus, John, you would *not* take my sons—not even *you* would take them in there. Especially not since the City withdrew the police from inside the walls."

"I've never had any trouble there." Never mind that he hadn't walked through Central Park in years; never mind that he'd never seriously thought of taking the boys there. "Irene, we didn't—"

"You have no right to put my sons at risk—"

"I didn't! Jesus Christ, Reen, I love them too! They're my sons too! Why the hell would I put them at risk for anything? What I did was say 'Hey, look, that's Central Park—' "

"Trying to get them to—"

"Trying to get them to do nothing. I *can't* get them to do anything, Reen. If I had suggested the Park, you've got them so conditioned they'd close down immediately."

She smiled. "Good. They listen."

"They *listen?* They've bought into your terror—it's no way to live."

"There is nothing wrong with the way we live. It's you. I'm the one who'll have to tell the boys you were killed on one of your damned walks. You don't think there's any danger, but people are killed all the time all over this goddamned city."

There was no point pretending that battle had not been joined. Tietjen felt sorry and defensive. Deeply, wearily familiar anger grew in him.

"Irene, you have no idea where I go—"

"Does it matter? One night you'll be killed somewhere. God, John, will you wake up? Out there—" She gestured with a fist toward the shrouded window. "People are living in a state of war."

"That's just what you read," he threw back. "You hide up here in this place and everything you know, you learn from the tabloids. You have no idea about the people you share this city with." He was at the edge of the pit again, about to fall in again, the same way he always did. Tietjen made himself stop for a moment, breathing as if he had been running, reaching for logic and reason and words that would explain.

The right words didn't come. Instead, "Irene, take a walk with me." Let the city explain it to her. Maybe this time it would work.

Their eyes met and held. There was a long moment of intensity, and the air seemed to shimmer between them. Then Irene shook her head. "You're out of your mind."

Tietjen was reluctant to let the moment go. "Really. Take a walk with *me.* I mean, really outside, away from the bus shelters and the cab stands. I can show you—"

Irene pulled away from his outstretched hand, jarring her coffee cup, and busied herself nervously mopping up spilled coffee. "Come on, John, I don't want to—"

"A short walk. You won't be gone more than an hour. You used to ask me where I went when I walked; I'll show you. You used to think my walks were romantic."

Irene shook her head, disowning the memory. "I can't leave the boys."

"Call a sitter," Tietjen said persuasively. "Let them go to the playroom—the attendant should still be on duty. Tell the guards downstairs you have to go out for a few minutes. What are you afraid of? The city can't reach in and grab them."

That was the wrong thing to say; he knew it as the words left his mouth. The denial that might have been the beginning of acquiescence changed to a hard, flat no in her eyes. Furious at himself, nothing left to gain, still he went on. "Reen, there are two men in your lobby who monitor security cameras all over this building twenty-four hours a day. There are six locks on your door. There's a brace of guards by the door downstairs itching for the chance to use the guns they're carrying. You and Chris and Davy could live out your lives in this goddamned fortress and never know there was a world out there, with people in it—"

"I don't *need* to know." She stood up. "I don't *want* to know about them. I know enough: there are people out there waiting to kill you if you give them a chance. That fucking world out there is killing people all the time. Out there—if you weren't here, if I could afford to, I'd take the boys and get so far away from New York—" She waved her hands disgustedly. "You keep your damned city; one of these days it'll catch up to you."

"I'd like my sons to know something more about New York than armed schoolbuses and security patrols." The coffee in his cup was stone cold.

"*I'd* like my sons to live long enough to make a choice about it," she countered. "I think maybe you'd better go, John." She turned her head to call down the hall: "Boys! Your father is leaving."

Tietjen went past her into the living room to wait for his sons. Davy came first, running as usual; Tietjen caught him and swung him in a circle that put the lamps and table at risk. Davy gave him a quick, sloppy kiss. "I had a real good time, Daddy. I love you."

Chris waited in the doorway until Davy was done, then ambled over, unconcerned, and unbent enough to give his father a shy kiss and a back-slapping hug.

"Love you guys. I'll talk to you tomorrow, okay?"

Finally, aware that Irene was waiting with broadly repressed impatience, Tietjen stood and followed her and waited as she unlocked the locks. "Good night, Reen."

She said nothing. The door closed behind him and as he walked down the hall he could hear the bolts slipping into place.

Tietjen left Irene's building without plan and began walking south, downtown, walking off his anger, walking into connection. The light was full of fading reflections, sunlight slanting orange through trees on Park Avenue; the air was warm and reedy with voices. He walked with his head up, recording buildings and people, feeling the anger and tension ease out of him as the first mile and then the second went by. Park Avenue—the square, residential blocks of unsurprising granite gave way to glass-faced corporate towers in the Fifties, and then the startling gilded pleasure of Grand Central below that. Tietjen walked through blockcops and peddlers, across to Fifth Avenue and past the offices and stores of Midtown, gradually toward Greenwich Village. He had grown up here before the tidy residential streets in the Village were sealed off by ornate iron fences and gates; now he did not try to chat with the guards who stood at parade rest behind them cradling rifles in their arms, or crane to admire the old brownstones. Instead, he skirted Washington Square, threading through the bazaars on MacDougal and across Houston, through SoHo and into Little Italy. Here the streets were the way he remembered them from his childhood: small buildings, people walking and talking freely, only an occasional policeman or brace of blockcops wandering through the crowds. Families together, mothers leaning out of windows into the soft, heavy June air to call their children in; a cluster of old men playing checkers and arguing sanguinely; kids no older than Chris teaching each other street moves: daring each other into tough poses, eyes lidded, high nervous giggling.

Tietjen walked among them, comfortably unnoticed, observing. A smell of cooking made him veer down a side street seeking the source. He found a street fair, hardly a block long; a few crafts booths, some rickety games, a sausage seller, a banner announcing the whole effort to be on the behalf of Our Lady of something or other. He bought two delicious greasy sausages from a wizened woman who wore an apron stippled with grease and charcoal, and they stood watching children playing tag between the legs of the passersby. He thought of Chris and Davy, wondering what they would make of the fair.

"S'okay, huh? S'good?" the woman beside him prompted. "The sausage. You want another?"

Tietjen licked the grease from his hand. "No more, but yes, it's very good."

"Another hour, pfff!" She made a sweeping motion with one hand. "Gonna be all gone. A week I'm making them, and in a hour they gone. You got to put the right spices in, see. You got to grind it all very fine." Tietjen listened, captivated, while the old woman described the process in exotic detail, her face lit from below by the flame from the grill she tended. The seasoning, the grinding, stuffing the skins—"the right thinness, you got to get—" He loved this about walking in the city: it seemed he could talk with anyone, with strangers, get past all strangeness and fear.

"Don't you worry, being out after dark out here?" he asked her, thinking of Irene.

"Here? In this crowd? It's my home, I live here sixty-seven years. Besides." She pulled her apron slightly askew, revealing the handle of a small pistol in her skirt waistband. The sight diminished Tietjen's pleasure in the conversation; he felt saddened, diminished by the sight of it. The old woman smiled at him, smoothed her apron down and turned to serve another customer. He stood a while longer beside her, watching the children, trying to recapture the comfortable companionship the sight of the gun had interrupted. At last Tietjen turned back to the woman and they exchanged good-nights. He started walking south again, toward the dark and quiet of the financial district. He would be walking late tonight, he thought, and he was suddenly eager for the windy echoes to be found farther downtown.

●   ●   ●

Broadway was empty, an echoing fault in the face of the city. Tietjen walked from streetlamp to streetlamp, skirting the steel-grilled plazas and peddler's sheds that surrounded the buildings, savoring the feel of soft air, the taste of salt, the way sounds traveled here. He liked the lightless faces of buildings, their evidence of busy occupation uncluttered by its substance. To the west the old World Trade Center rose out of a granite and steel surround, ugly and graceless and compelling. There were security grilles around all but the municipal buildings, where armed city cops swept through periodically to oust the sleeping homeless. The grilles, some of them quite beautiful, made Tietjen think of the buildings and courtyards they encompassed as walled cities, medieval keeps. There was comfort in the huge buildings that loomed over the streets, glass towers and gilded domes, caryatids staring down into atria. Alone in the middle of the street he felt a kinship with the thousands who walked there by day: bankers, messengers, court clerks and lawyers, peddlers and street people. Tietjen found himself smiling at the air and the buildings.

From time to time an armored police car cruised by, slowed to survey him, passed on. Weekends or at night, blockcops rarely stopped anyone passing the grilled buildings; people working late took their chances or hired guards. The street people who lived this far downtown kept to clannish packs, avoiding each other and the daytime workers. After dark a solitary walker like Tietjen was an anomaly; anomalies were best left untested.

He walked on, heading toward Battery Park. Turning a corner suddenly, he startled a covey of old men huddled together in the shelter of a news kiosk, passing a bottle around. The men drew back, muttered resentfully, powerless to do more than glower at the intruder. Tietjen backed off apologetically.

As he turned east, then south again, he considered making the trip to Staten Island. Years before, when he started his night walks, he would have taken the ferry across and back, reveling in the breeze and motion, the make-believe sea voyage. The old ferries had been retired for ten years, replaced by newer high-speed ferries, computerized, with plastic seats and air-conditioning and glass windows that kept the salt air out. No resonance, no history.

"Mister?" The voice was ripe as a broken grape. It was one of the men from the kiosk. Tietjen looked up, nodded. "Change, mister? You got a couple bucks?"

Tietjen nodded again and reached into his pocket. The drunk reeled closer, carrying a miasma with him, engulfing Tietjen.

"Thanks." The man took two dollar pieces. "You know you shu'nt go scaren people like you done."

"I'm sorry. I didn't mean to."

The old drunk insisted belligerently, his face shining red in the lamplight. "People get killt 'roun here. No'by ever tol' you that?"

Tietjen thought of Irene. "Yeah, they've told me."

The drunk stared a moment at Tietjen, sizing him up, trying blearily to read him: armed, not armed, carrying money? Who walked alone, strolling at this hour? "Fuggit, you fuggin' crazy." The drunk shook his head, shuffling back toward the darkness again. "We do' wan' no crazies 'n our neighborhood," he called back.

Tietjen watched him go, feeling almost affectionate toward the old man. Then he continued on southward to the Customs House just above Battery Park. Tietjen stopped a moment; firelight from the B-Park shacktown nearby cast flickering shadows on the elaborate Beaux Art detailing—paired columns, allegorical friezes, and four marvelous statues at the street level, draped with glittering security grating. At the base of the statues a few dark shapes were settled in for the night, unmoving, but beyond, in Battery Park, the shacktown moved, settled and resettled in the darkness, fires flickering, voices sounding loudly then dropping off. B-Park was one of the worst shacktowns: the most murders, the most drugs. B-Park was what Central Park had been, a decade ago, and now it was a mystery he knew better than to explore. Instead, he began to trace the winding, archaic streets that were all that was left of New Amsterdam's cow paths. A little after midnight he turned north and west again.

The air by the Hudson was cool, as fresh as it got anywhere in New York in June. Tietjen walked slowly, marking the sound of his own footfall, watching on his right for the small details of occupancy that occurred from time to time in the buildings near the water. To his left was the river, and the nest of parks and plush event spaces that had taken over the Lower West Side piers in fifteen years.

Lit by light reflected from the Jersey shore, most of the piers were ostentatiously off-limits to all but the wealthy, surrounded by grilles,
velvet ropes, and blank-faced security. Limousines glided up and
rolled away; the hush of money just made the grimness of the ware-
houses and factories across the street more profound.

A rustle, a padding noise warned him of another presence behind him on the dock. "Ey, man." Lilting menace, gang lowspeak:
the consonants softened to mush.

"Hey," Tietjen returned. He did not turn around. It was not the
first time he had been noticed or stopped by the docks. He made
himself still despite the silver whisper of metal and leather behind
him.

"What you doin' here, so late? Y'a cop? You some kinda Uptown?"

"Just walking."

A buzz of murmuring behind him, then a kid in piecemeal
leathers, his face obscured by one of the old leather "samurai" helmets favored by some street gangs, slipped up beside him, indicating
that Tietjen was to walk with him.

"Seed you here before, man. Whyfor you come walkin here?"

Tietjen smiled and spread his hands, but carefully, gently. "I like
it. It's good here, you know?"

The kid looked at him curiously, Asian eyes set in a Chicano
face, glittering in the Jersey light. "*You* know?" he echoed. There
was another whisper from behind them, a prodding. "Man, you got
any money?"

Tietjen nodded, tasting acid. "A little. You want it?"

The kid watched him, the whispering stopped. "Fuck *me*," the
kid said, and turned to grin at his followers. "Do *we* want *your*
money? Gotta pay the toll, man. Give here."

Tietjen reached slowly into his pocket for the mugger's roll he
kept on him—enough money to make the kids feel they'd made a
score, not enough to make them wonder why the hell he was there
in the first place and roll him for his watch, cards, everything else.

The kid counted the money. "Okay," he said at last, deliberately,
so that the rustling soldiers in the shadows could hear him. "You
crazy motherfucker, man, you know? No Uptown come walkin'
here, this Dogs' turf. What the fuck you doin'?" Before Tietjen could

answer, the kid answered himself. "You *like* it here, right?" His tone was heavily satirical, touched with just a breath of understanding and faith.

Tietjen nodded.

"Alri', we make you the—what the word? The mascot. You bug-fuck enough to come down here again, the Dogs know. Anyone fuck with you, we know. We take care'a you. Dog's blood, man." He held his right palm up to show a sloppily drawn star of scar tissue, looked over his shoulder and nodded to his soldiers. Then he smiled again. "Jus remember: bring the toll, man." There was a silver whisper behind them as the knife was sheathed.

Tietjen mouthed his thanks, uncertain what to say. He and the Dogs' leader walked in silence for a while, looking out at the gravelly moonlit plain of the Hudson. Tietjen missed the moment when the kid slipped back into the shadows again, but gradually became aware that he was watching the changing light on the river alone.

Looking around him as casually as he could, Tietjen called himself every stupid name he could think of. He'd got off again, still alive again. The lights of the Jersey shore glittered, their reflection in the Hudson glittered. Off the hook again. "Jesus," he breathed. At the same time, knowing better, "But I did it." He always came through, his luck was uncanny and always had been. In all his waking years he had never taken worse than a beating, never lost more than a hundred dollars.

"Expensive fucking hobby," he told the night air at last. Jersey glittered without response. He looked at the watch the gang had let him keep: going on for two A.M., and he was on West Street above Christopher. For the first time all night his feet hurt. Time to head for home. He turned right, making for the subway at Sheridan Square.

Dimly Tietjen remembered what this neighborhood had been like when he was growing up half a dozen blocks away: the bars and restaurants, a couple of theaters, cabarets, people on the streets all day and all night. Now it was—he searched for a word. Prim? The streets were empty, the houses and shops closed early. Even the homeless didn't seem to settle on Christopher Street anymore; what AIDS hadn't managed to do to the neighborhood, the "quality of life" campaigns of '02 and '05 had. The spirit of the neighborhood had been broken; everyone looked over their shoulders. Tietjen found these blocks architecturally satisfying but depressing. Good brick, bad spirit.

The Sheridan Square subway station was almost empty at this time of night: the attendant in the token booth was talking with the guard stationed inside the booth; another guard prowled up and down the thirty-foot stretch of platform directly opposite to the booth. Two tired-eyed women huddled together near the booth, watching Tietjen as he came down the stairs, clearly expecting the worst. He ran his fare card through the turnstile and walked through onto the platform, then started up toward the northern end of the track.

"Hey, asshole!" Tietjen turned. The guard patted his automatic absently. "Where the hell you going? This is the guarded area, right *here.*" He pointed to the length of platform he was pacing.

"Just stretching my legs," Tietjen said easily.

The guard looked at him blankly, trying to figure it out. Finally he shrugged. "Look, asshole, you wanna walk up that way, be my guest. Some psycho comes out of the tunnel and knifes you, I ain't running my ass off to save some asshole wanted to stretch his legs."

Tietjen nodded. "I'll be careful," he said. What else was he going to say? The guard shrugged again and turned away. Tietjen turned too and went up the platform, pacing slowly up and back, weaving around the stanchions. He was aware that the guard was watching him, and kept his moves simple and slow. Finally he stopped, leaned against a tiled wall, and listened. In the quiet, little noises bounced off the tile walls of the tunnel: a high-pitched "uh" from one of the women waiting near the entrance; a burst of laughter that leaked from the microphone of the token booth and echoed tinnily; the pat-pat sound of the platform guard's automatic slapping against his belt as he walked. The air was warm and moist and smelled like steel, and fire far away. Now and then the rails clicked or shuddered, but nothing appeared. Tietjen waited twenty minutes for the uptown local, and when it came he found it was a short train and he had to sprint back to get on board.

"See, asshole," the guard yelled as the doors closed.

Tietjen sat down; the car was empty except for a guard, hanging on to a handstrap, half asleep. All the way up to Seventy-second Street no one else got on their car. Tietjen sat at his end, reading the ads in Spanish and trying to make heads or tails of the Haitian and

Polish and Arabic ones; the guard stood holding on to his handstrap, coming alert for a moment at each stop, then dropping back to his doze.

At Seventy-second Street he had to step carefully over homeless sleeping on the island between Broadway and Amsterdam. Once he felt himself come down heavily on the hand of a sleeping woman, but she barely shrugged in her sleep. That didn't make him feel any better. He walked up Seventy-second street, doing the same delicate tap dance around the sleeping homeless who spilled out of doorways, and the wakeful ones who watched his passage.

Two of the streetlamps were out on his block. Time to complain to the DPW again, he thought. And they'd come and put in the high-intensity halogens that kept everyone—homeless and apartment dwellers alike—awake at night, and then there would be a fight about getting the bulbs changed, and eventually he'd wear them down and get the low-glo bulbs used on closed streets, but the fight would be a pain in the ass. The lamp nearest his own door worked, and cast a white moonish glow on the brownstone stoop and the steel grille set over the upstairs door. The basement tenant had had a steel plate welded over her outside door and used the inside stairway to go in and out of her apartment. In the front garden he could make out Maia sleeping, curled under a blanket in the shadow of the stoop; the street light glinted off the silver of her hair. "Hi, honey, I'm home," he murmured.

"About damned time," her voice, a sweet whisper, came back at him. "I waited up," she said. "I was just about to get worried about you." She pulled the blanket down from her face with one finger and peered up at him. "How're them boys?"

Tietjen smiled. "They're just what you called 'em, Maia. Little lambs."

She laughed in a whisper. "Those lambs kept you up till this hour? Or you just been walking out again?"

"Taking the air."

"Well, air is free, I guess. Must be, I get enough. You get some sleep now, John." Her finger curled around a corner of the blanket to pull it back over her face.

Tietjen said, "You're an angel, Maia."

She laughed again. "I know."

•   •   •

He didn't turn on the light when he entered the apartment, just pulled off his jacket and tossed it in the direction of the sofa, locked the door behind him by the light of the streetlamp through his window, undressed and brushed his teeth by Braille in the bathroom, and found his way to his bed. The sheets were cool against his back, and he closed his eyes and let himself sink heavily into the mattress. A scent like a thousand things, like the day just gone, clung to him: the dusty, metallic tang of the subway; the warm smell of sun on trees; the perfume of women passing by; sun on brick and sun on asphalt; the river smell of the Hudson, and rain not far off. Air that tasted like everything, forever.

As he fell asleep he thought, It will always be just like this, and I will live forever, just like this.

2
___

IN September Tietjen helped Maia rebuild her lean-to in the front stairwell. Under city law squatters could build against, but their structures could not attach to, private property. It was a peculiar design challenge, constructing a weathertight shack in the six-by-six area without totally obstructing the downstairs tenant's window, out of found material Maia had scavenged. He enjoyed the chance to use his architectural training almost as much as the chance to help his downstairs squatter. She wouldn't take wood or shingles from Tietjen; nails, the loan of tools, and his expertise and the skill in his two whole hands were all she would accept.

During a break they sat together on the stoop drinking lemonade Tietjen had brought downstairs. Food, Maia took without question.

"You build houses like these?" Maia asked. She waved her clawed hands to include the brownstone and brick buildings that lined the street.

He shook his head. "Nobody does houses like these anymore, Mai."

"Skyscratchers, then," she said. "Like that big glass building with the gold net on top."

He knew the building she meant, one of the office towers built over Lincoln Center, its security grilles glittering like gold lace in the sunset. "I don't do that either. This is about as much design as I've done in the last ten years."

"But you're an architect? Why they wasting you?" Her tone was suspicious, a little protective.

Tietjen shrugged. "I'm not a very good designer, actually. I'm better at getting them built than I am at designing them, so that's what I do."

Maia looked at him shrewdly. "That okay with you?"

Tietjen shrugged again and cracked his knuckles.

While the hot weather lasted, and if he was home before midnight, he always wound up downstairs. Sometimes it was talking with Maia. Sometimes Mrs. Harabi on the second floor would hear his footsteps as he went by and come out to the landing to ask something. Often one of the block squatters would stop him as he was coming home, asking a question or making a complaint. Some apologized for taking up his time; others approached aggressively, poised for abrupt dismissal. Tietjen knew most of the squatters on the block by name. He had to stop and listen.

He took walks when he could, but none as epic as the long walk from Irene's that night in June. There was never time. In the evenings when he got home late he climbed the stairs to his apartment, zapped something from the noodle shop on Columbus, and leafed through the mail as he pushed the food idly around his plate. If he was still wakeful he'd settle in the armchair by the window and listen for a while to the voices on the street; sometimes he turned off the lights. The light from the streetlamp outside his window squeezed through the slats of his blinds and cast long, bright patterns on the wall. In his sagging leather chair Tietjen would sink lower and lower, head tilted to one side so he could listen, pick out individual voices; gradually the exhaustion of the day would weigh him down so that he could not move. He fell asleep in the chair often, waking at two or three in the morning, just long enough to shuffle into the bedroom, take off his clothes, and fall onto the bed.

When Chris and Davy went back to school their weekends began to fill with homework and play-dates. Each Saturday the boys were cautiously glad to see him, had stories to tell—and by four o'clock were wondering whether this kid or that one had called about the game or the model or the new homework. Tietjen tried inviting the boys' friends along, but rather than bringing him further into their lives, the friends seemed to pull the boys further away from him. Each Saturday he brought the boys home to Irene and went back to his apartment to work or read or talk with a neighbor or, as likely, settle into the leather armchair and listen.

In October his firm got a new commission, a corporate head-quarters and manufacturing facility in southeastern Massachusetts. There was the usual infighting among the firm's designers, all jock-eying to lead the design team. The competition for construction ar-chitect was less bitter, but plainly most of his coworkers regarded the assignment as a plum. Weeks, months more likely, spent outside the city at the relatively clean, relatively rural site. A big project with the rewards in status and preferment that usually came with big projects.

"So what's wrong with it?" Irene asked when he mentioned it to her.

"For one thing, I wouldn't be around much on weekends. I wouldn't see the boys."

"They could visit," she said it as if it were the right thing to say. "They'd probably like it."

He thought of half a dozen objections—what would kids find to do in Whittendale, Massachusetts, stuck in his hotel room watching satellite TV when he was called back to the site, as he always was on weekends? They'd hate him for it; he wouldn't be able to do his job properly worrying about the kids. Where would he find someone to stay with them when he wasn't there?

Irene was saying something. ". . . time you have a job out of town you go through this, John. You know, there are places with flush toilets and electricity all over the country, it's not like you'd be going to the Kalahari or something." She stopped and began again. "This project would count for something with the partners, wouldn't it?"

He nodded.

"Then go for it. How else are they going to realize you're their best project guy?"

Tietjen smiled at her. It was the closest he'd felt to her in a long time. Still, "But what about the boys?"

"They have their own lives, John. They'll be okay. God, these days they hardly know I'm around—"

Tietjen heard the subtle emphasis on *I*, stressing his less-favored status. The warmth he'd felt a moment before flushed out of him and he was left only with Irene's common sense. It was a good proj-ect, a plum, regardless of the site, which wasn't Siberia. And it wouldn't be forever, wherever it was.

In late November he took the first of several trips to Whittendale. Construction wouldn't start until late spring, but there were always reasons why he was needed in Massachusetts. RaiCo's CFO liked him, said he was a "no-bullshit kinda guy," which meant Tietjen was sometimes sent where the design team might otherwise have gone. He got to know the route—rail to Providence to copter to Whittendale field to car to the site—and the inside of the Red Lantern Motor Inn, the nearest motel to the construction site, and the inside of RaiCo's conference rooms and company cafeteria. The trees and mechanically perfect landscaping around the old plant made no impression on him, except he noted that winter was setting in. The people were pleasant, hospitable even, inviting Tietjen to Thanksgiving parties and, on the next trip, New Year's brunches. Tietjen made the right responses, went out for beer at the end of the day, put in his time at planning sessions that went on too late into the night. He enjoyed the work. The people were friendly. He just wanted to be home again.

Each time he got back to the city it was as if he could breathe again. He never said that to anyone except Maia, who drank the coffee he brought her and nodded as if what he was saying made all the sense in the world. At work, the partners smiled on him: the reports from RaiCo were good. When a new meeting was scheduled in Massachusetts, there was some edged humor in the office about how tough John had it, going off for another long weekend in the country.

Each time he merely smiled and shrugged and went home to pack a bag.

But on the fourth trip, something felt wrong. He sat, staring out the window of a MetroRail club car, drinking gin and flat tonic, watching rooftops as featureless as cobblestones ripple past. They'd sent a man named Westley with him this time, a nervous, talkative, good-humored guy from Systems. There was nothing wrong with that, Tietjen thought. Nothing wrong with anything, only he had felt a vague sense of risk or threat all day, something that gnawed at him unassignably. What was threatened? What was endangered? He washed the taste of anxiety away with gin. Below, the city ebbed and receded into the dusk.

"Goddamn hellhole. Doesn't look so bad from up here, does it?" Westley began. Tietjen cut him off. He hated conversational gambits that depended on New York's bad character. He sipped his drink absently and stared out across the complicated pattern of park and highway, the elegant silhouettes of the skyscrapers. A ragged strip of sunset above the Hudson caught fire in the mirrored spire of an East Side tower. Four days, Tietjen thought. A week at most. *There is nothing to worry about.* He took another sip of his drink, watching out the MetroRail window until distance and dusk closed off his last view. Then he closed his eyes.

He dreamed and woke with a start, sweating and shaking. Passengers in the seats around him eyed him with a detached curiosity but kept a safe distance. At the end of the club car the steward, his arms akimbo and one hand resting lightly on the handle of a billy-club, was watching Tietjen. After a moment the steward relaxed. Tietjen rose to his feet feeling frail and off-balance; his stomach still churned, his heart was still pounding as he staggered toward the bar. What in God's name had he been dreaming of? Disaster. The end of the world.

He ordered another gin and tonic and found his seat again. There, grasping the glass as if it could hold him up, he peered into the car window at his own reflection. Westley said nothing, watching Tietjen curiously. Tietjen did not permit himself to drift into sleep again.

They were met late that night at the MetroRail station in Providence and coptered out to RaiCo's plant in Whittendale. Rooms had been booked for them at the Red Lantern. Westley wanted a drink and went off with the man who had met them. Tietjen found his room, tossed down his bag, and prepared to sleep.

Instead, he lay awake for hours, afraid that the dreams would return. He knew that in the morning he'd need to concentrate; he wanted to sleep, but could not. In the end he lay on top of the blankets, staring at the ceiling of the room which was without even the charm of cracks or blemishes.

All meetings were held in a conference room at RaiCo's assembly plant, around an oval composition table fashioned to look like wood. The chairs were uncomfortable and the acoustics so bad that words spoken across the table were a jumble of vowels by the time Tietjen heard them. From time to time he was aware of faces turned toward him expectantly, and he looked down at the paper before him and forced the words written there into focus. He had shaded cityscapes in the margins.

"I'm sorry, what?" he asked in response to a question.

"Are you hungry? Lunch?" the man next to him repeated. Tietjen nodded thankfully, but when the group rose to leave the conference room he realized that he was not hungry. Instead he returned to his motel. For the first time in the thirty-six hours since he left New York, he was able to sleep for an hour; when he got back to the plant he felt much better, queasy but alert. The managers and designers he had been meeting with were clustered together by the door of the room. He greeted them, raising a hand to wave at Westley, hoping he looked refreshed and ready to get to work.

He might have been invisible.

Someone was saying, "What do you mean? Try another station." Someone else said, "Bring the radio in here, for Christ's sake."

He followed as a radio was placed in the center of the conference table. The news issued from the speakers in staccato bursts: ". . . sketchy at this time, as some sort . . . ectrical interfe . . . missions. No telephone or broadc . . . ories from refugees are confused . . ."

"Refugees?"

"Jesus, from *where?*"

Voices rose, ebbed, rose again over the sound of the radio.

A brassy taste blossomed in Tietjen's mouth. Blood was pulsing at his temples, and his hands and feet throbbed with the beat. "It's New York."

"Shut up," someone said angrily.

". . . explosions may be from gas mains . . . cause of major dama . . . apparent paralysis of cit . . . no firefighting equi . . . in the uptown area looters have been sighted, there are reports of gunfights between block police and lo . . . ew Jersey has sealed access to all parts of Sovereign N . . . Manhattan may be hardest hit, but repo . . ."

He was right. Tietjen felt a cold wind sweep through him. "New York," he repeated dully. His voice was distant, it might have come from any of the shocked faces that surrounded him. "What happened?"

"They don't know. I mean, they keep saying different things. Just that it's *bad*."

The web of discussion, disjointed opinion, fears, maledictions, and prayers from the others grew more urgent and agitated, but Tietjen heard none of it. He felt wrapped up, separate from the others, in a shroud drenched with adrenaline. His ears were buzzing; he could feel the strokes of his heartbeat. All to one purpose: to get him home. He was hooked by an absolute need to get back to the city, to see for himself, to know. He almost screamed it at them: *I have to know!* The need made no excuse, brooked no delay. Somewhere inside him there was a voice, a thin, nervous keening. He was left with his own, only thought.

"I have to get back," he said urgently. At first his words did not register over the murmurs, the tinny noise of the radio. Only when he asked one of the designers for the fastest route back to New York did protests begin.

How? What good would it do? No one knows what's happening, you don't just walk into something like that. *Wait.* It can't be as bad as it sounds. *Wait.* They'll have asked for the National Guard, it'll be cleared up in a couple of days. Family? Hell, man, you can't help your family by getting killed. That's what the Red Cross is for. They'll get out if they have to. *Wait.* The police, the Guard. All media hype. Refugees, Jesus Christ. You don't want to walk into that. *Wait.* Have a drink. Think it over. *Wait.*

Tietjen shook his head and forced a cold calm over the terror, hoping that no one else could see what was happening to him. "What is the fastest way back to New York?" he asked again.

3

PROTEST grew from murmur to babble.

"Jesus, John," Westley said irritably, as if he had made a joke in bad taste.

"We can't do anything," someone said.

"Not until we know more," another voice chimed in.

"I'm not talking *we*," he said curtly. "*What's the quickest way back to New York?*"

He looked around the room, meeting each person's gaze and seeing their eyes fall before his gaze. I'm being rude, he thought. I don't care.

Finally, out of the silence, one of the engineers said, "The copter went into the shop this morning, you'd have to drive to New London—that's due south. The MetroRail to New York from New London will be fastest. If it's running. But look, you can't really—"

"I have to," he said. He did not want to waste time arguing, but no one seemed to understand. His mouth was dry and there was a low buzzing in his ears. Shock, he thought. "Christ, I'm not doing this for fun." Then, more quietly, said "I have a wife and two little kids there."

Someone nodded. "You'll need a car."

Tietjen nodded. He looked at Westley. "You want to come?"

Westley shrugged. "No point. Worse comes to worse, I'm down my CD collection and a couple of coleus. I'm staying until we know what the fuck happened. The news may be overreacting."

"Or not." Tietjen couldn't say how he knew it, but he was gut-certain that New York was in dire trouble, fighting for its life. "I've got to go."

•   •   •

In an hour he had crossed the state line into Connecticut, driving a shabby blue car with the RaiCo logo painted on the doors; the registration and single-passenger permits were in his breast pocket. The countryside was drab, the muddy gray of snowless March; here and there grimy white imitation colonial and saltbox houses dotted the landscape, and salt-rusted cars in blue or burgundy passed his. Tietjen saw none of them, thinking only of New London and the coast, the MetroRail ride back to the city. He kept the radio on, but reception was crappy: it gave only unsatisfactory bleats of information, and more than once chattered off into static completely. The low whine of the car's engine seemed to wind him tighter, focus him more completely on the road ahead and the trip home. He drove with ferocious concentration, as if that itself would save his life.

He got lost in New London in the mess of highways that wanted to bypass the town and take him across the Thames River to Groton or Providence. When he managed to get into the city itself, he got tangled up in the small streets that surrounded the downtown mall, always running one way away from where he wanted to go: the handsome old building that was the MetroRail station. The red-brick station had been designed by Stanford White, he remembered, but he could take no pleasure in it; the rest of downtown was characterless, the same as any other once-rehabbed, forgotten Main Street. Tietjen locked the car and circled the station looking for an open door. Instead he found an elderly man in a creased gray Metro-Rail uniform posting a sign at the front of the station.

Westbound service had been temporarily suspended.

Jesus. "What's the fastest way into the city?" he demanded.

"To New York?" The old man was plainly appalled. "Mister, you don't want to go there. You heard what they're saying on the radio?"

Tietjen wanted to pick the man up and break him in two. He clenched his hands at his sides and said as levelly as he could, "Of course I have. That's why I have to get back. My family is there."

The old man shook his head. "If they're lucky they're getting out, mister. Jeez, I'd stay out of it if I was you."

"You're not. How do I get back?" Tietjen's voice was icy.

The old man looked at Tietjen warily, as if he'd suddenly realized the man he was talking to was dangerous. He leaned back against the wall of the station, considering. "You'd have to drive all the way down, I guess, if you got a car, and the highway permits and such. But I hear the Guard ain't letting people past White Plains anymore, not till they get word from the city that it's okay. And they got their own hands full with people coming out, now. Better stay here a few days, maybe. There's a lotta motels out near the college—"

Tietjen's hands unclenched and he thanked the stationmaster over his shoulder as he went to find the car again. His hands shook as he unlocked the door, and when he was in and the door locked he sat for a long moment, just shaking all over, muttering "shit, shit, shit," in a low, automatic monotone. Inside him the cold wind blew, and in the wind there was the faint keening of fear, a sound like an animal trapped alone in the dark.

When his shaking stopped, Tietjen started the car.

He drove straight down I-95, occupying his mind planning a route into the city, willing the deeper thing into abeyance. From time to time the panic would jitter upward to the edge of his consciousness, making his blood buzz in his ears. Then Tietjen would breathe slow, shallow breaths, counting eight between each breath and willing his shoulders to relax. Each time the fear subsided he told himself he was done with it for good.

The first roadblock was just after New Haven. For about twenty miles the traffic heading east had been getting heavier; westbound traffic was much as it had been: trucks, the rare private vehicle such as his own. Despite his assumption of calm, Tietjen felt his stomach churning when he saw the National Guard cars across the road. They seemed to be letting people by, but, "Where're you headed?" the Guardsman asked.

"Greenwich." Tietjen lied smoothly and smiled, hoping for a sympathetic response. "My wife and kids are down there. I want to get them back up to Branford to stay with her sister until—"

"Yuh, right, right. Go on through. But watch out when you get past Stamford. There's refugees on the roads now, not enough places to put them all that close to the city, they seem to be just walking out on their own. Red Cross is going crazy. Most of them are on foot, and some of them are pretty nasty."

Tietjen nodded, asked casually, "Any word on what really happened?"

A trace of human feeling crossed the young Guardsman's face. "Mister, from what I hear, *everything* happened. Still happening."

Tietjen nodded and put his foot lightly on the gas as the Guardsman waved him on. He smiled, and cursed the necessity for amiable façade as he did so. What he wanted was to grab the Guardsman by the collar, to yell and demand an explanation, to know what was happening. Instead, he drove, listening to the persistent, howling rage of the voice inside him that was calling for home.

He saw the first refugees around Milford, and for a few minutes the sight shocked even the banshee wail inside him to sober quiet. Men and women and children, dressed in everything they could not carry. All of them were dirty, scarred with smuts and grime, wavering with exhaustion. They shared, in their different faces and styles, a look of incredulity, a shock that overwhelmed fear. Where were they going, he wondered. Who would understand them when they got there?

The walkers came in waves: a straggling group, then empty road, a few solitary marchers, then a mass of ten or fifteen again. It was in one of the empty patches of road that a woman stepped out from the shoulder into the path of Tietjen's car and forced him into a skidding stop, half into the other lane. Furious beyond caution, he got out of the car.

"What the hell are you doing?"

"Oh God, oh God, oh God—" The woman was small, haphazardly dressed. She had fallen on the asphalt and was crying.

He felt his anger, partly a product of the panicky sudden stop, fade. "Ma'am?" He went toward her to help her to her feet. "Ma'am?" In the back of his head a vague alarm was sounding, mixing with the terrible keening of the voice boxed up within him. But the woman was obviously in trouble, possibly hurt, and she was almost directly in the path of his car. "Lady." He bent to lift her up. She clasped his arms with panicked tenacity and almost overbalanced him.

"God, mister, I got to get away," she whined. "Please, you got to understand, I got to, I got to—" Her small, strong hands bit deeply into his wrists. Behind him Tietjen heard the scuff of feet on asphalt. The keening inside him screeched so high it was lost to his inner ear. As he turned his head, unable to shake the woman loose, a fist caught him at the side of the head. He dropped sickly and the hands released him with a quick sideways shove. Dimly he heard voices, saw a blur of motion toward the car, but his body, stunned by the unaccustomed violence, refused to move for him.

When he could stand again the car was gone, eastbound. Honest thieves: they had thrown his topcoat out of the car and, unknowingly, the RaiCo registration and private vehicle permits. There was little comfort in knowing that the woman and her accomplice would be stopped sooner or later. Tietjen dragged the coat behind him, made it to the side of the road before he was sick, damning himself for stupidity, wondering where his city smarts had got to. At last, shaky and cold, he shrugged the coat on and began to walk along the side of the road.

It took almost an hour to reach an exit to the roadway, and it was dark in earnest now. At the end of the ramp he found himself on one of the small roads that honeycombed Fairfield County: there would be fewer refugees and less chance of trouble. Walking, he tried to calculate his distance from Manhattan, coming reluctantly to the conclusion that on foot, he would not see home tonight. If he was sixty miles out it meant a minimum of twelve, more likely fifteen hours of solid walking. If he could walk that far. If he kept up his pace and did not stop once. If there was no trouble. If he did not run into more like the crazy woman and her friend.

Stumbling through the icy black night on the road he had chosen, Tietjen turned his thoughts over and over obsessively, worrying them like a sore tooth until the shock of walking into an abandoned car gave him a present pain to worry over. He leaned against the bumper of the car, unable to see the damage to his thigh, cursing roundly. A gust of wind cut through his topcoat; he ached for sleep, for rest, for the comfort of safety. Home, and the endless bass rumble of city noises like a heartbeat under his cheek. Fumbling. Tietjen found an unlocked door on the car and climbed into the back seat, tugging his coat over him. Better than nothing. Alone in the dark with the voice whimpering, demanding through his exhaustion, he closed his eyes.

The sun woke him the next morning, a reluctant, watery, dirty sun that glared from a dirty gray sky. He climbed out of the car and willed his legs to work, to take him home. The car, he saw now, had no tires; a good camping place, that was all. He had slept badly, when his imagination permitted it. Sleeping in ignorance, he woke resolved to know what the hell was happening in New York as soon as possible, to lay the ghosts and quiet the voices that had wakened with him.

He had been walking for almost an hour when the first car passed him, heading east, away. A passenger leaned out to shout something unintelligible as they passed. After that there were occasional cars, more occasionally people on foot, heading east. He tried a few times to talk with them; some ran away, one woman threw rocks at him, staring with dull, fearful eyes. The people who would stop to talk, sidling anxiously eastward even as they stood, told conflicting stories, as if what had happened to the city was so huge that no one touched by it could know the whole story. Fire, gas explosions, quake, bombs, flooding, riots, disaster. As bad as his dreams.

So, he asked himself when he had stopped for a few minutes. Why am I in such a goddamned hurry to get back?

The answer he'd given to Westley and the people at RaiCo, to the man at the train station, to the Guardsman below New Haven, was his family: Irene and the boys. Tietjen imagined himself as a hero, fighting his way in to save his sons from looters, perverts, dragons, or whatever the hell else there was in New York now. For a few moments, walking along in the cold morning light, he allowed himself to be mesmerized with the notion of a great rescue, but really, it was too ludicrous. He didn't have the tights and cape; what was driving him back to the city was not heroic.

When he focused on his kids, the idea of rescue seemed bizarre, anyway. All the images he conjured up were of the boys with him, in the city as Tietjen had left it. He balked at the notion that anything could get into the tower the boys lived in; it was warded round with Irene's terrified magic, her refusal to let anything from the city reach in and touch her or the boys. When Tietjen stopped forcing the issue and thinking about his family, he forgot them. So maybe he wasn't going home to be a hero.

When he really listened to it, the thing that was driving him on had nothing to do with Irene or his sons. The voice that welled with insistence every time he stopped to catch his breath was not heroic. It cried for home.

He kept walking.

The horn that sounded behind him, almost in his ear, jolted him out of his reverie and nearly startled him off his feet.

"Where're you going?" the old man called from the window of his car. Smarter than I was, Tietjen thought.

"New York. I mean, as far in toward Manhattan as I can get," he amended.

"You armed?"

"No." Tietjen winced at his own stupidity the moment he said it, but it seemed to be the right answer. The man made a noise that sounded like damned idiot. "Look, you want a ride in as far as I can take you? Tuckahoe if we're lucky, but that's only if the Guard's sleeping late."

Almost as he answered Tietjen was sliding into the car. When his hip hit something hard he looked down and saw the gun.

"I *am* armed," the man said conversationally, and stuck the pistol back into his coat pocket. "Just so you know. You can keep an eye out for the Guard. And for refugees."

They rode in silence for the first few miles. Tietjen let himself relax into the seat, weak with the pleasure of sitting. His leg muscles buzzed with fatigue. He had never known this particular kind of exhaustion, stress and panic on top of physical exertion. He felt unable to make conversation, but at last, feeling that some gesture should be made, he asked, "Why did you stop for me?"

The older man smiled. "Anyone foolish enough to be walking *toward* New York this time of the morning in the state things are in . . . must have an interesting story. Anyway, you wouldn't be a refugee, and they're the real danger now." He gave Tietjen a curious sideways look. "Which brings me round to asking why you *are* walking into the mess. I'm Corliss, by the way. Frank. And there's coffee in a thermos somewhere back there," he cocked his head toward the backseat. "Help yourself."

"John Tietjen." As he poured coffee into the thermos lid—luke-warm, too sweet, delicious—Tietjen tried to think of something to tell the driver. "My family is in Manhattan: my ex-wife, our kids."

"You plan to single-handedly go in and rescue them, astounding the world?" Corliss's tone was very dry. "Sounds fine, John. You have any idea what it's like down there?"

Tietjen ignored the sarcasm, swiveled in his seat to face the other man. "Do you? No one's been able to tell me what happened."

"I don't think anyone knows all of it. It's hard to get the big pic-ture, and nothing much is coming out of New York except people, refugees. One woman told me that she and her kids saw a gas main blow half a block away; some sort of explosive, maybe, but she wasn't sure there hadn't been an earthquake. One guy—poor bas-tard swore he'd seen dragons in the street, but the state he was in . . . Supposed to be fires all over the city, looters, flooding in the south end of the city, Manhattan and Brooklyn. Hurricane winds, earth-quakes. God knows what-all else. The news said that Washington's set up a task force, but they're waiting to send in the Guard or the Army until Sovereign New York asks for help, and no one knows where the city governor is, no one's heard anything from the city government since this-all began. A city as big as New York has a del-icate balance; one thing happens and whssst!—" Corliss made a flourishing gesture with his free hand. "Everything goes. I've seen some people who're leaving the city. I would think more than twice before trying to get back, myself." The dry note returned to the old man's voice. Something about his manner galled Tietjen.

"Why the hell *are* you going back in, then?" he snapped. "You don't look like a hero."

Corliss smiled wryly. "I'm not. Not much of one. Margaret—my wife—and I set out to leave Tuckahoe yesterday morning, but our daughter-in-law had to get out, and there were a few neighbors who couldn't get out of Westchester on their own. Suddenly Margaret was organizing a damned car service. I made one trip to Bridgeport, and when I got home she'd already talked to other people, kept say-ing she could wait. I made four trips from Tuckahoe to Bridgeport yesterday—our daughter lives up there—and Margaret is still home, holed up in our house there. This time I'm taking her with me and we're getting out of the salvation business. I'm too old for this."

Tietjen nodded, his anger gone. Images of fire, of quake, ripped pavement and shattered buildings, were starting up again in his head. The rising panic squeezed his chest; the blood rushing in his head made a ferocious buzzing noise.

He swallowed a few times, rapidly.

"You okay?" Corliss was asking from a distance. "John? Damn. Look, pull yourself together. We're going to have to do a little bulling and hope that they don't recognize me from yesterday." Corliss jabbed his chin forward, pointing. Ahead, Tietjen saw a roadblock and the familiar uniforms of Guard officers.

"Where're you headed?" the Guard asked wearily.

"Down to White Plains to pick up my family," Corliss began.

"I'm real sorry, sir. Traffic's been restricted again. No one past the state line anymore, up about as far as Armonk and across to Tarrytown. Refugees have been coming out of the city, taking over pretty much everything from Purchase across to the Hudson. If your family's down there I don't think—"

"Frank." Tietjen spoke quickly to cover the other man's shock and paralysis. "Margaret said if she needed to she could make it to Greenwich, remember?" He forced the words out of a dry mouth. Did terror show? "She'll have heard about the block past the line. You know Margaret, Frank. She'll meet us in Greenwich."

The officer leaned down to check Tietjen out. "Who's Margaret?"

"His wife. My sister." Tietjen smiled stiffly. "Hate like hell to have my sister in the middle of all that, sir."

"Yeah, well." The Guard checked over Corliss's license, the vehicle permits, their IDs. At last he waved them on. "Good luck," he called, but as if he doubted they would find any luck at all.

Corliss let out a gust of breath that kept time with the car's acceleration. "Nice, John. Nice. You've earned your passage, so to speak. The state line." Another exhalation. "Jesus, I hope Meggie's okay." Then, smiling curiously, "You didn't seem fazed by that Purchase-to-the-Hudson business."

"I don't know where Purchase is. Is it bad?"

Corliss laughed. "Damn, yes. Basically everything from the Connecticut–New York border across to Tarrytown and the Hudson, down into Sovereign New York. I'm glad you said what you said to him—I couldn't think that fast. Where in the city is it you mean to get?"

"Manhattan. As far in as you'll take me, and walk the rest of the way unless I can find another ride."

Corliss shrugged. "If we can get across the border I'll bring you down to Tuckahoe with me, but then—I left Margaret with an old .32. I think she'd use it, but I hope she doesn't have to. Purchase to the river. Jesus H. Christ."

But Tietjen was sinking into his own panic, hearing the bravado of his plans, wondering how he was going to get to the city and what he would find there. Not who, he realized. What. He felt a dim anger at himself; what about the boys, what about Irene? What the hell was wrong with him?

But everyone seemed to think them as good as dead. There would be time to mourn later. Now he had to know.

The keening voice under all thought insisted: Home.

For a while the two men rode in silence.

"We're getting close to Greenwich," Corliss said at last. "Looks like we'll have to run the line on one of the small roads. Hell, they can't have this whole area covered."

"You know it well?"

"Grew up around here. Hope I remember what I think I do." Corliss smiled a mirthless smile, ridges of white stubble bracketing his mouth. "We'll get off the parkway here and maybe I can find one of them."

"Is that what this was? A parkway? Doesn't look like much."

"The Merritt Parkway. Turns into the Hutchinson once we get into New York State. One of the few roadways they kept open when the second fuel crisis hit. It's suicide going faster than fifty on it, and there's only two lanes. Designed by Mickey Mouse in the late nineteen-thirties, expanded in the nineties and contracted right back again in '07. Used to be pretty when I was a kid: all green, lots of trees." Talking in a reassuring historian's voice, Corliss guided the car off the parkway and began to cut and weave down a series of narrow roads, making lefts and rights without any apparent reason. Tietjen knew they were still headed vaguely west by the slant of the sun, but that was all he was certain of. "Before they cut the big private tracts around here into development lots—ahh." A note of guarded satisfaction. "I think we're in New York, John. No sign of the Guard anywhere?"

There was no sign of anything at all. The silence was eerie. Certainly there was no sign of mass hysteria. Maybe it was all crazy, Tietjen thought. Maybe everything would be okay after all.

Corliss took the car left, right, then left again, kitty-cornering southwesterly. Tietjen was relaxed in his seat, watching the small, carefully tended houses as they passed them; a SCHOOL CROSSING sign that shone in the midmorning sunshine. The taut plane of Corliss's cheek was beginning to relax. They turned a corner and another. Then Corliss brought the car to a slamming, violent stop.

Three cars had been overturned and were on fire in the middle of a crossroad. The fire fed on itself in bursts of smoke, gusts of flame that plumed upward in the clear daylight. Worse was the bedraggled crowd of people that stood, mesmerized by the gouts of flame.

"Jesus God," Corliss whispered.

"Floor it," Tietjen ordered, low in his throat. "Frank, for Christ's sake, floor it. They'll turn us over too—" He did not finish. As the crowd turned toward their car Corliss stepped on the gas and the car tore a hole in their ranks, people scattering before it. Corliss had seen the arm that dangled, burning, from the window of one of the cars.

"Jesus God, Jesus," Corliss was whispering like prayer. "Meggie, Christ, all alone. Meg." His foot was pressed flat to the floor on the gas pedal; the car was taking curves on luck and inertia. "Christ, let me be home soon."

Tietjen was possessed by the voice; his terror welled up and choked him. *Christ, let me be home soon.* He would never see home again. Without thinking, without hearing what he said, he asked, "Frank, take me to the Bronx. To one of the bridges."

Corliss let up on the gas pedal a little, snapped out of his own trance. "What?"

"The Bronx. Take me to the Bronx. I'm not asking for Manhattan."

Corliss looked at Tietjen sideways with a sad half-smile. "Son, your family isn't alive in there. If they made it out they'll find you. Look, you can come out to Bridgeport with us, we'll find you a place—"

It was too late for Tietjen to explain about the howling voice in his head that drove him on, about Irene and the boys and the locks on their doors, about the city. Even if he had the words. Too late to allow himself to be affected by Corliss's offer. *It doesn't matter,* the voice howled. *Nothing* matters.

He repeated, "The Bronx, Frank. *Please.*"

Corliss shook his head. "I can't. I'm not a hero, John. I'm scared to death. I want my wife and I want to get out of this, as far away . . . look, I wish I could help you. I'll take you—"

The action was begun and completed almost before the thought had formed: Tietjen reached for the gun and in a moment had it, warm from its resting place by Corliss's hip, in his hand. "The Bronx, Frank. It won't take you long. I'm serious. I'm desperate."

"Yes." Corliss let his eyes flicker from the road to the gun to the road again. "If that's what you want, John. You've got the gun. But think about what you're walking into."

Tietjen thought about it, clenching his hand around the gun, feeling its weight.

"Your family can't be—"

"I know. Just drive, Frank. Please." Tietjen's voice was weary. Corliss drove and there was no more conversation.

Corliss drove with steady attention, as if he had made his agreement and meant to stick with it. Tietjen watched him, then the gun, then the road, then Corliss, then the gun, back and forth, feeling the cold weight of the thing in his hand, imagining what it would have been like if Corliss had forced him to use it. The image of that cluster of upended cars, of the one ghastly burning arm extended, played in his head. Looking down, Tietjen hated the gun, hated the voice that had driven him to use it as a threat.

"Frank."

Corliss did not turn his head.

"Look, Frank. I'm sorry." He stopped, looked down at the gun again.

Corliss relaxed the slightest bit. "I wish I could figure out what it is that's driving you. It's something more than your kids you're worrying about?"

Tietjen kept his eyes on the gun in his hand. "I don't know that I can explain it. I have to get back, that's all. Since I heard about this thing. It's crazy."

"John, you know the city's gone." Corliss made it a statement. No avoiding it. "Is that what you're going back for?"

"How do you know that? You said yourself, no one knows what's happening." Even to his own ears he sounded naive.

"And you're going to save the city." Corliss's voice was gentle. This time the older man looked quickly at Tietjen; the glance was half pity, half assessment. Surprisingly, Tietjen found he did not mind the look or Corliss's tone, the unveiling of his fears. The old man's face was sharp in the sunlight, features and expression clear. Tietjen looked at the gun in his hand; it seemed to have no reality at all.

"How old is your wife, Frank?" he asked at last.

"Sixty-three." Corliss did not ask why he had asked.

Tietjen thought a little longer. "Look, where are we now?"

"Far side of Saxon Woods, a bit below Scarsdale. Maybe twelve miles from Manhattan if you make it over to 9A and cross on the Henry Hudson Bridge."

Tietjen thought of the sun dropping like a heated penny into the Hudson River in the springtime; of the chatter of rails in the subways. Looked up at the old man beside him. "Let me off somewhere in here, Frank." He dropped the gun on the seat of the car.

Corliss stared straight ahead of him. "I can take you as far as Tuckahoe, that's five miles closer."

"And be worrying all that time that I'll grab the gun again. I'd be worrying too. Let me off here, Frank, while I've got the guts to be a gentleman about it." Tietjen smiled. "I hope your wife is all right."

Corliss slowed the car down. "I hope you can save something, John. Look, take the damned gun; if you're going to be on foot you may need it. God knows what you're going to run into."

Tietjen shook his head. "I really don't *like* the damned things, Frank. Thanks for the ride." The car came to a stop and he was out with the door shut behind him in a moment. Burning his bridges. "Thanks. Have a good trip."

"You too. Look, if you do get to Bridgeport—"

"Thanks for that, too, but I won't. Now, go." Tietjen slapped the fender.

The car started forward.

•   •   •

He stood alone, watching Corliss's car vanish, an icy sparkle in solid sunlight. Then Tietjen started walking after in what he hoped was the direction of Manhattan. His legs were as stiff as cardboard. I don't know where the hell I am, he thought, and for a moment that seemed almost comic to him. Let Corliss take off and didn't even ask which way to go, that's where virtue gets you: somewhere in Westchester without a ride. Still, it was pleasant to feel like a good guy, like he'd done the right thing; the warmth of it cut the March wind just a little.

Then the voice reminded him: you don't know where you are. You don't know what has happened in the city or when you will see home again.

The thought sobered him. He was walking without a plan, no way of knowing which way to take. The voice inside his head took up the low chant that urged him on. The image of those cars overturned, burning, came back to haunt him with a renewed sense of vulnerability. How could he be walking, just walking, alone, as if it were any time, any suburban road. The flat vista of the roadway made him more vulnerable; he missed the safety of granite walls rising on either side. For a moment he thought of turning tail, finding Corliss, reaching Bridgeport and the offered shelter, the kindness there.

There would be no kindness in the city. And no rest anywhere else. Tietjen turned a shoulder on retreat and continued along the road.

After an hour, certain that he had taken the wrong roads, Tietjen began to approach houses, hoping to ask directions. There had been no one on the road since Corliss's car had vanished from sight, and his fear had ebbed a little. The idea of reaching Manhattan seemed exhausting but possible; less absurdly quixotic than it had been that morning. But the first house he stopped at had been broken into: smears of blood on the door turned him back to brood as he continued on the road. There were others like that house, shutters askew, doors ajar. Tietjen avoided them. Other houses stood like fortresses on quarter-acre lots; he avoided them, too, after a round of shots was fired at him from an upper-story window. From behind a tree he had howled furiously: "I only want directions! Am I on the right road for Manhattan?"

The answer was another shot.

So he kept walking, trying to judge southwest by the sun, watching out for dangers one-eyed, preoccupied with thoughts. If Reen could see this: the world she had believed in, where everyone was a killer. What if Corliss was right and they were all dead? Irene would never have had the skills to save them or herself, and Tietjen couldn't imagine her trusting someone to help her. What if they're all dead, he thought again. And kept on walking doggedly along the narrow tree-lined road.

He was brought out of reverie by sound. It might have been the ocean, but the ocean was twenty-odd miles away. He listened, trying to make sense of the sound, until he realized that the deep, rumbling rhythm was made up of voices. The voices were angry, maddened, a sound of tidal wave. With little idea how far away the crowd was, Tietjen darted off the road and into a culvert, rolled down to a huge drainage pipe and crawled in, waiting and listening.

Like a wave, the sound rolled ahead over the road. It took forever—perhaps a quarter of an hour—before the first walkers from that surge of voices passed overhead. These were different from the refugees he had seen in Connecticut the day before: they were not in shock. The voices he heard, and the steps and the threats, belonged to the jungle: furious and vicious. Twice he heard fights break out, settled by blows that sent one dark form tumbling from the side of the road into the culvert. Listening, Tietjen understood the cars burning, the shots fired from shuttered houses. He pulled himself tighter into the drainpipe and tried to breathe as softly as possible.

The crowd passed and passed and thinned and filled again. He was cold and damp and cramped in the pipe, watching the shadows change and lengthen. Tietjen realized hollowly that he might not reach Manhattan tonight. Might not reach it at all. The feet fell and the voices rumbled overhead. Then the dark pile of clothes that had been tossed heavily over the side of the road began to move and Tietjen drew himself into an even tighter ball, watching the form resolve into a boy, a street kid in dusky green leathers, dark skin powdered with gray dirt.

"Ey. Ma'. Help me."

Tietjen squeezed farther into the pipe, hoping desperately that the kid had not realized that he was there, that the cry for help was to anyone. God, maybe.

"Ey, I know you dere," the voice wheezed. "You wan' I call 'em down'ere? Pull me in dere wit' you, ma'."

Tietjen weighed the risks and began to edge out to the boy. Getting him back toward the pipe was difficult, a scuttling, dragging movement. They accomplished the ten yards in silence, afraid that the voices would stop, that the crowd would hear them and descend and kill them both. Every inch was a victory; the boy had been slashed in the fight and was bruised and bloodied, one arm broken in his fall. Finally they were crammed, breathing each other's breath, into the drainpipe.

"Thans, ma'." The kid was shuddering with cold and shock. Tietjen tried to wriggle out of his topcoat and could not; the space was too small. In the end he managed to wrap the tail of the coat across the boy's lap, hoping that would help a little. They were quiet a long time, listening to the ebb and flow of the mob overhead.

The boy mumbled something. "What?" Tietjen asked.

"End of th' worl', ma'. Fuckin' end of the worl'."

"But what happened?" Tietjen felt a spasm of excitement: the kid must know something. "What happened?"

"Buildin's fallin'; fires; rats in the street like dogs and rain fallin' like shit. Monsters, ma'. 'M tellin' you, 's end of the worl'." The boy's face was shiny with cold sweat. "Din you see it? Or you come out early wit' Uptowns?"

"I didn't—I'm trying to get back—I was—" The words stuck in his mouth. "I was out of town."

The boy coughed, laughing, trying to keep the consumptive rattle quiet. "*Nob'dy* goin' in, baby." The word ended in another cough. "No*body*. New York dead. You don' go in'ere nomore."

"I do," Tietjen said.

"Hear 'em up there? Think 'ey leave, was somethin' lef' inna city?"

"They maybe don't want what I want." The boy thought about that for a while, his lips tight-pressed. Tietjen asked him, "You cold?"

"Shit, yeah, col. Wha' you think?" He seemed to have made up his mind that Tietjen was crazy or stupid or both. Turning himself with painful slowness, the boy stared out at the shadows of the crowd. Over his shoulder Tietjen watched the day grow colder and later.

Even when, hours past, the last wave of people had vanished, the air seemed haunted by an echo of voices. At last Tietjen tried to move the boy.

"Ey, where you goin'? You can' lea'me 'ere."

"I have to get to the city. Do you think you can make it on your own?"

The boy's glance was fretful and feverish. "I tol' you, assho'. Can' go dere no more. You can' lea' me 'ere neither." He paused, pulling his strength together. "You lea' me down'ere, I die sure." The boy's cockiness faded for a moment. "Jesus, ma', don' lea' me down'ere." His eyes, huge and dark in a dark face, searched Tietjen's without bravado. "Leas' you help me up dere, ma'. I be okay onna road."

Tietjen nodded. They began, haltingly, to reverse the process that had secured them in their hiding place hours before. The boy squirmed and Tietjen pushed, edging out behind him. When he shoved at the boy's shoulders he thought that the body, even through the leather jacket, seemed too tough and wiry for death. Still, Tietjen recoiled from the thought of the boy lying alone under the bridge in the cold of the night. Would he be any better alone on the road? Perhaps he should try to bring the boy with him, back to the city.

The choice was not his. When they reached the roadside the boy stood drunkenly away from him. "Gonna be okay, now, ma'. I make it all right." He gave no salutation, no backward look. He began walking, limping after the crowd long past.

Tietjen did not waste time watching the boy disappear. It was almost twilight, the light was nearly gone, and he had a long way to go yet.

It took him eight hours to walk twelve miles, through dusk and darkness. Through Mount Vernon, west toward the Hudson, trying to make out the faces of disfigured signs. Perhaps the boy had been right and that last, frightening parade had been the end, the last of the people of New York. Down the Saw Mill Parkway, past the empty tollbooths with signs hanging askew, dangling and rattling in ghost-town winds, and into the Bronx. New Jersey, when he caught glimpses of the river and the land across in the dark, glittered serenely, safely distant across the water.

It was a long, cold walk, and Tietjen was more aware of being alone than he had ever been in all his life. When he reached the bridge that spanned the Harlem River and was the last barrier to Manhattan he had no idea what time it was, only that it was dark and had been dark for hours; that he was hungry and had not eaten for almost two days; and that he was very nearly home. He saw stars overhead, the first stars he had seen over his city in years. By their light he could see shadowy obstacles on the bridge that stretched its crippled arms across the river. In the distance there was the uneven moving glow of fires, great Beltane blazes in the darkness.

I am home, he thought. *I am home.* For the first time in two days the voice that had driven him was quiet. Another hundred yards and he would be on his own ground again. He took the first step, but it was difficult to negotiate in the dark: the wind was strong on the bridge, and he could only see shadows and the moonlit glitter of twisted steel, things to terrify. So close to home he found himself wanting to wait until morning, when the shadows would be gone. Then he could see the city as it was. Make plans. Learn the truth.

For the first time in two days, common sense overweighed obsession and the driving need inside him quieted. He could wait until morning. The city was within reach, a fact. It would guard his sleep as he guarded it. Shivering in the March wind, Tietjen settled himself against a stanchion of the Hudson Bridge, pulled his grimy topcoat close, and huddled down to dream and to wait for the light.

PART TWO

1

J IT woke, recalled from a very long distance, breaking through the surface; very tired. His eyes fluttered open and yellow light from stolen Park Service lanterns washed over him. He had been dreaming about the door.

Slowly Jit sat up, rolling his head, touching big ears to sharp bony shoulders, staring down at his legs, willing them to move too. His knees were so knobby they made his legs look like pipes. He swung his legs over the side of the old wooden bench and dragged himself standing. He felt empty. Not hungry—well, always hungry—but *empty*. Something happened, he thought dimly. He could not remember what it was, but something had happened. Had he *done* something? He reached out, listening for the others.

There was nothing there. For the first time he could remember, he was alone. It made him panicky, like a man in the dark who wakes and thinks he is blind.

He reached out again, fumbling, and finally found something, a nice squishy disorganized thing: the taste of dried grass, *hungry hungry cold balance on the limb of this tree gray world*. A squirrel. Jit rarely heard the animals in the Park; sounds of people were always too loud, drowning out animals, sometimes drowning out Jit himself. He listened to the squirrel for a minute or two, comforted by the creature's small hungry warm thoughts. The silence wasn't in him, after all: he could still hear.

But where were all the others?

Usually when Jit woke it was to a dull roar of thoughts, *things*. They were in his dreams, too, always there. Good, sometimes, but mostly bad things. When the thoughts got too loud, too bad, when he could not stand them anymore, he threw them behind the door, slammed the door shut on them, to make them go away.

He had been dreaming about the door. In his dreams the door had been flung open, burst its seams, and all the things, anger and fear and murderous feeling, years and years and years of things, had come flooding through him, pouring out the door and through him, and back at them. He shook his head tiredly.

Hungry. The squirrel's hunger had quickened his own. Moving shakily on his stick legs, more awkward today than usual, Jit followed the tunnel to his kitchen. He was proud of the stove, which he had stolen from the cart of a hot-dog vendor who had been stabbed near the Park. The man had been hollow as an empty can, all the thoughts gone. Jit had lived high on hot dogs and rolls and sharp yellow mustard for a week. When he looked at the stove he could almost taste the hot dogs. Good memory. Now he lit the tiny lamp and looked over the small collection of cans and jars on his shelf. Soon he would have to make another raid on one of the food places. A good, scary thought.

He took a can of soup—he knew which foods went with which pictures—and opened it and put the can on the heat. The label around the can immediately lit and burned away to nothing as Jit watched. This quiet scared him. Even in the middle of the night he had never felt alone like this; there were the night people, the ones that walked in the Park, the ones that stalked the streets. Even sleepers' thoughts had their own sound, the noise of dreams a white whisper against the dark noise of the night people. Jit did not know the words for these things but he recognized them. There were the good things and the bad things. Only now, there were no things at all.

A hot sizzle from the little stove brought him back from thinking: the soup was beginning to bubble in the can. Jit looked through the magpie collection of spoons on his shelf, picked one that was not too dirty, and took the sleeve from a discarded shirt to wrap around the heated can.

Then he took his meal with him and clambered agilely to the upper level of the tunnel where the cold sunlight of afternoon filtered down from a grating thirty feet overhead. He settled himself against one of the stone walls, pulled his bony knees up tight to his chest, and spooned hot soup into his mouth.

He missed the people stuff. He had never tried to imagine what

it could be like without the thoughts canceling each other out until
what Jit heard was an undistinguishable roar of emotion, most of it
the loudest things: anger or fear. This quiet should be peaceful. But
the silence was not so nice. It was lonely.

Jit had lived alone as long as he could remember, making contact
with one of *them* only rarely; like the kid who had given Jit a name.
Jit had watched that kid play handball against the stone of the
boathouse face, watching first from the bushes, drawn there by the
rhythmic thud of the small pink ball; later he began to edge out behind the stone columns. The kid had seen him, talked to him, laughing. Up close, Jit had been able to hear him individually, decide to
trust him. The kid had seemed amused by the audience, called him
jitters or jitterboy or, finally, Jit. And Jit had liked the sound and the
boy enough to keep the name. He had a friend. He made sure to be
there every day in case his friend was there, watching from the
bushes until he was certain that no one else was around, ducking
back behind if a passerby interrupted the older boy's monologues.

"Jitters, why you so cra-zee?" the boy asked sometimes. Jit had
no answer, but he liked the sounds of the words. Sometimes, sitting
alone behind a grating watching people move warily through the
Park, Jit would repeat the words to himself: Jitters, why you so
crazy?

Some of the soup was burned on the bottom of the can. Jit
scraped doggedly until he had it all, burned or no. He glanced up
again, out at the deserted walkway and gray lace of the leafless
bushes. It had been light for a long time, he thought.

When he had finished eating and the soup was a warm liquid
ball in his stomach, Jit decided to scout the Park. Going out in daylight meant taking one of the crawl tunnels to the old skating-rink
house, and working himself through the boards that covered the
windows so that he could appear magically on the hillside behind
the building. Jit rarely left his home the quickest way; it was too
dangerous. It would be too easy for someone to follow him, find the
warren he had made for himself from old Park furnishings, scavenged bits and scraps, stolen things. He had a dozen routes from the
tunnel and could come up half-anywhere in the Park. Now Jit
grabbed an old jacket, sloppy on his stick frame, and climbed down
the ladder into the tunnel, making his way toward the skating rink
by memory in the dank, moist air.

Even out in the daylight the loudest voice Jit heard was that of the squirrels. There was a sense of wrongness that confused him; it took him several minutes to understand that something was wrong with the Park itself, something was sick. The unkept mass of trees and shrubs around the skating rink was dead, not just winter barren and gray but dead; the earth looked as if it had been scorched. Jit wrinkled his nose. There was a taste of fire in the air, something was wrong but he could not tell what it was. He wondered again: where were all the voices?

He didn't like the deadness. Jit picked up a stick that lay at his feet and switched it at the trees. Grow, he thought idly, angry at the deadness. Grow. In his hand the stick felt warm. As he watched, the rusty gray bark began to move, forming like clay into a tiny shoot. A leaf unfurled, and another. Jit stared at the stick in his hand, puzzled.

Grow, he thought again. Another shoot pushed from the stick, two more tiny leaves.

He turned his gaze on one of the dead trees, a bleached white skeleton of a maple. *Grow.* He thought wistfully of the tree full of green, boughs heavy with leaves, saw himself improbably swinging in the branches. Laughing. *Grow,* he thought again. In his imagining he was not hiding, the Park was not peopled by streetgangs and the babbling homeless, there were people under the trees picnicking, playing games; a young woman feeding a baby, the boy who had named Jit playing ball with other leather-jacketed kids, an older group of gang-kids circled and talking intently, removed from the pastoral; over all of them, high in the generous green of the maple, Jit himself watching like a benign godling. *Grow,* he thought one more time at the tree.

By the time Jit had turned his back on the tree, satisfied, a few fragile buds of green had begun to show on the white branches, and death was receding from the limbs of the tree. This was a new game, but he was very pleased with it. If the magic stayed, he would work on the other trees later. Now he set off in his nervous scuttle, dodging from tree to lamppost, exploring. A squirrel chittered by in the distance, its simple incoherent thoughts loud in the silence. Still no trace, no taste of people. The air was cold and clear and sharp enough to scour the skin inside his nose. There were no human smells, not the sour tang of ozone and exhaust, not the more localized odors of hot grease and meat from the vendors who ordinarily lined the Fifth Avenue wall of the Park; not even the individual scents of people, fearful, swaggering, sexual, that Jit normally picked up in the Park. The air was as dead as the trees. As quiet as the place in his mind where the voices usually were.

Gradually, Jit gathered the courage to walk openly on a pathway. There was no one to see, report him, turn him in to the Uniforms. Jit had no memory of how he had come to live in the caves and tunnels under the Park; it was as if he had always been there. Long ago there had been an old man who took slipshod care of him, but old Nogai had drifted away over time. And there was a woman who had wanted to take him home with her, who used to come to the Park every day and sit, staring straight in front of her and talking to Jit in a low voice of how it would be, how she would civilize him. She had stopped coming too, when the cops stopped patrols inside the Park walls.

Worst was the time when one of the Uniforms found him asleep inside a maintenance shed; Jit had wakened in the echoing din of a police station, washed in voices and thoughts, unable to make them understand his halting pidgin speech. There had been words about Homes and Law, questions that made no sense. *Whose Little Boy Are You?* Jit had heard a jumble of thoughts, perhaps well-meaning, all terrifying. At last he had blasted out at them, all the people who bent solicitously over him. He cut through *Who's Your Mommy* with his fear and his anger, knocking them all back away from him, and in the confusion he had escaped, run through the maze of corridors and out to the street, run until he found one of his hiding places. He had stayed there for three days, until hunger drove him out to forage, and he had never been caught again.

There were many people living in the Park, but Jit had the neatest hiding places, the best home. Those others lived in nervous packs; everything they did was makeshift, a pale imitation of life remembered from somewhere else. Jit only remembered the Park and his tunnel, a warm burrow, secure and comforting.

In the waning afternoon light Jit made a circuit of the lower Park, ready at any moment to dart behind a tree, disappear upward or downward at the sight of another person. No one. A few times he stopped and played with a tree, thinking at it until pale green buds began to cluster on the dead white limbs. The game grew easier as he played it. He heard thoughts, meatier than the squirrel's but not human: a pair of dogs running through the Park, disoriented without People, maddened by the subsonic howl of the earth in their ears. Briefly Jit thought a kind of peace at them, but the dogs' grief would not be quieted. He turned his attention back to the trees.

This was all right for now, the silence. But he would grow lonely. Where was everyone?

When darkness started to close in on the Park Jit returned to the skating rink, squeezed between the boards again, and started through the tunnels to his cave. He heated another can of stew—when he went to a food place to find food he would have to find cans of fuel for the cooker—and ate it in the sputtering yellow light of the lanterns. He made a fire to cut through the chill, neat stacks of dry twigs piled on the brick floor under the tunnel shaft. He fed the small blaze with carefully gathered and rolled sheets of paper. Every few minutes, staring at the shapeless shadows dancing on the far wall, Jit would reach out again, listening. No one there.

Finally, bored, he curled up near the dim glow on the hearth and went to sleep. He dreamt of the door again, closed on an empty room.

2

SUNSHINE woke him: Tietjen moved rustily against the stanchion, cold and stiff, unwilling to untuck himself from the tight curl that had kept the chill out. He shook out his shoulders and wiggled his fingers gingerly: they still worked, that was something. He had rarely slept outdoors. Irene loved camping; during their marriage she had kept brochures on trails and camping equipment; they were always going to spend a week walking the Appalachian Trail or camping in the Blue Ridge, her chance to impress him with the beauty of plants, water, and natural stone.

He looked at the gnarled mess of the bridge, whole girders skewed and twisted from position, cables waving in the wind. What would Irene make of this?

When his shoulders were unknotted, Tietjen rose, sliding his back against the girder. He flexed his legs, stiff and sore, discovering new muscles that protested as he crossed the road to look out over the side of the bridge. The day was beautiful, clear and cold like autumn, the sky china blue with large showy clouds that sailed effortlessly toward the Jersey horizon. If he did not turn his head, if he looked straight across the water at New Jersey, Tietjen could believe that nothing had happened. Then he took a deep breath. Morning air stung his nose; there was a strong acrid taste of fire in it, traces of gas, of other things less easily defined but no less frightening. He turned his head for his first daylight glimpse of Manhattan since leaving.

From the Hudson Bridge he could not see much; the barren gray of leafless Inwood Hill park blocked most of his view. Above the park a long flat bar of smoke hung across the brilliant blue of the morning sky, a gray slash interrupting the scudding clouds. Sunlight reflected crazily off the island beyond the trees, and the dazzle bounced off the smoke, creating an odd sandwich of dark smoke, light, and gray trees. He could see no details, only the layer of smoke from the fires of the night, and the underbelly of light.

His stomach set up a protesting growl. Tietjen tried to remember when he had last eaten. Breakfast in Whittendale, two days before. He was sure as hell hungry now. He looked one more time out toward New Jersey and the peaceful landscape there. There'd be something to eat in the city. The sooner he started, the sooner he would be fed.

The phrase caught him up short for a moment; it was an echo of one of Irene's maxims: "sooner begun, sooner done." She said it often to the boys.

He shook his head clear and began walking.

He had to step carefully around spots where the pavement was torn through; he could see the lower tier of the bridge below and, in places, the dull green flow of Spuyten Duyvil lower still. He had never owned a car, rarely driven in the city, but he had gone over the Henry Hudson Bridge enough times to know that its signs had not been in good repair for years. But the casual neglect he remembered was different from this: some signs were twisted, actually shredded, as if by some enormous hand that had crushed and torn them between thumb and forefinger. One, ripped in half and hanging in two pieces, welcomed him to New York City and demanded four dollars, cash or EZ-Pass. Tietjen caught himself, hand in pocket, reaching for his coins.

He reached the far shore and Manhattan without incident. The cold sharp air was eerily silent: no street sound, no cars, birds, not even the usually unnoticed bass hum of the city's functioning. Tietjen found it easy to believe himself the only living soul in Manhattan, an idea both terrifying and exhilarating. Inside, the voice that had driven him in panic from Massachusetts sighed: Home. More mundanely, his stomach growled again.

The Henry Hudson Parkway was badly torn up; in places where it would have been impassable by car it was nearly so on foot. Huge chunks of pavement thrust upward, guardrails scattered across the lane, burned out cars and—he turned his head but could not avoid the sight, nor the later memory—bodies scattered in the clear morning sunlight. One young man was curled fetally on the hood of a red sportscar, his face frozen in giddy rictus and his eyes wide open; there was not a mark on him. Looking east and uphill from the highway through the tangle of gray branches, Tietjen could not make out the tower of the Cloisters, but ribbons of color ran down the gray stonework that fronted the highway. Paint? he wondered. He had a vague notion that he might come back to find out another time; right now he couldn't stop. He trudged on.

The parkway followed along the Hudson River, curving back and forth on itself; the leafless trees hid, then revealed, the broad untroubled breadth of the river on one side, and the gray stonework of the MetroRail tunnels to the other. He became a little hypnotized by the curves, the sensation of being hidden away from the danger of the city here on the road; he didn't look up ahead. When the road curved to the left again and he did look up, it took him a long moment to realize that the big blocks of stone that littered the parkway had fallen from the overpass that led to the George Washington Bridge. One had hit a car passing underneath; Tietjen kept his distance from the car, his head craned backward, gawking. He was so close it was hard to make sense of what he saw. Suspension cables, tangled together or swinging free and deadly in the breeze, made a low, rumbling song. The upper deck of the bridge, and its bases, looked to be intact, but the stanchions that rose above were tilted, nudged left or right. The whole thing looked frighteningly unstable. Tietjen sprinted a hundred yards or so, just to get out from under the overpass. Then he continued quickly south, turning again and again to look backward, up at the bridge. Earthquake, he thought. Nothing else could have done such a thing. What he didn't understand was why the parkway showed no signs of it.

A while farther south, a complex of public housing buildings was burning in a slow, leisurely way, flames blackening the old brick, twisting the aluminum fixtures, while the dry wood of the trees planted along the pathways burned fast and hot with sooty smoke. No bodies visible there; it looked like a ghost town on fire.

Riverside Church, where he had once taken Irene for a concert, rose tall and elegant to overlook the highway. Only, when Tietjen looked back at the delicate tracery of the spire he saw something that made his skin crawl: the church had been neatly sliced in half, one side left standing and the other side crumbled, a spun-sugar decoration on which someone had dropped a brick. The rubble spilled out in a puddle in front of the modern annex to the church itself.

Then the highway disappeared. The road itself suddenly twisted sharply to the left, crossed over the northbound lane in a maneuver never imagined by its designers, and dropped down into the narrow park that separated the highway from Riverside Drive. Looking south there were only trees and a muddy riverbank for blocks, until the river curved around out of sight. Tietjen stayed on the road as it arched up and curved east, until it met the grass and earth of the shoulder and became part of it: the asphalt of the highway seemed to grow out of the patchy grass and gray dirt, guardrails and lane dividers and a lone abandoned car rising out of mud as if by magic. It was so weird Tietjen could hardly take it in: a sort of numbness overtook him. He felt distantly curious: what the hell could have done that?

He headed east for a while, trudging uphill toward Central Park. He had expected to see bodies, but there were very few here; only a smell—what Tietjen imagined must be the smell of death—followed him as he went. On Broadway, Amsterdam, Columbus avenues as he walked along 104th Street he saw comprehensible, almost comfortable disaster. Building grilles fallen from the huge old apartment buildings lay like crumpled tinsel, glittering in the sunlight. Burned-out storefronts, cars, trucks, and buses piled into each other, the streets churned and broken by earthquake. The Art Deco marquee of a movie house lay on the ground, blocking entrance to the theater. Wares of a small greengrocery were mashed and rotting in front of the otherwise undamaged store. Everywhere there was a smell of rot and decay, diluted in the cold clear air, but strong enough. Tietjen's nose wrinkled with the effort to filter out the scent of death and transmute the smell into something bearable.

The feeling of walking through someone else's dream increased; buildings he passed looked as though they had been hit by bombs, flattened by hurricanes. Tietjen thought of old photographs he had seen of Hiroshima and Beirut, London after the blitz. Sometimes there were bodies; he didn't look too closely. Other times there were just the buildings and their dust and rubble. From time to time he thought he heard laughter from the buildings; he hoped it was just the wind.

Central Park was a gray maze of trees not just bare of leaves but dead, skeletons reaching for the sky. Despite the bravado with Irene, Tietjen had not walked in the Park in years; he paused before he entered the Park, and once inside he walked quickly, trying to scan around him, uneasy in the silence, expecting the worst there. The hair on his neck stood up, his heart beat in heavy strokes, and he was certain something terrifying was waiting for him in the Park. There was no one, not gangs, no homeless camps, nothing. The emptiness was more frightening here than it had been in the littered, shattered streets. Tietjen was grateful when a gaunt squirrel, the first living creature he had seen in New York, eyed him from one of the bleached limbs of a maple tree. Hopefully, he made clicking noises, wishing he had something, crumbs, an apple core, to offer it. The thought made his own stomach growl again. He and the squirrel watched each other for a long moment; then the squirrel turned, chittering angrily, and disappeared down a bole in the trunk.

"Hey, wait—" he began. I've been reduced to begging for the company of a Central Park squirrel, he thought. But he didn't want the squirrel to go: something about the empty Park made him subtly uneasy in a way that was worse than the horror of walking among the ruins of the buildings. But except for the ashy barrenness of the trees there was nothing visibly wrong in the Park that he could see— nothing like the wreckage of Riverside Church or the eldritch twisting of the West Side Highway. He was thankful when he reached Fifth Avenue.

He continued east on 102nd Street. There were more bodies here: some looked as if they had dropped in midstride, others as if they had battled with each other for their lives. They all had the gray, bloated look of death, and the smell was appalling; Tietjen stayed as far away from the bodies as he could. Someone should be picking them up, taking them away, he thought. It was weird that they were still lying there.

More weirdness: half a block in from Fifth Avenue, a new block of condominiums with tattered red, white, and blue bunting in the windows, across the doorway and stringcourse, and on the steel security barrier a pristine sign that read MODEL UNIT OPEN FOR VIEWING. GRAND OPENING. Behind the sign the building was split in two, crumbling in on itself: grand opening. Tietjen found himself chuckling. The sound was shocking. He stared at the building for a long moment before he turned again toward Third Avenue and the building in which Irene and the boys lived.

The building was less damaged than many others he had passed. The steel grille that had made an ornamentally protective shell around the plaza and bottom stories of the three towers was crumpled, melted in places by the blast of an explosion that had ripped out the northwest corner of Irene's building. The outer door, inches thick and made of dull-finished steel to resemble the door of a vault, lay on its side propped against the wall of the building; the inner doors, more decoratively fashioned of steel and glass, were shattered. From across the street Tietjen could see the security desk with its banks of blank video screens; slumped over the top of the desk was one of the guards—he could not remember the man's name—with a hole several days old in the top of his head.

Trembling, Tietjen looked up past the two-story-high gape in the building where explosion had ripped through the concrete and brick and steel, up and up to where a fire was still burning, the flames randomly visible in one window, another, throughout the top ten stories of the building. The dark brick of the building was blackened, and smoke hovered over the building like a black halo, like a setting for the tongues of orange flame that reached up through the windows. The fire was frightening: it raged slow, fluttering in the midmorning air with eerie deliberateness, picking and choosing what it would destroy. The air around the upper stories rippled in real time with the slow-motion heat.

The fourteenth floor, where Irene's apartment was, was dead center in the fire. The corner of the building where the fireproof stairway had been had been ripped open, and the stairs hung into open space eight stories up. If Irene and his sons had been in the apartment when the fire began, they would have been trapped in the fire.

Tietjen did not know at first that he was crying. Tears coursed down his face through the grime and soot, and fell on the fabric of his topcoat. When he heard a wet choking noise Tietjen started and looked around him, stunned to realize that he had made the sound himself. He staggered back a few paces and leaned over the hood of a car, his empty stomach clenched on grief.

He cried for a long time, and afterward he stood, looking mutely up at the dark orange flames that licked casually from the windows of the fourteenth floor, dull against the blue sky. He tried to tell himself stories of how they might have survived, but all he could imagine was death. It was a long time past noon when Tietjen looked around him, thinking dimly that he could not stay where he was forever. He felt lost, dispossessed. He had returned to the city to do something, and now could not remember what it had been or why it had seemed so important. His stomach gurgled with the hollowness that follows long, harsh weeping.

If I stay here any longer I'll never get away. There was a siren call to the burning building, a silent lure that could draw him in and keep him; he took a few steps toward the gaping doorway before he stopped himself. The urge to surrender was very strong: what else had he come home for if not to find out what had happened to his family? Now he knew, and he needed something: a place to go and something to do when he got there. He'd come back with a purpose: somewhere the city was still home. He could not imagine anything else.

He decided at last to head for his own apartment on West Seventy-sixth. It meant crossing Central Park again; that very nearly turned him against the whole idea, but after a moment he looked away from the burning building, from the guard—his name was Larry, Tietjen remembered—slumped over the security desk, and turned back toward Park Avenue.

After so much crying and fear he now felt . . . light, empty. He catalogued disasters as he saw them, but without much feeling for what he saw: fire; explosion; quake; flooding. Madness, he thought, when he saw a storefront shattered by gun blasts. Then he realized that the stuff littering the doorway was human bodies, and the shock of it cut through his lightheadedness. He stood stock-still for a moment, watching for movement, but there was none. In the middle of the street a tangle of electric cable was threaded through a manhole and lay bared for thirty feet of the crosswalk. It had electrified an MTA bus; the big blue and white bus was still humming with electricity. Once Tietjen thought he heard laughter again, but he saw no one when he looked down Ninety-third Street toward the East River, toward the sound.

At Park he started south again. A few minutes later, through the ruined grille of the Eighty-eighth Street gate, he saw a whole row of town houses pushed askew and leaning, perfectly ordered, at a forty-five-degree angle, windows and doors in neat slanting parallels. This morning the impossible things had been to him curious but real; now he began to doubt his eyes.

So much of the destruction he saw was things that couldn't have been done by man—like the skewed buildings. He saw some signs of looting, but most of what he saw seemed to be purely acts of God. Then, as he came down Park Avenue, he looked east, down a gated side street. The two-story mesh fence was intact, and from it someone had hung severed human hands, feet, legs, and arms, some still wearing shreds of clothing. They were hung with rope and wire and even ribbon. At the top of the fence a whole body had been hung, a man whose feet had been forced through the holes in the mesh; his ankles were broken. He was grimacing joyfully.

Tietjen turned and ran south, stumbling blindly, until he was several blocks distant from the fence. Then he stopped, chest heaving, and threw up.

From then, he walked on with a kind of tunnel vision, taking in details of specific horrors, but not letting them surprise him. So he didn't see what he was walking into until he was almost upon it; ten city blocks had collapsed into the ground, leaving a sea of stone and concrete nearly level with the street. The subway, he thought dimly: the Lexington Avenue tunnel must have collapsed and brought all of this down with it. The apricot glow of afternoon light made the rubble shimmer slightly, moving in the windless air. Without more than a moment's thought Tietjen turned west again, toward the Park, to walk around the crater.

He rested on the steps of the Metropolitan Museum of Art. The building looked untouched, comfortably ordinary, banners still fluttering between the paired columns; only the settlement of street people who lived on the steps and plaza was gone without a trace. Maybe, he thought, they'd gone inside. Maybe the place to find people would be in public buildings like this: the Red Cross would set up in large buildings, housing the homeless and tending to victims. Surely survivors would come to places like this, to the museums and armories and courthouses.

He was hungry for people. He was hungry for talk. He wanted

to tell his story and hear others', to talk about what he had seen and find out where the madness lay: in his mind or across the streets of the city.

Tietjen rose stiffly from the step and climbed the stairs to the museum doors. What, after all, did he have to lose?

The main doors were locked, the glass unbroken. Behind them Tietjen could see the dim vault of the museum lobby. Neat signs stood at the doors: MUSEUM CLOSED. HOURS:. He checked each of the side doors and the last moved ponderously at his touch. For the first time since he had left the bridge that morning, something going right. Cautiously, Tietjen entered the museum.

The air was dusty. He heard echoes, but when he listened there was no sound save his own footfall. He put it down to the resonance of empty space, and cautiously started across the lobby, through the arched metal detectors and past the information desk with its bright fans of brochures in French, Spanish, Korean, Tagalog. The security doors to the left, leading to the Greek and Roman art and the Rockefeller wing, were ajar. The stairs ahead were empty expect for the statuary on the landings. The immense floral arrangements that sat in granite urns were wilting, decaying sweetly.

Not too loudly he called out. "Hello? Anyone here?" The echo in response unnerved him, and for a long moment he waited, wondering which way to proceed. Then another sound answered the echo of his call. He went left, toward the Rockefeller wing. He thought the noise might be a voice answering his.

He had to stop inside the door to let his eyes adjust to the darkness; without artificial light the hallway was filled with steely shadows and black shapes. Tietjen made his way cautiously along the left side of the hall, one hand skimming lightly along the surface of the wall. The hall let onto another hall, and another, finally ending in a smaller stairwell that glared with afternoon light. He stood blinking for a moment, until a sound of footfall behind him made his stomach lurch. Tietjen swallowed and turned.

"You're real! It's hard to know when a noise is a *noise,* if you know what I mean." The man was tall and bone thin except for a sloping paunch; he wore a suit that struck Tietjen immediately as professorial, curiously dapper under the circumstances. His manner, too, seemed cocktail-party sociable, but his voice was steady and the hand that he offered to Tietjen did not tremble. Tietjen held out his own hand, bemused, feeling like the old joke about English gentlemen dressing for dinner on a desert island.

"You hear things in an old building like this when it's empty. I'm glad you're real and not just another shifting block of granite." The man turned in the direction he had come from. "Come on, I'll take you downstairs. Are you hungry? Of course you are. You'll want to see what I've been able to save, won't you? I was the Assistant Curator for Eastern Art, but of course now I'm sort of Curator Pro Tem. Until things get sorted out, you know."

Tietjen revised his first estimate; okay, a little crazy, but benign. The curator's eccentric cheer made Tietjen feel more solid. What had the man called him? Real. And it rather cheered him to think that in the midst of all the destruction someone was taking care of the Met's art treasures. "I'm John Tietjen," he said, matching his stride to the curator's.

"Tietjen. Is that Dutch? Down these stairs. The emergency generator is working downstairs, so there's light, but I'm afraid that the main stairs are flooded below this level—thank God most of the doors were sealed and nothing was badly damaged. This area is for staff only; acquisitions and restoration. Dutch, right?" He turned to smile again at Tietjen. "I suppose you're hungry."

While Tietjen listened to the stream of chat, the curator led him down the narrow stairs. When the upper floors cut off the daylight from above, Tietjen heard for the first time since the night before the voice inside his head, a vague unhappy whine.

He ignored it. I have to trust someone. Maybe he knows what happened.

"Let me see, let me see," the man was murmuring to himself. "Let's feed you first, then we can see about getting you settled. It's rather a responsibility being in charge of the whole museum. Of course, it's more like a field promotion, as it were. I think the Board will approve what I've done, on the whole."

"I'm sure," Tietjen said politely. "Look, were you here when all this happened? Did you see—"

"Here in the museum? Lord, no, I was on my way home—I live in Greenpoint, but when I heard what was happening I turned right around and came back. Thank God I did, too. On my way back in I saw what was happening at other museums—bricks through the windows of the Whitney; the tower fell right in on top of MOMA—sort of poetic justice, I thought—" the curator nattered on.

"I mean," Tietjen broke in doggedly. "Did you see how all the—the damage started? What happened? Where did it start?"

"Start? I don't know. I was on the bus, but I got out—at an unsecured stop, too—and came right back. Someone had to stay with the museum. Here we are." The man stopped before a large door marked STAFF ONLY, and opened it with a key from a janglingly overfull ring. Inside was a cluttered office furnished with gunmetal gray cabinets, files, desks. An old bulletin board covered in clusters of old notes and paper notices hung by the door, with a newer electronic board hanging beside it, its backlit screen dark; one desk had been turned into a makeshift kitchen with a pair of hot plates, a small store of dishes, glasses, and silverware, and neat stacks of cans and packages. In a corner behind two filing cabinets Tietjen saw blankets laid out precisely against the wall, with several books and a lantern neatly arranged on an upturned carton.

"What would you like? There's soup, stew, the usual things. I'm afraid it's not haute cuisine, but it's food."

Tietjen was suddenly giddy with hunger. It had been two days since he had eaten. "Anything at all. Do you have anything to drink?"

The curator emptied a can of stew into a pot and put it on the hot plate. "There's bottled water. I hope that will do. I took most of this from the restaurant kitchens. They do have a wine cellar, but I don't want to encourage drinking during the crisis. One never knows where it might lead." The stew began to bubble thickly, filling the close room with the smell of beef stock and onions. Tietjen's mouth began to water. In a few minutes the man spooned the contents of the pan into a delicate porcelain bowl and handed it to Tietjen with a beautiful, delicate silver spoon, beaten so thin it seemed a touch would bend it. Seeing his guest examine the bowl and spoon, the curator laughed. "From one of the exhibits upstairs. Georgian. They were made to be used, after all. Besides, no one's going to complain: the woman in charge of housecrafts and jewelry was crushed under an Apollo on the second floor. Eat up."

Tietjen ate, unquestioning. The stew was gone too soon, but it left a warm glow in his stomach and he found himself able to focus again on what the man was saying.

The curator had stopped talking while Tietjen ate, and sat with his ankles crossed, watching his guest with a musing stare. "All done?" he asked. "Splendid. Would you like to see the others?"

Tietjen looked up. "You're not alone down here?" He felt suddenly edgy, cautious. He wanted to trust the man, the first person he had met in the city. *The guy's okay.* Defiantly, *I'm okay.*

"Of course I'm not alone. I'm just the curator. Come on, I'll show you." Tietjen stood to follow the other man. Back out to the corridors again. Deliberately, the man pulled out the weighty key ring and locked the office up. "It's going to take a long time to get the collection back to where it should be." He murmured to himself. "Dutch, you did say Dutch?"

The curator started off deliberately down the hall and stopped before another locked door. "The Asian wing was badly damaged. It's going to be a problem." He seemed preoccupied with other thoughts. Again he brought out the key ring and went through a self-important process of unlocking the heavy door. "Hello! I've brought someone."

The door swung heavily open; Tietjen smelled dust and the faint trace of decay he was beginning to recognize. He blinked in the dim light of one yellow emergency light at the back of the room. It was a large storage space: frames and exhibition easels stacked against each other, a few canvases, their faces turned to the wall, shelves that divided the room into small aisles. There was movement from different sides of the room; farthest left Tietjen saw first a glitter of eyes in the amber light, then a restless, shrugging motion. Tietjen stood, disbelieving. The voice cried in his head: *too late, too late.* Behind Tietjen the curator clicked a switch and an overhead light flickered on.

"Hello," the curator repeated amiably. "How are you today?"

The man he addressed, swarthy, young, dressed in the institutional whites of a food services worker, stared at the curator with dumb hopeless eyes. A rope was tied to one of his wrists and to a heavily laden metal shelving unit. The knot could easily have been untied, but the prisoner looked in shock and quite helpless; Tietjen doubted he was capable of it. He stole a look at the curator, who was professional, enjoying the role of docent. *Be easy,* Tietjen told himself. *Wait for the right moment to run like hell.*

"Italian, but not the best. Primitive." The curator pushed aside a box that stood partially in front of one of the small areas to reveal a black girl, maybe seventeen years old, dressed in street leathers. The gaunt beauty of her face warred with feral rage in her eyes. There was a dark slash of dried blood across her forehead and both her hands were tied. Tietjen would not have vouched for his own life or the curator's had she been able to free herself.

"Primitive," the man behind him repeated appreciatively. "A little damaged, but still quite valuable. Actually, there are three, but the other two are damaged."

Tietjen looked beyond the girl to see a grotesque grouping against the back wall. Two black men, one in the same leathers the girl wore, the other somewhat older and dressed in a business suit; they were obviously dead.

The girl followed the curator's movements, her eyes flickering like a cat's at every gesture. "Bastard," she muttered. "You wait, bastard. Gon' rip you bare-hand; gon' drink you blood, mother-fucker bastard. Bastard—"

It was as if the curator had not heard. From another aisle a woman's voice, quiet and ironical, said: "Don't waste your breath. He won't answer us."

This time it was Tietjen who pushed aside the boxes to reveal an older woman, her hands tied behind her, sitting on a carton. She was still blinking in the light. Her glance at Tietjen held sympathy and—weirdly—faint amusement, as if she were embarrassed to have been found in such a condition. She and Tietjen looked at each other for a long moment; he liked her. For a moment the nightmare unreality of this cellar room, the mad curator close enough behind him so that Tietjen could feel his breath on his neck, the harsh mutterings of the black woman, faded in the face of this older woman's rueful smile. Then her expression changed. Before he had time to understand the message her eyes conveyed, or to hear the warning she yelled, something heavy came down on the back of his head. He heard the curator behind him drop whatever he had used as a club; the older woman's shout rang in his ears, mixing with the black girl's stream of threats and abuse. The sounds together flowed into the high keening in his head: *too late, too late.* Tietjen lost consciousness altogether.

3

JIT woke to the buzz of voices: faint, very far away or very weak or very few. He was so glad for the noise in his mind that for a moment he missed everything about the voices, the bad things even, the feelings so complex and hateful and angry and frightened that Jit had wondered how he could live, hearing them. He was lonely without the feelings. He was frightened. For the first time in his life Jit was hearing his own thoughts in a peculiar clear way, like pennies dropped one by one on a stone floor. Nothing filled the emptiness, he could not hide from it in games, talking back to the squirrels, making the dead trees leaf again. The fuzzy echo of the voices in his mind now was welcome. He croaked a laugh, sitting up before the cold ash of his last night's fire, and stretched for the voices, welcoming them, seeking their direction.

Outside it was still dark. The voices were dark, confused, angry, strange. Not the night voices of the park dwellers, he knew those well enough. They had been angry, violent, crafty in the way that the squirrels and rats were crafty. But there was a flavor to these new voices that Jit liked but did not understand, dangerous but curious. The voices tasted like anything could happen. And for once he could easily pick out individual voices with individual feelings, clear and distinct. That was something new: from his first memory Jit had been awash in so many voices, so many feelings, that he had only been able to pick out strands of meaning, themes.

"Hello," he said to the darkness, to a mad voice that was howling somewhere in the night. Someone was locked up in a dark room, listening to someone else crying and muttering.

Jit giggled. He reached out for something else. A voice full of pain, incoherent with it, its owner ground beneath some heavy thing—a piece of building—was slipping in and out of consciousness. Jit played tag with the voice until it whispered away to nothing. Bolder still, he flitted from voice to voice, tasting each, stopping long enough to sample the different, singular flavors, all a little crazy, all a little strange in the darkness.

The novelty did not wear off until the morning light began to seep down to Jit's tunnel and the voices became quieter, the game less exciting. Jit was hungry. If the voices were true, something had happened outside the Park, and he was curious. He had met images of emptiness, open streets, skyscrapers brought down and lying like fallen giants. A new playground, a wonderful new place to explore. It was time he found more food, anyway; even the squirrel that chattered when he reached for its voice knew that the hot-dog and souvlaki men would not stand on Fifth Avenue today.

The day was clear and bright. Instinct urged him back to the tunnel in daylight, but the voices said he would be safe today in the city. Jit experimented, walking coolly down the center of a path, watching from the corners of his eyes but claiming the path, the whole Park as his own.

He went west. When he listened particularly he could hear new voices, not so interesting as the night voices, but good. A woman was trapped somewhere in the dark, facing a sea of tiny eyes. Rats, Jit knew. Did she? Yes, he could taste her funny terror as they surged forward, burying her in musky scent; the tiny scrabblings of their feet against her skin before they went to work and tore into her.

That reminded him that he was hungry. For that, best to go farther north on the West Side; too far down was only towers and stores filled with things whose uses Jit could not understand. The security walls of steel mesh and old brownstone were crumbled into each other where Jit reached the Park's edge, at Sixty-seventh Street. He scaled the pile of debris, moving agilely from displaced stone block to a doubled-up steel column, making a game of it. As he climbed it seemed the wall itself was playing with him, growing higher as he climbed. It took longer to reach the top than he had thought. In places the steel mesh grew out of the stone like a weed.

At the top of the wall Jit balanced carefully, scanning along the street, Central Park West, looking for movement, people. Uniforms. People in uniforms had taken him that one time. Now he saw nothing but the occasional skirl of a piece of paper or the lopsided roll of a hubcap down the center of the street. Emboldened, Jit slid down the face of the wall and started a cool saunter down Sixty-seventh Street, toward Broadway. At the corner, gazing across the broad knot of avenues, he stopped. There was a circle of people in the plaza, handfast and moving in a slow, deliberate dance, crying out in low voices. Jit could not hear their words, but touched their minds and found confusion and pain and a somber, bizarre hope that the dance they did round the fountain in the plaza would placate an angry god. Jit understood that; his world had always been ruled by dark forces, erratic gods. Still, he stayed clear of the dancers.

Fifteen minutes' walk up Broadway brought him to the neighborhood of small shops, butchers and bakers and greengrocers. Ordinarily Jit would have found these places just after dark, stealing and running in the confusion of closing time. This was a different world, and he gawked and peered in the shattered windows and wrinkled his nose at the rank smell of spoiling meat, rotten vegetables, the dusty smell of stale bread and pastry. He was hungry enough to snatch a few rock-hard doughnuts from a baker's counter; when he bit in he found tiny black bugs cutting tunnels in the sugary cake, and threw the doughnut down.

He kept walking. A fireplug gushed water into the street and down the steps of the Seventy-ninth Street subway station. Cars and buses were piled into each other, turned on their sides or completely over. Looking up once, Jit saw something dangling from the railing of a fire escape down Eighty-first Street: a child dressed in jeans and a knit shirt, hanging by one ankle, unmoving. The boy was wrapped or tangled up in clothesline; Jit could see towels and underwear still clinging to the line. Jit watched the dead child curiously, without horror or amusement.

Finally he found a supermarket, both doors slammed open invitingly. The air inside was heavy with the same ripe, sickish smell of rotting food he had met in the butchers and greengrocers. The frozen food was defrosted and spoiled, and what meat there was left was silver-green in its wrinkled plastic wrapping. The bread was gone, and the milk that had not been taken was bad. Jit fought through the thick foul smell around the dairy case and stuffed packages of cheese into the bag he had brought, different colors and shapes as they caught his eye. A few aisles over he found Saltines and animal crackers, brightly colored bags of chips and cookies, and started pulling them down from the shelves into a pile. He would have to find a way to bring it all back to the Park. Did he dare take one of the shiny plastic carts with him? Jit grabbed the handle of one and tugged it over toward the crackers, tossing things in, watching with satisfaction as the cart got fuller and fuller.

Canned foods. He selected by picture and color: gave preference to the red and brown foods and took fewer of the yellow and green foods. Soups and stews, anything with meat in them. Fruit in sticky syrup, tiny black beans in heavily spiced sauce, corn and olives and anything else he remembered by label or illustration. The cart moved more and more slowly as Jit piled things into it. At last he thought he had enough. Opening a box of sugar-dusted cookies, he munched on one while he tugged the cart one-handed toward the door. There was an anti-theft barrier there, wide enough for Jit to pass but too narrow for the cart. Jit looked anxiously around, afraid someone would come and try to stop him. At last, quickly, he emptied everything from the cart, bent and crawled under it and slowly stood with the thing on his shoulders. The barrier did not extend high; Jit brought the cart through the barrier, then went back through and laboriously transferred the food to the cart again.

Then it was a matter of pushing or tugging the cart through the streets, watching for people, guarding his treasure. He crossed east and entered the Park at Eighty-first Street, reaching out for voices nearby. But there was no one near, no one in the Park at all, only a few voices on the edges, someone huddled under the gratings that hid the Columbus Circle entrance, voices from the east side where someone was crying. Jit reached out to find that voice and explore it, keeping his hand and half attention on the cart he was pulling. The crying came from the dark, a mind as small and terrified as one of the Park squirrels, watching as things changed and moved in the dark. People in the shadows, one voice dark and rich with hatred, muttering words like those of the Park people Jit recognized. He changed his focus from the small keening mind to the angry one.

A woman. Something was—she couldn't move her hands; the world looked strange, yellow-colored and oddly refracted through her eyes. She hated, she wanted to kill, visions of bright blood and vengeance drove the words away. For a moment it felt so familiar to Jit that he welcomed the anger. But it was too strong, undiluted, washing through him so that he could hardly see his own reality: the blue plastic cart before him, the gray earth and bristle of leafless trees. He recoiled, trying to untangle himself from the voice, but it followed, hating him as much as the others, all the others, everyone. Itself. The hatred burned hot and fierce, a pain that lanced through his head. Jit pushed, shoved the cart away from him, trying to shove the voice from his head. "No!" he yelled, and his voice echoed baldly among the trees. "Stop! Stop!"

Blindly, he did what he had always done, reaching inside himself until he found the door. He would put the voice there, with the others, the bad feelings. There was something about the door—he had dreamt about the door, what was it? He found the place in his head, frantically swept up the killing rage that filled him and, finally, opened the door to put the rage behind it, away with all the other horrors and terrors and furies.

There was nothing there. From inside the swirling anger that filled him, Jit saw: the place behind the door that had always been dark with the emotions he had placed there was white empty. Where did it go? For a moment he stood still, around him the Park and the clear bright day, inside him the woman's anger churning, and farther inside, a kernel of dry curiosity, wondering what had happened to the door in his head and the feelings he had hidden there. Then Jit got smart. He could not bear the anger: put it behind the door and slam the door shut on it and do not worry where the other things have gone to. If the things did not come back to trouble him, why should he care?

His head hurt. Jit blinked in the sunlight and saw the blue grocer's cart rattling in the breeze ten feet away, where he had shoved it. He should get back to his place before someone found him. He shoved the cart in front of him. He tried to eat another cookie, but his stomach hurt, clenched hard with the anger that had swept through him.

What had he dreamed? He tried to remember again. The door burst open, swept open by the force of what he had put behind it.

"Wha' you do?" he said aloud to the door, as if it somehow had destroyed itself. "Wha' happen?"

No answer. It was too much to think about, the door spilling all those things out again, back into the city. Filling up people with all their old angers, with new angers. "Wha' you do?" he asked again, accusing.

The steely afternoon sun shone on him, on the grocery cart with its burden of good eating. There was nothing he could do if the door had burst its seams. All he could do was take his food home and put it away. And eat, his stomach reminded him. He could eat. "O-kay, Jitters, you gon' eat," he said aloud. The words whispered all around him in the air of the Park; he was not alone. "O-kay, Jitters!" he shouted, and the words rang in the trees. He started trotting with the cart pushed before him, singing tunelessly under his breath, thinking of what he would eat when he got back to his place.

He had always known about the voices; he had to be taught about the door. Old Nogai had told him about it, and the wall, and the places in his head to find the feelings and put them. Old Nogai had lived in the Park for a while when Jit was small, and had talked to Jit with a funny singsong, all the time drinking from a bag and twisting pieces of paper into shapes. Jit had found Nogai one afternoon, twisting paper and talking to the pigeons that paraded arrogantly around the Wollman Rink fence. Ducks, he called them. In a high-pitched singsong he rebuked them for laziness, for disrespect. "Bad ducks! Whyou come bother an old man, ducks? Away!" For a while Nogai, as shy as Jit himself, had refused to talk to the little boy. Gradually a few words were spoken from the side of the mouth and the two had edged together. Old Nogai called Jit Duck as often as not, and Jit would giggle way up high.

"Bad feelings all over this city," Nogai had said. "Bad feelings, you find them, boy?"

Jit had nodded solemnly, not at all understanding what the old man meant.

"Sick feelings, make your gut hurt, you understand, boy?"

This time Jit did understand, sort of. The things that washed through him, they made him hurt sometimes. Did they belong to the city?

"Only one way for bad feelings, boy. You find the place somewhere and bury them deep quick." Nogai threw a handful of pebbles at the uninterested pigeons. "Find a wall and throw them bad feelings over. You find a door and lock them safe away. You understand me, boy?"

Jit had giggled high, shaking his head in imitation of the old man. Nogai wheeled around fiercely: "You understand, you duck?

Bad feelings get all twisted up in you, make you old like me. You pitch them bad things 'hind the door, you understand?"

"Understand?" Jit echoed. The old man's mind was rich with a thousand confused, scented images: the searing taste of the liquor he drank, the baffling flurry of movement from the pigeons, even Jit's narrow white face. Everything itched with the irritable need to be understood. Jit tasted old Nogai's thoughts and wondered at them. "How?" he asked at last, less about the door Nogai spoke of, than about the old man's thoughts as a whole.

Nogai had told him. Then, and later, and again and again, over and over, the door, the wall, take the bad feelings and the bad thoughts and throw them away, hide them somewhere safe behind a door, get rid of them. "Or they eat you up, boy-duck, you hear me?"

"Eat you up, boy-duck," Jit echoed.

For a while, until Nogai had disappeared (everyone Jit knew in the Park went away sooner or later), the old man led Jit through the shadowy dim places in his own head, looking for the wall, the doors. By the time Nogai had been swallowed up by the city, Jit knew the old man's trick so well that it was automatic. And it worked: nothing had eaten him up. But now the bad things had found a way out of the locked room, had broken down the door, splintered the frame and twisted the hinges, spilled out into the city again.

A squirrel chattered angrily as Jit passed. "Don't care!" Jit called to the squirrel and the dying afternoon light. "Don't care. Go way, duck!"

The squirrel, more easily intimidated than Nogai's pigeons, fled at once. Jit was pleased by the victory. He found the access tunnel he wanted and quickly unloaded the grocery cart, putting everything off to one side of the tunnel, thinking as he did of the food he would eat later, savoring the choices to be made. Something big had changed the city, but if that meant the food places would be wide open to him, Jit did not mind. Then Jit clambered up again and shoved the grocery cart down the path, watching it rock and sway and clatter downhill, away from Jit's tunnel so that no one would know where he was.

Then he slid down into the tunnel himself. Around him, the thin air had begun to take on the flavor of slowly waking voices. Jit pulled out a heavy blanket, piled his goods on it, and began to drag it slowly down the tunnel toward his home.

4

TIETJEN was only faintly surprised to wake with his hands bound. His head hurt ferociously. He struggled into a sitting position, trying to ignore the pounding ache that movement increased. Blinking in the dim wash of yellow light he made out the form of someone sitting above him.

"You awake?"

It was the older woman. Tietjen tried to remember what she had looked like in the light: white hair, a heart-shaped, tanned face; eyes blue or gray, very steady; spare, rather fine-boned features but not—he struggled to find the word—not patrician, exactly. It came to him at last: if Irene had aged thirty years—gracefully—she might have looked like this woman. There was something comforting in her presence, someone so abundantly normal-seeming sharing the nightmare with him.

"Lie still for a little bit, if you can," she was saying. "I don't think you'd have come to so fast if you were concussed, but frankly I don't know enough to tell."

"How long?" he asked thickly.

"Only a few minutes. He tied your hands and dragged you over there, and left just a moment ago. He's getting better," she observed dispassionately. "He killed the older man when he hit him."

Tietjen became aware of a constant murmured litany of expletives and threats from the black girl. "How long have you been here?" he asked.

"I don't know exactly. Two days, maybe. The poor man over there was here when *he* brought me in. The others came after."

"You're very calm about it," Tietjen said.

"I've had nothing to do but achieve calm. If you can convince me that panic would help, I'll gladly panic." Her voice trembled slightly in the darkness. "I'd take just about any excuse. In the meantime, when you think you can move, we should see about getting out of here."

Experimentally, Tietjen tried to shift onto his knees. It was not difficult: his feet were not bound, but each movement made his head hurt fiercely. "I can move," he said at last. "But as for getting out—"

She laughed briefly, a startlingly lovely sound. "Piece of cake, if you can move. I've been waiting for him to bring in one sound-minded person. If you can get your back round to me, I'll see about untying your wrists, then you untie mine, and we leave."

"Just like that? What about the doors?"

"Old secret about these doors: you need a cardpass or a key to get *into* the offices, but they're meant to keep people out, not in. I used to do volunteer work at the museum," she added, almost apologetically.

Tietjen stared up at the woman's silhouette, wishing he could see her face. "Why haven't you left before this?" With some difficulty he braced himself against the wall and slid upward to his feet. She made room for him on the packing crate she sat on, and for a moment they concentrated on getting into a position where she could work on his bonds.

"Needed someone who would be able to untie me after I untied him. And willing to," she added. "That girl over there is so crazy for blood I was afraid she'd kill me and go after him. Sort of defeat my whole purpose. Acchh." She stopped talking and concentrated on the knots at Tietjen's wrists. "There," she said at last. "Wriggle your hands a little. Can you get loose?"

Tietjen shrugged his shoulders, flexed his wrists, and found that the bonds were loose enough for him to work his way out. "How'd you learn to do that?" he asked.

"Untying years of Merit Badge practice; den mother, scout leader, all that stuff. Your turn." She sounded a little less certain as she presented her bound hands to him. Tietjen realized that she was not as sure as she pretended that he would not leave her there. He bent in the yellow light to unknot the rope.

"Okay, all done," he said after a moment, and watched with satisfaction as the rope dropped away from her wrists and she flexed her arms, sighing with the pleasure of unrestricted movement. She turned to face him, flexing her fingers, and held out her hand. For a moment he thought there was some other knot he was supposed to untie.

"I'm Barbara McGrath," she said.

Tietjen took her hand. It was very cold. "John Tietjen. Feels like you're freezing."

She laughed again. "Rotten circulation. Being tied up does nothing good for it. Look, I'd really like to get out of here. What should we do about—" She waved a hand to indicate their companions. "We have to set them free, I think, but the dishwasher isn't capable of taking care of himself, and that girl—"

"If we set her free I think she'd go after . . ." Tietjen rolled his eyes upward. "I don't think she'll go for us unless we try to stop her. The younger man was with her?"

"Yes. But even before that, I think she was a little crazy. These street kids—"

Tietjen thought of the boy he had helped the night before. Years ago. "You know how to spring that door?"

Barbara McGrath grinned. "No trick." She went to the door, pushed a button to the side of the knob, turned the knob, pulled, and the door swung heavily open, carried by its own weight. "Stone walls do not a prison make."

"Nice. What shall we do with him?" Tietjen was untying the dishwasher's bond. "Bring him along?"

"He'll slow us down," she said thoughtfully. "But someone has to take care of him."

"I guess so." Cautiously, Tietjen moved to where the black girl sat, huddled against the wall. The girl's eyes followed his movement, her head turned almost 180 degrees to watch him as he bent to untie her. "I wouldn't stand too near the door," he murmured to McGrath. And the moment her hands were free enough to pull out of the rope the girl was across the room and out. She had no weapon but her hands; Tietjen doubted she would need any. He felt a shiver of guilt at what would happen to the curator if she found him, but, "Let's get out of here," he said.

"Right." McGrath took the dishwasher's hand and started to lead him out of the dim room. But the man refused to be pulled toward the hall. For a few moments she tried to talk to him, calmly, soothingly. When that did not work she let Tietjen try. The man pulled his hand from McGrath's and backed away, settling against the wall as if that were all the safety he knew.

"We can't wait too long," Tietjen murmured. "If she finishes with him she may remember us and come back. I don't want to fight her."

"Or anyone, with that bump on your head. I know. Dammit, man, we're trying to help you." McGrath tried one more time, impatience barely hidden by brisk kindliness. The dishwasher stayed where he was, only his eyes tracking from one of them to the other. "Hell, we'd better go."

Tietjen was the first out into the hallway. "You know the quickest way out of here?" he asked. When she nodded, he stood back and let her lead him through the hallway, up a narrow flight of stairs to a metal door set at street level. The door moved reluctantly. When they pushed on it together it opened with a grating sound that rang down the hall behind them: shards of steel mesh from the security grating littered the ground around it. An automatic alarm blared for a moment, then was abruptly silent. Tietjen thought he heard a sound of laughter somewhere, and stifled the impulse to run: the curator surely had problems enough to distract him from their exit.

Central Park stretched to their left, Fifth Avenue to the right. The air was cold and clean after the mustiness of the lower hallways. Tietjen breathed deeply, turned to look at his accomplice again. She was panting a little, grinning. She had had the presence of mind to grab a jacket—probably hers, since it fit—as they left the storeroom. She was dressed in a red turtleneck, navy blue sweater, darker red skirt, low-heeled boots. The jacket, which McGrath now began to fasten, was lined with synthetic fleece. Tietjen eyed her with a little envy: he had left his topcoat in the curator's office, and was not about to return to look for it.

"Well," McGrath said. "Where to now?"

There was something infectious about her matter-of-fact good humor. Tietjen found himself returning her grin. "I don't know. You hungry?"

"I'm always hungry. My family were embarrassed by me for years: I can always eat. I *like* food. And I'm rambling, aren't I? Yes, I certainly am hungry."

"Let's go find some food, then. I think a celebration is in order. You're the first—" He searched for a word but found none that worked. "You're the first person I've met in three days who was dealing with this, right in the middle of it. Who wasn't crazy or trying to get out. Or trying to die."

"I'm not the dying sort. About crazy, Gordon might have had something to say. Tell you what: you find the food, I'll pay. Least I can do for my hero. I just hope they take plastic."

Tietjen laughed. It felt wonderful. The sky was blue-gray in the wake of sunset. He felt guilty, laughing: so much death, so much devastation. It did not matter; the kidding around was as nourishing as food to him. "Well, as to who rescued whom . . ." He led them away from the still-disturbing vibration of Central Park, eastward.

They found a delicatessen Tietjen remembered on Lexington. It was empty, the security grill across the door was torn but still in place. The sidewalk door into the basement of the place had been sprung by a quake and they pried the door open and crept in, up the stairs into the restaurant. The power had been off for several days and all the prepared food was spoiled; the kitchen area stank of sour milk and rancid meat. Downstairs in the basement there were candles, labeled FOR EMERGENCY. "I think this qualifies," McGrath said dryly, and lit several while Tietjen closed and barricaded the delivery door against intruders. Then they investigated the industrial-size cans of fruit, soup, vegetables that were stacked in neat rows beyond the door.

"Sit down," McGrath said, making a mime of dusting off her hands in businesslike fashion. "The least I can do is make you dinner."

"Definitely the best offer I've had all day." He watched while the woman emptied a can of juice down a drain, efficiently cut chimney holes in the lid and a small opening in one side, then started a fire inside.

"Where did you learn to do that?" Tietjen asked, admiring the neat stove.

"Two girls in the Brownies, and a son who was the Cub-Boy-Eagle Scout to end all Cub-Boy—you get the idea. You learn a lot of things I used to regard as utterly useless. Look, can you see if there are any vegetables around here that don't come from a can and haven't gone bad?"

Looking, Tietjen found bags of onions and potatoes, a few

scrawny carrots. As he investigated the shelves he felt like a child at Christmas offered the run of a toy store. At last they sat down to a huge meal of stew, then soup, a dozen little packets of crackers, packaged pound cake with syrupy Royal Anne cherries.

"God, I feel sick," McGrath said contentedly. "That was wonderful. All I want now is a nice zinfandel and some Schubert in the background. Ummph." She leaned back against a packing crate, one leg still tucked under her in half-lotus. "What I'll settle for is something else again. Uff." She shifted a little. "I could do with a walk, but I don't think this is the night for a midnight stroll."

"Maybe not tonight." Tietjen gave a quiet little snort.

"What's funny?"

"My wife would have loved to hear that. It was a kind of running battle between us: she didn't like it when I walked around town; she hated it when I took our kids out almost anywhere; she was sure I'd get them killed." He trailed off, thinking again of the flames that he had seen licking from the windows of Irene's apartment that morning. A quiet tremor shook him. He did not cry, just sat and shook for a moment.

"What happened to them?" There was no laughter in McGrath's voice, just a kind detachment that made it easier to speak.

"I don't know. Irene probably kept them in her apartment until it was too late. I saw what happened to their building. If they were in there I don't see how they could have survived."

"You don't know, then."

He thought about it for a moment. "I know. They're dead. I don't know how I know, but I'm certain of it."

She didn't question the statement. "You weren't with them. You and your wife divorced?"

"Almost four years ago. No, I wasn't there." It felt like a confession, enormously difficult. "I was away when this happened. It took me until this morning to get back into the city. I was so certain that nothing could really touch them in that goddamned fortress they lived in. The boys—" he stopped. His throat was thick with anger. "Shit. I should have been here."

"You don't think you could have kept it from happening, do you?" For a moment Tietjen heard Frank Corliss's voice in McGrath's words. That same dry common sense puncturing his self-pity. "I saw it, some of it. Even if you'd been in the city, downstairs in the lobby of their building, even, there might not have been any chance for them. It was too damned fast. Random. And too—" She stopped.

"Too what? What did happen? What did you see?"

"All I saw was what happened in the subway. And only in that one station. I mean, I don't know what happened in other places, other subway stations. By the time I got out—"

"What happened where you were?" Tietjen interrupted. "I've been trying to understand, piecing things together that I've seen."

"I was going downtown to a harp recital at NYU. A friend of Ellen's was playing and she sent me the ticket. Ellen is my younger girl; I was staying at her apartment, sitting for Dermott. I don't imagine Ellen ever took the subway when she could avoid it, but I rather like them; must be because it's a novelty for me. Country girl. Do you know the Lexington Avenue station at Seventy-seventh Street?"

Tietjen nodded.

"I thought I'd given it plenty of time: that line is always slow. There was quite a crowd waiting. More as the wait went on—late rush hour, you know. Both the guards were up at the token booth chatting with the girl in the booth—I remember because I thought they'd be in a hell of a lot of trouble if they were reported. After a while I thought I heard the train coming; I could see the light reflect on the tiles at the end of the tunnel, you know the way it does. It took me a moment to realize that it wasn't right. It sounded wrong. What I heard was angry voices, kids' voices, like a whole group of kids walking in the tunnel."

Tietjen thought of the crowd that had passed above him in Westchester, that angry roiling sound of a human sea. He nodded again.

"I thought someone should make them stop. I thought, they'll be hurt when a train finally comes. But the guards didn't seem to hear anything, just went on talking with their rifles slung over their shoulders. And it got more wrong. I really wasn't sure if I was just going crazy or what. Something changed about the air in the station, or the light, everything seemed to be moving, the air shimmered around everything. I couldn't tell if the motion was a train coming; it just felt like a rumbling in the air itself, just a motion, as if the air was rippling through me. I'm not saying this well."

"You're saying it just fine. Don't stop."

"I thought maybe I was having a stroke: my ears were ringing.

Things had an aura. I knew that what was happening had to be more than just a gang of kids on the track. And there *were* kids on the track, not a handful but dozens, carrying lanterns. That's what the light was. I saw them just before it happened. Gang boys in leather jackets and headbands and those helmets, carrying lanterns and flashers, yelling."

McGrath stared at nothing as she spoke. Tietjen shook his head, not disbelieving, trying to follow the vision that held her.

"I started backing away. At last the guards came down from the booth and had their rifles out. I didn't want to be in the middle of that." She pushed a lock of white hair behind her ear in an absent gesture. "You know that birds and animals are supposed to know when an earthquake is going to hit? The dogs howl and the horses become frantic, birds startle and just keep flying? I felt like that. I knew something was about to happen. All I could think of was that I had to get away from that track. That's probably what saved me: I was already up the stairs and crouched down beside a big metal garbage bin. When it really started I could hear the screams of those kids on the tracks; the last thing I saw was the walls of the tunnel just closing up on them like a hand. That was when I really thought I was going crazy."

"Why?"

She did not answer immediately. "For a moment. For just a very little moment, *I* was closing that hand on those boys. I could feel them between my fingers, I could hear them screaming. I was *glad* to feel it. Then I saw what was happening, and I knew it wasn't me, but I couldn't stop it happening, and— A girder hit the garbage bin and wedged me in between it and the wall. I thought that was it. Everyone around me was dying."

She rubbed insistently at a patch of tar on the back of her hand. "When I got to the Met, do you know what that crazy man lured me in with? Hot running water. And he didn't even have cold water. Do you think there will ever be hot showers again?"

Tietjen thought of places distant from New York, the Connecticut countryside he had driven through, no signs of disaster save those which the refugees brought with them. That might have changed too, by now. "I'm sure of it," he lied.

She looked at him, saw him this time. She smiled.

"How old are your kids, John?"

"Chris was seven. Davy was five." He did not notice the shift in tenses from her present to his past. "Good kids, you know? Sound, I mean. As good as any kids with parents as far apart as Irene and me." He let himself see the boys, Davy's face shining up at him, open like a small, serious flower; Chris watching him sidelong, looking for small cues and shared secrets. He relaxed against the crate, thinking. Then roused himself. "But you must have lost—what, a grandson? How old was he?"

McGrath looked puzzled. "Grandson? Oh no, Dermott: Ellen's cocker spaniel. I was dog-sitting. Since Ellen was away it was a nice opportunity to come into the city. Better than bringing the damned dog out to Cos Cob—"

"That where you live?" He pictured orderly houses on half-acre lots; quiet streets. He could see a neat white-haired woman living in one of those houses, being mother, Scout leader, volunteer. What he did not see was McGrath as that woman. Too many odd angles and unexpected corners, despite the smooth exterior. An oddball.

She was talking. "—wouldn't get out under any circumstances. Never saw a lazier animal in my life. As for grandchildren, none of my kids have had kids. Makes you wonder, doesn't it? I thought I was a pretty good parent, all those years. Ellen's in Majorca on a company jaunt; when she hears about New York the first thing she'll do is think of Dermott. The second thing she'll do is to arrange to move to San Francisco. New apartment, new dog." Her tone was almost painfully dry.

"Ow." He could not think of anything else to say.

McGrath leaned back next to him, gingerly at first, as all her motions seemed to be, testing the reality of the structure before she would trust it. Then she relaxed fully. "I'm being honest. I love Ellen, but I don't kid myself about her. Kids do take you for granted, and that's okay. But it can get to a point where it's not okay, and it went way past that point with Ellen and me, years ago. My fault; probably all my fault. I hold on to hope too long."

One of the candles flickered, then guttered out. The basement room seemed colder in the dimness. Tietjen could not think of anything to say; when he thought of his own kids what he remembered most clearly was their expression that said he was unfathomable; loved but unfathomable. He would never have a chance to make himself understood.

"So, what do we do tomorrow?" McGrath asked out of the dimness, startling him with her assumption of complicity.

"I hadn't planned anything specific. Start salvaging and wait for rescue troops to show up, I guess. You have any ideas?"

"Salvage sounds good. I could use a little of that. How long do you think before the army or someone—"

Tietjen shrugged. "The last thing I heard, the president was waiting for a formal request from the city governor. Wherever he is."

"In other words, we're probably on our own for a few more days." McGrath stretched. "Then definitely, some sleep is in order. How wonderful to sleep lying down—that was the worst thing about being tied up, I think."

It was as if her words triggered all his muscles into a state of rubbery fatigue. "Shall we camp here tonight?" He hoped she would say yes.

"Of course. I'm too tired for any adventuring right now."

Better the devil known than something worse unknown and unplanned for. "Let's see what we can find to make this place a little homier." He offered McGrath his hand. After a moment she took it and got to her feet carefully. They began to investigate the cellar again.

There was not much of help: some bundles of ancient newspaper, dank and yellowing; three split cushions from the banquette seats in the dining room, the stuffing plumed out of the tears and smelling of mildew.

"Better than nothing," McGrath said doubtfully. Tietjen nodded. While she tidily stacked the dishes they had used to one side of the stairway, Tietjen laid out the cushions, covered them over with a thick layer of newspaper. "Wish this were the sort of place that used tablecloths," he muttered. McGrath grunted agreement.

At last they bedded down. The cushions were every bit as uncomfortable as Tietjen had expected they would be. He lay in the dark, listening to unfamiliar sounds of near silence, the woman's breathing, a dripping of water from somewhere.

"John?" Her voice was young in the darkness. Tietjen wondered how old she was.

"Yeah?"

"Go to sleep. We'll start in the morning."

Tietjen fell asleep.

5

TIETJEN and McGrath found an apartment building on Fifth Avenue and East Seventy-second Street, one he had admired for years for its graceful entry, the granite stringcourse that separated the second and third floors, the hokey cast garlands and escutcheons above the windows on the upper floors. They stood on the street looking at the building, trying to read it.

"Does it have what we need?" he asked McGrath.

"What do we need?" she asked back. From a pocket she took out a pen and a distressed, scribbled-on envelope and made ready to take notes.

Tietjen thought. "Space. Water. Drainage. Adaptability. Power's probably impossible right now, so don't worry about that. Uh—ease of cleanup—" A squeamish way of saying Not Too Many Dead Bodies. "Can you think of anything else?" he asked.

"Not really. I won't know the stuff we overlooked until it's critical." She smiled crookedly. "Should we go in?"

They slipped in between the fractured steel grating that webbed the first floor, and went exploring. The lobby was dim; no power meant no lights, and the grating and debris in front of the building kept out much of the sunlight; still, they could see enough, and in the doorman's desk they found flashlights. They played the lights over a civilized grouping of couches and armchairs, the marble-fronted doorman's desk, fake Art Deco light fixtures, marble-tiled floor. The lobby branched left and right to two stairways; the elevator was on the right. There was an elderly woman, several days dead, wedged in the door of the elevator; her coat was soaked with blood but Tietjen didn't see a wound. His stomach lurched at the sight, and he knew they would have to get her out, carry her body away.

"I hope I can do this," McGrath said, a step behind him. "Let's—let's come back to her, shall we?"

They backed away and found that the left-hand stairway led to the basement. They went looking for the super's office, and found it and the super himself, a neat, white-haired man slumped over his desk, unmarked by death. The master keys for the building were in a case over his desk, carefully labeled. Twelve floors, seven apartments per story on all but the first, which had three—eighty all told. For a moment the two of them stood looking at the keys and the super, knowing they'd have to lug him up from the basement. Eighty apartments, maybe with bodies in all of them. Tietjen quailed at the thought, but said as briskly as he could, "Let's check the rest of the basement first, then go up to the top and work our way down."

The rest of the basement was clear. With jumbles of keys in their pockets, Tietjen and McGrath climbed thirteen stories—and then another: Tietjen wanted to check out the roof. The building had a good-size water tank; Tietjen climbed up the rickety steps to peer in and was pleased to see that it was nearly full, and that the water didn't seem brackish. Even better: the building next door, which was several stories higher, also had a water tank. Maybe they'd be able to siphon water from it, too. McGrath sat on the roof, leaning against the doorway, her foot holding the door ajar just in case, and watched him without comment.

"So, is the news good?"

Tietjen smiled. "So far, the news is good. We've got a starter water supply."

It was nice on the roof, the sun was shining and gave a little warmth, and the wind wasn't too stiff. If he went to the street-side he had an unimpeded view across the gray, skeletal shadows of Central Park, and beyond to the West Side, which was a mystery of silent buildings that glittered in the sun. Tietjen was reluctant to go downstairs hunting for bodies, but the day was already several hours old.

"You game?" He offered McGrath his hand to pull her up. She took it with a firm, cool clasp and stood at once.

"I kinda gotta be, don't I?"

So they started searching on the twelfth floor. The first three apartments were empty, but in the fourth they found another body. Like the super, this one looked peaceful and there were no marks on him that Tietjen could see. It wasn't pleasant, though: the smell in the room was nauseating, and the body was bloated, pale, and icy cold. Tietjen found himself swallowing over and over again, just looking at the thing; he had never touched a dead human. He turned to look at McGrath, and saw that she was rummaging through a closet. He thought for a moment that she was deserting him, losing it, having some sort of justifiable breakdown at the thought of moving the body.

"Sheets," she said tersely. She was pale, and kept her eyes on Tietjen when she worked, but she found a couple of sheets, shook them out next to the corpse, and knelt at its feet. "Let's roll him up, and we can carry him by the ends."

Tietjen blinked, then went and knelt at the head of the corpse. "You're brilliant," he said as lightly as he could—while not breathing through his nose.

She shook her head. "Squeamish. On a count of three?"

They rolled the corpse onto the sheet, rolling it over and over. Tietjen kept expecting arms and legs to break off or the belly to split open and spray them with blood and ichor, but the body was cold, solid, and—as they found out when they started to drag it out of the apartment—very heavy. They left windows open when they left, to air out the smell, then went down the hall to look for more bodies.

In the end, they were lucky. The next two bodies they found were like the first—awful, but normally awful. Then they found one which was something much worse: a young woman with tumors all over her body, gray, semisolid things that grew out of bloody sores. One tumor spread across the lower part of her face, and Tietjen thought she must have suffocated on it; it was scarred, and her fingernails were bloody, as if she had tried to rip it away. Neither Tietjen nor McGrath said anything for a moment. Then McGrath mumbled "Excuse me" and went out into the hall. For a minute Tietjen stood where he was, afraid to interfere but just as afraid that she might run. He followed and found her in the hallway, crying. The ghostly white shapes of the three sheeted corpses they had dragged down from upper floors lay near the stairway, and seemed in the darkness of the hall to give off a dull light.

"I'm sorry," McGrath said. "I'll pull myself together."

Tietjen patted her shoulder awkwardly, not knowing what would help. "I was hoping you'd let me cry too," he said as lightly as he could.

She turned her face up to him and smiled tearily. "That is very sweet of you. You can cry if you want to, but I'm okay now, really I am. If you want your turn at bat—"

He shrugged. "Well, maybe I'll cry later. I want to get this done today. I don't want to sleep with *that* in the building."

"Amen," McGrath said. They went back to work.

There were only fifteen corpses, and of those, only three were stomach-turning grotesqueries. It took them until midafternoon to search the whole building, wrap the corpses, and drag them downstairs to the lobby. Tietjen's stomach was growling, but he could not handle the thought of food with so much death around them.

"So now what?" Barbara asked.

"Get them out of the house, burn 'em," Tietjen suggested.

They found a building across the street where one side had collapsed, leaving a pile of rubble and a small clear space. Tietjen found a furniture dolly in the basement, and they loaded up the corpses three at a time, rolled them over to their burning pit, and went back for more. Every muscle in Tietjen's body ached unbearably, and he was so used to the sickish smell of decay that the cold air outside was almost a shock. They stacked the bodies on top of each other, and Tietjen realized he didn't have matches.

"Go and get some," McGrath said. "And if there's any kerosene or anything like that—I don't know what these things will need to burn." She bent over and picked up a cobblestone-size rock and put it near the stack of corpses, then another and another. "Go on, let's get this done."

He went, found a lighter and a gallon of lacquer thinner, which he hoped would work. What did it take to burn a human body, he wondered. He refused to think about how awful the question really was, and made his way back to find that McGrath had neatly ringed the burning pit with stones and rubble. "Fire containment," she told him. "Boy Scout Merit Badge."

A gallon didn't do it. The sheets and clothes charred and then burned sullenly. It wasn't until Tietjen went back and found several more gallons of lacquer thinner and turpentine that they managed a satisfactory blaze.

The light from the fire was golden in the fading daylight.

They decided at last to head back to the diner on Lexington Avenue to sleep, and to forage for provisions for the next few days. Tietjen went downstairs to the super's office to leave the bundle of keys he had been carrying. When he came back he found McGrath arranging the soiled couches and chairs in the lobby in a semicircle facing the doorway, as if offering a civilized place to sit and chat. It was almost entirely dark inside now.

"What is this?" he asked.

McGrath stopped as if the question confused her. "I'm not certain," she said finally. Then shrugged. "I'm building a conversation pit in Dante's Inferno. No, I'm—decorating—trying to make this place as inviting as I can. With small materials, might I add. We're going to need a lot of lanterns." She propped up another sodden cushion from a pile they had found in a flooded storage locker in the basement.

It was nuts. It made all the sense in the world, Tietjen thought. Like everything they were doing, like opening this place up wide. He laughed suddenly: "Department of Futile Gestures. D'you realize we're going to have to find a way to clear away all that crap out there"—he gestured to the grates and rubble that blocked the window—"and then find a way to seal it all up again?"

McGrath stared at him for a moment, then cracked up. When she got her voice under control: "So much for my career in interior decorating. Groo go out and kill something for dinner. Tomorrow Og try to figure out how to make the cave secure for the night." Still laughing, and almost staggering with fatigue, they left the building together.

They took to calling the lobby and apartments on the lower floors the Store, as if they had set up to sell something. They began opening apartments on the first few floors, removing extraneous furniture, dragging mattresses and beds down from higher floors to make dormitories of them. The first few nights they slept in separate rooms in the same apartment, taking comfort in nearness. In a couple of days they had the building set up to their satisfaction, enough to handle a first wave of survivors.

They brought down whatever packaged and canned food they found in the building, collected spoiling food to be buried or burned nearby, and worried over the problems of water for drinking and cleaning. Bottled water now, until Tietjen could figure out how to tap into the water in the water tank on the roof. Sanitation. First aid. They set up an infirmary in a three-bedroom apartment at the far end of one first-floor corridor and stocked it with the first-aid supplies and medicines they had found in bathrooms throughout the building.

"But that won't last long," McGrath said as she looked over the inventory at dinner that evening. "John, have you ever taken CPR or first aid, anything like that?"

"First aid in high school. I remember a little: you keep people in shock warm, that sort of thing. Cold water on burns. I didn't pay too much attention."

McGrath nodded grimly. "I took a CPR course about fifteen years ago and had some first-aid training when I volunteered at the hospital. If you had a heart attack I could probably keep blood flowing to your brain until I died of exhaustion. But I don't remember very much about the real mechanics of first aid. I hope to God we don't get any really grave stuff walking in here before I can get to the library or a bookstore—"

"Barbara," Tietjen said gently. "The *really* grave problems will have taken care of themselves by now." He saw the look of pain that crossed her face and felt like a heel. McGrath had an astonishing range of odd, useful information and skills, but he didn't know how deep those skills ran, or what she would do when her skills failed her.

She was saying something and he had not heard. "What?"

"I said there will probably be more serious injuries in the next few weeks. Or a pregnant woman with a breech delivery. Food poisoning, or cholera or diphtheria or whatever pestilence is supposed to overtake cities that get hit by disaster. People with chronic illnesses. People with HIV failing without their meds." She tossed down the clipboard and stood up. "I don't like being helpless, that's all."

He had no comfort for her. "We'll cope," he said at last, inadequately. "We'll be doing something, anyway. There'll have to be a doctor left somewhere in the city. And *they'll* be coming soon," he added lamely. *They* were the Guard, the Army, the Red Cross, rescuers, and day by day Tietjen grew more sure that they were not coming, not soon anyway. But he couldn't say that to McGrath. "Meanwhile, we'll get some books or something."

"*Brain Surgery for Beginners. Plague for Fun and Profit.* I know, I know," she waved his response away. "It's better than nothing." She began to collect plates and silverware. They had taken the kitchen fittings from one apartment and moved them into another, emptier of utensils and dinnerware but larger. They were still cooking on McGrath's makeshift can-stoves, but Tietjen was hoping to find a wood-burning stove somewhere. The apartment they cooked and ate in was earmarked as the office and meeting place; it stood just off the lobby. Each of them had chosen an apartment upstairs, sparingly furnished with other people's belongings, McGrath's on the second floor down the hall from the infirmary, Tietjen's above her on the third floor. At the end of the day they would sit in one apartment or the other, going over their lists by candlelight, making plans, talking about the old city.

Sooner or later, the conversation always came back to the same question: *what happened?* McGrath wryly suggested a cataclysmic breakdown in communication. "You know: all those agencies that were holding New York together just went on strike at the same time?"

"And blew up the city?" Tietjen remembered his walk through the patchwork rubble of the West Side and shuddered.

"Not *all* of it. Just enough to prove their point. They're probably waiting for the union negotiators to show. The joke's on them." McGrath looked up from the sink and saw that Tietjen wasn't laughing with her. Gently she asked, "What do you think, John?"

He shrugged. "I don't know. Someone told me on my way back here that *everything* had happened. Sure as hell looks that way. Or maybe all the stuff I got in school was right."

"What stuff? Which school?" McGrath asked, smiling again.

"When I was getting my architecture degree. I took some planning courses; about fifteen years ago there was this vogue for chaos planning. Guy named George Lymach had this whole theory of what would happen to an urban system if it got too big, that it would self-correct down to a more manageable size through a series of disasters. But this feels too damned deliberate to be chaos."

"The wrath of God? Wouldn't any right-thinking deity hit Los Angeles first?"

That startled Tietjen into a laugh. "That's what I'd do if I were God," he agreed.

McGrath snorted. "John, I'm going to bed. Long day." She held out her hand. Tietjen took it and they stood, handfast but not shaking hands. More like recharging batteries, a nighttime ritual between two adults who were not close enough to kiss, but felt something was required to seal and acknowledge their bond.

"Thanks, Barbara," Tietjen said, as he did every night.

"Sleep well," she answered, and left him.

Sometime after noon on the fifth day they got their first recruit, a ragged, skinny young woman with dark, tangled hair falling into her eyes, who hovered uncertainly near the lobby doors for the better part of the afternoon and, when she did come in at last, spoke only to Barbara. She was dirty and bruised, with a glazed, shocky expression; she jumped at noises and watched Tietjen move about the lobby with suspicious concentration.

"Raped, I think," Barbara told Tietjen later. "Maybe she'll tell me something after she's a bit more . . . accustomed. Until we have more women staying here I'm going to have her sleep in my apartment. And I guess—here's something I didn't even plan for. We're going to have to do some kind of informal counseling."

Tietjen recoiled at the thought of sitting quietly and listening when there was so much work to be done. Something of it must have shown on his face. Barbara snorted in amusement.

"I'll do the hand-holding, John. You think about generators, you *guy*, you."

Tietjen grinned and ducked his head, a little embarrassed to be understood, and forgiven, so easily. He thought about generators. And fresh water. Sanitation. Simple things taken for granted in last week's world. He began to make lists of places to scout and things to scout for: drugstores, stationery stores, hardware stores, supermarkets. As he thought of new things he made notes on slips of paper and each night pinned the day's collection of notes to his wall until it bristled with little islands of ideas. McGrath, he noted, had found a clipboard somewhere, and took her own notes at the end of each day in firm, briskly arched handwriting.

Their first recruit's name was Elena Cruz. By the end of her third day with them she was cooking over the can-stoves and talking easily with McGrath; Tietjen she still eyed uncertainly, and she started at sounds and watched the shadows.

She and Barbara were working in the lobby when a boy appeared as if out of nowhere. Elena shrieked, an eldritch wail that brought Tietjen down the stairs two at a time from the third floor to reach her. He found Barbara in the center of the lobby with one arm behind her, wrapped protectively around Elena. Across the room, shadowy in the light from the doorway, was a kid with freckles and a shock of sandy hair, a magazine advertisement for boyhood—except that his eyes moved too quickly from place to place. He stood stock-still, as scared by Elena's scream as she had been by his sudden appearance. Finally he croaked in a voice breaking with nerves and adolescence, "My name is Greg. Do you have anything to eat?"

That broke the lock. Barbara shooed Elena up to the kitchen to get something to feed the kid; Tietjen brought the boy in and sat him down.

"This is nice," the boy said finally. He sat carefully on the edge of his chair, feeling out what was expected of him by way of company manners. "My name is Greg," he said again.

"I'm John," Tietjen said. He had a million questions, but could not ask any of them. His hands were sweaty and it was difficult to make himself sit still. "Barbara will be back in a minute," he managed at last.

The kid smiled. "Great." He looked to be thirteen, maybe fourteen.

The silence fell again. Tietjen made himself ask, "Where have you been since . . ."

It was all the invitation the kid needed. "I was in my house for the first couple of days, but Mom never came back, and I ran through all the food there, and—" he went on, telling about the game he had made of survival, an adventure that would have sounded glossy and exciting in a boy's book. But there was a harsh, manic ring when he spoke of his game, and Greg was obviously relieved to have an adult to turn to, to tell him what to do. Tietjen sat and listened, edgy and anxious, wanting to get back to work and, more and more, wanting to get away from the kid.

Finally Barbara came back. She had a plate of biscuits and stew; a thick brown sweater hung over her arm. "Here you go," she said comfortably. She spared Tietjen a look of concern, then sat down matter-of-factly next to the boy and took over. After a few minutes Tietjen got up quietly and went back upstairs to where he had been working. There, he sat, folded over the grief he thought he had wept out, and shook. The boy was probably twice Chris's age, there were no similarities, but "Mom never came back, and I ran through all the food." Could his sons even have opened the door to their apartment, with the bristle of locks Irene had insisted on? He remembered again their building and the fire in the windows, the crumpled fire stair, and the mournful certainty that his sons were dead ran through him like a current.

But the boy in the lobby was alive, and the Store had done what it was supposed to do, attract survivors. Tietjen would make sure the kid took his instructions from McGrath, he decided. And hope there were other recruits soon to dilute the pain of the boy's presence.

On the evening of the day that McGrath and Tietjen declared the Store officially open for business, a fair-haired, chunky middle-aged man approached the doors, hallooed, but did not come inside. Tietjen went outside to talk with him.

"You're crazy, advertising this way." The man gestured at Tietjen's neat hand-lettered offer of sanctuary, posted by the door.

"Figure it's easier than dragging people in off the street," Tietjen said calmly.

"You're making yourselves sitting ducks. If you're for real." He paused, looked around him. "I've got family out there. I won't tell you where," he added, before Teitjen could ask. "I want to watch you. I don't want to walk into anything—after what I've seen."

What have you seen, Tietjen wanted to ask. "What can we show you?" he said.

"Nothing. I'll be watching. Maybe I'll bring them down here if I think you're okay." He turned belligerently away and left Tietjen standing in front of the building, bemused.

Whatever the man's criteria were, he was back the next day. The Store had passed: he had a woman with pale curling hair and a girl of seven or eight years with them. Tietjen went out again to greet them, and returned to the office grinning this time.

"Well," McGrath prodded.

"Tell Elena to put on a lot of whatever she's cooking," he told her, as proud as if he had created the Hochman family himself from the asphalt and sawdust in the street. "Three more for dinner."

With Hochman, his wife and their daughter, the boy Greg, and Elena, the Store had five recruits that night. Just before McGrath turned to follow Elena into the apartment where she slept, she said, "See? It's begun."

Tietjen went about the routine of securing the downstairs areas. They had worked out some precautions: the Store stayed open in daylight; at night the doors and windows were closed, the front doors blocked off with a barricade of furniture and plywood. As Tietjen heaved the boards into place he thought of the boy in black leather, the street kid he had spent so many hours curled up next to in the culvert. Months ago. Years. Only a little more than a week. There might be more kids like that boy, maybe. The madness had receded from New York like a tide, but Tietjen did not doubt that there were pockets of it still, and people who were no crazier than they had been before the disaster, ready to face ruin for a chance to rule or destroy.

When the planks were secure he went through the first-floor apartments, checking doors, thinking. Overhead the Hochmans slept in one of the dormitory rooms; Greg was in the room next to them. Tietjen had watched at dinner as Greg vacillated between Barbara McGrath and Sandy Hochman, playing orphan-son to each. In the end Tietjen thought Sandy Hochman would win the contest; McGrath was too amused to play Constant Mother to the boy. But Greg would get a mother of sorts—and Tietjen wouldn't have to deal with him. The Hochmans were asleep by now, probably. The boy too, and Elena Cruz and Barbara McGrath above him.

Now he thought of Barbara's words—"It's begun"—and something wordless bubbled up in him. He was too rusty to recognize it at first as pure joy. It had begun; he wanted to share the feeling.

In the end he took his exaltation where he had always taken it. Twelve flights up, climbing until the ache in his legs was no longer even passably pleasurable; he found a window at the end of the hall, opened it, and sat on the sill breathing the frosty night air, looking out over the city. There was a moon and the sky was clear. What New York had become was spread out before him, a view southwest over Central Park, velvety in the moonlight, and beyond that the wreck of cityscape as far as he could see, some buildings still straight and upright, others wholly demolished, still others spiderweb skeletons glittering distantly. The old Central Park statue of Alice and the Mad Hatter shone in the moonlight, lifted entire from its old place near the boat pond and plopped down on Fifth Avenue at the Inventor's Gate to Central Park. What did *that?* Tietjen wondered. Far to the west there were a few flickering lights that reminded him that he and Barbara weren't alone. He wondered about his old apartment, his street, but there had not been time to look—and he couldn't face crossing the Park yet.

Below him nothing stirred. No movement, no streetlamps, buses, late-night bustle of carousers and their hired guards, taxis drawing up to enclave gates, street people skirting the patrols of block cops.

Tietjen looked out, wanting to make an offering, a demonstration of good faith. He counted up the people sleeping below him: one, two, three, four, five, six. He said to the night: "Tomorrow there will be more."

After a while it got too cold to sit any longer with the window open. Reluctantly he gave up the windowsill and went downstairs to his room.

The kid, Greg, proved to have a genius for finding things. Some of the stuff the boy brought for Tietjen's approval was useless: a smashed camera, DVD disks, two boxes of holographic name tags from a convention that had been held at the Armory on Sixty-seventh Street: magpie souvenirs of a life of plenty. But Greg also brought a full set of screwdrivers, two rolls of baling wire and, emptied one by one out of his many pockets, a set of two dozen crayons. The boy had dropped them into Missy Hochman's lap, and with each one the little girl's sober expression warmed until at last she was grinning delightedly. With the proven knowledge that his foraging was appreciated by his new family, Greg went after it with a vengeance, making two or three trips a day.

Teitjen had not got over his first feeling of discomfort with the boy, although Greg clearly wanted his approval. He tried to be friendly to the kid, but felt awkward and uncomfortable. Let McGrath be comfortable, let Sandy Hochman or Elena or Allan Hochman. He had other things to think about.

But it was Greg who told Tietjen there were monsters in the streets.

Three children and a dark, thickset man staggered into the Store one morning. The children were bruised and dirty, the man feverish and on the verge of collapse with exhaustion and blood loss. He had a deep gash in his side and dozens of puncture wounds in the fleshy part of both arms. Hazy with fever, at first he would not let anyone near him to clean his wounds; even when he let Sandy Hochman and McGrath treat him, he refused to let them remove his pants. Barbara thought he was afraid he'd have to run at any moment. Finally, deciding after three days that he and the girls with him were safe, he let go an iron control and fell into coma-sleep. Barbara tended to him, finally dressing all his wounds—though in the name of preserving the man's privacy, she would not tell Teitjen more about the nature of his wounds except to say that they were . . . disturbing. Sandy Hochman took charge of the three little girls who, solemnly quiet, refused the first day to go far from the man's room. Greg and the Hochmans, McGrath and Elena worked individual magics; by the end of their second day at the Store the girls were all playing docilely with Missy Hochman. The eldest was talking, as best she could, to Greg.

"It's weird." Greg told McGrath and McGrath told Tietjen. "They're sisters, they lived down on East Sixtieth. I *think* that's what she's saying, but she talks really funny."

"They've been through a lot," McGrath told Greg gently.

"No, I don't mean like that. I mean, like suddenly they don't know how to speak English, like half their words were turned inside out. And it's not the way they used to talk, cause it's driving Karen nuts. She's the oldest one. Their names are Karen, Colleen, and Kathy . . . uhh, Calvino. Karen says—"

McGrath heard a good deal of what Karen had said. The girls had been waiting in a guarded bus shelter when the disaster struck; the man with them was a guard, and he had taken care of them afterward. For four days it had been just them. Then they had found what Kathy called the monsters.

"I think you'd better tell Mr. Tietjen about this," McGrath said at that point. To Tietjen she said, "I thought you should listen to this. I mean, kids exaggerate, but if there is some organized group of vandals or something out there, we need to be prepared for them."

What it was was worse than that, if Greg and the Calvino girls were to be believed. "Didn't *you* know about them?" Greg asked. "The monsters? I just saw them once, and I stayed clear, and then I found you and Barb—Mrs. McGrath, and I figured they wouldn't come near *you*. But I figured *you* had to know about them, Mr. Tietjen." Tietjen was not much comforted by Greg's confidence. The boy went on: "They're scary, sir. Like really scary, awful. Like something out of a horror movie, monsters and stuff. Like, they just want to kill things, like they're really crazy. If those kids and that guy ran into them, they're really lucky they got away. Mr. Tietjen, you don't think they'll come here, do you?"

No matter how Tietjen and Barbara pressed, they couldn't get Greg to explain what he meant by monsters: did he mean a chain-saw-wielding psycho from a slasher film or something more monstrous? But Greg slid away from explaining, and asked again, "They won't come here, will they?"

Tietjen said something reassuring and sent Greg back to his chores. Kid's stories, Tietjen decided. More likely gang kids, mean as hell and crazy too. They need not be physical monsters to behave monstrously: the people he had seen on their way out of the city had been monstrous—but human, too. Tietjen persuaded himself it was more of the boy's imagination, but as an afterthought, he called after Greg and told him not to wander too far from the Store in his foraging. And that night he talked to McGrath about tightening security around the Store.

He and Allan Hochman worked, boarding up lower windows, setting up a system of night watches, reinforcing the front doors; when, after a day or two, nothing happened, he began to feel sheepish at having worried. He told McGrath, as they sat talking one night, that thinking about security was probably long overdue; sooner or later someone was going to want to challenge them for what they were building.

There was a daily trickle of new people to the Store. After the third week Tietjen stopped trying to remember all the names as he was introduced to newcomers; names would come back to him at odd moments. Strangely, he could never remember someone's name to refer to that person; McGrath teased him that he thought everyone's name was Whatsername, but whenever he had to say thank you, the name came immediately. McGrath laughed when she saw it happen, and told him he lived a charmed life. He believed it.

"The thing that's weird," McGrath said: "Everyone talks about when the Guard shows up—but I don't think anyone really expects it."

"It's been a couple of weeks with nothing but us, Barbara."

"Well, where the hell are they?" she asked peevishly.

Tietjen shrugged. "Stuck in traffic?" There was no real answer. Not one person among those who came to the Store gave him enough information to imagine an answer. It didn't make sense. Thinking about what had happened and why the outside world hadn't arrived to help yet, Tietjen felt as if he were dealing with blue-sky puzzle pieces—no shadows, clouds, straight edges, nothing to give a clue about how they fit together or what the picture really was.

Once the bus guard, Bobby Fratelone, began to heal, his recovery was quick. Tietjen liked him: he looked like a thug, and talked slowly, as if each word had to be brought out specially, but he was polite, almost courtly with McGrath, brusquely tender with the little girls he'd brought with him. Whenever Tietjen stopped in to talk he found the three Calvino girls in or near the room, chattering in high-pitched gibberish or sitting in a solemn semicircle on the foot of Fratelone's bed. Finally Tietjen decided he'd have to outwait the girls, and strolled into the infirmary just after dinnertime. The man sat up in bed, laboriously reading a comic book aloud to the girls, one thick index finger moving from picture to picture. Tietjen sat down and began to read a first-aid pamphlet. After a while Fratelone finished reading the comic and gently shooed the girls out of the room. "Go play or something. Ask Miz McGrath if you can help out." The girls nodded and went.

"So?" Fratelone asked.

"I wanted to give you a little time," Tietjen began. "But I need to ask you some questions. We need to know what's out there. What hurt you."

Fratelone's face closed up. He looked past Tietjen, out the window. "I don't know. I mean, I was half-dead, they almost kilt me. How the hell d'I know what I saw?" His face was still shadowed with pain and fatigue; the stubble on his face was not much shorter than his cropped black hair. "Look. I got jumped, they tried to torture me. You don't take notes, things like that happen to you. I kept the little ones safe, didn't I? Their mother didn't make it. . . ." Fratelone stared blankly out the window and said nothing more. Tietjen had a feeling that the man did remember something, but he didn't know how he could question him any further. He had been through enough.

When Barbara at last declared him well enough to leave the infirmary, Fratelone appointed himself Tietjen's lieutenant and would-be enforcer. McGrath he treated as a combination of Mother Superior and nagging librarian; Tietjen was Boss, and Fratelone gave him an unswerving loyalty that Tietjen found unsettling. He spoke as though Tietjen had saved him, but Tietjen didn't understand that; Fratelone had made it in to the Store on his own power, and all Tietjen had done was to have it waiting there. The only other bond Fratelone acknowledged was to the Calvino sisters. They were his: his responsibility, his family, and his way with them was unfailingly gentle. The girls had obviously adopted him, bringing their questions and fears to him, speaking still in the half-gibberish that Greg and McGrath were beginning to understand.

By the end of another week most of the dormitory apartments were full. The Hochmans had taken over a two-bedroom apartment on the second floor and Greg was living with them, tacitly adopted. The Calvino girls slept in the living room of McGrath's apartment with Elena Cruz, and Fratelone slept lightly in the apartment next door. People discovered the Store in ones and twos, dazed and apprehensive when they arrived, and Elena or Barbara or Sandy or Allan Hochman took them in, comforted them, showed them where they would stay, and gave them work to do.

The rules were simple. For as long as you stayed you worked, scavenging or building, helping in the kitchen under Elena's supervision, cleaning up the apartments upstairs or in the neighboring buildings. This last was a job left to hardened recruits, since no day went by without the discovery of more dead. Some were badly decomposed, some seemed eerily well preserved. The worst were bodies deformed or amputated. McGrath was the one who found a body with no head: skin had tidily grown to cover the stump of a neck, the head nowhere to be seen. Tietjen found her afterward, sitting, her back to the macabre corpse, white-faced but in control. "The damned weirdness doesn't stop. Just when you think it's over, things are getting back to normal, it just—starts up again." But she got to her feet and she and Tietjen dragged the body to the charnel cart themselves.

He did not know what he would have done without Barbara Mc-Grath. She was fifty-eight to his thirty-seven, but she kept the same hours, often rose earlier, and did the same physical work. She had a touch with people that Tietjen knew he did not have, a knack for close attention and immediate caring. Newcomers to the Store gravitated to her at once. The humor and common sense that he most valued in her kept the others on an even keel when the work they were doing was most depressing or difficult. Together, after others in the Store had gone off to sleep, Tietjen and McGrath sat up and planned, while Fratelone sat silently by, listening.

When he looked at Barbara, tough and unruffled in skirt and boots, with her hair neatly combed, framing her face, Tietjen felt a vague awe, as if he was in the presence of a force of nature, a timeless goddess of the hearth, her warmth unerring and seductive. Then McGrath would leave a smut of dirt on her forehead while gesturing, or say something flatly sensible, and the illusion shattered; she was Barbara, his good companion, old enough to be his mother.

They had each taken some work for their own, so Tietjen was surprised when McGrath appeared at his door one morning, tight-lipped and anxious, and asked him to look at something in the infirmary with her. It took him a moment to realize that she still wore yesterday's clothes, that her eyes were dark-ringed as if she had not been to bed.

"It's the littlest Calvino girl," Barbara explained. "Bobby Fratelone brought her up last night. She had a limp, remember?"

He didn't remember; if someone had mentioned it, he had not paid much attention.

"She's got a scratch on her leg and it's infected. Her damned sisters don't have a clue when it happened—could have been days ago, even. They didn't pay attention, didn't even tell Fratelone until yesterday morning when Kathy couldn't get out of bed, why the smell didn't get to them I don't know, and the damned leg's swollen up like a grape and about that color—" She made herself stop. "It's bad, John. I got out the books and read them last night and it's blood poisoning and I'm scared."

Tietjen swallowed. "*I* don't know anything—"

"For Christ's sake, *nobody* knows anything!" McGrath took a breath. "John, I have to share this. If we don't do something the kid's going to die. If we can't help her, we've got to get her to someone who can. Outside New York."

The fear in her voice got through to Tietjen like nothing else. "Okay, let's see her." But the thought occurred to him: Barbara had seen it coming. This, or something like this. He had listened to her worrying about cholera and dysentery and tetanus, and hadn't taken it seriously, but Barbara had. She'd known all along this would happen.

He followed McGrath to the infirmary apartment. The smell of alcohol and disinfectant in the hallway masked something dying. Kathy was in a room alone. The smell was like a wall, and as hard to get through, but Tietjen swallowed and went to her bedside. Seven or eight years old: her skin was flushed, tendrils of dark hair hanging around her face were lank and dry-looking. She barely moved. Her leg had been left uncovered; it was red and swollen, with a darker streak of savage red stretching toward the groin. The cut was a small, ragged gash just below the knee, crusty skin broken in places where pus oozed out. The child stirred a little and made a high, unhappy sound. McGrath, behind him, echoed it.

Sickened, Tietjen turned away, turned back to McGrath. She stood there, arms at her sides and her mouth pressed thin.

"We've lanced it twice. Those streaks on her thigh mean lymph-node involvement, the book says. Which is bad. And the fever—nothing we do brings the fever down, John—" Her voice broke. McGrath was not crying; she was furious. "Dammit, she's just a baby."

"What does the book say?" he asked helplessly.

"Drain it. Keep it clean. Apply antibiotics. Keep the fever down. Hospitalization as soon as possible." Her voice was mirthless but she said it as if it were a punchline.

"Do we have antibiotics?"

"We were going to. Remember? We were going to find drug-stores, a hospital somewhere to get drugs and antibiotics and maybe some better first-aid books, if we couldn't find ourselves a doctor to bring back with them. Every single goddamned drugstore in a ten-block radius was flattened, burned out; the stuff we found, we can't identify. I can't just give her a pill and hope it's the right one. We don't have *anything*." This time anger vied with tears.

Tietjen touched the skin around the wound. It felt tender and frighteningly hot. He reached up and put a hand on the child's forehead, but the skin there was only slightly cooler. McGrath circled around the end of the bed and began soaking the towels in water and placing them on Kathy's face and neck.

"If we had antibiotics would you know how to use them?"

"These days they mostly come in premeasured doses, freeze-dried. You add distilled water." In answer to Tietjen's bemused look she said defensively, "I was a hospital volunteer."

"Thank God for it. Look, I'll take some people, we'll make a run over to—" He thought for a moment, which hospital was closest. "New York Multi. Ought to find everything you need. Uh—" He thought for a moment. "Can you tell me what you want us to look for?"

McGrath made him a list: antibiotics, antiseptics, bandages, reference books, splints, tape, "anything else that looks useful. Bring a lot." She raised one eyebrow. "Bring a doctor if you find one."

As if the act of setting things in motion had somehow made her nursing easier, McGrath smiled and went back to Kathy's room.

Fratelone insisted on going. Tietjen would have been happier had the man stayed as Barbara's backup at the Store, but Kathy was his kid, Tietjen could hardly tell him no. Two others volunteered: a gawky teenaged boy named Ted and a dark, slender, muscular woman who called herself Ketch. Tietjen suspected that Ketch was looking for good scavenging; Ted was looking for a way to impress Ketch. Fine, so long as both did what they were supposed to when he needed them.

The party left the Store about noon. McGrath was left in charge, but Tietjen doubted she would leave the infirmary except in direst need. Allan Hochman would back her. "See you in a little," he told Hochman at the door.

At the end of the block, Tietjen turned to look back at the Store. For a moment he thought he saw McGrath at a window, watching. Dumb notion: he shrugged it off and fell into step with Fratelone, east down Seventy-second Street.

6

"**W**HICH hospital are we going to?" Ketch asked Tietjen. She was exotic-looking; long hair pulled tightly into a knot at the nape of her neck, long body, tight-pressed lips and narrow dark eyes. Her voice was low-pitched, her diction clear but slightly accented. She wore black: a heavy street fighter's jacket and narrow black pants that accentuated her thinness. Her intensity made Tietjen a little uneasy, but she seemed comfortable to follow his lead.

"New York Multi, Seventy-first and York. They're big, and we've got a big shopping list."

"What do we do if we find someone there?" Ketch pressed.

The question made Tietjen impatient. *If there were someone at New York Multi, we would have heard; if there were someone at New York Multi, they would have come out to help.* What he said was, "If there's a doctor there, we bring her back to look at the little girl. Anyone else—we'll figure it out when it happens."

Ketch nodded, apparently satisfied.

The sun shone with hard brightness in a brittle blue sky, and the air had a taste of river in it—salty water, mud, and chemicals. The breeze came and went, scattering scraps of paper and pebbles, exploding clots of brick-and-stone dust into clouds that stung the eyes. Tietjen walked slightly ahead of the others, not to establish himself as the leader, but because, as often, he could think of nothing to say. Except with Barbara, there seemed to be nothing he knew how to talk about, nothing he knew how to ask about, except the progress of the Store.

Fratelone followed after Tietjen by a pace or two, as quiet as Tietjen but angry. The man had gone dead quiet when McGrath explained why the antibiotics were needed; except to announce that he was going on the hospital raid, he had said nothing since. Fratelone's trust in him—wholehearted and unquestioning—made Tietjen a little nervous; he didn't feel he'd earned such obedience. Still, he had to admit it made him feel better to have Fratelone at his back on his first real foray outside of the Store's neighborhood since he and Barbara had set up there.

Behind them, Ketch strode along as if she enjoyed the motion of her arms and legs, the sensation of moving strongly; she watched sharply from right to left, looking everywhere except where Ted, the fourth member of the raiding party, was. The word gangling was invented for this kid, Tietjen thought; and his awkwardness was in no way helped by his crush on Ketch. Ted kept trying to talk with her; Ketch maintained a pained silence. Tietjen, listening to the boy's nervous chatter, found himself grimacing sympathetically.

The streets were filled with quiet echoes. They passed a fire in a mesh trash can that flared, died out, then flared again, over and over as if it were on a timer. Each arm of flame reached out to them with bright fingers, imploring, grabbing out desperately before it was withdrawn into the fire's hot core. They passed doorways sealed uselessly against the disaster, and doorways caved inward, displaying shattered walls and tumbled furniture. They passed two streetlamps that arched to meet and intertwine like courting swans.

As they walked east Tietjen felt his stomach churning and tasted a sour, rotten taste in his mouth. Nerves, he thought. The strokes of his heartbeat got louder, heavier, until it felt as though his ribs were vibrating with the beat; the blood pounded behind his eyes, in his ears. Each step made it worse: he felt sweat beading at his temples and under his arms; a sense of dread began to work in him, rising up and burning in his chest. Heart attack, he thought, listening to the rapid heavy pounding; stroke, he thought, feeling the hard pulse of blood in his neck. I'm dying. He wanted to run, turned his head to look behind him. The kid, Ted, was wild-eyed and shaky, stopping and starting, he lagged far behind him. Ketch was still walking, but she led with one shoulder as if she were cutting through a gale-force wind, and her face was ashy and streaked with rivulets of sweat. Only Fratelone appeared to be unaffected; he kept up the same steady, angry pace. Tietjen turned forward again, the hardest thing he had ever done.

Every step they took was through some heavy medium, a gel of fear. The air pushed against their forward progress and when they reached Second Avenue Tietjen was astonished to find how long it had taken them to cover the one block. He raised his eyes from the pavement and realized they would not need to go farther.

From Second Avenue the land sloped into the East River. A dozen blocks south Tietjen could see the FDR Drive twisting out of the water to resume its course downtown, and the shore was dotted with buildings below that point, but from Sixtieth up to—he turned to look up the bleak new shoreline—up to about Eighty-fifth Street, there was nothing but a thin ribbon of land which looked as if the buildings that had stood there had slid or been dragged into the water, leaving behind a soft trail of muddy disturbance. First Avenue, York Avenue, the FDR, all gone. New York Multihospital had vanished.

They backed up through the miasma, back along Seventy-second Street. Tietjen felt the sickness and terror recede with each step they took away from the river. No one said anything about what they had seen. Only when they reached Lexington Avenue again did Ketch speak. "I'm going back to the Store."

"Me too," Ted said quickly.

Ketch looked at him. "Okay, kid, if you want."

Tietjen held out a hand as if to keep them, but did not know what to say. "We still need the medicine."

"You guys can carry enough medicine for the kid. The kid's nothing to me." She looked sullenly at Tietjen.

"Me neither," the kid echoed.

"Some goddman earthquake knocked the hospital into the river. So it's creepy. Baby's still sick." Fratelone looked hard at Ketch, then at Tietjen, as if it were his responsibility to take the party onward. It was, Tietjen realized again.

"We'll go on to Mt. Sinai, up on Ninety-eighth Street. We're still going to need people to carry things. Ketch, anything not medical you find, you keep; that goes for the rest of you. But this isn't a scavenging trip: the Calvino girl is sick, and sooner or later someone—one of us, maybe—is going to need medicine we haven't got at the Store yet. So we go. Now." Tietjen watched the tightness in Fratelone's posture ease slightly, watched Ketch make her decision.

"Isn't there somewhere closer?" she asked.

"All the smaller private hospitals that used to be around here—Lenox Hill, Doctors, they got incorporated into New York Multi. Metropolitan is—was—too close to the river. We can't be sure it's not like this." He waved a hand eastward, toward the disappeared landscape. "I've seen the nineties around Fifth Avenue; I know Mt. Sinai is still standing. There isn't another hospital between here and there."

Ketch tilted her head to one side, studied the sky, then shrugged and nodded. Ted watched Ketch, reluctance warring with the wish to impress; finally he nodded too.

"Good. Let's go. We're wasting time."

They started north on Lexington Avenue.

The same silence reigned, out of which echoed their footsteps, the occasional scatter of pebbles and dust. The small shops, cramped in between bigger chain stores, had been crashed and trashed; there were spills of expensive clothing, piles of books, waterlogged stationery, shoes. As they passed an expensive women's clothes store, Tietjen saw Ketch casually reach in and unwind a heavy scarlet shawl from around a mannequin and wrap it around her waist. Most of the larger stores were screened and grilled, sealed off from casual attack, but they passed one where the security grilles had kept the people inside from getting out, and they pressed, like flies caught in amber, against and through the grilles with grimaces of terror and rage on their faces. They were weirdly well preserved, but not all the bodies they passed were; sometimes they saw bodies several weeks dead, gnawed by vermin and decaying badly; sometimes only the familiar, sickening stench told Tietjen they were passing the dead.

There were many dead, but no one alive. From every half-ruined apartment building or house, ghost-town sounds echoed: loose pipes and posts creaking in the March wind, plaster falling, bricks slowly sliding away from their mortar, dropping into beds of rubble. The sounds shocked and frightened Tietjen. He had begun to believe, seeing progress at the Store, that the same progress must somehow be taking place everywhere in the city. The dust of decay filled his nostrils and powdered his hair, made him suddenly angry.

"No," he said aloud. "Goddamn."

"Boss?" Fratelone at his shoulder. "Hey, Boss?—"

Tietjen relaxed and turned to the others, embarrassed. "Thinking aloud. Nothing. Just thinking about all the things that have to be done."

"At the hospital?" Ted asked.

"Right. At the hospital," he lied. For a moment he cursed the city for being so damned big. It was going to be near impossible to learn the extent of the damage without more people, more competent people he could send out, who would report back, bring news of downtown, Brooklyn, Queens. And most of the people who had come to the Store just wanted to rest there, safe, and survive.

Think about it later. Now, "Anyone ever been to Mt. Sinai?"

No one. It would have to be potluck, take their chances and stumble on what they needed, wherever they could find it.

At Eighty-first they went west to Fifth Avenue to skirt the crater that had sent Tietjen toward his disastrous visit to the Metropolitan Museum of Art. He kept them on the far side of the avenue; Central Park made him anxious; he remembered the icy feeling of death in the park the morning he had walked across it, unrelenting eeriness that made the skin crawl and the hair rise. Looking across into the park he was surprised to see trees flowering, not just the first tentative springtime greening of new leaves, but extravagant masses of blossom.

He would have sworn that the trees in the park had been dead a month ago.

Finally, Ninety-eighth Street. At random they chose one of the newer buildings to start with—the Zimmerman Pavilion. There was no sign from the outside that the hospital had been occupied since the disaster; inside they found nothing, no one alive, no bodies, the population of the hospital might have been magicked away. The air was stale and chilly, but there was no decay, no stench. The long hallways, with their gurney-width doors and linen wallpaper, might have been chambers in a modern pyramid. The first floor was all offices and lounge areas, useless. On the upper floors they found doors with MEDS. LOCKER—RESTRICTED stenciled on them. Each door needed a combination as well as mortise key and cardpass. On the fourth floor Tietjen stared in frustration at another door he could not unlock, and felt the others watching him.

"Boss?" Fratelone nudged Tietjen aside. "Let me give it a try."

It took him two minutes, and the door swung open. "Pussy locks," Fratelone said disdainfully. Tietjen blinked, startled as hell.

"Okay. Fratelone, you go downstairs and start work on the door down there; Ketch, you look around and try to find where they keep things like bandages, cotton, that kind of stuff. You follow me," he said to Ted, as the kid started off in Ketch's orbit. Reluctantly the boy turned back and Tietjen began to read through McGrath's shopping list.

She had torn pages from a home guide to prescription drugs, circled names, whole categories of drugs, made notations in the margins. Tietjen read the list aloud: penicillin, any kind; tetracyclines, any kind. Aspirin. Darvon, codeine, ibuprofen, acetaminophen, Demerol. Anticoagulants. Dramamine, Benedryl, any antihistamines. Insulin and any antidiabetic drugs. Cortisone. Anitspasmodics. Nitroglycerin. Barbiturates, antidepressants, tranquilizers, amphetamines. Antipsychotic drugs and immune-system boosters. Distilled water. Antiseptics, cotton swabs, bandages, suturing needles and surgical thread, scalpels, forceps—did McGrath know how to use any of this stuff?

Ted was dropping bottles into the plastic bag he carried with gleeful abandon. There was a giddy pleasure in grabbing everything in sight and carrying it off; Tietjen felt it himself. "There're labels on those bottles?" he asked. "We don't want to have to sort them out later and give someone the wrong stuff. And we want all the antibiotics they have, anything at all, IV or pill, whatever."

It took them fifteen minutes to empty the shelves, checking against McGrath's list. Ketch returned before they were ready, pulling a wire cart with deep canvas bins. MT SINAI LAUNDRY was stenciled on the sides.

"I didn't think the hospital would mind." She grinned. She had almost filled one of the two bins with cartons and bags of bandages, swabs, alcohol and iodine swipes, and sponges. "We should probably find out where Emergency is. They'll have things like splints and tools—needles and thread and stethoscopes and like that. You guys ready?"

"You know your way around emergency rooms?" Tietjen asked as the three of them negotiated the laundry-cart into the stairwell and down to the next landing.

"They're not that tough: they label *everything*. I used to be on the streets a lot, spent some time in the ERs. Nothing uptown like this place, though." For the first time Tietjen heard the lowspeak lilt in her speech. He looked at Ketch with new interest, imagining her as a street kid, knife or billy hanging negligently at her side; she'd come up a way since then. She was too old to be street now, had probably been away from it for half a dozen years. Still, he thought: interesting.

Fratelone had unlocked the door of the medications locker on the third floor; his bag was almost full when the rest of the party joined him. As Fratelone finished up, methodically reading each label before he dropped a box into his basket, Tietjen scanned the shelves quickly for anything they had missed upstairs. Then he turned his party back to the stairwell, where the laundry cart waited. Fratelone's bag went in with the other treasure, and they went to look for the emergency department.

It took nearly an hour to find; Mt. Sinai was spread over an area five blocks long. Emergency was in the basement of the Annenberg Building, a dark rectangle sealed away from the street, hidden behind the buildings that faced Fifth Avenue. An ambulance had been thrown through the glass and steel mesh of the front doors there, so that the signs that marked it as the ER were illegible, but the stench was unmistakable. All the other hospital buildings had been empty, or had seemed so. Here in Emergency, the smell of death and decay was everywhere. Tietjen and his people wrapped scarves and bandages around their faces, smeared mentholated salve on their upper lips, trying to drown out the stench. Then they climbed over the twisted steel and fiberglass of the ambulance, through the maze of steel and concrete and glass that filled the Emergency area lobby. There was a sea of bodies there, swollen, soft and corrupt. Many looked as if they had been brought in during the disaster and left to die, others looked as though they had died instantly, in a breath of fear or rapture. Ted threw up; Ketch's dusky skin turned ashen. Tietjen felt faint himself. Only Fratelone waded in, unnoticing, looking for drugs.

Splints. More cotton. Slings. Stethoscopes, most taken from the pockets of corpses. Suturing needles and thread. Surgical tools from two of the examining rooms. Sealed sacks of alcohol and distilled water. Vaccination guns, hypodermics. Ted found another laundry cart and they filled it, more cotton, more swabs, thermo-strips, aspirin, a cache of vitamins. All four of them became frantic, giddy, grabbing everything, tossing it into the cart, calling to each other from the examining rooms: what was this, could they use it, did they want it?

"MAST pants?" Ketch called to Tietjen.

"What are they?" Then he remembered: inflatable pants that would force blood from the legs back into the body, give a shock victim a transfusion of his own blood. "Forget 'em." No point in being able to stabilize someone with a ruptured spleen if you couldn't fix the spleen later. They took more iodine and bandages instead.

They were at it a long time, filling a second cart. The light outside was fading when they emerged from the alley that led to Madison Avenue, tugging carts so heavily laden that the canvas bottoms scraped the pavement. The hectic flush of work faded slowly in the chilly air; all of them felt sheepish suddenly, a little edgy.

"Let's get home," Tietjen said.

He took point, with Ted and Ketch navigating the carts just behind him. The carts, on hard rubber wheels, barely made a sound as they rolled over the uneven sidewalk; the wire frames creaked and rattled, and sometimes the contents of the carts settled with a rustle. Fratelone brought up the rear, his square bulk casting a menacing shadow on the sides of the buildings. As they walked past the gutted boutiques on Madison, Tietjen kept hearing things, small sounds, disturbances so slight he wondered if he'd heard them at all, really. One footstep. The note of a high-pitched giggle, cut off immediately. A flurry like the beating of giant wings somewhere behind the shadows. Imagining things, Tietjen thought. He felt hollow, hungry and scared and tired, now that the adrenaline of the hospital raid was fading. Just imagination.

"I heard something." Fratelone had come up from the rear to mutter at Tietjen's shoulder; he was half a head shorter than Tietjen. "*I heard something,*" he said again. It frightened Tietjen to hear a quaver in Fratelone's voice; he thought of the guard as a rock, as unflappable in his way as Barbara McGrath was in hers. But she was upset over the little girl this morning, he remembered. And Fratelone had been taken and tortured by someone in the dark of the city, probably still had scars to show for it.

"Let's get off the street for a bit," he said. They struggled with the awkward bulk of the laden carts, lifting them up a few granite steps to a doorway that had been destroyed, creating an artificial courtyard. The building above was simply not there—looking up, Tietjen saw the first dusty scattering of stars. Fratelone and Ted pushed the carts behind one of the walls; then the four of them peered out into the street.

Darkness seemed not to descend from the sky with the dying of daylight but to well up, infusing the shadows with an unnatural ink-iness. There was nothing but the blackness in the street, nothing to make Tietjen's skin crawl as he scanned the street for motion. He forced himself to relax slightly, leaning against the crumbling gran-ite of the old portico and taking measured breaths.

"How long're we going to stay here?" Fratelone muttered after a few minutes. "Baby's sick."

Tietjen flushed with irritation. Fratelone had been nervous, and now he wanted to go. No pleasing some people. "If it seems clear in another few minutes we'll go," he said. Almost as Tietjen spoke he heard a high thin wail of a laugh. He couldn't judge where the sound came from, but suddenly he was aware of a murmuring, a distant crowd voice.

"When are we heading back?" Ted echoed Fratelone.

Tietjen resisted the hand at his elbow, the urgency in the boy's tone. "I don't want to go out there until we know what that is."

"What *what* is?" Fratelone snapped, but he looked on the street fearfully.

Ketch shook her head at him, at Ted. "Don't you hear it? Tietjen's right; listen."

The swell of sound continued, echoed from the faces of the buildings. The blackness at the end of the block was impenetrable; something was advancing within it. Behind him Tietjen felt the oth-ers pressing forward, looking. A chunk of stone chipped from the portico and fell at his feet.

"Stay back," Tietjen whispered between his teeth. He turned to look at them all over his shoulder. "Just keep back, will you?" Ketch nodded, pursing her lips fiercely so that the skin stood in white ridges; Ted stood looking at her, listening for something he was not sensitive enough to hear. Fratelone was listening too, with cold in-tensity. He was terrified, Tietjen realized. He knew something about what was happening out there.

High-pitched laughter rolled giddily down the street. Just behind the laughter the blackness rolled forward, a fallen cloud of oily darkness that pulsed. The pulses resolved into motion, the motions became separate. There were people out there.

"No," Fratelone breathed behind them.

He was right. What was out there was not human. From the shifting mass of darkness, something resolved. It was appallingly human at first glance, standing upright on two legs, its narrow tapering shoulders sloping into two unnaturally long arms. The head was long and tapering, insect-like. A praying mantis? But it was, or had been, human; it was almost as tall as Tietjen, and still wore the tweed jacket and corduroy pants cut to fit a human body, now hanging around its spindly limbs. The large eyes were reflective, glittering slightly as the thing moved its head. Tietjen drew back farther into his own shadow, pressing his lips tight to suppress a cry of terror. Behind the insect Tietjen could see the shape of a head, but where the features should have been there were only teeth, grisly pointed canines radiating in a long mouth; as the thing raised one arm Tietjen saw that it had no hand, just a single hooked claw.

Jesus.

Something with huge wings that beat slow as bellows, as if marking time. Two skeletal bodies linked like chain, moving awkwardly forward with the crowd. Misshapen flesh, skin that draped and quivered, deformities he couldn't make sense of at first, miscolored, scaled, feathered; a man, apparently normal except for the bright ring of blood around his smile, smeared across his cheeks, down his neck. From the inkiness that welled up around the creatures' feet something slithered forward, a dusky cloud, a tangible gibbering shadow with smoky amber eyes and the smell of death. There was no physical trace of humanity in the black form, only the hungry rage of the eyes.

Dear Jesus God.

Tietjen shuddered convulsively, wanting to deny what he saw. *You're not real!* He clutched the stone at his left and a piece crumbled in his fingers. *This is real and I am real, the city is real. . . . You things . . .* He stared at the creatures but they did not vanish in the face of his outrage. And they—he and Fratelone and Ketch and the kid—had one pistol, a couple of knives, and two carts full of drugs and bandages. Defenseless. Tietjen wanted to turn to the others and tell them not to breathe so loud; it seemed he could hear them sweat, hear the echo of his own thoughts ringing clearly through the street.

He turned away from the street, pushing the others back with him. "Back—quietly," he whispered, and they moved as one for the shadowy protection of a half-fallen wall.

Fratelone moaned almost soundlessly and sagged against the wall. "I thought I dreamed it, I thought—" The man closed his mouth tightly.

"Tietjen, how long are we going to stay here?" Ketch whispered. "We can't defend this place—"

"Shut up. The only way out is right past them. We have to wait till they pass. And goddamned keep quiet."

They pressed together, huddling for warmth in the purple dark, listening. In the street the high laughter continued, the muttering. Now and then a word or two of chillingly normal conversation drifted in to them, spoken in unhuman voices. "Is he bringing her?" one voice asked.

"He's got her," another confirmed. "I can feel it."

Tietjen could not explain the horror in those words, the way they made him shudder. Fratelone sat on a chunk of granite, as still as if he were cut from the stone; the others leaned with Tietjen against the wall, breathing carefully, waiting and listening. With a peculiar obstinacy that Tietjen prayed was not deliberate, the crowd of monsters had stopped in the street almost in front of their hiding place, and were waiting there.

"Is he bringing her?—" someone asked again.

"I hear it." Another voice.

A distant, thin wailing played on the air, a woman's voice wavering between terror and hysteria, beyond pain. "I hear it too," another voice said with satisfaction. The whine grew closer, the murmurs of anticipation and satisfaction rose: he's bringing her, she's coming, I hear her.

Tietjen edged past Ketch, motioning the others to stay still. Slowly, so as not to cause the least disturbance in the dust and stones under his feet, he made his way to the gray darkness of the shattered doorway. He was there to watch as they brought the woman in. The monsters lounged in a semicircle fifty feet away, like an audience waiting for the curtain to rise. The darkness still puddled and pulsed at their feet like a living thing—Tietjen believed that it *was* alive. At the end of the street a man emerged from the darkness, carrying a woman over his shoulder like a sack of grain. The man was enormously tall and thin, with lank dark hair that brushed his shoulders, and skin so fair that he had an almost greenish glow in the new moonlight. Among the creatures that had been waiting for him he looked comparatively normal, until you saw his eyes: the sockets were black pits rimmed with red and there was no eyeball. And yet he could see, it was obvious with every motion: he read his crowd, turning his head to acknowledge the presence of one, the hunger of another. That he was the leader was obvious in the way the others yearned toward him, followed his movements, let loose a breath of release at his arrival.

As the eyeless man reached the group of monsters he slung the wailing woman from his shoulder and draped her on the hood of a car, the altar of her sacrifice. She was stocky, hair a pale tangle and her skin pasty white with shock. Faced with the horror that ranged around her, she seemed unable to do anything but weep and laugh. She did not struggle, even when one of the creatures drew the hook that passed for his hand slowly, deliciously across her throat. No blood was drawn, but there was a sigh of satisfaction from the monsters. The eyeless man smiled broadly at his followers.

Unable to watch any more, Tietjen returned to the others with infinitely careful steps; it seemed he was hardly breathing. "We can't go anywhere," he told them, low. "They've got someone out there and—we can't do anything." Just be quiet. He thought longingly of the Store, of New York before all this, of his walks undisturbed through the cool air of uptown Manhattan at midnight, and he silently, venomously hated what had happened to the city. In the street the prisoner screamed. There was a low mutter of laughter. Against his will Tietjen listened, and watched the muscles bunch and release in Fratelone's arms as the man clenched his fists rhythmically. There were sedatives in the laundry cart, Tietjen thought, looking at the other man. The search for them would make too much noise; if they had to run or fight, he did not want to have Fratelone drugged. Fratelone would have to cope. Like all of them. They could not go anywhere, they could do nothing except listen and wait.

Tietjen was so absorbed in the wait, straining to hear the smallest sounds, trying to drown out the larger more horrifying ones, that he missed the moment when the prisoner stopped screaming and the creatures began to drift away. Not until the silence they left behind them became a sound itself did Tietjen break out of his trance. Ketch was stock-still, leaning against the wall with grimy tear streaks down her face, her eyes closed. Fratelone stared into space, still clenching and unclenching his hands. The kid, Ted, was snoring slightly, sound asleep.

"Come on," Tietjen said very gently. "Let's get back home. Barbara's waiting for us."

1

JIT flitted from voice to voice, from mind to mind, listening, tasting, playing with his new power, seeing through other eyes. He had always been kept down by the wave of feelings that pounded him, waking or asleep. Now he could separate the voices, savor them individually. Parts of the city he had never seen—which was most of the city—were now unfolded to him in a scattered collage. He saw the flooded south of Manhattan, the waters stopped by a wall of brick and stone washed from the offices of Wall Street. He saw the delicate outlines of midtown towers and understood, with someone else's knowledge, that these skeletons had once been concrete honeycombs filled with activity and expectation. He heard the wind fluting between splintered skyscrapers and remembered the strains of a serene Mozart clarinet, winding together and almost interchangeable in the mind of his contact. Jit saw a street littered with carrion, thousands of dead rats like a plush carpet gone to seed, and felt the squeamish horror of his host. Sitting in his tunnel, back pressed against the chilly stone wall, Jit could travel all over the city.

There were things happening that Jit did not understand. He heard voices full of light, of hope and faith that made him briefly yearn for what they loved, even when he did not understand it. Others were black dark, filled with rage, madness, and strangeness, imagery that pleased Jit's casually bloodthirsty soul even as it pleasurably frightened him. Until the strangeness grew too rich, Jit would tease those thoughts, playing with them. Watching through hosts he had seen people dancing wildly to a new god; Jit amused himself by making a big voice that he pushed through one dancer, and then another, so that the others thought it was magic, their master.

But after a while it wasn't enough fun just to sit in the darkness, listening. He began to explore on his own, ranging outside the Park in daylight, wandering at noon through streets he had formerly seen only after dark, hidden in doorways, tossed by the inner thunder of voices. He walked with growing confidence. No one came to the Park except the squirrels, gaunt for lack of pickings from the street vendors' scraps. Jit found no human being alive in the Park, little evidence of the old Park dwellers' enclaves. There were strange things, though, strange to rival anything his voices told him. The carousel was gone—by the look of what was left it had been twisted out of the ground like a top—and the monument that old Nogai had called Bolivar was a puddle of frozen bronze. The bronze sled dog that Jit had often stroked and patted in the dark was gone too, without disturbance, leaving its footprints in the cracked pavement.

"I wan'," he said once, loudly, waiting, but was not sure of what he wanted. The dog back, perhaps, something to touch and murmur to safely in the night. Nogai or the kid at the handball courts, even the old crazy woman of the park benches. The furtive community of street people which had populated the Park. "I wan'," but nothing came to him, and he began to venture even farther from the Park.

He was searching for one voice in particular, a voice surrounded by others: one voice like a strong old tree bearing apples; another voice brown and strong like a fine-fleshed nut; voices that sought and voices that worried and voices that simply were, uninteresting except that they all relied on and yearned for that central voice. Jit was drawn to the voice that drew so many others to it. He reached for it, tasting fear and sorrow, hard determination and confusion, as if its owner was not sure of how to get what it had determined upon. A strong voice uncertain of its own strength.

Through this one's eyes Jit saw the others, children, a dark woman with her face beaded with sweat, a kid Jit's own age, a short blocky man with an unsmiling face, an old woman, a young woman with narrow dark eyes. Not one of them followed the Man for a reason that Jit understood. And the thing that Jit wanted in the Man was not something any of the others seemed to share. He had found it there at the first touch: the Man needed the city. And Jit did too.

Until the change Jit had never understood loneliness except as a bleak sharp note among the voices. But the day and night of silence had scared him, the reedy thinness of feeling where there had been a rich soup scared him. For the first time in his life, Jit *wanted* people; wanted the Man, whose need and love was so encompassing that Jit himself might be included in it. When Jit reached out and found the Man he sighed with satisfaction and for a little while he was not lonely. Now, when he left the Park, he walked with a half-hope that he would find the Man and be taken in.

As it grew warmer Jit wandered the transverse roads south to the avenues and walked, no longer bothering to efface himself against the buildings. He passed bodies, some of them ripely foul-smelling, others gray and neat and without a scent; the smell didn't bother Jit, but they seemed in the way to him, so he made them go away. That was a good new trick, but he was sure he would learn more as he walked; there was so much to learn: in honey-colored afternoon he peered through shattered glass and twisted steel mesh, trying to make sense of what he saw. Things. Tools for doing and making, things that had no use at all. Clothes, bright colored cloth and oddly shaped shoes; Jit took a long scarlet skirt from one window display and, tearing open a seam, had a cloak that swept from his shoulders to trail in the stone dust that was everywhere. One window was filled with bottles and jars and plastic packets, electric banners hanging unlit and illegible. Jit was curious enough to reach through the grating and take one of the jars displayed there, but was disappointed to find only small yellow and white pills. He tasted one, spat it out: it was dry as dust and tasteless.

Without thinking, Jit reached out with his new talent—the thing that brought the trees in the Park back to leaf—and made the bottles on the shelf explode, their contents spraying dust until the store was hazy. Satisfied with this small revenge, he turned to continue, tucking the jar he held into the pocket of his jeans. Every now and then he spilled out a pill, tossed it into the air and exploded it, enjoying the tiny puff of dust and sound.

As he walked, Jit sensed someone watching. He was being followed, but he could not see, could not hear, could find nothing when he turned his head. It took long moments for his body to let him know that he was scared; then his hair bristled and his heart sped in weighty thumps. Jit made a sudden sweeping turn, trying to surprise something. The scarlet cloak snapped around behind him as he moved. He found nothing and kept walking.

After a block or so he pulled a handful of the pills from his pocket and started tossing them into the air, exploding them, showing off for the unseen audience. He walked resolutely ahead, away from the safe containment of the Park, into a part of the city he did not know at all, rather than turn and face what was not there. Gradually, as he became accustomed to the sensation, the prickling at his neck and back of his hands subsided. He walked on, exploding the pills.

"Do it again!"

Jit swung around, but the voice did not come from behind. Swiveling back, he saw a girl, thin and knob-jointed, with the pale skin of a night person and a tousle of red hair, sitting in a doorway. Maybe she was a woman: when she stood up, hands in the pockets of denim overalls, and moved close, Jit saw deep lines around her mouth and eyes, one eyebrow drooping lower than the other. Her arms and shoulders and throat were bare, goosefleshed in the cool air. She grinned at Jit. "Do it again."

Jit reached and found her voice in his head, flat and unpleasant; she was waiting for something. Harmless as the people in Lincoln Center, dancing to dead gods.

Jit poured a handful of pills into his palm, threw them in an arc over his head, and made each one erupt in a cloud of white powder. The woman's grin widened, showing close white teeth and too much tongue as she laughed. Jit's own laughter bubbled up briefly; he was hopelessly pleased that someone else liked his trick. "Know what Jit can do?" he asked her, thinking of the leafing trees in the Park.

She was not interested. "Again!" she commanded. Jit did it again. "More!" He exploded the pills again, but the trick was beginning to bore him. When she asked one more time, Jit shook his head and turned on his heel, walking back the way he had come.

She followed him.

Up Seventh Avenue, past the fallen marquees and shattered glass that had sifted through the gratings; past a miraculously unbroken window behind which holographic mannequins still gyrated. Once Jit turned around and waved his hands at her angrily. "Go 'way, you Ducks!" She still followed him, and drew her hands from her pockets and waved them in return, only she had no hands, just three long tentacles at the end of each arm, each with a claw at the end. Jit stopped in his tracks, curious. The woman should have tasted wrong, but when he let his mind lick out at her he found no sense of her own wrongness in her. What he found in her voice was dull, matter-of-fact rage; sly curiosity; and something else, a fearful hoping about Jit himself. He did not understand it.

"I can do a trick," she called to him. She took a step toward a doorway, reached down, and the tentacles on her left arm snaked out to grab something and pull it toward her. It was a body, one of the bad ones, gray and patchy with decay; a man in a suit. Something had been chewing at its face. "Watch me!" the woman said. The tentacles on her left arm held the body by the neck with the head up; one tentacle slid across the cheek until it caught on the upper lip. She began to work the mouth as if the man were a puppet: "Hello, how are you?" she faked a deep, pompous voice. "Are you having a good walk?"

Jit laughed once. But the woman kept on going, didn't make the body say anything funny, just "Hello, how are you?" over and over. He shrugged and turned away.

"Don't go!" she called to him. "Wasn't it a good trick?"

Jit turned, shrugged again. "Whyfor you after me?" he called at her.

She blinked at him. "Do me your trick again!" she said. And, "Gable told me."

Jit shook his head in disgust; he understood none of it. "You go 'way," he said again.

She stared at him with an empty smile. Jit read something beyond the smile, something beyond the woman herself, and it made his stomach turn. "Lea'me alone. Go 'way."

Her smile broadened. "Gable told me; you're the one." She stepped forward again, reaching out to him with one arm, each of the tentacles reaching out as well with a little life of its own. "Gable told me so. Come on, come with me. Gable's waiting." The voice Jit tasted in her warmed at Gable's thought.

Jit shook his head, annoyed. *He* was the master of voices, the master of Central Park and the city. Whoever this Gable was, Jit did not like him. "Go away!" he called again, waving his hand at her. He turned his back and started off toward the Park.

She kept following. The sky faded to dull lavender edged with pink as the sun went down, and her pale skin glowed pink and mauve. "Gable said—" she began. In her mind Jit read an uncomprehending confusion: Jit was not acting the way she believed he would.

"Don't *know* no Gibble-gabble. You go!" Jit yelled.

When she kept walking Jit reached with his mind and pushed her, knocked her to the ground hard enough to take the breath out of her, and held her there while he walked away. Enough of *that* game.

He made it back to the safe enclosure of the Park without the sense of watching, but the encounter with the woman still bothered him. She was harmless enough, the bad strangeness of her arms was nothing, even the anger that Jit had found in her was vague and dreamy. But the taste of the man Gable on her, and the idea that someone knew of Jit, that was frightening. The boy shinnied down the side of the ladder to his home cave, started the fire and the stove and opened a can of soup for his dinner.

When it was hot he leaned back against the wall, stared into the fire and, between bites, reached out with his mind, searching the city, trying to learn about Gable and the woman from the safety of his cave. He found others. Somewhere an old woman was kneeling, lighting a candle, muttering *Blessed art thou Eternal our God, King of the world, who has sanctified us by thy commandments and ordered us to light the Sabbath candles,* her head lowered and tears running down her face. Somewhere a man was laughing, hoarse and panicky. Jit touched the Man briefly and was tempted to stay with him. But now he was safe, and now he was curious.

Jit reached around the city, touching and discarding voices, searching for the individual flavor of Gable's woman. At last he found it: dull and angry except when she looked at the one she called Gable. Then her hunger rose and a warm fusion of wanting and fear lit her. Jit let the woman be his eyes, saw the crowd of people, each twisted by wrongness and sculpted into something strange. In the center of a crowded circle was a fire, and just to the side of it was Gable. He was tall and very pale, as if he had never seen the sun, and his eyes—the burning darkness where his eyes should have been—glowed like a torch in the firelight, sparked and beckoned to the others. He was speaking; Jit listened.

"They are ours," Gable was saying. His voice was hoarse. "I've *told* you they are ours. The city is ours, we just have to take it from them! When we take the city, the *maker* will come to us and we'll rule forever." The blind man looked over the crowd and stopped, looking at the woman in overalls. "Carol Ann found him today," he announced. "Carol Ann was the first to find him."

Jit tasted a hot blossom of joy in the woman as she was singled out, and the confusion of hope and arousal and fear. Gable would remember her now, she would be special, Gable would love her. The flush of feeling was powerful. It took Jit a long moment to understand who it was Carol Ann had found: himself.

Gable went on: "We will kill the others, the stupid ones, the ones who didn't take the maker's gifts. *Gifts!*" he repeated. With one long arm he pointed to a face that was all teeth, then to a dark shadowy figure flying overhead, then to a blocky man with one eye in the center of his forehead. "What were we before? Now we *deserve* to have the city, that's what the maker did for us. Those others, they're nothing, they're *food*." The blind man gazed round the circle, nodding his head, agreeing with his own words, fixing that agreement with his audience.

Jit reached into Gable, testing. Through Gable's eyes he saw faces watching him from the firelight, felt the strength of their need, their reliance. Jit tested deeper, for a moment nearly swept away by the erotic thrill of Gable's power. Then, through arousal, Jit felt the blind man's mind answer him.

Jit sat bolt upright against the wall of his tunnel; no one had ever found him before. The blind man opened to Jit, welcomed him, brought him into a black storm of rage, the deepest core of Gable's being, which he offered to Jit, waiting his praise. *Master*, Gable thought. *This is your place.*

Jit felt the blackness swell up to drown him in its tarry substance. *Bad.* He panicked. He fled, drew his mind back. He would not be the master of that. Those were the things he had hidden away, those were the things that broke down the door. Those were the things old Nogai had told him would kill him.

In the flickering light of his fire Jit cowered against the wall, staring at the coals, waiting into the dawn to see if Gable could find Jit as Jit had found him.

8

A LITTLE before dawn Tietjen's party got back to the store. Allan Hochman was on guard in the lobby. His eyebrows were drawn together furiously, anger the best defense against worry.

"Where the hell have you been?" he began. When he saw Tietjen's face, and the faces of the others, "What happened?"

"I'll tell you in the morning. I don't want to talk about it right now. Is Barbara asleep?"

Hochman shook his head. "She's up with the little girl. Did you get penicillin?"

Ketch said wearily, "We got *everything*. Look, if you don't need me—"

"Go sleep," Tietjen said. "Thanks."

"I'll go to bed, but I'm not sure I'll sleep," Ketch said dully. "I don't want to dream."

"If you have trouble, come up to the infirmary and Barbara'll find you a sleeping pill," Tietjen offered. "Ted? Bobby? You want something to help you sleep?"

Fratelone and the boy refused. Ketch stood looking at Tietjen for another moment: "It's been a slice. Can't think of anyone else I'd rather have stayed up late at the horror show with. Later." She smiled wanly, then shrugged her shoulders and went off down the lobby. In another moment Ted followed her, shambling down the hall after her, without a hope that she would notice him.

"Let's get this stuff up to Barbara," Tietjen said, and he and Hochman and Fratelone worked on maneuvering the carts up the stairs one at a time, and through the hall to the infirmary-apartment. McGrath stood in the doorway with the light behind her.

"We were worried," she said grimly.

"Yeah, well. I'll tell you about it some other time. How's the little girl?"

McGrath chose her words carefully. "Rotten," she said at last. "What drugs did you find?"

Tietjen echoed Ketch: "*Everything.* I think the antibiotics are in the first cart." He began to dig through the cart, but bending over made him dizzy; it occurred to him that he was tired.

McGrath's hand was on his shoulder. "I'll find them. You get some sleep, you look like hell. I'll manage here."

"How much sleep have *you* had?" he asked her.

"Some. Go lie down, will you please?"

"Yuh, Boss, get some sleep. I'll stay and help," Fratelone said behind him. Tietjen had forgotten he was there. " 'S one a my kids in there, right?"

"*Go*, John," McGrath said.

I must look really bad, Tietjen thought vaguely. "Okay. Call me in a few hours. You manage everything all right?"

"McGrath smiled lopsidedly. "Manage better without you in a dead faint to liven things up," she said.

Tietjen climbed the stairs to his room and collapsed on the bed and fell immediately into dreamless sleep.

He slept for nine hours. The room was filled with sunlight when he woke, and for a moment Tietjen lay in bed feeling the pleasurable schoolboy guilt of having slept too late. Then he remembered. He rose, splashed water on his face and brushed his teeth, dressed in fresh clothes. He had an impulse to burn the clothes he had worn on the hospital raid, as if that would burn out the memory of the monsters and their victim. He shook his head to clear out the memories, just for a little while, time enough to catch his breath. Then he went down to the lobby, toward Elena's kitchen. There were half a dozen people sitting around, talking. They stopped when Tietjen entered; he saw Ted sitting in one corner talking to three others. God only knew what he was telling them.

Elena handed Tietjen a plate with rice and beans on it. "Barbara needs you upstairs after," she said. Tietjen thought it was the first time she had ever said anything to him directly. I'm moving up in the world, he thought. He ate quickly.

Fratelone was asleep in the living room of the infirmary, his mouth slightly open, showing square, powerful-looking teeth. Tietjen went through to Kathy Calvino's room. The smell of dying flesh was like a wall. Tietjen swallowed hard on the rice and beans that threatened to come up again, and stepped in.

"Morning."

Barbara McGrath looked up from the pot in which she was soaking a cloth; she had tied a cloth around her face, but it had slipped down and hung casually around her neck. "Hiya. Feeling better?"

"Much. How's she doing?"

"I was just about to drain the wound again. See if that helps. I don't know, though. I'd like it if you'd look at the books and tell me what you think."

"About what?"

"I thought the antibiotics would do it, but with this mess—and I lost an hour realizing that I couldn't fake doing a venipuncture, so I've been giving her antibiotics by mouth, and I'm not sure it's going to work. The book says two point five million units—but I don't know what that translates to with pills. If I had *time* I could look it up, figure it out, but I don't know how much time we have—" Her look shifted from the girl on the bed to a metal cocktail platter that held an array of surgical and kitchen knives, razors, a bottle of alcohol, some matches, and, beside them, a stack of books and pamphlets. "I *hate* this," McGrath added flatly.

She looked *old.* The sunlight that filtered through the blinds lit her face in lemony splotches; the smudges under her eyes had deepened. There was a jerkiness to her motions, as if she was so in control of herself that the control itself had become a burden. She wore a white smock spattered with dots of blood and pus.

She laid another cloth on Kathy's forehead, then took a pan from beside the stainless-steel platter, dumped the knives and razors into it, and came around the foot of the bed. "I'm going to boil this stuff and try to lance the wound again. I'm glad you're home."

She disappeared around the corner for the camper stove that had been set up in the kitchen. Tietjen watched her go. *Glad he was home?* Why? What in God's name did she think he could do that she or someone else had not? For a moment he was furious, staring down at the medical dictionary and the first-aid books on a chair where McGrath had left them for him.

He flipped open the top book and started looking at it, sat down and pulled the book into his lap and flipped through looking for information about blood poisoning.

"Anything?" McGrath was back with the pot held out at arm's length; the steam that rose from it made the neat waves of her hair kink up into a soft white froth around her face.

"According to the book, we should have taken her to the hospital two days ago. Failing that, wait and watch. Want a hand?" Tietjen dumped the books on the floor and reached for the pot, but she pulled away from him.

"You'll burn your hands. You *could* lance the wound this time." She put the pot down on the table, where it sizzled slightly, scorching the plastic surface. "You'll have to wash up first."

He regretted that he had said anything, opened his mouth to say no and found that he could not. Not looking at the slope of Barbara's shoulders and the tight set of her mouth. So Tietjen followed her into the bathroom, washed his hands four times with soap and water, as McGrath did. Back in the sickroom, she took a place at the girl's head, both hands hovering near her shoulders. "I'll hold her down if we need. Bobby did it for me while you were asleep."

The sheet was pulled away from Kathy's leg. It had swollen since yesterday, and taken on an ominous purple color. There were small blisters across the skin, and the red stripe that stretched toward the groin had widened and deepened in color. It didn't look like something human; it didn't look like anything that should be attached to a little girl. When Tietjen's hand hovered over the knives and needles McGrath had removed from the pot onto a piece of cloth: "The parer works best." She nodded when he picked up a three-inch kitchen knife with a wooden handle. "That's it."

She told him what to do, and Tietjen slowly opened the wound again. It was nearly impossible to make the first cut, slicing through the scab and skin to suppurating flesh to release a slow ooze of pus. The cutting got easier; Tietjen clenched his teeth and ignored the lurching of his stomach. Probed farther. Barbara poured a thin stream of Betadine solution into the wound, mopping it up with gauze before he went on again. At last, unsure that continuing would help, and not in any case sure that he *could* continue, Tietjen stopped, laid down the knife, and stood away. Through it all Kathy had not moved or made a sound.

"Think that will do?"

"I guess. You're braver than I've been." McGrath's hands were still on the girl's shoulders; she moved one now to smooth the lank dark hair from Kathy's face. "It's okay, sweetie, that's the end of it for a while, you rest now. That's my good girl." There was no sign that the girl had heard.

"Now what do we do?"

She looked up from the child's blank face and smiled. "It's time for another round of antibiotics—unless you know how to put in an IV? Damn. Okay, another pill. After that, who the hell knows?" Again the tight smile.

"Then go get some rest, Barbara." It occurred to him that as long as he sat here, he did not have to deal with the monsters outside the store.

She smiled again, and it was the familiar Barbara. "I could stand to change my clothes—maybe you've noticed?"

"Then go change them. I'll stay and watch for a while. You could even sleep a little."

She did not argue. When she was gone Tietjen picked up the books and continued to read. The *Physician's Desk Reference* was studded with slips of paper: when he opened it Tietjen saw notes in Barbara's neat writing, dosages for Cephalexin, Dolsephexin, Cafazolin, Clindamycin. He put down the PDR and spent the next hours picking up information he hoped he would never need to use. The medical dictionary, for example, listed ninety-six separate types of amputation. He looked up from the book and stared at the little girl on the bed, shuddered, and flipped the pages ahead: carbophilic, carboxy-lase, carbuncle, carcass . . . enough of that. He put down the dictionary and picked up one of the first-aid handbooks, a fairly comprehensive one. The entry on infected wounds and septicemia ended, "Hospitalization may be necessary; your physician will advise."

McGrath appeared with a plate of stew for each of them. Tietjen ate hungrily, so used to the smell in the room that he barely noticed it. When they had finished eating, she tried to get Kathy to drink some fruit juice with her pills.

"Come on, darlin', come on. Have to have some energy to fight this stupid infection on. Come on."

Kathy seemed to rouse a little, swallowing, muttering. Tietjen couldn't remember if he'd ever seen the girl before this. She was how old? Maybe eight; near Chris's age. Don't even think about that. She looked nearer a hundred, like a paper doll no one had bothered to color. When she finished the juice McGrath settled her with her head raised a little on the pillow and combed out the limp dark hair, smoothing it gently away from the child's forehead, keeping up the murmur of inconsequential, soothing words. "When you're well again we'll find you some ribbons and tie it up pretty for you, you'll like that, won't you? What's your favorite color?" No answer, a pale flicker of smile that might have been deliberate. McGrath went on. "Mine is yellow, which is a shame because it looks terrible on me. Makes me look a like a lemon. You'd look nice in yellow, it would be pretty with your hair. . . ."

She kept up the murmur for some time. Tietjen felt as if he was intruding, listening and watching her. Finally he turned back to the books, reading about German measles, swollen glands, lice, heart attack, an overwhelming array of ills. At the bedside McGrath put the comb aside and sat down, staring aimlessly across the room.

An hour or so later they gave the girl another dose of penicillin, took her temperature, looked at the dusky purple, swollen flesh of the thigh, the blackening, crusty skin near the wound, and the nasty, pus-filled blisters that surrounded it. No change, despite the antibiotics.

An hour after that, McGrath cleared her throat. "We have to do something."

Tietjen looked up from the dictionary. There was a morbid fascination in reading the entries. "Is it time to drain the wound?"

"John, what's the difference between septicemia and gangrene?"

"Ask me something hard." He thumbed through the book in his lap. "Septicemia is blood poisoning—infection that's spread to the blood. Gangrene is the death of tissue, uh—" He paged through the dictionary. " 'Usually in considerable mass and associated with loss of vascular supply and followed by bacterial invasion and putrefaction.' " With each word he felt a little sicker. "Barbara?"

She looked at him. Tietjen felt he should put his arm around her, give her a shoulder to lean on. He could not. What he wanted more than anything was to walk out of the room, out of the Store, into the streets that were filling with dusk, into the March warmth. And he couldn't. All he could do was sit in this room watching a ten-year-old kid die of septicemia and what looked like gangrene. McGrath was holding Kathy's hand. Tietjen closed the medical books on his lap. Thinking.

"Boss?" Fratelone edged in and hunkered down next to him, eyes on the bed. "How's the kid doing?"

"Lousy." Tietjen grimaced.

"All that medicine didn't help?"

"We aren't sure, Bobby. What we need is a doctor or a hospital or someone who *knows* something."

Barbara spoke. "I shouldn't have wasted time sending you out for drugs. We should have just sent her out of here on a stretcher, to Westchester or Jersey or somewhere. We could do it now—"

Tietjen shook his head. "She wouldn't last the trip, Barbara—"

"Dammit, John, what else can we do? Do you really want to sit here and watch her die? I *can't*. We've got to get help for her—"

"Boss, I'll take her," Fratelone started. "I can hot-wire a car—"

"Shut up! Christ's sake, Bobby, Manhattan's a fucking island. The bridge I came in on you could hardly walk on. You going to load the kid into a car—if you can find one that'll run—and cruise around trying to find a tunnel or bridge that's passable? Build yourself a raft and float across the Hudson? She'd die before you got to the river. . . ." Tietjen trailed off, remembering the overwhelming dread that had hung over the East River like a fog.

Fratelone hung his head. "Then whadda we do?" he asked. "I told them girls I was takin' care of them from now on." He was stroking the child's hair; his big square hand was larger than her face.

"*What can we do?*" Barbara echoed. "If she died on the way out of the city, at least we'd have tried something. What else can we *do?*"

"You can't let her die, Boss. Shit, she's only a baby. I promised them."

The fury that filled Tietjen was overwhelming. At Bobby Fratelone and Barbara, at the girl, at everyone who had got out and left the city, at the city itself, at whatever had happened—

He wheeled around, strode into the next room, and kicked at a closet door until it hung by one hinge and his foot hurt like holy hell. The adrenaline subsided. Reason, or something that felt close enough, returned. Tietjen limped back into Kathy's room.

Barbara and Fratelone watched him warily. Neither one had moved.

"I'm okay," he said tersely. Tietjen looked from Fratelone to Barbara McGrath, and finally at Kathy Calvino, unaware of them all. For one more minute he wished that he could chuck it all and go back to the streets, wished that he had come back a day later, or a week, that he had not left Massachusetts and come back to the city. No, not that, but he wished.

No use wishing.

He took a long breath. "Bobby, I want you to find some things for me." As Tietjen started to list what he needed, Fratelone began to shake.

"Ah, God, Boss. No, there's gotta be something else you can—"

"Like what?" Tietjen asked. "Just get everything together and bring it back here. We don't have time to go around the block on this, Bobby. Okay? I don't like this any better than you do."

There was a great release in having made a decision, even with the consequences that flowed from it. "Barbara?"

She nodded. There was fear and reluctance in her look, and sorrow, and trust that terrified him. "We have to *do* something," she affirmed. "If there's no help, we'll have to do it ourselves. What will we need?"

He could have damned everything on the face of the Earth just then for making him the decision maker, but McGrath made it easier by not asking questions, protesting, acting squeamish. She came around the bed to his side, put her hand on his for a moment, then reached for her clipboard.

She took charge of sterilizing the tools: a hacksaw, the kitchen parer, a few scalpels, suturing needles and thread, all the surgical clamps they had brought back with them, and two steel spatulas that could be heated for cautery. From somewhere, a pile of miraculously clean towels. Bobby had found a folding massage table upstairs and brought it down to the infirmary, where it was swabbed with alcohol and draped with sheets to make an operating table. A ring of high-beam lamps stood a yard's length from the table, all connected to a single battery.

•   •   •

As Barbara and Fratelone set up the room, Tietjen sat by Kathy's bed, rereading the descriptions in *Dortland's* of amputations, checking the skeletal and circulatory charts. Poring through *Rosen's*, the emergency medicine book, trying to plan. What kind of amputation it was, exactly, that he was planning? Callander's? Carden's? Farabeuf's? Flaps cut from where to where, sewn how? Bleeding to control from the femoral artery, the deep femoral, saphenous vein— a moment of panic: *I can't do this.* Sutures: vertical mattress, over and over, Lembert, lock stitch, Halsted, horizontal mattress stitch. Methodically Tietjen worked it out. Watch for the femoral artery, which might retract to a place where he couldn't find it: clamp it first, then cut. No anesthesia: if Kathy was not unconscious with the fever the pain would knock her out. Tourniquet to cut down the flow of blood while he located, clamped, and tied off the blood vessels—

"John?" McGrath's voice startled him. "We're ready."

"Right." This time she followed him to the bathroom, where Bobby Fratelone was scrubbing his hands with angry attention.

"'S my kid. You and Barbara might need a little help."

Tietjen decided not to argue, and started washing his own hands. One book prescribed twenty soapings, twenty rinses. Soap was too precious, hot water in too short supply. After five cycles they rinsed their hands in alcohol, then went back into Kathy Calvino's sickroom, hands held up before their faces to dry in the cool air of early evening, and snapped on latex gloves. Allan Hochman had moved Kathy to the operating table and stood in the hallway, guarding the quiet of their work.

First the tourniquet, a narrow belt with the insignia of an expensive designer. Fratelone wrapped it around the girl's leg, high on the thigh. "Like that?"

Tietjen nodded. "Draw it tight."

Afterward he remembered very little of what he'd done. When he took up the scalpel it did not seem possible to use it on another human being. At the first cut Kathy strained against Fratelone's hands, shuddering. Then she went limp.

"That's taken care of," McGrath observed dryly. She was calm, and followed Tietjen's orders briskly, as if she had trained for her job since childhood. Fratelone, at the head of the bed, had slumped back on his stool when Kathy fainted. "Don't faint, Bobby," McGrath said quietly. Fratelone shook his head and sat still, hands on the child's shoulders and eyes trained on her face, not looking at what was happening.

He'd plotted it out beforehand, but despite his planning the operation wasn't neat, wasn't tidy. It took forever, cutting, clamping one artery and then another, sewing, cauterizing, cutting bone. The sound of sawing bone made Tietjen's stomach lurch; it reminded him of sitting in the dentist's chair listening to things he couldn't see. Now he could see, and wished he couldn't. Tietjen made it work by thinking like an architect, envisioning structure, systems, making a puzzle out of the little girl's leg.

At last he finished the cut with a long flap from the thigh, pulled the skin over the blunted edge of the stump and began to suture it into place in the front. McGrath took the tools he had used and dropped them into a bucket on the floor. Fratelone relaxed just enough to pat the child's shoulder clumsily. Tietjen put the needle down and swabbed the stump with alcohol and iodine.

"I don't know," he said into the silence.

"I do," Barbara said. She took a sheet nearby and tenderly wrapped the leg he had amputated, for disposal. "There was nothing else we could do. I don't want to hear any nay-saying. I'll stay in here for a while—you guys go get cleaned up." She frowned at Fratelone when he shook his head. "Don't give me any trouble, Bobby; you're white as a sheet. John, drag him out of here. She's going to live, okay?"

Tietjen took Fratelone with him, wishing he were as sure as McGrath.

Allan Hochman was still at the door. "Wait and see," Tietjen told him, and pushed past him into the hallway to find everyone— Elena, Ketch, Ted, Sandy Hochman, the other Calvino girls, the thirty-odd others who were living in the Store, waiting there.

"Oh, for Christ's sake!" They looked at him expectantly. "It's over, she seems to be okay, we don't know. Don't any of you have work to do?" They looked at each other but no one moved. "Go away. You'll breathe up all the good air! You'll leave all your nasty germs around. Christ!" Sandy and Allan exchanged sheepish looks and Sandy turned, taking the children with her; the others began to move away. Tietjen felt a little guilty at having yelled at them.

"Damn sideshow," Fratelone muttered beside him. The two of them went off to the men's showers to wash the operation off.

It was dark when Tietjen was finally clean, changed, and a little of the adrenaline had dissipated. He went into the lobby, where two of the men were putting up the shutters for the night, peered out the door, and decided against a walk. Instead he started climbing stairs, up to the fourteenth floor, to sit in a window and look out over the city. He sat there a long time, not really thinking, forgetting about Kathy and McGrath, about the monsters he had seen the night before, forgetting about anything but his own exhaustion and the delicious sensation of sitting with the breeze on his face.

"You pull a couple more stunts like that one and you're going to be a legend in your own time." A woman's voice came from behind him. "Between last night and today—definitely mythic stuff." Ketch stepped closer.

"Come on," Tietjen said uncomfortably.

"Yeah, well, that's what the hero is supposed to say, no? Shucks, ma'am, 'tweren't nothing?"

"It was *something*. I don't know if we did more harm than good. As for last night . . . I didn't do anything heroic last night. Stood there pissing myself and praying."

"And kept the rest of us from freaking and running out and getting ourselves killed. Can't get out of it, *Jefe*; you're developing a reputation." She moved closer and Tietjen swung one leg down from the sill, making room for her. She sat down easily, leaning against the sash. "It's nice up here. You could almost forget some things. Have you told anyone about last night?"

He shook his head. "I haven't had the time. I thought maybe tomorrow we'd call a meeting, try to decide what to do."

"They'll do what you decide to do," Ketch said. "Better figure out what you want."

What I want? Tietjen looked out over the streets. "I want things the way they were," he said.

"Really? Street kids and peddlers and thieves and blockcops beating on anyone they don't like? You don't look like the type. You should be the armored-cab-from-door-to-door type with sixteen locks and a gun under your pillow. Upward mobility, all that."

He smiled. "That's why my wife married me. Didn't think I'd run against type. I thought you said you were a street kid for a while?"

"A while. I got tired of looking over my shoulder all the time. The times I didn't, that's when I got to know the inside of ERs so well."

"Then what were you doing before all this?" He waved a hand to indicate the ruins below them.

"Law at NYU—educational ward of the state. Which meant I did a lot of shit jobs for the state while I was getting my degree." She sounded as if she did not want to be asked. "You?"

"I was a project manager, an architect. Lived on the West Side. I wonder if my apartment is still there. I should go look sometime."

They sat quiet for a while. "Your wife didn't make it?" Ketch asked at length.

"I think not. The building she lived in was burning when I got there."

"You weren't together, then." She sighed and stretched one arm above her head. Her fingers were very long and ended in long, bluntly shaped nails. "You know, I meant what I said yesterday."

Tietjen didn't remember. "Yesterday?"

"Yeah. You know: no one else I'd rather be stuck in a nightmare with. You held us together—the tough guy looked like he was going to lose it, and I was damned near wetting my pants, and you just looked—strong. You got us through it."

Tietjen blinked and thought about that. He hadn't felt strong, if anything he'd just been concentrating on keeping himself together.

Ketch leaned a little closer. "I might as well ask. You sleep alone?"

"Alone?" It took Tietjen a moment to make sense of the question. "Yeah. Who would I sleep with?"

Ketch smiled whitely. "I don't know, that's why I asked. Ms. McGrath, maybe, or Elena-the-rabbit. Or the tough guy, Fratelone. No telling. Think of it as a rhetorical question. Like, a proposition."

He had figured that out, at least. "I'm flattered."

"Don't be flattered, say yes or no. Or not tonight."

"Uhh. Tonight I don't think I could do justice—" he began.

"Okay. The offer stands." She stood up. "Go back to your stargazing. I'm on the second floor, if you change your mind."

He watched her turn and start for the stairs. He flirted with the idea, feeling an adrenaline rush at the thought. Couldn't just let her walk away. "Wait a minute. What's your name, first name?"

"Luisa. You can call me Li. Does it matter?"

Now Tietjen smiled. "I like to know. Second floor?"

"Yeah." Ketch stood by the stairway, a shadow in the darkness, her head tilted to one side as she watched him.

"Maybe you'd better show me where," Tietjen said at last, and left the windowsill.

9
—

IN the morning Tietjen ate breakfast with McGrath. She was exhausted, her skin the translucent white of vellum . . . but Kathy Calvino's fever was down. McGrath was certain the little girl would live; she sounded like a drunk in love with the world. "You were wonderful!" she slurred, stirring her oatmeal. Barbara leaned toward him and repeated, "You were wonderful. *We* were wonderful!" It was as if the surgery had bound them together in some new way. But Tietjen had woken early, unused to another body in the bed, left Ketch's room silently and crept upstairs to his own to wash and change, thinking about the monsters. The operation had allowed him to put off thinking about what to do next. Now the operation was over, and he was going to need Barbara's help. If he closed his eyes he could hear that woman screaming again; he thought sickly that it was the call to battle.

"John?" Barbara was looking at him, had obviously said something that required an answer. "I said I hoped you got enough sleep?" McGrath gestured wryly at herself. "I must look like I slept in a barrel, but we did it. The kid's going to make it, I'm sure."

"I'm glad, Barbara."

"*But* . . ." she prompted. "But what, John?"

"There are some things I didn't get around to telling you yesterday. Barbara, we saw something out there when we went to the hospital—"

He was interrupted by a hand on his shoulder and in his ear Ketch's voice. "Hey, early riser. Can I join you?" Her breath was very warm.

He waited while Ketch settled herself at the table, caught be-

tween adolescent embarrassment and an equally adolescent pleasure. She could corroborate what he had to tell McGrath.

Across the table McGrath looked momentarily disconcerted,
pursing her lips as she watched Ketch sit down. She smiled politely.
"Good morning, Luisa."

"Ms. McGrath." Ketch turned back to Tietjen. "I didn't hear
you go."

"Uh, no." Tietjen felt his face go hot, and he willed Ketch to understand that this was not the time for morning-after chat. As if *she*
read his thoughts, McGrath made a little noise of impatience and
began gathering up her plate and silver to leave.

"Barbara, wait, we need to talk. We have to tell you—" He
turned back to Ketch. "I'm glad you made it down; I was about to
explain to Barbara about the, the people—"

"Oh," Ketch said dully. "Right." Her smile dimmed.

"The people?" All the tired ebullience that had characterized
McGrath five minutes before had faded. She made no move to leave,
but neither did she put her silverware and plate down. "John, later?
I need to get some sleep."

"Barbara, five minutes. Look, I'll walk you up to your room. Li,
you come too, you can tell her—"

McGrath shook her head. "I'm too tired to listen now, John.
Give me a couple of hours; maybe then." She walked away without
a backward look.

"Barbara!"

"John, let her go." Ketch had her hand on his sleeve and urged
him back into his seat. "Like she says, she's tired."

That was not it, though. Something else was going on. "We need
her to understand about what we saw out there. We have to get the
Store ready: those things're going to come down on us and we have
to be ready."

Ketch pushed her fork through the beans on her plate. "They
won't try to take the Store. We're dug in here, we're fortified. They'd
be crazy to try anything."

"They *are* crazy." Tietjen looked at the knife in his hand. "Oh
shit, maybe *I'm* crazy."

Ketch looked at him levelly. "A little, maybe. Tilting-at-wind-
mills crazy. Look, baby: most people here don't give a shit except

that they've found a safe place. Unless that's threatened you're not going to find a lot of fighters here, John. Everybody's too tired."

"You too tired?"

Ketch said slowly. "I heard that woman screaming. But she was one woman, alone. They won't come here, after us. There's a lot of people here. And I tell you: when I think of fighting those things I want to dig a hole and crawl in. Maybe take you with me, since you obviously don't have the sense to run yourself." She raised a hand to his neck in a light caress to soften the words.

He shrugged under the touch, aroused and discomfited by the casual intimacy. "So you think we should play business as usual unless the—what can we call them? Unless the monsters come after us?"

"When you get a better plan, let me know." Ketch dropped her hand, made a face at her plate, pushed it away and stood up. "I'm on cleanup again. See you later."

Tietjen waited until she was gone, then cleared away his plate. Something was going on with McGrath and with Ketch, and it was distracting him from a threat to the Store, and he couldn't have that. Trying to think through that knot, he left the dining room for the building next door, where Fratelone had started workers clearing and cleaning out living space.

When he cornered Fratelone the man said, "We don't need to go after no more trouble, Boss." He waved Tietjen away and refused to hear anything more. The gawky teenager, Ted, looked pleased to be asked to advise, but he said the same thing, only with more words. "Jeez, Mr. Tietjen, like, they aren't gonna bother us here, we're, like, established. Nobody here wants to go after them, right?" The boy looked at him as if to see if he'd made the right answer. Tietjen could not tell him.

He filled the day with hard work and went to bed too tired to think. The next day was filled with work, and the day after that. The harder he worked, the less time to remember. Tietjen persuaded himself that Ketch was probably right, the Store was too strong for the nightmare people to attack.

After eighteen hours of sleep, McGrath had returned to work. Back to normal: competent, cheerful, dryly humorous. Much of her time was spent with Kathy Calvino, nursing and comforting; Tietjen did not know how Barbara had explained the loss of her leg to the eight-year-old, but when he went to visit her she was meekly polite and more cheerful than he would have expected. Barbara, standing by the end of the bed, was triumphant.

Sometimes Tietjen thought McGrath watched him when he was with Ketch; he thought she was laughing at his awkwardness around the younger woman. And Ketch was—herself. Since Irene he had seen other women, taken them out and gone to bed with them, but he had never lived with one or worked with one on the day-to-day level of life in the Store. When Tietjen expected Ketch to be possessive, she laughed and walked away, then surprised him by expecting responses he neither understood nor anticipated. And it was weird, living publicly, being watched as the leader. Ketch played the role of his lover comfortably, with a relaxed sense of what she could and could not grant on Tietjen's behalf. She was not much of a talker, fairly handy with tools, and willing to help find and dispose of bodies in the buildings nearby. She was an active, rather fierce lover, and told jokes well. Tietjen liked her.

Still, without McGrath's amusement to stiffen his spine, he might have been embarrassed into breaking with Ketch.

He and Fratelone and half a dozen others were in the basement of the building next door, clearing away rubble so they could examine the water heater. Hot and dirty, Tietjen sent Greg Feinberg back to the shop for a jug of water or juice, and called a break. In the sputtering yellow light of the lanterns the people sitting there, wiping sweat from hairlines with a forearm or a sleeve, looked like old sepia-tinted photographs Tietjen had seen of mine workers.

"Mr. Tietjen?"

Greg stood in the door to the boiler room, framed in more of the yellow lantern light from the basement hall. His voice was urgent. "Mr. Tietjen, can you come upstairs?"

Tietjen swung easily under a low hanging pipe and straightened up, wiping his hands on his pants as he went. "What's up, Greg?"

"Can you *please* come upstairs, sir?" the boy repeated. His voice trembled, and he was pale beneath the freckles and slight tan. Tietjen did not argue with what he saw in the boy's face. He let Greg lead him up the stairs and through the long marble lobby. In the doorway the sun was an assaultive glare. Tietjen blinked as he approached it, blinked as he looked outside.

Across the street, sitting with his back to the base of a fallen streetlamp, was one of the monsters. He was a little man, bandy-legged, dressed in a red T-shirt and black Bermuda shorts, with a round head with a fringe of dark, greasy-looking hair like an unkempt monk's tonsure. And no features except for a huge mouth, lined with narrow, needle pointed teeth. The mouth watched them like a Cyclops' eye for a moment; then, like a wink, the mouth smiled.

Tietjen felt the world tilt. He thought sickly: *We left you alone; you're not supposed to be real.*

"Jesus fuckin' Christ," Allan Hochman murmured, behind him.

"What *is* it?" Greg Feinberg asked. His voice wavered and cracked; Tietjen felt the boy's stare and the urgency of his attention. "Mr. Tietjen?"

He made his voice very calm, dry, matter-of-fact. "I don't know. We'll have to find out." He ignored the twisting of his gut and took a step forward; someone had to do something. *He* had to do something, God knew what. What could he say to a thing like that? *Hey there, how ya doing?* Another step; I'm getting brave, he thought with detachment. Or stupid. Another step and he was in the street, poised before the doorway with one hand raised. Maybe it wants to be friends. Immediately he remembered the screams of the woman he had heard tortured. Stupid.

"Yes?" he said.

The thing grinned wider. There was no sound except a soft whistle of wind through the street.

Tietjen raised a hand, a sort of halfhearted wave, a signal of good intent.

The blast of sound from behind him was so sudden that Tietjen thought for a moment that he was the one who had been shot. Across the street the thing with no face jerked suddenly, then sat rock still for a moment, braced against the streetlamp base. Then it slumped sideways and Tietjen saw the red on red of blood seeping through the creature's scarlet T-shirt.

"Jesus."

Tietjen spun around and found Allan Hochman behind him, staring; others stood behind Allan. Beyond Allan, in the doorway, Bobby Fratelone stood with a rifle under his arm. He was white-faced and his grip on the gun was not casual. "Teach 'em," he muttercd. But he held the rifle out to Tietjen. Tietjen stared at it mutely for a moment. "That'll fuckin' teach 'em," Fratelone repeated.

"Will it?" Tietjen asked. "Come on, we've got to finish what you started."

He directed two men to drag the monster's body to the cremation pit. Everyone else he herded back into the building. When Fratelone would have said something more Tietjen shook his head. "Later, Bobby. We need to talk later."

Fratelone did not come to dinner. Tietjen had sent him back to the Store to get some rest while he and his work crew finished clearing the basement of the building next door. At dinner he sat between Ketch and McGrath, trying to talk with Barbara on the one hand; trying to amuse Ketch on the other; trying, with a show of self-conscious leadership, to set an example of good-humored calm for the others. By the end of the meal he felt like he had been through a battle more unnerving than merely walking out to face the monster that afternoon. Not a single acrimonious word was spoken by Ketch or McGrath, they seemed to go out of their way to be polite to each other, but it was a laden, terrifying politeness. He stood up from the table feeling wrung.

"Look, we need to talk," he muttered to McGrath.

"All right," she said coolly. "When?"

"Half an hour? Let me collect Bobby. Can we meet in your room?"

McGrath relented, smiling. "Of course."

Twenty minutes later Fratelone, still groggy from a nap, was in the hallway outside McGrath's room. "Gotta throw some water on my face." He gave Tietjen a nervous sideways glance.

"Make it fast, Bobby. We'll wait for you."

While they waited for Fratelone, Tietjen explained it all to Barbara. Not just the incident that afternoon, but the surreal horror show he and the others had witnessed near Mt. Sinai. By the time Fratelone joined them Barbara was as quietly frightened as Tietjen could have wished.

She was for shoring up the Store's defenses and waiting. "Don't borrow trouble."

Fratelone ducked his head and did not look Tietjen in the eye.

"They won't come after us here again," he insisted. "They want easy kills; 'f we go after them they'll pick us off. We showed 'em today; they'll have to leave us alone now."

Tietjen bit back his first angry response. Bobby was working from terror; even talking about the monsters had him working his hands together, rubbing and clenching, cracking the knuckles. Bobby the tough guy couldn't face fighting the monsters. For the first time in weeks, Tietjen heard the warning voice that had accompanied him back into the city, wailing, insisting that he make the others understand.

"They *will* come," he said at last. "You heard them that night: they won't be happy until they've wiped us out or we've killed them all."

"John, how can you be sure?" Barbara asked.

"I *know* it," he insisted. "If I were one of them it's how I'd feel. They're a part of what happened to the city, Barbara, the thing that hates the city. I've walked around more than you have since the disaster, you've worked closer to the Store, you don't know—"

McGrath drew herself up, cold as death. "Don't pull that I've-been-in-the-streets crap with me, John. I've seen what's come in here; I've nursed people who've come to us and they've talked to me. I know what happened to the city was weird, John, but don't try to pull experience points on me. I stayed *here* because you asked me to."

Tietjen looked at her, exasperated. "I'm not saying you shouldn't have stayed—"

"Just that I can't know what's going on out there because I'm not used to crawling around the city on my belly the way—" She broke off and began again, obviously getting her temper under control. "John, I told you what I saw, the day it happened. You think anyone else saw anything, *anything* weirder than I have?" There was something else going on that Tietjen did not understand, something that was making Barbara angrier than she should have been, and that scared him because he needed her and he had to make her understand what had to be done.

"What we heard out there was twisted, those damned things out there are twisted too, and sooner or later they're going to want to bring the Store down; everything we're doing is directly opposed to what they want. They *won't* peacefully coexist. Unless we expect them they'll win. Barbara—" He held his hand out to her. "I need you to back me on this. First thing is, we have to make sure the Store is safe. But after, we have to go to them before they come to us."

"I have to think," she said at last. Her voice was steady again, without the steely tone of control. She was working on making a good decision, Tietjen thought. "Let me sleep on it; I can't decide all at once."

Tietjen nodded. "In the morning."

Fratelone shambled from the room with his head down. "N'a morning," he muttered, and headed toward his own room.

McGrath and Tietjen watched him go. "John, I don't like what this is doing to Bobby," McGrath murmured. "Look at him."

"I am," Tietjen said. "I don't like what this will do to any of us. What those things out there would do would be worse. Sleep on it, Barbara."

He left her in her doorway and climbed the stairs to his own apartment, feeling manipulative and melodramatic and desperate. He reargued it all under his breath, worrying that he had left something unsaid. When he reached the landing and opened the door to his living room, Ketch was waiting for him.

In the dark later, with Ketch's breathing a noiseless rise-and-fall against his side, Tietjen lay awake, listening to laughter that seemed to thread its way through the streets to find him.

He sat with Barbara at breakfast again and tried not to push too hard for her answer.

"I still don't know," she told him at last. "Everything, *everything* I know says that you reason with your enemies. Last ditch, you defend yourself. You don't go out and kill preemptively—"

"Dammit, you can't reason with monsters—"

"Loaded word." McGrath watched Ketch settle at the table on Tietjen's other side. He refused to be sidetracked.

"Call them whatever you damned well like. We wipe them out, or else they're going to wipe us out, and every normal person left in the city." He was sounding panicky and high-pitched; Ketch was nodding beside him, but he was afraid he would lose Barbara by being too shrill. "I'm not telling this right. Shit." He paused. "Look. I do remember what you told me the night we met. About the subway tunnel. The kids, and the tunnel squeezing shut, and the feelings you had. I remember that guy at the Met that was collecting people. Those were a *part* of it, Barbara. These things out there are a *part* of it."

Beside him Ketch murmured, "Tunnel?" Tietjen ignored her, concentrating on Barbara, willing her to believe. He watched the memory play across her face.

"Really like that?" she whispered.

"Like that. Whatever did that made these things."

"Then they *will* come," Barbara said.

Tietjen released the breath he had been holding. "They're organized, they have a leader, the blind one. If they're bringing people in to torture—they don't want to live and let live, Barbara."

"No, I imagine they don't," she said dryly. "They're the ones that hurt Bobby?"

"I'll back John up," Ketch said.

McGrath nodded coolly. "*He* won't want to fight them, John."

"We need him—we don't have many real fighters; Bobby's as close to an enforcer as we've got."

Barbara nodded and leaned back from the table to wave at one of the Calvino girls who was passing. "Karen, can you find Mr. Fratelone for me?"

The little girl hesitated for a moment, then pillowed her head on her hands and made a snoring noise. "Sy—ee—pin'," she managed, and Tietjen remembered that McGrath had said the girls had some sort of speech problem.

"Yes, dear, but I need him a lot. Can you wake him up and tell him that Mr. Tietjen and I need him—" She paused. "Up in my rooms, okay? It's important, sweetie."

Karen nodded and left them.

"Closed conference, Ms. McGrath? Maybe someone else has an idea could be useful." Ketch looked at Tietjen from the corner of her long eyes.

McGrath smiled politely. "We're not shutting anyone out, Luisa. Just chatting about how to . . . present this to the Store. Do you have any thoughts?"

Ketch made a face. "*Please.* John, I'm going upstairs."

Tietjen was too grateful at having won his point with Barbara to worry about Ketch just now. "Li, we'll talk later, okay?"

"Okay, baby." Ketch ran a negligently affectionate finger along his collar, gathered up her plate and fork, and left them. McGrath watched her go.

Bobby was groggy and resentful. "Stay where we are, don't go looking for no trouble," he repeated stubbornly. It took all Mc-Grath's calm persuasion and Tietjen's restrained passion to make him agree to take the fight to the monsters, and even then Tietjen believed his agreement came more from Fratelone's loyalty to them than belief that the monsters could be beaten. The three of them separated after an hour and went to spread the word of a meeting that evening.

Looking across the lobby that night Tietjen was startled at how many people the Store had recruited—he hadn't seen them all together at one time in weeks. They sat crammed one-too-many onto the couches, perched on the coffee table and useless radiators, sat cross-legged on the black and white marble floor, leaned against the walls or against each other. Fifty, sixty people, kids, adults, talking low in the torch and lantern light, already friendships and families forming within the community.

When he cleared his throat they—all of them—turned immediately to listen. Tietjen felt a flash of fear—*don't look at me that way!*—that came and went too fast for him to think about. He cleared his throat again and cast about for the right words to say. So much of what he did seemed to be finding the right words.

"Everyone's probably heard about the—uhh—visitor that Bobby Fratelone killed yesterday. Some of you may have seen these things around town before you got here—" A ripple of agreement in the crowd, as if he had struck a chord many would as soon have forgotten. "Bobby and Ketch and Ted and I ran into some of them last week when we went out for medical supplies. Until yesterday we hoped they'd leave us alone; I guess we could still hope for that, but I don't believe it." He paused and looked from face to face. "We know they've found us. I think the—thing—out front yesterday was sent in just to make us nervous, let us know they've found us. War-of-nerves stuff."

He could feel the weight of absolute attention and picked his way between over- and understatement. "Look, people. Those things are monsters. I mean physically, sure, they look like Halloween walking. But we heard them torturing a woman, the night we were up at Mt. Sinai; we heard them talking. They hate us, they don't want to be reasoned with. So first we have to make sure this place is damned well fortified. Then we're going to have to fight. We have to win the damned war once, or be prepared to fight and keep on fighting."

A hand went up. A youngish woman with pale brown hair and a round face stood up. Tietjen did not know her name. "What about when help comes? I mean, they won't matter then, I mean, won't the Guard or somebody take care of them? I don't know how to fight anything, that's what I pay taxes for, for the Guard and the Army and that. When *they* get here—" She looked around her for agreement. Some people nodded.

Behind Tietjen, McGrath spoke gently. "Gail, it's been almost two months since the disaster. The only person I know of who's come *in* to New York since that time is John, here, and he came in two days after. I don't know what's keeping the outside world from pouring in and starting the biggest damned relief program in the history of the modern world—all I know is that we've been on our own for two months, and we'd better plan on being on our own indefinitely. This isn't an adventure; it's *life*. Ask Kathy Calvino. That's why we're planting the garden and working on this place—we don't know when—if—we're going to be helped. If these monsters are as bad as John says, we have to count on dealing with them ourselves. I'm not a fighter either," she added gently.

"Yeah, well." A man stood up, someone from the cellar work crew. "How do we know these things are so dangerous? I mean, yeah, they're frightening-looking, but the only word we have is Tietjen's." He looked at Tietjen apologetically. "If I'm going to fight, I need to know that I *got* to fight. I saw that thing out there yesterday, but it didn't look dangerous to me. Just ugly."

There was a murmur of amusement, agreement.

"Don't take my word for it," Tietjen began. "Ketch, Bobby, the Calvino girls, some of the rest of you must have—"

Fratelone cut him off. "He's right. The Boss is." His voice was hoarse. "They had me for a while. Them things. It ain't just they want what we got, even that they want us dead. They *like* killing. They like the pain. They were going to do me real slow, then the kids. Look." Fratelone ignored Tietjen's cry of "Bobby, *don't*." He turned his back to the crowd and, startlingly, loosened his belt and dropped his trousers. Standing in front of the man, Tietjen could not see what made the crowd behind him gasp. "I'm sorry," Fratelone said punctiliously to the cluster of older women who sat on one of the couches. "But you got to see it, and understand what those things are. I don't want to go near them, but the Boss is right. They want to go after us."

He turned around, pulling his trousers up as he went; Tietjen caught a glimpse of sickeningly new flesh on the back of Fratelone's legs, pink and shiny as if it had taken the place of skin flayed away. He bit back his own nausea and stepped forward. He needed them to fight, but he didn't want panic. "I guess other people have stories they could tell—" He raised one hand to forestall them. "Anybody has any doubts, they can talk to Bobby later, or me, or Ketch . . . but for now, we have to decide what to do."

A voice from the back of the room, quaveringly: "Kill them." Voices rang out in agreement.

Tietjen shook his head. Looking out at the faces turned up to his he thought distantly that it was easy, dealing with a crowd, if you had made up your mind in advance what must be done. If you didn't worry about what was fair. It was a dangerous, unsettling piece of knowledge.

"Before anything else, we have to make sure the Store is defended. We have to make sure this place is tight as a drum, that we have food and medicine and water stored up just in case." There was murmuring as the meaning came through. "People who don't know how to handle a gun but think they want to help will have to learn."

McGrath added her voice to his. "We're going to have to stop building for a while, until this is settled. The gardens, and repairs in this building, and regular chores—we can't lose what we've started to gain. But no new projects until we know we're safe."

She was right, but Tietjen felt a fresh wave of fury; they should be building, not playing guerrilla freeze tag with a bunch of freaks.

"Okay. Barbara's the organized one. She's making lists of people who are willing to go on foraging raids—for food, for medicine, bottled water, hardware and batteries and anything else anyone can think of that we'd need in case of siege. Bobby has the list of people who want to learn how to handle a gun; anyone who knows how, or knows any other fighting skills well enough to teach, see me after the meeting. We'll start taking names in a minute."

There was a rustle of motion and whisper.

"Listen up, just a few more minutes. No one, and I mean absolutely no one, is to go out alone anymore. I don't care where you're going or how well you know the route, or whether you think this whole thing is a crock, or what your excuse is. Just don't do it. Teams: two, three at a time, better still four or five. Someone with a gun should be part of each team."

They were all watching him, deadly serious.

"Okay," he said. "Anyone who wants to sign up for foraging, see Barbara; anyone who wants to learn to shoot, talk to Bobby. Anyone with skills or ideas you think may be useful, see me. The floor is open, ladies and gentlemen." And, lest he seem to be compelling them too openly, Tietjen looked down, studying the scrawl on his notepad.

Embarrassed silence, the scrape of shoes on the marble floor. Tietjen looked up and saw that Greg Feinberg was standing before Fratelone, muttering intensely. Allan Hochman was behind him. Slowly, the lines began to fill, in front of Barbara, in front of Fratelone.

Ketch, two behind Allan Hochman in Fratelone's line, called out to him, "Hey, John, street fighting and a little cutting count for anything?"

Tietjen smiled; the atmosphere lightened slightly. "Anything counts. You want to teach?"

She smiled grimly. "Just watch me. Anyone wants to learn, it's Bring Your Own Knife. And be serious. But I'll teach."

10

SOMETHING was trying to break inside.

The sunlight on the floor was the syrupy gold of afternoon when Jit was wakened from sleep by a touch that lanced through him like a hot needle. Reacting from the well of dreams, he struck at the thing that threatened him.

Jesus, what a wind. Where'd that come from?

The sharp otherness of the outsider's thoughts was choppy, fragmented. Reaching for it, Jit tasted curiosity and fear, a hint of bravado, and the bloody taste of horror. Through the outsider's eyes Jit watched fingers quickly flipping toggles and levers, correcting for the killing breeze. Saw the drawn concentration of the pilot before the thinker turned away to watch the city below.

The strangers flew above the city, far above it, looking down on a wide ruined plain of rubble blackened by fire. Everything was dead. *The Bronx*, the watcher's thought echoed in Jit's head. The thinker looked bleakly across the Harlem River with a sick expectation of worse to come. Jit was pleased by the start of pleasure the man gave when he saw the green richness of Central Park.

The pilot's mind was concerned with keeping the whirling, chopping, fiercely loud thing in which they were flying upright and on course. *Don't look down*, Jit heard him thinking. *You don't want to know.* This one had a sorrow eating at him, someone he loved had been in the city: Jit remembered a shadow face, a cloud of sweet-scented red hair, felt a remembered smoothness of skin. *You don't want to know*, the pilot thought again, trying to shake loose from the memory, watching green-lit displays as they changed.

"Tommy, let's swing down south of the island," the other man said.

Jit felt the tight flexing of muscles in the pilot's nod. The man kept his eyes on the lighted display or on the close-by blue of the sky; he did not look down.

The other man was pressed against the cool plastic of the door, his excitement rising as he watched. He knew what the island should look like, no longer looked like; as the man peered down at the drowned southern tip of Manhattan Jit felt his horror—an impersonal marveling thing—and pleasure. *Wait till we get back and tell them*, the man thought. *Man, what'll I be able to sell the photos for! This is Pulitzer stuff.* The thought of reward warmed the man, diffused the awe and horror that was still with him. *Jesus, will you look at that?* he thought, as the tide splashed up and down the length of two immensely tall buildings that now lay side by side in the bay, steel and glass estuaries. *When the troops come in*, the man thought. *Jesus, won't they have a job?*

Jit shared the man's imagining: men, crowds of them, in uniforms like and unlike those of the police and blockcops the boy recognized, swarming into the city, disturbing the quiet, taking it away from him. His *no* was a peal of panicked denial that rang in his own head and clamored like thunder across the sky above the city.

The sweeping rage of Jit's anger fragmented the thoughts of the men in the helicopter; the pilot could barely see the changing displays before him, his partner shook his head, trying to see through a glare of pain. "What the fuck? Tommy, are we in trouble? What's happening?" the watcher yelled, rubbing his eyes.

Jit tasted their sudden hot fear with pleasure: *I'll stop you.*

He reached into the heart of the flying thing and froze it still in the air. Then he unwrapped himself from his tight huddle and clambered up the ladder to the surface of the Park. It took a moment for his eyes to adjust to daylight; then he scanned the sky until he found it, a dark blot hovering in the southern sky.

Inside the machine the pilot and passenger were frozen too, unable to move, hanging impossibly at an impossible angle, a thousand feet above the city. Jit touched them again and found the pilot looking down, staring into the splintered ruins of Midtown, dazzling in sunlight; again, the memory of a smile and scent, sure knowledge that his beloved was dead, somewhere in the ruins. The pilot wept and his tears dropped down from his unmoving face.

The passenger did not weep; he was frantic, trying to make

something logical out of his captivity. *I'm dreaming*, he thought. *Lack of air, something, this can't happen, something . . .*

Me, Jit thought. *Me*. But the voices did not know that.

Jit watched the dark blot as he unfroze it and pulled it down toward the ragged gray surface of the river. He'd done this before; he knew what to do, not to listen to the cries that reached out to him in disbelieving cacophony. It took a long moment for the falling shape to be lost behind the ruined skyline to the southwest; another minute and the voices rose to screaming halt. Orange light flared behind the trees and died and Jit nodded.

He was not sorry. He had defended the city before. "No men. No so'jers," he said aloud. No intrusive faces, no shrill, reedy questions: whose little boy are you? where's your mommy, son? where do you live? None of that. He was not sorry.

Still, he walked through the afternoon, waiting for the disquieting churning of excitement to die down in him. He amused himself by listening to the mindless thoughts of the squirrels, making a score of them follow after him with plumed tails raised high, bobbing in precise rhythm. His followers, his soldiers. That made him think of Gable. The thought was bleak and awful, but insistent. At last, emboldened by his triumph over the invaders, Jit sat down beneath one of the trees he had brought to flowering life, and reached out with his mind.

He searched gingerly, as one of the squirrels would have tasted around the edge of something foreign; he waited for the foul taste of Gable's thoughts to mingle with his own, for the dulled hunger of Carol Ann or Gable's other followers. Nothing in the first seeking. He reached farther, the reaching a thin net barely scented with his own thoughts, nothing that would alert Gable or Gable's people. Dim pictures, thoughts, and sensations skittered through the net like mice, commonplace and restless. Jit was relieved and hopeful at the easy silence, but he could not leave it alone, kept searching, invading dreams, sampling. Then he touched a dream filled with blood hunger, and another that was nothing more than a smashing of things, over and over and over again, a whirling dance of smashing.

He had not imagined Gable.

Hastily Jit retreated lest they sense him. For a long time he simply sat. He thought briefly of reaching out for the Man, but Jit was afraid of what he might find in the seeking. It was safer to sit huddled into himself, hugging bony knees to chest, his cheek cradled on one wrist. So he sat and watched the sun set, and when full darkness had fallen and the Park was filled with the viscous shadow Jit knew best, he made his way back to the eastern edge of the park, near the place where the Man lived.

The Man and the people around him had been taken up with a new game lately, something with a silvery taste of urgency and danger. Jit had half-listened, enjoying the pulse of excitement that ran through everyone's thoughts: the Man himself, the women and men and children who surrounded him. None of it made much sense to him, the work of carrying and hammering and dust, the acrid smell of sweat that hung in the air, the tastes of pulpy stew and rice and water that was never quite fresh. And fear, all the time, and resolve and a warm core of camaraderie which left Jit hungry.

He stood on the stone wall that faced Fifth Avenue, his long white fingers laced through the wire mesh that rose above the stone, and peered at the flickering lights of the Man's settlement. Jit wore a black sweater and old black leathers: pants and jacket pulled in, hacked off, made to fit or grown into. In the darkness his hands and face floated, caught by the moonlight.

After a time Jit wanted more than light from the settlement. He reached out for the old woman—she was easy to find, a rich, warm pool of thought. She was stroking someone's hair, a girl, smoothing the cool, dark length of it and listening to her. Jit felt a pang as he felt the weight of the girl's slight body against the woman's arm; he did not bother to make sense of the child's words. The old woman was making nice with some baby-girl. So what? But he knew from the child's mind that the gentle touch of those cool, roughened hands was very good. Gradually the girl slept, and the old woman drowsed too, her own soothing magic too powerful to resist.

She drifted, somewhere between sleep and waking, warm with recall and faint melancholy. Jit slid down the mesh to perch more comfortably on the stone fence, curious. What did the old woman see? It was herself, younger; the white hair was red-brown and longer, her face more angular, the touch of impatience about her full lips softened by sleep. The younger self had her head pillowed on someone's shoulder, a man's shoulder. Jit could not see the dream-man's face, but the old woman knew him. *Gordon.* The name was a loving sound. *Gordon.* Jit savored the shades of affection and regret and puzzlement and gratitude.

To lie that way, her head awkwardly on the man's shoulder, while her right arm went to sleep under her and her shoulder knotted with a tension she would carry throughout the next day. It was heaven. The memory was from long ago, but the feelings of it were real and immediate. The old woman's breathy thoughts were half laugh, half weeping. Briefly a smile, a man's grin, took the place of words, a smile of hush-and-never-mind and easy love.

Gordon. A slow swelling heat rose in the old woman's belly. She stirred in her dozing the way a cat stirs to catch rays of midday sun. Jit felt his own belly rumble and recognized the feeling as hunger he had encountered before, a thousandfold in a night, and never understood. He rested in the old woman's thoughts as they tossed and darted from a lock of dark hair to the shifting planes of a shoulder, fingers touching, the press of flesh. She lay still with the girl child half-cradled in her arms, remembering. The memory of pleasure made her smile. Always, the image came back to the first one: her younger head pillowed on that shoulder.

At last, *Gordon, my dear.* The image shifted, tracing the pulse under her cheek, the veins in the neck. Her pulse quickened again, a quickening of nervousness or fear as the focus of the image followed from shoulder to throat to chin, until his whole face was revealed. The warmth in her abruptly became a fire of dismay and desire and confusion. It was the Man's face. *John,* the old woman thought. *Oh, God.*

She wakened and opened her eyes.

Barbara, you old fool, she thought angrily.

Jit, still listening to her thoughts, trembled. He was leaning into the mesh fence, his cheek pressed to the wire, shivering in night air, which had not seemed cold before. The old woman's hunger still churned in his stomach. The boy did not understand it, or the shame and confusion that went with it. Something to do with the Man, something to do with the other man, the Gordon.

The old woman shifted the child's weight in her arms and tried to order her thoughts. *I won't let him see me watching him like some imbecile kid. John*—the name was an ache. The image that Jit shared with her, of a dark woman's fingers lightly brushing the Man's jaw, hurt. Jit tasted guilt, and desire and self-anger. The thought of the Man's face was a warm tangle of desire and love and amusement and, again, anger at herself.

Then, as he listened, the old woman forced a moment of calm, as if she had closed her eyes on a light too bright to stand and stood now in darkness. *For God's sake, Barbara, stop the agonizing*, she thought. She laughed almost silently. *He doesn't see any farther than his nose about people. Poor Luisa Ketch probably had to jump him to get his attention. John, John*—no ache now.

Jit slid down to sit at the foot of the wall, thinking. The cool silkiness of the little girl's hair under the woman's hand still played against his palm. The old woman wanted the Man. For what? And, he wondered, did the Man want her? He left her, still stroking the child's hair, shaking her head at her own foolishness, letting the strong feelings of her dream drift away; he reached for the Man instead.

Jit found him in the dark, wrestling with the dark woman, tasting her sweat, the pressure of her skin against his, heat flowering between them. Even with his mind crowded with sensation, with immediate intention to touch, to feel, there were pockets of thought that claimed the Man's attention: worry about the soundness of the south wall and how the marksmanship class was doing and how long they would have until the monsters came back. Jit ignored those thoughts; the pleasure, the foreign knowledge of what his body was doing, was overwhelming. He wrestled as the Man did, felt the woman's touch on his back and her breath in his ear. When the Man's back arched, Jit's did too, and he cried out, his eyes closed. Panting, Jit fell off the wall.

He lay at the bottom of the wall, feeling heavy and tired. The ache in his belly was gone and his butt was sore where he had landed. After a moment Jit reached for the Man again.

"God, John," the dark woman was saying. Her voice was slow and tasted pleased.

The Man lay still, as winded as Jit. A trace of memory, of a dark street freshened with breeze, fluttered in his mind for a moment, and Jit heard him wonder again about the south wall. He reached for a blanket and pulled it up to cover them. The Man's pleasure was as heavy and languorous as Jit's or the dark woman's, but already he was pulling away from it, thinking of streets again, and Gable's people, and work. "You cold?" he asked the woman.

She shook her head. "You gone already?" Voice teasing.

The man shook his head as if to clear it, and pulled her close. "Right here," he said. Only Jit knew that he was lying.

Their conversation did not interest Jit; he tasted the images that played in the Man's head, the city things. Then he remembered his curiosity earlier. The old woman's wanting. Carefully, Jit reached into the Man and searched for those feelings. Some of them he found, but they were there for the dark woman beside him, tangled now with the buttery taste of release. For the old woman there was warmth, gratitude, affection, and no ache of hunger.

Jit wondered what to do with this new understanding: the old woman wanted the Man; the Man wanted the dark woman. Jit stood up stiffly and began to walk back to his tunnel mouth, thinking.

Jit wanted the Man too, the way that both of them wanted the city. He wanted him as he missed old crazy Nogai, wanted a friend. None of this belly-aching confusion, although a shiver of pleasure ran across his shoulders at the memory of it.

John, they called him. Jit spoke the name aloud. John. The other name, Tee-jin. "John, John, John. Tee-jin, Tee-jin, John, John." No magic in those syllables, nothing to conjure with. Nothing to scare away the demons that haunted his city. The Man was the Man. That was enough.

He had learned things tonight. Jit had tasted a passion in the Man, hotter than sensation, colder than the air on sweaty skin. The man wanted Gable and his people dead and out of the city. Jit had savored that fire, that ice, the deliciousness of that hunger. The Man wanted, and Jit would help. Then the Man would want him, too.

As he threaded the dark pathways, Jit raised his head and cried "Tee-jin, Tee-jin, Tee-jin," like a battle cry or a challenge.

Above the park the Man slept.

11

IT took a week or so for the focus of the Store to change. There was less building and more training, repairing, shoring things up. Tietjen hated the change he had insisted on, as the Store concentrated on survival today and tomorrow, and put the future aside. The foraging parties went out armed, and a part of everyone's day was spent learning to shoot or fight; Elena Cruz, in charge of the kitchen, turned out to be fast and dangerous with a staff, of all things, and gave classes every afternoon; Ketch taught what she called "the cutting arts," anything to do with knives. Fratelone was their expert with guns. Tietjen found himself frustrated with Fratelone; he would have put the man in charge of defense, made him the general in their army, but Fratelone refused the responsibility. "I can't do strategy and stuff," he said. "I'm a soldier, Boss. I don't know how to do that other stuff."

What other stuff? Tietjen wondered. He would have kept after Fratelone and nagged him into taking the job, but Barbara talked him out of it.

"It's a wise man who knows what he can and cannot do," she reminded him, late one night when Bobby Fratelone had slouched off to bed.

"He's the closest thing we have to a real fighter, Barbara. We need him."

She shook her head. "John, would you really feel comfortable following Bobby into a fight when he was calling the shots?"

"Sure, of course—" Tietjen said.

"*Really?*" Her tone was very dry. "Think about it for a second."

He did, and came to the crux of the problem. "*I* can't do it! I don't know anything about fighting—"

"But you know about *planning*," McGrath said. "You're the strategy guy. Bobby's the—what do you call it? The enforcer."

Tietjen gave up trying to change the way things were.

When they weren't learning to fight, they were making the Store secure. From buildings on Madison a party wrestled away whole sheets of shop-grade security grating, brought them home and secured them over the windows on the first few floors, arching the grating back at the top so that no one could climb up the grating itself. They found inner doors for the lobby that could be secured with chains rather than by piling furniture against them. The roof was ringed round with razor wire, and the alley behind the building, where the children played handball and hopscotch and other games too arcane for Tietjen to identify, was sealed up with grating and razor wire too. Tietjen was uncomfortably aware of the prison feel of the Store these days. When he stood in the street, looking at the graceful garlands and friezes, the stringcourse hidden under security grating, Tietjen made a promise that as soon as the threat was over he would set the building free again.

And there was foraging, and storing, and cataloguing, and the making of ration plans in case of siege. It was unbelievably complicated; every time Tietjen thought of one thing they hadn't done, two more things sprang from it. At the end of a day he trudged up to his room, shirt clinging wetly to his back, wrung with sweat. He and half a dozen others had been stowing treasure: a cache of two hundred five-gallon mineral-water bags brought in by a foraging party. His arms and legs hurt, his back was sore, there was a permanent crick in his neck from looking: looking at fortifications, watching Ketch's knife-fighting class go through its paces, peering down Fifth Avenue or Seventy-second Street during his guard stint, reading Barbara's daily notes, inspecting, approving.

He was exhausted. Well, Barbara was exhausted, Bobby, Ketch, the Hochmans; Elena, who was cooking for eighty people, maybe more now, with assistance from the older Calvino girls that Tietjen suspected was more hindrance than help, and an occasional hand from someone else. Everyone was exhausted. We should add people to the regular kitchen rotation, Tietjen thought. And infirmary duty, too; Barbara was doing too many things; she was cheery and brisk as always, but her eyelids were purple with fatigue.

He was always making lists: things they needed, things they wanted, things to be done. As he reached the top of the stairs and started down the hall he was revising the rotations: guard duty, kitchen duty, infirmary, messenger. The gardens, cleanup, trash burial. He was searching his mind for more when a shot rang out.

He was on the ground before *I'm not hit* sank in. Cautiously be began to sit up, looking for the source of fire. If the shot was fired *in* the building that meant the monsters had somehow broken through all their sentries, killed them, probably. Who was on watch? A couple of new people, he remembered, and felt an instant flash of relief that neither Ketch nor Barbara had been out there. But if the monsters were in the building, everyone could be dead by now. Except him.

Another shot, and a fainter ringing sound he recognized as ricochet. The fire was not in this hall. But the source sounded near. One of the apartments? How the hell had they broken through without a warning, at least a warning? Had they been betrayed to the monsters?

As he crawled down the hallway toward the utility stairs there was another shot, sounding closer, as if he were moving toward it. What the hell? Then voices, chattering, normal voices, and one he thought was Bobby Fratelone's: muffled, but recognizable. He figured it out. *Jesus H. Christ.* Tietjen stood up, rigid with anger, and went back down the hall, down the stairs, strode through the peaceful lobby of the building, nodded to the woman standing guard at the door, and went into the building that had just been cleared out next door.

He found Fratelone and his class down one hallway on the fourth floor, targets tacked to the far wall, a mismatched assortment of handguns and rifles laid out on the floor. Two teenaged girls were lying prone on the floor, giggling nervously as they aimed at the targets. They, and the others in the room, had bits of cotton stuffed in their ears.

As Tietjen watched, the girls fired. One bullet glanced off the wall, hit a metal doorframe, and buried itself in the opposite wall. The other hit the target, within six inches of its bull's-eye. As the girls got up from the floor, the sharpshooter reminded her friend to put the safety on.

"Very nice," Tietjen heard himself saying. Preserve the image: *el Jefe reviews the troops*. He smiled at the two girls, at the others crowding around them, then turned to Fratelone. "Bobby, can I have a word or two with you?"

He pulled Fratelone into the stairway.

"Kids're doing pretty good," Fratelone began sunnily. "Some a the older people are—"

"Bobby, aside from scaring me to death, what the hell are you doing in here?" Tietjen asked very quietly. "What the hell are you do-ing teaching these people to shoot indoors? Did you see what the girl's bullet did?"

"Almost hit the fuckin' bull's-eye—" Fratelone said. "Can *you* shoot that good?"

Tietjen spoke very deliberately. "Not *her* bullet. The other one. Didn't go near the target: bounced all over the place. This hall is too narrow to use as a shooting range, one of these times a ricochet is going to kill someone. For Christ's sake, Bobby, use a little sense!"

The big man sulked. "Where the hell you think I should be teaching them? Too windy out in the street. Where else is there room? In the lobby, with all that marble and brass stuff? I ain't stu-pid, Boss. I was trying to do the best I could find. Jesus."

"Bobby—" His adrenaline was lower. Tietjen took two breaths before continuing. "Look, Bobby. I'm sorry I came on so strong. I was going up to my room and heard the shots. Scared me shitless." He remembered himself, flat on the floor of the hallway, trying to find the sniper that wasn't there, and grinned. "I think we need to re-locate you somewhere safer."

Fratelone nodded. "Yeah, well. We could go out to the Park, I guess."

Tietjen still had a weird feeling about Central Park as he re-membered it, dead and maleficent. It was green now, blooming, and no one else seemed to feel it, but the place still gave him an unsettled, queasy feeling. "There's wind in Central Park, too, Bobby. How about the basement?"

"The basement?" They sat in the stairwell, discussing how, and how quickly, one of the basements could be turned into a shooting range. Fratelone broke off once to stick his head back in the hallway.

"Take a break, you guys. Fifteen minutes. Then come back; we're moving this stuff downstairs. I think."

Too much was happening like that, Tietjen thought regretfully as he climbed the stairs to his room that night. Ketch had pled exhaustion and was in her own room, polishing her nails and reading by flashlight. We're making decisions too fast, we're not planning things properly. We're going to regret some of the things we're doing now, and those goddamned *things* have forced us to panic. He felt a sudden urge to take a walk, a long desultory walk around the city, as he had in the old days. He needed to clear his head, and that had always been the best way; only now it wasn't safe, wasn't even possible.

"John?"

When he turned he saw Barbara on the landing below; she had a thermos under her arm and two mugs in one hand. She had changed into a clean sweater and skirt, and loosened her white hair around her face; but the small vanity had not erased the bruised look of her eyes.

"Barbara, what is it?" He took a step down, then another, down the stairs. "Jesus, you look like hell."

She winced slightly, then waved a hand at him and smiled. "One of these days I've got to get my hair done. No emergency, John; I'm sorry if I scared you. I just—couldn't sleep, and thought I'd bring some coffee up and go over some things. If you don't have other plans. . . ." She peered up the stairwell, as if trying to make out Ketch's form in the shadows.

The light in Barbara's face, tired and drawn as she was, dimmed more before Tietjen pointed out that he was alone. "I was just going to sit and look out the window. Come on up. I've been thinking about organizing rotating duty for the kitchen." He held out a hand companionably, a gesture of invitation. Barbara looked at it for a moment, as if she couldn't tell what it was for; then she handed him the thermos and started climbing the stairs.

Tietjen took a couple of kerosene lamps from his apartment, and the two of them walked up several more flights, until they were both slightly breathless. Then they found an open apartment with a view and went in. There were three chairs, a coffee table, some paintings; most furniture from the upper floors had been brought downstairs for use in the communal living areas. Barbara put the mugs and thermos on the coffee table and went directly to the window that looked west over Central Park and south toward Midtown.

"It's so black," she said softly. "Just pinpoints of light; I wonder what they are?"

Tietjen came and stood beside her. The street below was washed with light from theatrical spotlights from an uptown warehouse, running on emergency generators: anything to keep the approach to the buildings well lit and secure. Beyond the splash of yellow light there were shadows, then darkness. The lights Barbara spoke of flickered in the distance. Tietjen calculated that one was in the vicinity of Lincoln Center, another farther downtown, at the edge of Central Park near the Fifth Avenue entrances, another a reflection in one of the office buildings in the Forties, just a dim glow. Probably a nest of monsters, he thought.

"Pockets of civilization, you think?" Barbara asked dubiously.

"Wish I thought so. Hey—" He put a hand out to get her attention. "Did you see that?"

She shook her head. "Nothing," she murmured softly.

"There," he breathed. "Across and over by the Park wall. It looks like a smear of white until it moves."

After a long moment Barbara nodded slowly. "Just one person, I think."

The pale blur moved closer to the light and suddenly Tietjen could see what it was: a man, or rather a boy, stick-thin and pale in the wash of yellow light, wearing dark clothes that made his hands and face seem to swim out of the darkness, phosphorescent. The boy looked up toward them, and Tietjen had the feeling he knew they were there, that the boy was listening to them.

"He's looking for us," Barbara echoed his thoughts.

Tietjen shook his head. "He could be one of their scouts or something. If he's okay he'll come back in the morning."

"If he's alive in the morning, John. If he's come to us for help, shouldn't we help him?" McGrath turned toward the door. Tietjen put out a hand to stop her, but she was already halfway out the door. "I'll get a closer look before I let him in, John."

He found himself following after. Common sense said to leave the kid out on the streets until morning, when they could get a better look at him. But Barbara was right: by morning the monsters might have torn the kid limb from limb. Beside, daylight was no guarantee against peril; the thing that Bobby had killed had come during the day.

In the lobby Barbara was having an argument with the man and woman on guard duty. Tietjen resolved the question by backing her up: "Unbar the doors so we can get out, then bar them again quickly, and listen for the signal—" He rapped out a tattoo against the door sill. "Don't let anyone in unless they give you that signal, okay?" The guards nodded doubtfully. "Let me borrow your pistol," Tietjen added after a moment's thought.

While he examined the gun to make sure the safety was on (it was not; he made a note to speak to Bobby tomorrow about weapon safety) Barbara was helping the guards wrestle the bars off the door. She was halfway out the door when he stuffed the pistol into his back pocket and followed after her.

"He was over that way, wasn't he?" she asked.

He nodded. "Don't go out of the range of the light, Barbara. We can't afford to lose you."

She smiled as if this pleased her, still scanning the edge of the darkness for movement. When it came it was so slight that they almost missed it. At the edge of the Park, by the old stone wall that had been reinforced with sloppily applied concrete and razor wire, something moved again. After a moment Tietjen realized it was the kid they had seen, scraping roughly at his nose with the back of one hand as if trying to suppress a sneeze. His pale skin was streaked and smeared with soot and earth; he had bitten his lip and there was a rough scab on his mouth. He stood leaning into the stone as if, if he pressed into it hard enough, it would absorb him. Yet what Tietjen sensed coming from the boy was not fear but shyness. We've startled a wild animal, he thought. There was a smell of earthiness, an unwashed animal smell, that came from the kid, not pleasant but not awful, either.

"Hi," Barbara was saying, softly. She took a tentative step forward, one hand held palm out, as she might have reached to an unfamiliar dog. "Hello. My name is Barbara; this is John. Are you okay?" Tietjen could not see her face from where he stood, but he imagined her smiling, not too broadly, as tentatively as she held her hand out. "Are you alone? Is there someone taking care of you?"

Tietjen heard no reply, but she continued as if the boy had responded: "You take care of yourself, right? Do you live in the Park?"

The boy flashed a brief smile, rubbed at his nose again, looked at Tietjen over Barbara's shoulder. Tietjen smiled back without any awkwardness; the kid was maybe twelve, thirteen. A short, scrawny kid dressed in pieces of clothes meant for someone larger, as if he had been patched together out of spare parts from a Salvation Army thrift shop. Younger than Greg Feinberg. He didn't stop to wonder why he immediately felt closer to this kid than to Greg. "Do you live alone? Are there other people there?"

The boy just watched Tietjen, as if he didn't understand the words. Barbara tried again. "Would you like some cocoa? Something warm to eat?" The boy shook his head. He was staring at them, Tietjen realized, as if he was trying to hear their thoughts. "Are you cold?" Barbara asked. Her voice was gentle enough so that the questions sounded merely curious, not intrusive or threatening. She kept one hand extended but did not move any farther forward. The boy watched her cautiously, but Barbara did nothing to spook him. Again he turned his attention to Tietjen.

"Do you know about the—" He broke off, unsure of what to call the monsters. Would the boy understand him? "Do you know about the ones that are trying to kill everyone else?" he finished lamely. "The scary ones?"

The boy nodded, and an expression of distress crossed his face. Misinterpreting the expression, Tietjen stepped forward quickly, thinking to tell the boy that they would protect him. The kid withdrew into the shadow of the wall, and Barbara turned briefly to frown at Tietjen. "No sudden moves, okay?" she whispered. Tietjen nodded.

"Would you like to come stay with us?" Barbara asked slowly. "We have lots of kids staying with us, and we'll protect you from the monsters."

The boy said something in a low-pitched, furtive mumble. It sounded like "Jokay."

"I didn't hear you," Barbara said gently. "I'm afraid I don't hear everything I used to," she added regretfully, gracefully. "What did you say?"

"Ji' be okay," the boy repeated.

"Are you Jim?" Barbara asked. "I'm Barbara and this is John," she said for the second time.

"Jit," the boy said clearly, in accents unlike the street sound he had used before, in an accent much like Barbara's, Tietjen realized. "Jit be okay, you ducks." He hit the *d* in ducks hard and grinned broadly, as if sharing a common joke.

Tietjen shook his head. "It's very dangerous right now. I think you should come back with us—" Again he took a step forward. This time the boy started; with an expression like a rabbit caught in headlights, he stood frozen for a moment. Then he dashed forward, collided headlong with Barbara, reeled back a few paces and then charged forward again, knocking Tietjen down as well. By the time he and Barbara got to their feet the boy had vanished into the shadows cast by the big lights in front of the Store.

"Damn," Barbara murmured mildly.

"Will he be all right?" Tietjen asked. "It's chilly tonight."

Barbara shook her head, but answered in the affirmative. "I think he's been fending for himself for a long time. But where does he come from?"

Tietjen's turn to shrug. "At a guess I'd say his parents were part of that homesteading group in the Park from ten, twelve years ago. Who knows how long he's been on his own."

Barbara shook her head fretfully. "He's not connected to anything, is he. This is a dangerous time not to have a connection." She turned to Tietjen. "Give me your coat, John."

"You cold?" He took the fleeced-lined flannel jacket off at once and would have draped it over her shoulders, but Barbara took it from his hands and started toward the shadows.

"I owe you a coat," she said quietly. Then she raised her voice. "Jit! If you're there, this is for you, to keep you warm." She paused to let her words sink in. Then, "And remember, if you need help, you come to us. Okay?" She bent in the shadows, a shadow herself, to lay the coat on the ground. Then, without a pause, she turned back and marched past Tietjen toward the doors of the Store. "Come on, John. He's not going to get the coat with us standing out here."

Shivering, Tietjen followed after. Neither one saw Jit dart from the shadow of the Park wall to grab the coat. Neither saw the boy drape it over his shoulders, or saw the ridiculous way it hung, sleeves a good six inches too long, shoulders drooping comically, the whole thing looking like Daddy's clothes on a six-year-old. Neither saw the way Jit stroked the fleece and nestled his chin in the collar, or heard him murmur "Teejin, Teejin," as he disappeared into the Park again.

12

AFTER the first flurry of fear and hard work at the Store had spent itself, the hardest thing was waiting. Everyone became twitchy, restless. Sentries cried out at paper whisking down Seventy-second Street toward Central Park; quarrels began and ended in the space of half an hour; and Tietjen woke at least twice a night, listening for something that hadn't yet come, hearing only Ketch's even breathing and the faint whicker of breeze in the curtains. It was exhausting, being always on guard. Where Tietjen had worried before if they could be prepared enough, now he worried that they were too prepared, that they'd be worn out with waiting if something didn't happen soon. People who had resisted getting the Store prepared for a fight were now nervously talking about taking the fight to the monsters, "no matter what Tietjen and Barbara say."

It was almost a relief when the attacks began. New refugees had brought word of a sporting-goods store on Fifth at Forty-third, unlooted so far because an MTA bus was wedged between its front doors. Freeze-dried camping stores, bags of water, water-purifying tablets, sleeping bags and camp linen, first-aid kits . . . and weapons and ammunition. They had to have it. Five people set out, including one of the new people; Tietjen didn't know many of them by name yet—McGrath was good with names and somehow managed to make Tietjen look as though he were too—but Bobby Fratelone vouched for all of them when he talked with Tietjen about the expedition. They took the two large carts from Mt. Sinai, plus a few carts liberated from a supermarket, and set off on a muggy gray day, armed to the teeth but with a holiday air.

Four hours later, working in the back of the building, where a crew was bolting steel plate onto the alley door, Tietjen heard a commotion before it found him. Bobby had a woman by the arm, supporting her weight. She was bruised and shocky-looking, blond hair streaked with dirt, dirt and blood on her face and arms. With difficulty Tietjen recognized Bobby's sharpshooting student from the upstairs hallway: Susie something.

"They were waiting for us when we started back," she said, low, in between long breaths. "I got away to come for help. The others— I don't know. I don't know if they're still alive—" Her voice broke, then steadied again. "We took cover in the lobby of a building on Fifth, a little below St. Pat's. I can show you." She showed no fear at the thought of returning to fight again, just a fearful hurry. "There were so many of them, please, we have to go *now*."

As the girl spoke Barbara had appeared in the hallway. She would have led Susie away to get cleaned up, to rest, but Tietjen stopped her. "Can you go out again?" he asked as gently as he could. Barbara frowned and shook her head; he ignored her.

She nodded. "We have to. There's so many of them, they just came out of everywhere." Her voice cracked again. She turned and smiled wanly at Barbara, then turned back to Tietjen. "We have to get there soon."

Bobby was calling his people together; when Tietjen reached the lobby a dozen men and women were waiting, and others joined over the next ten minutes as Fratelone and Tietjen explained what they were doing and where they were going. Most carried rifles or guns, a few had lasers, a few carried cudgels or spears or shiny decorative swords taken from a martial-arts school on Eighty-third and Third. Looking at them Tietjen was frightened. He had no idea what he was doing, if he could fight, whether he would be able to kill one of the monsters if he had to. They looked to him to set the example. Aw, for the love of Christ, he thought.

It was easier when he saw Ketch leaning against a pillar in the back of the lobby, wearing a dark, heavy leather jacket, leather pants, heavy boots. Her hair was braided and wound close to her head. She smiled at him and gave him a self-mocking thumbs-up sign, then turned to answer a question from one of her knife-fighting students.

"Elena and I'll be seeing to defense," Barbara said behind him. She too was in dark, heavy clothes, hair pinned rigorously back.

"Somebody has to mind the store, John. Come home safely." She smiled at him, a smile of trust and confidence that was somehow girlish and inspiring. He could do this, the smile said.

Well, he had to. "We stick together," he said again. "Susie knows where the raiding party is holed up, she's our guide, but basically we're going down to Fifth and Fifty-first or -second. We're going to get our people out and we're going to get back here—we're not going to take this fight to them unless we have to, is that clear?"

Nods, shrugs, from the thirty or so people in the lobby. He turned again to Barbara. "See you later. Lock up after us, will you?"

"We will. Safely home, boys," she said to Tietjen and Fratelone as they turned away toward the door.

They went east to Park Avenue, then started downtown, hoping they could get close before they were noticed. Susie Gollancz walked with Tietjen at the head of the troop; Ketch walked just behind with Bobby Fratelone. No one said much. The way was mostly clear, and there were almost no bodies; every now and then they'd move through an area that smelled bad, smelled like death; in another block the air was sweet and humid. It shouldn't work like that, Tietjen thought. You can't zone out decay. But the fact remained that some blocks smelled of death and others did not.

At Fifty-second they cut west again, now walking single file, close against the building faces. As they crossed Madison Tietjen heard something, a gentle crowd sound punctuated by hoots and cries of excitement. For a moment his knees went watery; he was back uptown the night of the hospital raid, listening to the monsters torturing their captive, unable to help. A sideways glance at Ketch and Fratelone showed them as unnerved as he was; Susie Gollancz, at his side, was pale and grim. The rest of the troop seemed unmoved by the noise; he had to pass the word back to keep quiet. Then he said, "I'm going ahead to scout it out. Keep back."

Fratelone opened his mouth to say something, then closed it again. Ketch's face went blank.

Tietjen edged forward as silently as he could: each scuff of toe against concrete sounded loud to him, and twice he had to climb over the twisted mess of fallen security grilles that blocked the sidewalk, and the metallic *clung* of sound sent a shiver of panic through

him. He reached the corner, peered gingerly around to look, pulled
back fast, looked again.

There was a ring of them, perhaps a dozen. He had expected
more. The monsters stood in a semicircle twenty yards from the
doorway of a cut-price jeweler's; as he watched, one of them broke
from the ring and advanced on the door with odd, dancing steps.
His head, shoulders, and arms were huge and heavily muscled; his
torso and legs seemed almost wasted in comparison. A few steps and
he stopped, then began to dance, tap-dance. He looked like a gorilla
doing Fred Astaire. Tietjen couldn't see his face, but it sounded like
the hoots were coming from the dancer.

Then a volley of shots rang out from the jewelry store and the
dancer stopped, twitched and shuddered, then danced back to the
rim of the circle, one shoulder held higher than the other, bleeding.

"Christ," Tietjen murmured, and backed along the wall, backing all the way to Madison, where Bobby and the others were waiting.

"You okay?" Ketch asked.

He didn't answer her. "There are about a dozen of them; one's
wounded. Our people have some ammo left—they fired the shots. I
can't tell if they—the monsters—have backup nearby. Susie, how
many did you say there were?"

She looked confused. "I don't know. More than a dozen, but I
don't know—"

He nodded. "So there may be more around here somewhere.
Okay, I think what we're going to have to do is draw their fire, some
of us. If about half of you wait, close to the corner, we can go in and
deal with the ones that are there. You guys watch our backs in case
it's a trap. Okay? Bobby, you're in charge of the rear guard."
Fratelone frowned; Tietjen ignored him. "You, you, uh, you guys"—
rapidly he chose ten people to come with him. Susie attached herself
to that group, unasked; Ketch was with Bobby and the rest. "Okay,"
Tietjen said at last. "We go."

They filed up the street, making too much noise, moving clumsily over the steel grillework. Tietjen didn't believe this was happening. He was leading these people, nice normal people, with guns and
a rifle and two spears and a golf club and trash-can lid brandished
like a shield, into a battle. At the corner they stopped behind him.

"*Shit. Shitshitshit!*" he murmured. Then, loudly, "We go."

They spilled out into the street. Susie darted ahead of Tietjen, flopped onto her belly and starting firing a pistol at the nearest monster. He dropped, and she stopped firing, startled at what she had done. "Don't stop!" Tietjen barked harshly. She looked at him blankly for a moment, then, with a blink, turned back to shoot again. Behind him Tietjen felt the others fanning out, those with guns shooting at the monsters, who turned away from the door of the jewelry store slowly, as if the shots were not enough to distract them from their prey. By the time they had turned, three more were down. The others charged Tietjen's group. The apish dancer darted like a broken-field runner, dodging bullets, waving one huge fist like a club while the other arm hung uselessly at his side. He dodged toward Tietjen, who ducked away from a blow aimed at his head; the next moment there was a meaty thud behind him, and Tietjen turned to see that the thin, reedy woman with the golf club had hit the dancer square between his eyes.

Another monster darted through the bullets, coming for Susie again. As he fired, Tietjen realized that he recognized this one—his arms ended in thin, sharp claws. Tietjen's shot missed the claw-man, but hit another monster who squealed and ran. A shot fired from the jewelry store dropped the runner.

Then something grabbed Tietjen and he was rolling on the ground, staring up into red-rimmed eyes; ringlets of blond hair bounced around her face as the monster struggled, trying to bounce Tietjen's head against the pavement. She had no mouth, no nose, just nostrils planted flush in her face like blowholes; her breath came in hot jets that scorched his face. She was strong. It was only luck that when they rolled to the side of the curb he had the leverage to bash her head into the stone, then her neck, then her head again, until the red light in her eyes dimmed and she let him go. Her breath rushed out, hot and foul.

Tietjen rolled away in time to see the claw-man scuttling away, claws red with blood. He didn't see who had been hurt, just rolled for his gun and fired at the claw-man. On the fifth shot he dropped. Tietjen awkwardly jammed a fresh clip into his pistol and rolled to his knees, trying to see what was happening. It was over.

Across the street a face appeared cautiously in the door of the jewelry store. Then a face, and a voice. "Mr. Tietjen? Are they gone, sir?"

He looked around. Behind him, waiting in the cross street with the rest of the group following, Bobby Fratelone nodded all clear. Ketch was just behind him, smiling broadly at Tietjen, her eyes wide and bright. Tietjen waved the raiding party forward, and they left the building, three of them, pulling carts as they came. "There's two more carts left in the store," the leader of the party said. Then his eyes lit on something and he said, "Oh shit."

Tietjen followed his gaze. Susie Gollancz lay on her back, face upturned, her throat slashed cleanly from ear to ear, so deep that he could see the bones in her neck. She was dead, but there was no blood. Tietjen swallowed hard to keep from throwing up; he thought the clean bloodless slit was worse than a gory show would have been. The damned *weirdness*, he thought, unable to get close to his real feeling. Aloud he said, "Damn." Then he looked around him to see if there were other casualties. The woman with the golf club had a bruise starting on one side of her face, and the blank, stupid look of emotional shock. The others were all right, though Tietjen wondered if they felt as nauseated as he did.

"We have to get home," he said at last. He felt, rather than saw, Ketch appear at his side; she put her arm around his waist for a moment, and the contact warmed him, even as the public closeness made him uncomfortable. He heard Fratelone giving orders to have Susie carried back uptown with them, heard him send a couple of people to get the heavy carts that remained in the shop across the street. When someone balked at pushing a cart, Tietjen said curtly, "People died so we could get this stuff. *You* want to leave it here?"

Leaving probably only took minutes, but it felt long to Tietjen, hours instead. He was sure that more monsters would arrive soon, that an alarm had been sent out, that they would never make it back to the Store alive. "Come on, come *on*," he muttered under his breath, hands jiggling at his side. Finally they started uptown again, a somber caravan.

They had won. He heard words being whispered behind him: "We beat the motherfuckers!" The words made him sick. *Yeah, we won. Except for poor Susie, who was the best shooter we had.* "Let's not get cocky," he said coolly. *Don't sound angry, it's not their fault, it's normal to crow.* "Not until we walk in the front door of the Store."

They walked up Fifth, in the center of the avenue. Tietjen was wary of what might suddenly appear in a doorway; he assigned lookouts on the left and right at the head, middle, and end of the caravan, and hoped to God they would notice any little movement, any shadow, any breeze. As they walked, he talked with the leader of the scavenging raid, who agreed that the pack of monsters that had jumped them had been larger than the dozen Tietjen and his people had seen.

"When they saw how few of us there were, I think they lost interest," he said. "Do you think they're around now?"

Tietjen shrugged and tried to smile. "Do I know? Safest to assume they're out there and keep our heads up."

Past St. Patrick's Cathedral, badly quake-damaged, where a pile of precious vessels—gold, silver, brass—blocked the gaping doorway. Past Rockefeller Center—Atlas had fallen from his pedestal and lay draped over the globe as if it were a torture rack. Past the Plaza, flakes of gilding clinging to its massive security grilles. A doorman's top hat with a chiffon hat band dangled from the hand of the statue in front of the Plaza.

Every time a scrap of paper fluttered past, or a pebble was kicked, or a leaf fell from one of the greening trees of Central Park, Tietjen and his people flinched.

At Sixty-fourth Street Tietjen stopped so suddenly that Ketch, walking behind him, stumbled into his shoulder. At her murmured apology he held up one hand to silence her and the others. He listened.

The sound was like a kitten mewling or a baby whimpering. It came from the door of an apartment building, behind a brushed-aluminum frame that masked the security grille. For a moment no one moved or spoke. The sound came again, more like a baby crying. Ketch took a step forward, looked sideways at Tietjen, and stopped.

"It's a kid," she whispered between clenched teeth. "Maybe we can help."

"Do you know it's a kid?" he hissed back.

Then, as if on cue, a child peered from the doorway. She looked about five or six, about Davy's age. She wore a sleeveless shift, grubby and torn at the hem; her pale red hair was dirty, and there were streaks of dirt across her face, arms, legs; there was a healing scab on her forehead. Her eyes were large and pale and her mouth was pursed worriedly. Tietjen was flushed with a sense memory, remembering the weight and warmth of a small child's body in his arms.

"Honey?" Ketch took another step toward her, one hand held out. I wouldn't have taken her for the kids type, Tietjen thought. Something still felt subtly wrong and dangerous. "Wait," he said. Ketch didn't even turn, but held her hand out farther and repeated, "Honey?"

The girl took a few steps forward toward Ketch, whimpering softly.

A voice behind Tietjen: "Jee-zus, lookit her hands."

Tietjen saw it. He had thought she wore mittens or something. But her hands were encased in shells, black casing. No. Her hands were shells, or claws, or something. She was a monster. He reached to grab Ketch back but she was already halfway to the girl.

"Li, get back here," he said, as quietly as he could.

She and the child had met. Ketch stooped, picked the girl up. The girl reached her arms around Ketch's neck, with exquisite care, and tucked her claws under her arms, out of harm's way. She stared at Tietjen over Ketch's shoulder, serious and beseeching. Then Ketch whirled and came back, carrying the girl.

"What's your name, sweetie?" she asked.

"DeeDee," the child whispered in return. "You better not stay here, the bad people will come 'n' get ya."

"The bad people?" Ketch whispered.

"Luisa, dammit—" Tietjen began. "We can't—"

"For God's sake, John, she's just a baby. You think she's some kind of spy?"

"The bad people'll come soon," DeeDee repeated. "They killed my daddy and Mickey ran away." Up close, Tietjen could see a network of fine scabs on her face, where she must have scraped and cut herself with her claws.

"Is that credential enough for you?"

Fratelone came up from behind, "Boss, what's the holdup? We're getting antsy back there."

Tietjen felt like throwing something. "Li, are you suggesting we bring her back to the Store?"

"John, they already know where the Store is. And what can she do, even if she is with them—"

"They killed Daddy and Mickey ran away, and they wanted me

to go stay with them, but I wouldn't." The child looked uncertainly from Ketch to Tietjen. Looking at her, he believed as Ketch did, that the girl was a baby, not part of the monsters' gang; looking at Fratelone he thought of the eighty, ninety people at the Store. What right did he have to extend trust on their behalf?

"Boss, we gotta get going," Fratelone repeated.

"Okay, okay. Li, you'll stand for her good behavior, right?"

"I'll be good," the child said earnestly. "I can even set the table the right way."

Tietjen smiled, smoothed the dirty hair away from her forehead. "Can you, honey? The right way? That'll be a big help. Okay, let's get going."

They went on. He sent the word back to close up the line; they were more spread out than he liked. At Sixty-eighth he heard cackling from the side street, but saw nothing. The group continued on watchfully, eyes left to the Park and right to the doorways, waiting. A flash of color, of something moving, but Tietjen couldn't tell if it was something live or a plastic bag tumbling in the breeze. He thought they were being followed but couldn't see anyone. He didn't want to send anyone scouting. We stick together, he thought. That's the only way.

At last they were home. Barbara was at the front door to welcome them back. Her eyes lit when she saw DeeDee, clouded when she saw the girl's hands; then—Tietjen could see the process—she decided that it made no difference, and opened her arms to hug the girl. DeeDee gave Ketch a backward glance, then went with Barbara. Ketch, with the girl safely home, seemed to lose interest.

Susie Gollancz was taken to lie in state in the mail room until they could cremate her the next day; it was too dark by the time they got back, and everyone wanted a ceremony, something to honor her. She was one of their own, not one of the faceless dead they fished out of buildings and burned. Elena saw to it that there was always someone to sit with the body, which they draped with an embroidered throw; they used too many of their precious candles to light the room. The supplies were shelved, the weapons they'd taken were assigned to fighters, and the ammunition stored away until needed. Tietjen was called to inspect the welded plate at the alley door and gave it his approval. Elena served dinner. Everyone ate, and by the light of the lanterns they had gained from the camping stores, the story was told and told again, and Susie was each time braver, a better fighter, more remarkable. When the heat and the rushy hiss of the lanterns made them sleepy, one by one the people of the Store went to bed.

In the darkest part of the night the voices started, one at a time at first, then two or three together in ragged chorus, then a single voice, then a jungle of calls and laughter from the street. When he looked out his window he saw nothing. Ketch had got out of bed behind him when the noise started, and stood peering groggily into the darkness. "What the hell is it?"

In the hallways below his floor Tietjen thought he heard the question being echoed: "What is that? Who's doing that? Why?"

Tietjen knew: it was a song of war.

13

WE have the advantage of stronghold, Tietjen thought wearily, the next morning, after the funeral service. Sometime in the night blood, which had not flowed from Susie Gollancz when her throat was cut, poured out of her, and in the morning there was a sticky, coppery pool of drying blood all around her, like a moat. The blood had been cleaned away, the marble floor of the mail room scoured, and finally they had carried Susie, wrapped in the bloody coverlet that shrouded her, to the place where they burned bodies. Barbara said something appropriate that Tietjen barely heard. Then the body was drizzled with kerosene and a torch was touched to the sodden coverlet. It went up at once.

We have the advantage of stronghold, Tietjen thought. But how long will that last? A few hours after the funeral, a raiding party from the monsters' camp swarmed down the street from the east. The sentry Bobby had posted on that corner saw the monsters, four of them, and turned and ran, getting himself safe inside the Store before he managed to tell someone to pull anyone *else* outside off the street.

The other sentries and two women who had been securing a floodlight over the grille entry were brought in safely. The doors were barred, the Store on alert, and Tietjen stood in the lobby watching the street, wondering what the monsters would do. Behind him, low, Tietjen heard Bobby giving the sentry who had run—a heavyset Asian man about Tietjen's age—holy hell for deserting his post; he did not interfere, but he wondered what he would have done had he been the one on the corner. Every time he had to fight he had to battle his own incredulity first—how could this be me, I can't do this stuff, I don't know what I'm doing.

There was a sound of breaking glass. One of the raiders, a huge, muscled man with a tiny head like a little girl's doll, was throwing rocks at the windows of the building across the street. Then another crash, somewhere above in their own building.

"What's that?" he asked.

After a moment the answer was relayed from one of the sentries above. Arrows. The raiders were shooting arrows up at the face of the building. They'd hit a window.

"Jesus. Tell everyone to keep well away from any window that isn't sealed off."

If he listened he could hear the rhythmic clung and whir of arrows being loosed, and usually a dull clatter as the shafts bounced against the granite face of the building. In the next hour he heard two more crashes: two windows hit. He passed along instructions to the fighters on the upper floors. No firing down on the raiders, not while what they were doing was more an annoyance than a threat. No one knew how many friends the monsters might have waiting, just around the corner on Madison Avenue.

He hadn't realized how tightly strung he was until, three hours after they appeared, the monsters retreated, sauntering back down the street, turned the corner, and vanished. He and Bobby decided not to sound all-clear at once, but a sigh seemed to run through the entire building all the same.

"We outlasted 'em," he heard someone say triumphantly.

"*Outlasted them?*" He wheeled around furiously. "A couple hours, that's outlasting them? We don't even know if they just took a break to go to the john, for Christ's sake. You think we won the whole damned war just by hiding in here? Jesus!"

A dozen faces stared at him, frozen by his anger.

"Ease up, John," someone said. It was McGrath. "None of us have ever done this before."

"Neither have *I*. Oh, Christ. Bobby, keep the lid on down here, will you?" Disgusted, Tietjen slammed up the stairs, heading for his own rooms.

We have the advantage of stronghold, he thought again, as he looked down from his window to the empty street below. We can withhold a siege for three hours. In fact, Sandy Hochman, their quartermaster, had gone painstakingly over the stores of food, water, ammunition, medical supplies. With what the scavenging trip to the sporting goods place had brought in, and their other goods, they could withstand a siege for as much as a month, maybe more if real rationing was set into effect. If they didn't all go stir crazy. If no one got seriously ill, contagiously ill. If there weren't too many dead bodies to deal with safely. If there were no more than the usual demands on supplies, time, energy.

In other words, "We're trapped," Tietjen said aloud. "We *have* to take the fight to them."

That evening, in a council of war with Bobby, Ketch, Allan and Sandy Hochman, and a few others, he repeated the words. "We're trapped here unless we take the fight to them." Barbara was busy in the infirmary, but had promised to join them as soon as she could. He felt the lack of her keenly. Barbara always understood what he wanted to do, but he wasn't sure he could make sense of it to these others. "We have to take the fight to them," he said once more.

But no one needed persuasion. "Okay," Allan Hochman said. "How do we start?"

"Thing is," Ketch said, "most of us aren't fighters by inclination, let alone by training. We have to take the fight to them, sure, but who do we take *to* that fight? That lard-ass who left his position this morning?"

This time Tietjen defended the man. "If I were alone, even just down the block alone, and I saw four of those things coming straight for me, I'd probably run too. It makes a difference, being alone." Ketch shook her head dismissively. "Okay, Li, so you're nominated for all the solo kamikaze missions. Happy? I'd have run too, believe it. But you're right. Do we have enough people to make a fight with?"

Bobby nodded. "Yeah, if we gotta. It's not like we got a choice. And we ain't going to get no more, anyway, with those fuckers out there cutting us off."

"Bobby's right," Allan agreed. "Sooner or later we have to take the offensive, or we're dead."

Ketch was right, Bobby was right. Allan had written Web code before the city went down. Barbara had been a housewife in the suburbs. Ketch had been a law student—and reformed gang girl. She and Bobby probably made up the Store's entire warrior class.

Tietjen had a flash of memory of a night when Chris had croup, in another lifetime. He and Irene had worried through the night, taking turns holding the baby in the bathroom while the shower ran hot and steamy. The fear that they might make a wrong decision, that a mistake might harm that small life . . . It came to him in a flash that the people he sat with were dear to him. How do you make the right decision?

"*If* we have the people, how do we take the war to the enemy?" he asked at last.

"We have to find where they are," Barbara said from the doorway.

"Their base," Tietjen agreed, and pulled a chair into the circle for Barbara. He was sitting in an old armchair, and Ketch was perched informally on his left. As they talked, Ketch braided black cord with speed and inattention, her hands a blur of strong movement.

"If they have a base," she said, and nodded at Barbara.

"They have one," Bobby said grimly. "I was there. Only I don't know where it was, exactly. Somewheres downtown, but I dunno how far. I was pretty messed up when we got out of there."

"Could the girls tell us?"

Bobby shook his head. "I don't want them messed with any more," he said. "They couldn't tell you nothing."

"I doubt they'd remember anything useful, John," Barbara agreed. "The way they perceive has been stood on its ear: they can focus on a color, a logo, a shape, but not a whole thing."

He sighed. "Okay, so we storm the monsters' base, somewhere downtown. If you were a monster, where would you be?" he asked singsong. "Anyone got any ideas?"

There was one overhead light, a Coleman lantern, hanging low over the table; the faces in the circle were bleached by the light, and shadow pooled behind them. They looked from one to the other, Barbara to Bobby to Allan to Lo-yi to Ketch to Beth to Sandy to— Tietjen ran out of names—until the gaze fell on him again. The light seemed to draw them all inward, close to each other. Tietjen felt a charge building between them. But no answers came out of the light;

he was about to shrug his shoulders at the impossibility of it when Ketch said, "It would have to be a big place."

"That's half of New York," Barbara said dryly. But, "Big, with a lot of open space," she added.

"Yeah, but with hiding places. Some of them want to burrow, to hide out."

"Tunnels, maybe," Sandy Hochman suggested.

"The leader, the man we heard that night. He'd want someplace special," Ketch said. "Not just big but grand. Marble and crap like that."

"Palatial and baroque," Barbara suggested. "High ceilings." Ketch nodded.

"Not too far downtown," Lo-yi Quan said.

"Or uptown," said Beth Voe.

"A place everyone knows."

"A place they could feel they'd grabbed from the normal people."

It was as if they were building up a rhythm of conjecture, each contribution speeding the rhythm slightly. "East Side, West Side?" he asked.

"East," Barbara said.

"East," Bobby agreed.

"Why East? Bobby, you remember something about it?"

Fratelone shook his head. "Maybe. I dunno. East feels right to me."

"East Side, Midtown, a place everyone knows. Palatial and baroque, a place seized back from the normal people." The rhythm built, like an incantation.

"A powerful place," Alan said.

"A place full of stars."

"And darkness."

What the hell is this? Tietjen wondered. The group turned to him as if he knew the next line in the incantation. He was about to ask, "Where did this bullshit come from?" Instead, he heard himself say, in the same singsongy way, "East side, Midtown, a place everyone knows. Palatial and baroque, a powerful place, full of stars and darkness, taken from the normal ones. A place of tunnels." He broke off. "Tunnels and stars." What was he thinking? The words came out of him from nowhere; he felt as if a channel into the dark had opened up inside him, and the words had come tumbling out. And the words sparked something: images from architecture classes, urban history. Tunnels and stars. Brass and marble and vaulted ceilings, tunnels and stars and stars and stars. . . . When he closed his eyes, Tietjen could see a vaulted ceiling with stars, constellations gilded across it, dimmed with years. He knew. It was as if the knowledge had been waiting in his brain, just waiting to be set free.

"It's Grand Central."

The others looked at him blankly. Then Barbara nodded. "The painted ceilings. The tunnels. The marble and brass." One by one the others nodded. Again Tietjen had the sense of some kind of telepathy, as if they were literally on the same wavelength. The room had a pulse and they all shared it. Each of them looked around at the others, exchanging glances, excitement building into a silent earthquake.

Then Bobby asked, "But how could we take out Grand Central?" The glow and energy faded, even the overhead light seemed to dim. "Those things could hide out in the tunnels. We'd never find 'em, then they'd come up and kill us."

Tietjen felt the welling excitement diminish until he felt too small for the armchair he sat in. "There are two levels of tracks, all underground, and tunnels clear out to Harlem. Offices. Catwalks. Crawlspaces. Stairways. Bobby's right: there's no way we could put Grand Central under siege—and if we went in after them hand to hand, they'd go to ground in the tunnels; they'd all get away."

Into the silence Barbara said, impatiently, "John, you're thinking like a damned architect. You know too much, you're letting what you know defeat you."

Ketch, on his left, bristled. "Knowing too much isn't the problem, Ms. McGrath."

Barbara ignored Ketch's tone and grinned. "It's exactly the problem right now. John knows too much about Grand Central, so he's decided it can't be defeated. You have to be a little ignorant, like the bumblebee."

Beth Voe asked, "Bumblebee?" Her breathy voice made her sound bewildered.

Tietjen finished Barbara's thought. "That old saw: the bumblebee can't fly, but it doesn't know that, so it flies anyway." He turned to face Barbara. "Okay. So tell me."

Her grin grew wider; he had a feeling she was enjoying this, enjoyed having answers. "We don't know that Grand Central is the same way you remember it, John. It could be in ruins. The tunnels could all be flooded, or collapsed. Even if it's still just the way it was, you're thinking like we're going to fight them one-on-one. Maybe we will, but why start out that way? Let's cheat. Doesn't anyone in this place know how to make a bomb?"

Tietjen found himself grinning in response. "Do you?"

"I could fake it. I *was* a Scout den mother." Everyone laughed. Then Barbara continued, "So what kind of wholesale mayhem can we come up with?"

Sometime in the next few hours Elena brought up coffee. Tietjen was not sure how long after that the meeting broke up, but when they left each of them had tasks, people to talk to. Tietjen, McGrath, and Ketch walked down the hall together; at the stairway there was an awkward moment when he and Ketch turned to go up the stairs to his room and Barbara headed down to the infirmary.

"Good night, Barbara." There was something else he wanted to say to her. "Thanks for keeping me honest."

She smiled warmly. "Goodnight, John. Luisa."

"Ms. McGrath." Ketch stood at Tietjen's elbow, one foot on the stair, anxious to go up. Tietjen turned to follow her, feeling like he should say something more.

"Good night," Barbara said again, and left.

Jit sat on a rock in the middle of the Park, his back against the fallen body of a bronze falconer, the textured metal cool through the fabric of his shirt. He had taken the sweatshirt off the body of an old woman, and wore black pants rolled up so his ankles showed whitely. In his hand was a grubby square of cloth he had cut from the coat the Man had given him, which he worried absently. There was the faintest slip of moon over the park, and no other light. Jit paid no attention to the moon or the darkness. He was listening to the Man and his people.

They wanted to fight Gable's people, but didn't know how. Jit floated from the Man to the old grandma woman to the others, around from mind to mind, tasting their helplessness. They couldn't see as Jit did. So Jit told them something. He raided the thoughts of Gable's people and passed the thoughts, the images and tastes and smells, on to the Man and his people. High ceilings, marble, shiny brass; the musty scent of the tunnels that smelled like safety itself; high black caging on the windows; painted ceilings. He let the Man and his friends savor the taste of that place until they knew it and gave it a name. *See?* Jit thought at the Man. *Jit your friend too. Jit your best friend.* The first rich flush of their pleasure and excitement made Jit laugh giddily, drunk secondhand on their triumph.

Then they began to doubt again.

Even knowing where Gable's people were, the Man wasn't sure how to fight them. And Jit wanted them gone: the thought that the monsters claimed him made Jit sick. He didn't like the taste of their rage; even the attractive weirdness about Gable and his people didn't compensate for having to wade through anger that tasted like before, when he was always near drowning in a broth of the voices' rage.

The Man would stop them. As Jit listened, the grandma woman said something that made them laugh, and the Man and the others were suddenly hopeful, even happy. Jit wanted to be a part of that, to say *I give you one gift, I give you another.* What gift could he give? He cast through his memories, the memories of the voices he had touched before and after things changed for the city. What would please the Man? What would help him fight? With his eyes closed, Jit rifled the memories, finding warriors and kings, gunmen and soldiers, creatures from other planets, winged men with flaming swords. Angels.

Give them an angel, he thought.

There was one. He had found the angel a day before, a woman who flew over the park like a bird, who had no hate in her, just joy. Jit had stolen into her mind to ride with her as she swooped over the city, watching what was below. She was one of Gable's people, he thought at first, one of the twisted ones. When she flew her arms were extended, wings webbing from her wrists to her back, filling and spilling air; there were three clawed fingers at the end of each arm. She wore a long knit dress that fluttered around her skinny legs. Every part of her was skinny, like the bird she seemed to be, except her face, which was broad and fleshy with lines by the eyes and around the mouth. Her body was twisted out of human form, but her mind was clear and sweet.

Her thoughts tasted like the sunshine that warmed her back as she flew. She swooped and arced across the sky, looking down on the ruined buildings, the lake that glittered in the sunlight where Hell's Kitchen had been. In her, pity for the people who were gone was mixed with her own triumph. *I guess I* am *an angel,* she thought. Jit wanted to stay with her forever. Then she banked eastward, went into a stoop, and dived through an opening in a vaulted roof. Looking through her eyes Jit saw the misshapen bodies, rapacious faces. Gable's people.

But she wasn't like them, he thought. He jumped away from her, deeply frightened and furious. He would have tasted the bloodlust if she were one of them. The others were filled with it; she was not.

After a while, tentatively, Jit had reached out to the Angel again, and found what he had found before: love, and pity, and joy. The monsters were her kin, and she was sorry for them. Maybe understood them. But she was not one of them. This made him wonder, were there others like her, who had been changed and twisted on the outside only?

Gingerly, because he did not want to draw Gable's attention, Jit began to sample the thoughts of the people around the Angel. Most were what he remembered and expected: black as tar, filled with hunger and rage. But a few, a handful, were like the Angel, gentle or loving or filled with a liberated joy in their transformations, living with Gable's people because they were their kind and it seemed to be the place for them. All of this Jit tasted and savored and understood, although he had no words for it.

Now, in the leafy darkness, listening to the Man and his friends plan Gable's destruction, Jit thought again, *Jit your friend. Jit give you an Angel.*

14

THERE was a peal of laughter from below, rising up from the alleyway behind the Store. It was a delicious sound, totally at odds with his mood. Tietjen went to the window and looked out to see DeeDee, Missy Hochman, and the Calvino girls sitting together on the pavement playing a game with stones and a ball. Jacks; he was surprised to realize girls still played jacks. DeeDee, with her claw-hands, couldn't play, but seemed to take pleasure in tossing the ball or the stones for the other girls. They all sat cross-legged except for Kathy, who sat on a box, the stump of her leg still wrapped in gauze. She didn't use a crutch; one of her sisters was always there to support her.

Tietjen winced, looking at them all. He thought of his sons for a moment, but he had to *make* himself remember. Chris and Davy seemed less real to him now than the cluster of girls three flights below him in the alleyway. He was healing, or he was growing new calluses.

"Kathy's doing pretty well," Barbara said behind him.

Tietjen didn't turn. "I never want to do anything like that again, Barbara." He said it as lightly as he could.

"Then we have to find a way to get the real world back in here." She did not sound angry, but inexorably matter-of-fact.

This time Tietjen did turn and looked at her. There was no trace of accusation in her eyes or in her voice; they both knew that finding a way out of the city had been the lowest of Tietjen's priorities from the start. He believed that he did not care if the real world came or not—he was where he wanted to be, doing what he wanted to do, but that stance was dangerous to the Store, and couldn't be allowed to go on for long. Still, every time the subject came up, he had turned it aside. He did now. "After we've dealt with the monsters, Barbara. It won't be safe to try before that. Anyway." He nodded at the stack of shabby books she held, pages yellowed and fraying, paper bindings taped. "What's this?"

She held them out to him, grinning. *The Anarchist's Cookbook. Organic Chemistry. Steal This Book.* "Is there a theme here?"

"Bombs," Barbara said simply. "It'd be a hell of a lot better if we had a working laptop and access to the net, but hard copy's a start. Have a good time: I understand fertilizer is very handy for making bombs, if we had any. Gas would work, if we want to waste it on mass destruction instead of running the generators. But, hey, it's your call. So I brought you a little light bedtime reading—if Luisa lets you read in bed." There was nothing in her tone to make him uncomfortable, but he was.

"You don't like Li, do you?" he asked.

Now Barbara flushed and made a flicking gesture, as if to push the question away. "I like her well enough. I don't think we'll ever be best friends."

He had to leave it at that. Barbara turned and left, and Tietjen wondered briefly if the strain he sensed between Li Ketch and Barbara McGrath was in his mind. He opened *The Anarchist's Cookbook* (Fifteenth Edition) and began to read.

Late that afternoon he was up on the roof, helping string more loops of razor wire across the roof, to cut off access from adjoining roofs. It was hot; the unseasonable chill of the last month had ended. Tietjen and the other men had taken off their shirts; the women had stripped down to T-shirts. He cut his arm open on a piece of wire, and stood watching the others work, feeling like an idiot while Elena treated the cut. He didn't think the wire would keep the enemy out, but if most of the Store's people were going to war, they needed to buy the ones who stayed behind as much time as possible, every way possible.

"Nice work, John," someone said. He turned to see who had spoken. He was looking out over Seventy-second Street with the roof's edge just a foot or two from his heels. The voice had seemed to come from above the street itself. Echo, he thought, and turned back. "John?" It was a woman's voice, familiar to him, and it came from directly over his head. Elena swore softly. Tietjen looked up. What he saw almost broke his heart.

"*Maia*." She was maybe thirty feet overhead, swooping back and forth in figure eights, winged. Her hands, which had been missing a few fingers before, now had three fingers each, a sort of bird's claw. Her knobby, sinewy feet looked the same—all of her looked the same except for the wings that webbed her arms to her body. She wore a brown dress that somehow went over her wings. With the sun behind her her wings glowed, translucent, the color of a gilded rose.

"Oh, Maia, no." She'd become a monster.

"John?" Her voice was the same as it had always been, raspy and humorous. "See, you were right. I'm an angel." She laughed, teeth white in a dark face.

Someone behind Tietjen threw something at the winged woman. Maia swerved, spilled air and had to swoop around to come back to her position overhead. Tietjen waved his arm at the people behind him: stop, wait.

"I'm not with *them*," Maia called down. "With Gable and the others. There's some of us that's changed but aren't like them. You know. Sick in their hearts."

He wanted to believe her. Maia was a part of the old days, the only part left. She meant something, like the city itself.

"Can I come down and talk? It's hard to stay in mostly one place this way."

From behind him there was protest. He told the others to go downstairs. "I knew her before. I'll talk to her." When one of them—the kid who'd come on the Mt. Sinai raid with him, Ted—started to give him an argument, "Just go downstairs, will you? Look, we know one—" He hesitated. "One changed person that's not a killer, the little girl we brought in from the raid. Maybe there are others. Maybe she knows something that will help us. Go downstairs. *Now*."

Elena took Ted's arm and pulled him toward the roof door.

"Come on down, Mai," Tietjen called.

She banked, swooped down, and landed at his side. She was smiling. Her pleasure was infectious.

"Best thing that ever happened to me," she said. "These wings are."

Tietjen looked around him. "Can you sit?" He pointed to the tar-and-shingle sill of a skylight. Maia nodded, folded her wings primly at her sides, and sat down. With her wings folded her elbows were pressed tightly to her ribs, and she kept her clawed hands in her lap. "So what happened to you?" he asked after a while.

Maia shrugged. "You been back to our block? Don't bother. The whole thing's sort of a puddle: I guess some water main broke somewhere. And a bunch of the buildings on the block, it's like they just sunk right down into the ground, like the water melted their basements right out from under 'em. That big five-story 'partment building right across from our house? All you can see is the top three floors, now. I was asleep in my place till the water started flooding, but then something dropped down—I think it was one of those big iron grates over Carolyn's windows?" She made a face; neither he nor Maia had liked his downstairs neighbor. "It sort of locked me into my place, in water up to my belly button. And cold. I could smell fire, but I don't know where that was. After a while I got sleepy, and I guess I went to sleep. Didn't think I was going to wake up." She looked at him shyly. "I missed you."

"Jesus, Maia." He wanted to ask what had happened, but felt weirdly reluctant, shy, as if it were too personal a question. Maia made it easy for him.

"When I woke up, my place was all collapsed around me, all my stuff was washed away, and I was covered in mud. I hurt all over, like I'd been beat up. I had to break through the wall, kind of kick my way out. My arms—I didn't know till I got out and got some of the mud off me. My arms hurt the most, and my back. When I got out and cleaned up some, I was like this."

"An angel." His Maia. He didn't know that any of the others would accept this. If he hadn't known Maia before, had only seen what the other monsters could do, he might not have trusted her. "But what have you been doing since it happened, Mai?"

She smiled again. "Flying, mostly. Looking round the city. Roosting with the other changed folk at night, mostly." As if in answer to his thought, perhaps only to a change in his expression, Maia added, "It seemed like the place for me, John. The couple few times I saw any normal folk, they threw rocks at me, like one of your people did just now. The changed ones, they let me alone."

Tietjen thought of his own people; who had thrown the rock at Maia? "Would you stay with us, Mai?"

She looked away from him, across the roof, at the buildings that fronted Fifth Avenue and faced the Park. "I see you're set up to take care of people pretty good here, John."

"We're trying to," he agreed.

She nodded, still looking away. "What happened to your little boys, d'you know?"

It didn't feel like a change of subject. "I think—I *feel* that they're gone." He told her what he had found, Irene's building in flames, the first day back.

"You haven't gone back to make sure?" She sounded unbelieving.

"I *know* it—Mai, you know what the city's been like since it happened. The weird things you see, the things you suddenly just know? I *know* Davy and Chris are gone, Maia. I know it." The words felt as if chips of rust flaked off each word as it was spoken, as if the words would shatter if too much weight was put on them. "I know it more every day. It's settled into my bones: the boys are gone. I can't even cry about it."

"John," Maia said gently.

He *was* crying. It started with silence and tears filling his eyes. Then he began to shudder, as memory went through him like floodwater: his sons were dead. He cried without words and without apology. Maia sat beside him and said nothing until he was done, and words had dried up with the tears.

The sun was slanting across the rooftops, and a fine breeze cut the afternoon heat. For a while it seemed like there was not a sound in the city except the faint whicker of breeze among the loose shingles. Then he heard the children laughing again, twelve stories below.

"You're takin' care of people here," Maia said.

"Trying to," he said again. "Filling the holes."

Maia smiled. When he looked at her face he could forget about the rest of her body. "Whose holes?"

"My own," he said baldly. "I need to get the city back, Maia. I have nothing else."

She cocked her head to one side, birdlike. "Would your folk take me in?"

"They will when I explain."

"Would they take the others? There's more like me, John. Not all of them, mostly they're like Gable, full of hate. But there's some like me, that don't hate. Some of us stay with Gable's folk down at the terminal—"

"Grand Central?" It was confirmation of that weird group insight from a few nights before.

"Yeah. There's four of us there that I know of. And three others down south, camping by what's left of the arch in Washington Square. *We* don't none of us want to fight you, John. But Gable's got the others thinking they got to."

He shook his head. "He's right, now, Mai. There's no way we can live in peace in this city until we settle it with the monsters."

Maia sighed. "I know that. Would your folk take us in? If we stay out of the fighting, will they come after *us* later?"

"Not if I can help it. I can't promise anything until I talk to people. But Maia—how much of the city have you seen? Flying, I mean."

"Whatever's left." She told him. Lower Manhattan was seven or eight stories under water. "Houston Street's still clear, but you get a couple-three blocks south, it's like everything just dropped way down. Both the Trade Center towers lying in the Hudson like a couple of logs—"

"That's not possible," Tietjen interrupted, thinking of the infrastructure of the towers.

"Maybe not, but it's so," Maia said blandly. "Looks like someone just swatted 'em right over, snapped off at the street." Brooklyn and Queens—as much as she had been able to see from Manhattan, anyway—were under water too. The South Bronx, risen from chaos twenty years before when the Police Academy and the Medicare hospice settlements had been built there, was burnt out again. "Like someone dropped a real dirty bomb. Melted and burnt." In the rest of what was left of Manhattan, the damage was more localized. It seemed, Maia told him, as if each neighborhood had been struck differently, by a different set of disasters. Some areas didn't look damaged at all: there just weren't any people.

"And there's places you just don't want to go, by the riversides, especially. I don't know why, but it's like they give off this signal telling you to keep clear."

Tietjen remembered the feeling of dread and hopelessness he'd felt on his way toward the East River the day they first encountered the monsters, and he nodded.

"And some things would be funny if they weren't so damn queer."

Tietjen didn't ask what; he was certain he didn't want to know. "Your friends, the ones you say aren't like the monsters—"

"Don't call them that, John. Am I a monster?"

"No." His denial was quick and vehement. "You're changed. But you're not a monster. You're one of us."

"I don't know your folk would feel that way, John."

"I'll tell them. It will be all right. But if it comes down to war between the—Gable's people—and us—"

"Which side am I on?"

He nodded. "And your friends."

"Can't answer for them till I ask the question, John. Want me to ask?" He nodded. "Then I'll go ask. If it comes to war between you and Gable's folk, I'm with you. If you people will let me live peacefully, me and the others." Maia stood up and rolled her shoulders, as if sitting for so long had made her wings cramp up.

"We will," he promised. Already he was thinking of who he would have to talk to, persuade, convince. Barbara, Bobby and Ketch, first. Alan, Sandy, Beth . . .

"John, you okay?" They hadn't heard anyone open the roof door. Startled, Maia lost her balance and Tietjen put a hand out to brace her. He caught her wrist, and his fingers felt the warm, leathery flesh of the wing, the fineness of bone. He loosened his grip so he wouldn't break her in two.

"Jesus, Barbara, don't sneak up that way, will you?" Behind McGrath, who stood just outside of the doorway, arms tense at her side, he saw Ketch. Hochman and Fratelone were behind her. "Maia's an old friend," he told them.

"You talk to 'em, John. I'll go talk to my friends." Maia straightened her arms and dropped her wrists so that her wings were half furled. She looked back at the doorway again. "You sure got a lot of love around you, John. You take care of it." She smiled at him, then smiled more broadly as she raised her arms so that the light breeze belled her wings. She took the few steps that brought her to the roof's edge, then stepped off the roof in a shallow dive, banked, and was somehow above him again.

"Take care, Mai," he shouted up.

Some were more ready to accept Tietjen's explanation about Maia than others. Elena: the silent, frightened woman who had barely spoken a word to Tietjen or anyone but McGrath since her arrival, had become the children's champion; the little girls, even DeeDee with the clawed hands, were her special charges. They played in the alleyway behind Elena's makeshift kitchen, running errands, their laughter bubbling up behind the Store. Elena believed in Maia and in her friends. "Look at Dee," she insisted to McGrath. "She's a sweet girl. What happened changed her hands, not her soul. They should come to us; we are not going to turn them away."

Ketch, who had faced Tietjen down about DeeDee in the first place, was ready to believe there were others like her among the monsters. Oddly, Bobby Fratelone believed too.

"I'd have thought you wouldn't be able to forget what they did to you, Bobby," Tietjen said.

"The little girl didn't do it, Boss. Hell, Kathy and Colleen and Karen are as changed as anyone; they can't talk like normal no more. But I know they're good kids. Besides," he added, almost shyly. "You trust the flying lady, yeah?"

Tietjen nodded. "Yeah."

"Well." Bobby shrugged as if the question was settled.

Tietjen was unnerved at how many people seemed willing to leave it at that: if he believed in Maia and her friends, that was good enough. Again he wondered if it was just wishful thinking on his part, if Maia was a Trojan horse, a way to breach his defenses. Again he worried about making the right decision.

In the end he had to trust his instincts. Two days later, someone came to tell him that the "bat-lady" was circling the roof. Maia had a friend with her, waiting a block away, just beyond their sentries.

"Can I bring him in?" she asked.

"*Fly* him in?" Tietjen asked, momentarily confused.

Maia laughed. "He's way too solid for that; I'd never get him off the ground! I just meant, can you tell your people, the guards and that, to let him come? I'll drop down low where he can see me; that'll make him feel a little safer."

Tietjen reminded himself that he and the people of the Store were as much on parole as Maia and her visitor. "I'll go out myself," he told her.

Bobby and Ketch didn't want him to leave the shop, and insisted on going out with him. Barbara did too, brushing off Tietjen's suggestions and Ketch's that she stay behind, "just in case." They stood just outside the doorway and watched as a short, stocky man walked carefully through the debris on the street, with Maia swooping back and forth just over his head. From a block away it was difficult to tell what about the man was changed: he wore a red shirt and dark red, oddly fitted pants, and moved with a peculiar, mincing gait. It was Barbara McGrath who first realized what she was seeing.

"Good lord, a faun," she breathed. The baggy pants were legs covered in coarse reddish fur. As the faun drew closer, Tietjen realized that he wore a breechcloth, and had tucked the red shirt into it. He looked back and forth between Tietjen and the people behind him, but always his eyes returned to Maia, hovering overhead, as if she were a touchstone.

Maia made the introductions. "This is Mack. Mack, this is John and some of his friends."

Tietjen offered his hand and the faun shook it. His feet were small and delicately cloven, but he hadn't the goat's horns of a classical faun. *Oh for God's sake,* Tietjen thought. *Mack the faun?* Barbara might have had the same thought, for when she stepped forward to shake Mack's hand she was grinning broadly. Mack's grin answered hers: his face was round and ruddy, his nose short, his eyes small and gray-blue. A good Irish face, Tietjen thought. Just what you'd expect from a creature from Greek mythology. Tietjen wanted everyone to come meet the faun; he couldn't imagine anyone seeing a threat in Mack. But when Bobby stepped forward Mack shied back and stood as still as a wild animal scenting the air, and looked up for Maia. Tietjen realized that the Store was still on trial with Mack.

"Ask Elena if she'll come out," he said to McGrath.

Ketch shook her head. "She won't come, John."

Tietjen insisted. "Tell Elena we need her. Ask her to bring the girls."

In a moment McGrath was back, with Elena following, and the little girls with her. Kathy Calvino now walked with a crutch, her sisters flanking her.

"DeeDee, uhh—" Tietjen looked around helplessly until Barbara murmured their names—"Kathy, uh, Colleen, Karen, this is Mack."

DeeDee smiled up at the faun and clacked one claw at him, as a wave. "Hi, Mack." The Calvino girls smiled and said something in their garbled language. All four children hung back slightly, but from shyness, not fear. At least, that was what Tietjen saw.

"Hi, DeeDee and Kathy and Colleen and Karen," Mack said. He sounded like someone who had spent a lot of time with children: friendly but not pushy. His voice was a musical tenor, his diction was precise but casual. Under it Tietjen thought he heard traces of the flat vowels of the Midwest.

"It's okay, girls. You can go inside again. Thanks, Elena."

Ketch, clearly impatient with the whole sequence, murmured, "What was that? You using those kids as some sort of litmus test to see if we can trust this guy?"

"No," Tietjen whispered back. "I'm using them to show him *we* can be trusted."

Mack watched as the girls followed Elena back into the building, obedient as ducklings. "They've taken good care of them," he said to Maia, above him.

"We try to take care of everyone who comes to us," Barbara said quietly.

Mack nodded. "Maia trusts you. Trusts him, anyway." He jerked his head toward Tietjen. "And I trust Maia. Must say, though: you're more my type." He smiled at Barbara. Tietjen realized after a moment that he was flirting with her. *Flirting with Mc-Grath?* he thought, astonished. It felt like sacrilege.

But Barbara was clearly delighted and unimpressed. "Flattery will get you dinner. What else can you do?"

Mack gave a howl of laughter, threw his arm around Barbara's shoulders, and drew her toward the Store. "Where shall I begin?" he said. From the back their heads—his dark and her silvery curls—tilted together like cups for a toast.

"Mack," Maia called sharply. "What shall I tell the others?"

He turned back to her. "That you left me here and came to bring the rest of them. That the coast is clear. That they'll take us in. Quote from 'Little Gidding,' for heaven's sake, but tell them to get their butts in gear; they should all be here before nightfall. When

Gable figures out we've joined the enemy, he's going to be pissed as shit. Now." He returned his attention to Barbara. "Did I ever tell you about my childhood in the IRA?"

She pulled back for a moment, assessing him. "For real?"

"For sure," Mack lied cheerfully. "Right before my stint in the Foreign Legion, but shortly after my service as an international espionage agent."

Barbara kept up without missing a beat. "And you gave up all that glamour?"

"What glamour? I hate martinis, can't stand the desert, and—"

"God, you're an actor, aren't you?" Barbara linked her arm with his.

"You needn't sound so dismayed. I was actually a rather decent actor."

Barbara shrugged. "But can you make a bomb?" she asked.

Mack raised his eyes to Maia, still circling above them. "I'm in good hands, dear. Swoop off to the others, then come back to me. I'm off to dinner!" He turned back to McGrath, affecting a thick brogue. "Darling woman, can I make a bomb? Where's me dinner? I build no bombs before I'm fed."

Speechless, Tietjen watched Mack and McGrath enter the Store.

"He ain't always like that," Maia said, grinning. "Sometimes he's worse."

"And the others? What are they like?"

"He's the only whatsit—faun? He's the only one. And he's got the biggest mouth on him. The others—shit, I oughta go after the others now. Couple of 'em move a little slow, and if they going to get here before dark—"

Tietjen nodded. He watched as she took a few steps, extended her wings, and launched up. Like a bat, he thought. Like an angel.

15

THEY were as ready as they could be. The war parties were assembled, plans were made and remade and rehearsed, and weapons gathered. The night before their attack on the monsters' stronghold Tietjen sat with his planning group long after they had run out of details to rehash. Finally Ketch had dragged him away, saying something about a good night's sleep. When they reached Tietjen's room she curled wordlessly on the bed, waiting for him to fold around her, and they fell asleep without saying a word.

The raiding parties set out just before dawn, when the light was warming toward a turquoise still inky in corners and alleys. The Store's army was armed with knives, axes, short staves made from spare wood or piping, chains, a pair of theatrical broadswords found in one of the fifth-floor apartments. The few guns they possessed had been distributed to Bobby's best marksmen. Tietjen wasn't one: he carried a machete, some rope, and a club Ketch had whittled from a two-by-four.

One group, Ketch's, had carts in tow, filled with sacks and cans of flammables: paint thinner, oil, anything they could find that would burn. Two cases of Chablis bottles filled with precious fuel siphoned out of old non-electric city buses, the bottles stuffed with rag wicks. Six boxes of old-fashioned kitchen matches, Barbara's idea. And several dozen packages of "instant logs"—the sort of thing you put in a dummy fireplace and lit to provide the illusion of a real fire: doused with paint thinner or gas, the things became astonishingly volatile.

Ketch and her group went straight down Fifth Avenue, planning to cross east at Forty-fifth and enter Grand Central from Vanderbilt

Avenue. Tietjen and the others crept through the streets, across Madison and Park, where Bobby took another group south; then across Lexington to Third. Then Tietjen turned them south, moving as quietly as they could: too many people, only roughly trained as fighters. Two more small parties broke off at Tietjen's direction, to accomplish preset tasks. The war council had stayed up for three nights trying to plan as much as possible, structure the attack in the same way that Tietjen once designed houses, laying the foundation, considering requirements, flow of movement, available material, cost.

The faun, Mack, had drawn floor plans of Grand Central and the way Gable's people were using it. To Tietjen's relief, they seemed to be concentrated mostly in the main concourse and waiting rooms; Mack said the eastern face of the station was mostly in ruins, the hallways caved in and the stairs down to the lower concourse and platforms impassable. On the western side of the building there had been no collapse, the hallways were clean, but the tunnel of the defunct Times Square shuttle was flooded, and Mack said that while there was access to the lower concourse and platforms, most of Gable's people avoided the tunnels. It wasn't enough to go on, Tietjen thought, but they could wait forever for enough to go on.

For weeks, every time Tietjen thought that his people's will to fight the monsters might fade, something new had happened. In the last week, two of the monsters had got past a sentry to lob burning waste into the windows of the building next door to the Store—the fire had taken three hours to put out. A new group of survivors had appeared one night, bloodied and fearful, to tell their story: all of them tortured, and two of their group dead at the hands of Gable himself, before they escaped. Tietjen, Bobby, Ketch, and Barbara, convinced fighters all, had done their best to remind the others at the Store what they were fighting for. Soon there was little need to remind anyone.

So now they were making their ways east and downtown in groups of ten or fifteen. Almost thirty people stayed behind, mostly kids, four of them over seventy, and a few like Elena and Sandy Hochman who could keep things going if Tietjen or Barbara didn't make it back. They had to win. Tietjen walked on, following paths he had taken once on his night walks, everything the same and entirely different. Barbara walked a little way behind them.

"We started this together," she had told him. "I'm not splitting off now." He had not argued with her.

More than once they passed through eddies of the same despair Tietjen had met on the streets, the hopelessness so overwhelming he could feel it squeeze his heart, making the blood roar in his ears. The sensation was faint, but corrosive. Only the thought that he had to set the example kept him walking during those patches. That, and the sight of Barbara, when he looked behind him, walking easily, a rope coiled and worn like a bandoleer over her shoulder, her hair a silvery halo. She smiled when she saw him look at her, then her face relaxed into a look of concentration, a faint frown, her lips pursed and gray in the predawn light. Should I have made her stay with Elena and Sandy? We can't lose Barbara.

In the end he drew strength, as he always had, from the streetscape through which they moved, watching for the enemy hiding behind the ornamented security grilles that ringed most of the commercial buildings, but seeing, too, beloved details, architectural flourishes and signs of the old city's life. He imagined the streets filled as they had been, with vehicles and with people in hurrying clusters. Remembered the smell, the heat, the sound of them. He was comforted.

At Fifty-fourth Street he looked at his watch, stopped, and motioned everyone in the party into the shelter of a courtyard beyond a brass-tone security grille. If the other parties were on time, they were all stopping too, to take a few sips of water, eat the fruit or chocolate or cookie that Elena had packed for each of them. Tietjen thought suddenly of Chris, provisioned for a school trip just so, with cookies, fruit, chocolate. When he looked at Barbara he wondered if she was remembering packing such bags.

"Okay," he whispered. "Time to go. The others'll be trying to get in to the terminal from Park and Vanderbilt while we're on Forty-second, so we may not see them till we're in. Everyone okay?"

They nodded.

"Okay. Good luck, okay?" He started to rise, but Barbara stopped him, took his hand and held it for a moment in both of hers. The gesture started a silent chain reaction of handclasps, shoulder-squeezing, hugs, among the others. Tietjen found himself embraced and kissed, hands clasped. He returned the embraces awkwardly, waiting for it to be over.

"Let's go," Barbara said finally.

Tietjen was first to the door of the gate, scanning the street. There could have been a dozen of Gable's people hidden behind each of the grilles or façades of the nearest buildings, but it seemed clear, and seeming was all he had to go on. He waved to the others to follow him, and stepped out onto the street. Nothing happened. He released the breath he had been holding and started walking again.

Within five minutes he knew something was wrong. He couldn't tell what; there was no sense that they were being watched or followed. Wordlessly Tietjen motioned the others in closer.

"*What?*" Barbara asked.

"I don't know," he muttered back. "Just listen for a minute."

The light was the thin overcast gray of just past sunrise, and half the street was still in shadow. The dozen of them waited, listening, straining for a sound.

"There," someone said, a stocky pale-haired woman in black shorts and a pullover who carried a bow and a quiver of arrows. "To the west."

Tietjen listened hard. In his mind he saw Bobby Fratelone, pinned under a block of stone or something, swiping one handed at an attacker who danced away from his blade and laughed. The others of Bobby's party were fighting frantically as other attackers swarmed out from behind the grilles of a looming Art Deco building. There was no sound to the vision, but when he heard a real cry, distantly, he knew it had been made by the man he had seen take an arrow in the thigh.

"Bobby's in trouble," he told Barbara.

She didn't ask how he knew. The sounds of a fight grew clearer, more cries, the sounds of breaking glass and impacts.

They ran single file along Fiftieth Street, dodging around the wreckage of a three-car, two-bus pileup on Lexington. The sounds grew louder, the high-pitched hooting and shrieks Tietjen associated with Gable's people bouncing off the windows. Where were they? Tietjen had glimpsed a building with shabby gilded sconces and an Art Deco portal, but which one was it, and where? On Park, where Bobby's group had gone? What cross street? On a guess, Tietjen turned down Lexington, still at a trot, and went down two blocks before starting west to Park Avenue again. The cries were so loud now it sounded as if they were surrounded. A hundred feet from the corner Tietjen stopped and sent a stocky blond woman with a bow slung over her shoulder up to see what was happening. Her name was Allis; he had watched her target-shooting behind the Store last week.

She was back in a moment. "They're halfway down the block. It's Bobby and them. Shit. There's a whole mess of them—"

"How many?" Barbara broke in.

The woman stopped and thought carefully. "One . . . three . . . and six . . . then the ones on the other side of the street. I don't know. Thirty, maybe?" They were outnumbered.

"Anyone hurt from our side?"

"Bobby's caught under a door, looks like they dropped it on him. He's gonna be killed if someone doesn't get him out of there fast. Tom Severin was bleeding, but he was fighting, too. I couldn't tell how badly he was hurt. And someone was lying down, but still moving. I think it was one of ours."

"Well, that makes it easier than attacking in cold blood, doesn't it?" Barbara murmured to him. She hefted the stick she was carrying, five feet long and almost two inches thick.

"It does," Tietjen said simply. "Go."

Then everything was a blur, things happening too fast for him to take in. They ran up the street and turned the corner, all of them screaming. The monsters, startled from their attack, turned to meet Tietjen's people. Allis, the archer, stood at the corner long enough to take one of the monsters out with an arrow before she followed the rest of them. Tietjen found himself parrying a piece of telescoping metal—an old-fashioned car antenna—with the club Ketch had made him, before he swiped at his attacker with the machete he carried in his other hand.

A spray of blood: the man wasn't dead, but hurt badly enough to fall back, grasping with his one hand at the cut across his face. Before Tietjen could step in and finish him, another of Allis's arrows cut him down. Tietjen barely had time to realize what was happening before another one, a stocky woman with stringy hair and mad-woman's eyes, came running at him. In each of her three hands she held a knife, and she swung her arms in circles, like a cartoon buzz saw. Tietjen raised his club to parry at least one or two of the blows, but did not need to: in her rush across the avenue the woman tripped and fell, caught by two of her own knives.

He looked around. Someone had got Bobby Fratelone out from under the door that had pinned him, and he was methodically shooting at the enemy, his rifle steadied on his wounded arm. He watched as two women squared off against each other, golf club against chain; the tall, Asian woman with four eyes was one of Maia's friends; she wore a blue shirt with OURS painted on the back in case of confusion—Barbara's idea. Her opponent was an elderly woman with lizard's skin and eyes; spit collected in the corners of her mouth, so that with each shake of her head she released a spray of saliva. The lizard-woman took a hit in one shoulder and kept coming. Then Tietjen got distracted by his own trouble. There were more of them rounding the corner at Forty-eighth, running northward to take up the fight. *Outnumbered*, Tietjen thought again. They were going to lose.

He kept fighting, slashing with the machete, parrying with the club. The club was heavy; he wasn't used to using muscles this way. He parried, left arm raised above his head to fend off one blow, but was too slow to avoid it completely. The baseball bat his enemy carried grazed the side of Tietjen's head and he fell back, dizzy, with his ears ringing.

For a moment that was all there was, the roaring in his ears and the pain, the hopeless sense that they were going to lose. *Crap. My fault.* When he could focus again he saw that everyone, human and monster alike, had stopped fighting to listen. At first he thought the sound was the sea-sounding roar of people, the noise he had heard months ago on his way back into New York. Then he realized that what he heard *was* a roaring, a real sound of animals coming closer, maddened by the smell of blood and the sweat of battle.

The first lion turned the corner onto Park Avenue and stopped, looking from side to side, raising its head to smell the air. Its twin followed a moment later, trotting lightly. Both stopped when they saw the human battlefield and roared again.

"Jesus Christ, Patience and Fortitude," Barbara breathed, nearby.

They were made of stone. Pink marble, and taller, standing up, than he was. Of course he had never seen them standing. They had been carved in 1911, Tietjen remembered; they had flanked the main branch of the Public Library for over a hundred years. *Patience and Fortitude.*

One lion looked back over its shoulder and growled, rolling its head with a "come on" gesture. Three other lions, two of iron, one of stone, padded up behind. Then another behind them, of chipped and weathered brownstone, and behind it in the distance more lions loping toward them, pacing, waiting. Stone, iron, one of glass. It was so impossible Tietjen only believed it because everyone seemed to be seeing the same thing he was. They stared and gaped just as he had. Then the woman with the snake eyes called out, sweetly, "Here, kitty, kitty."

The lions turned toward her.

"Here, pussies. Father sent you, didn't he? Come and get 'em, kitties." She waved an arm to include all of Tietjen's people. "Come and get 'em."

Delicately, one of the great lions advanced, walking sinuously up the street. Tietjen could see the muscles ripple under the impossibly fluid granite covering. The woman kept up her crooning, but no one else seemed able to move, even when the cat began to run, eating up the space between it and the woman with a few long strides. Not until the lion was almost upon her did the snake-eyed woman realize that *she* was its prey. The lion brought her down with a swipe of one paw, smashing her into the pavement. Then it stood, raised its head, and roared again.

Everyone began to run. There was no order; monster and human scattered toward the grilled plazas on either side of Park Avenue. The other cats ran forward to join in the hunt. Tietjen ran, fell, rolled, stood and ran again and darted into a nest of crumpled steel and aluminum grating. He watched a brownstone lion knock down one of the monsters, then stand on his chest, batting his head back and forth between its paws playfully. Looking up, he saw Barbara lying in the street, pinned by the dead weight of a monster woman. Tietjen watched, horrified, as one of the library lions walked leisurely over, raised its head to catch Barbara's scent—then walked past her.

Without thinking he ran from cover to help her up, then stopped as the lion saw him. Tietjen froze again, as it paced toward him. Standing before him, the lion was immense. He looked up at its perfectly curling stone mane, felt its hot, impossible breath on him, and knew he was about to die. Then the lion knelt before him.

When it lay on its belly the thing's eyes were on a level with

Tietjen's own. It looked at him calmly, the stone eyes speaking to something in him. An ironwork lion came up beside him, knelt too, and watched Tietjen silently. Then another. *What the hell is this?* A word came into his mind: trust. Was he to trust them, or they him?

Finally he reached out a hand to stroke the mane of the great lion. It was cool and gritty to the touch, but moved as silkily as any fur he had ever felt. Tietjen raised his head to meet the great cat's gaze. Trust.

"They're with *us*," he said clearly. In the morning silence his voice carried and echoed against the buildings.

The monsters began to run, dodging around cars and the median park strip that ran down the center of the avenue, trying to get past and away from the cats. The lions did not follow at once; not until their prey were half a block away did one, then the next, then the entire pride launch after them, covering the distance in powerful strides.

"Jesus, they're *playing* with them," someone said, awed.

Tietjen nodded, bent to help Barbara up.

They only took a few minutes to patch up the wounded, assess the damage. Two dead, one badly wounded. Almost everyone had bruises, cuts. Bobby Fratelone's left arm was broken, Barbara said, but Bobby refused any more help than a sling to brace it with. "I can still shoot," he said. "You need me." Tietjen did not argue. Their timetable was shot to hell, and Ketch and her group might be in position by now. If they hadn't been ambushed too.

"John," Barbara said, low.

He looked up. One of the library lions stood at the end of the street watching him with an air of expectation. A roar came, and another and another, not from the lion waiting there, but from all around them, hundreds of rough, terrifying calls of triumph. Every ornamental lion's-head, sunk in stone, decorating a newel post, lying broken in the street, sounding the cry all at once. The noise built to a final, thunderous crash, then stopped. In the empty silence Tietjen looked around him to gather his force together.

"Something is on our side," he said quietly. It is the city itself rising up to help us, he thought, but he did not tell them that. It was enough to know that whatever it was, it was on their side. "Let's go," he said aloud. He started south down the avenue. When he reached the lion it turned south and walked along flanking him on the right.

According to the plan, his group was supposed to enter from Forty-second Street, but their escort would not have it. The lion resolutely guided Tietjen toward Vanderbilt Avenue, on the west side of the terminal. There, crouched by the door and guarded by the rest of the lions, were Ketch and her group: all of them, unhurt. Tietjen waved a hand in silent greeting; she rolled her eyes at the lions as if to ask What? How?

He shook his head, mouthed, *You okay?*

She nodded, made a thumbs-up, but looked sideways at the lions again.

Tietjen made a hand sign of reassurance, then nodded toward the doors of the terminal: *Ready?* She nodded: *Do it.* Allan Hochman, behind her, nodded. Barbara, Bobby, and the others nodded one by one in final agreement.

The door moved easily in his hand. They went through the vestibule, then through the door to the balcony.

Inside the terminal, Tietjen blinked, trying to accustom his eyes to the shadows after sunlight. Gable was in one of those shadows. Downstairs on the main concourse the marble was banded with strips of bright sunlight that filtered in through the gated windows. The pile of rubble and dust that was the east end of the concourse was lit with a narrow blaze of sunlight from a hole in the ceiling of the terminal—Mack had told them that the Met Life building above the terminal was a gutted shell that channeled the sunlight into the terminal like an airshaft. Two of the stories-high cast-iron grates from the arched windows on the terminal's south side had fallen, and plants were growing in the spaces, like a parody of a formal garden—or a parody of the gardens at the Store. There was some sunlight from the south and west windows, the dazzle of light on the rubble, and torches everywhere. Like something out of an old *Dracula* film, Tietjen thought. The light made the creamy marble of the terminal glow warmly.

To Tietjen's left the old commuter bar had been cordoned off with velvet ropes, and heavy red velvet drapes were hung from ropes and rods. The effect was like a lush Bedouin's tent from an old movie. Gable clearly liked things theatrical.

He had stood inside the inner doorway only a few seconds, taking it all in. Then something came swooping down at him from the center of the terminal. It was so far from human that Tietjen thought for a moment that it was a bird or something—not one of Gable's monsters. But as it came it shrieked "Bastard! Bastard!" in a torn, painful baritone.

"Jesus—" Someone behind pulled Tietjen down in time to avoid the harpy's talons. He had been mesmerized by that voice, and the human eyes that had locked with his as the harpy swooped at him.

"Don't look at its eyes," the man said over his shoulder. It was Allan Hochman crouched behind him.

"Thanks," Tietjen said.

"A pleasure. Where do you want us," Allan asked. "Up? Down?"

Tietjen shook his head. "Some up, some down. Some of us have to go in *there*." He jerked his head toward the tented bar. "That's where Gable is." No one asked him how he knew; no one asked questions like that anymore.

"What about that thing?" someone asked, pointing at the harpy, which hovered over the tent, eyeing them. Tietjen did not have an answer until he looked across the concourse and saw something diving in through the hole in the ceiling. Maia's shadow swept across the floor, breaking the bands of light and darkness as it passed through them. The harpy swept down to meet her, talons extended. Maia had something in one hand that glittered, a knife, maybe. She looked like something out of Blake—fierce and unforgivingly righteous.

"Good luck, Mai—" he breathed. He couldn't stay to watch; Maia was buying them time. "Let's go."

Then a swarm of Gable's people poured out of the tent and they were fighting hand to hand. There was no time to think or make plans or even to worry—everything was reactive, it was all about saving his own life, helping the people around him if he could. When he realized that the one he was fighting was one of the monsters he'd watched torture a woman, weeks ago near Mt. Sinai, Tietjen shrank back for a moment. Then the hook-handed monster moved in on him and Tietjen brought the club up and smashed across his jaw. The monster struck out. Tietjen dodged, not far enough, and his left arm went numb from the force of the monster's blow. With his right he slashed up with the machete and its tip caught just behind the enemy's chin. When the monster jerked backward Tietjen thought he would lose the machete; the creamy stone floor was slippery with blood. Then the monster crumpled. Tietjen loosed his machete and went on.

There was fighting on the floor of the main concourse; Tietjen thought he saw Ketch turning and weaving, faking out her opponent. Tietjen looked away and kept moving. From the noise of fighting behind him and shadows dancing on the floor he knew that Maia was still in the air, still battling with the harpy. He pushed into the tent.

Again the darkness, broken in wavering pinpoints by candles. The tent was broken up by carpets and curtains hung up to create little rooms, and there was the smell of dust and corruption everywhere, permeating the curtains. No one stopped him. When he looked around one hanging carpet he saw two women, almost naked, curled together like kittens, sleeping. One had no mouth, just blank flesh below her nose. The other had no hands or feet, just— not fins, but webbed bird's feet. As she slept she whimpered. The other woman woke and stroked her hair softly. When she saw Tietjen she did not react.

In the next cubicle he found bodies, five or six. The skin had been neatly flayed off in strips which hung drying on a rack nearby. On a table a set of kitchen knives, immaculately clean and shining, waited. In a handsome brass tripod plumes of incense burned, mingling smells of decaying flesh and sandalwood. Tietjen gagged.

"Jesus," he muttered.

"You don't like it?"

Tietjen turned, startled sick. He had not heard anything behind him, and here was—with a shock he realized it was Gable. He towered a good foot over Tietjen, pale, almost emaciated, in a billowing red silk shirt that opened in the front to display his ribs. Lank, dark hair hung almost to his shoulders. Eyeless sockets glowed red as his shirt, and he was smiling, a narrow crescent below his narrow, patrician nose. His teeth, Tietjen noted in one of those weird dispassionate observations, were very bad: uneven and badly stained.

"No," Tietjen answered. "We don't like what you do."

Gable shook his head. "But it's not your city anymore, John. The old days are gone. We have the power now." Gable stood in the doorway, talking as if he had all the time in the world. He spoke past Tietjen, his blind eyes focused on the pile of bodies. "It's our city, to do with what we like. You pathetic bastards kept us down for long enough, but now it's ours. The Maker gave it to us."

"No one gave it to you," Tietjen said. "You have no right. We would have left you alone if you'd let us be—"

The grin on Gable's face widened. "You don't get it, do you, stupid bastard. We don't *want* to let you alone. We want to kill all of you sad pathetic little bastards. We want to make you hurt. We look the way the city looks now, and the city looks like us. The Maker gave it to us."

"Maker?" Tietjen looked past Gable, watching for sign of one of his people, or of the monsters. Nothing.

"The One who made the city new. Our Father who took us when we were sad pathetic bastards like you and made *us* new. Powerful—"

"Twisted and ugly, you monster. That's not power; it's your own sickness hanging out all over you." Tietjen hefted the machete in his right hand. The feeling had come back in the left, but it hurt like hell, and he couldn't count on that arm to save his life. *Where the hell is everyone else?* He took a small step to his left, toward the table with the knives.

Gable moved also. "I'm going to kill you," he said matter-of-factly. "Then I'll kill your women. Or maybe I'll let the young one live, John-bastard, so she can remember you each time I take another piece of skin—"

He struck out with a staff Tietjen had thought was another tent pole. Tietjen dropped to avoid the blow, and his bad arm stung as he hit the floor. He rolled and reached up, grabbing the staff at the bottom and overbalancing Gable. The monster fell hard, flailing, almost on top of Tietjen. The two rolled over and over. It was like a schoolyard fight: the sort of punching, kicking, wild striking out of eight-year-olds. There was nothing planned or heroic about it. Finally Gable grabbed one of the hanging rugs and pulled it down, tangling Tietjen in it. By the time he was free, Gable was gone.

Tietjen followed the monster's retreat, winding through the curtained tent, looking for some sign of his own people, following the fluttering edge of a rug disturbed by Gable's flight, a table knocked down, curtains torn aside. Then he saw light, outside of the tent. Gable was out on the terminal balcony again. When Tietjen emerged, Gable was standing near the marble railing, watching the fighting on the concourse. The vaulted ceilings echoed hoarse cries and the clang and clatter of metal against metal. There was fighting on the balcony, on the stairs, on the concourse; everywhere.

"They'll die," the monster said. "All of them." He smiled cruelly. "This whole fucking city is *mine*, John-bastard."

Something broke inside Tietjen.

Rage rose up in a flood that filled him with red light, and he ran headlong at Gable, machete raised to cut him down. Still smiling, the eyeless man jumped up onto the railing, balancing there. The railing was a foot wide and gracefully rounded; a backbreaking drop to the concourse floor. Gable danced back and forth mockingly, beckoning Tietjen to join him. Tietjen followed, staying on the balcony, looking up at Gable, moving the machete in his hand in a crossing motion from left to right, trying to anticipate which way the monster would jump.

"Scaredy cat, scaredy cat," Gable sang lightly. He danced soft shoe on the railing, his balance flawless, his eyeless gaze focused on Tietjen. "Come on, Tee-jin," he taunted. "Come on up here and dance."

Tietjen shook his head. "I don't dance." He lunged for one of Gable's legs, but the monster stepped out of the way, impossibly quick and balanced. "Come on down here," Tietjen offered, breathing hard.

Gable looked past Tietjen. "Your woman's dying, you know. The dark one . . ."

Almost, Tietjen turned to look. Then he remembered he'd seen Ketch on the concourse below them, not behind him on the stairs. "You are a lying sack of shit. And a fucking coward, and we're going—"

Gable leapt on him.

The machete went flying. Tietjen and the monster rolled on the floor, so close Tietjen could feel Gable's heart pounding through the thin silk of his red shirt. Gable's bony arms wrapped around him, one at the shoulder and one at the hip; Tietjen couldn't move except to roll, but neither could Gable. They crashed into the base of the stone railing, rolled away again. Tietjen felt like the whole world was right there, concentrated in a few feet: Gable's wiry, ferocious strength, his fetid smell like something rotting, the thunderous beating of his heart; the cold of the stone under them, the roar of fighting echoing all around them. Then Tietjen stopped rolling and listened and smiled. The roar of lions. First one, and then another, nearby, just outside the doors. Something is on our side, he remembered.

Gable had stopped too. Now he reared away from Tietjen and grinned broadly. "Reinforcements," he murmured. "The Father's sending help to *wipe you sad bastards out.*"

"Wrong," Tietjen panted. "They're on my side." He rolled sideways and away from Gable, up to his feet. Now he and Gable circled each other slowly. Tietjen's eyes were still locked on Gable's face; he was afraid to look anywhere else. The lions roared again, closer. "They're coming to get you, you fucking monster."

Gable scrambled back onto the railing again, and this time Tietjen followed him, a few yards away, balancing carefully as he moved closer.

He was almost to Gable when something grabbed Tietjen around the waist and swung him down, grabbing one arm, the other, holding him exposed to Gable, who came back along the railing, still smiling. The mouthless woman handed Gable a knife. His smile broadened.

Then something swept out of the air, knocked Gable off balance and crashed into whoever was holding Tietjen. Gable fell forward onto the balcony, dropping the knife, and Tietjen, fallen sideways, grabbed the knife and rolled to his feet. There was a groan behind them, but Tietjen didn't turn to look. He advanced on Gable, who stood with one leg bent, leaning against the stone railing, a trickle of blood on his chin.

"Why don't you just give up?" he said. "You won't kill me." He pulled himself onto the railing, sitting, then standing, looking down at him. "You won't kill me," he repeated.

Tietjen's hand trembled. Was he right?

"John."

He turned his head for a second: Maia lay on the floor, unable to raise her head, bloodied and crumpled, her wings torn. The mouthless woman was pinned under her, dead: a knife stuck from her throat.

A cry tore out of Tietjen's throat, wordless and brutal. The cry drove his arm up, drove the knife across from Gable's hip to shoulder, slicing him open and pushing the monster backward, off the railing. Gable's arms flailed as he fell, and he screamed. Tietjen looked over the balcony long enough to see Gable, on his back, broken upon one of the stone lions, staring sightlessly upward, slashed open where his knife had cut.

Then he turned back to Maia. As gently as he could, Tietjen lifted her off the changed-woman's body and cradled her on his lap, but the gentleness made no difference. She smiled and died in his arms and he did not even have the chance to thank her for what she had done.

"Oh, John. . . ." It was McGrath. He raised his head to look blankly at her. There was a streak of blood painted across her face; she looked ferocious, but her eyes when she looked at Maia were filled with pity. "John, I'm so sorry. Gable?"

"Dead," he said. "What's happening?"

She smiled, her teeth white against the blood. "We've won."

16

THERE was still some of Gable's people left, but with Gable's death the rage to fight had left them, and most simply ran away; the fires set by Ketch's team had kept them out of the tunnels, and the lions had caught many of them. From what Tietjen could tell, at the moment of Gable's death all the lions had returned to stone, or iron, or glass again, as if their job was done. There were only a few, a dozen at most in Grand Central itself, but when they left the terminal later they found more, stone lions lining the streets, converging on the terminal, frozen in the act of joining the fight.

"Wow," Barbara said when she saw them. To say the least, Tietjen thought.

Some of the monsters they let escape. Without Gable Tietjen believed that they would be no threat. There were not many.

It took a long time to find and gather in the wounded and the dead. Tietjen wrapped Maia in a velvet curtain as if it were a shroud, the first of their honored dead. They worked in teams to find the others. Allan Hochman was among them, a wooden stake through his neck. Tietjen thought of Sandy Hochman, waiting at the Store with their daughter Missy and Greg Feinberg, who had taken to calling Allan Dad. There were thirteen dead all told, and nine more wounded badly enough to need carrying back to the Store.

"It's a damned miracle," Barbara muttered as she dressed Bobby Fratelone's wounds. "We were outnumbered. Did you see the fighting, John? Our side was *trying*, but it's a damned miracle any of us are alive." Now that the fight was over, McGrath's grin had been replaced with a frown as she moved from one of the wounded to the next. She was rigid with anger, as if the sight of so much human damage offended her. Tietjen and Ketch stood to one side and plotted the best way to get their wounded and dead back to the store.

"She's okay," Ketch said, watching McGrath bandaging one of the fighters. "Ms. McGrath is all right." From Ketch, who had bristled each time Barbara was in the room, it was great praise.

"Yeah," Tietjen said. It hardly felt adequate, but nothing felt truly adequate.

The faun, Mack, was badly hurt. Tietjen saw him, sitting up on a plank, waiting to be carried up the terminal stairs to the street: someone had hacked at one of his thighs; the fur around the bandage was stiff with blood.

"Hey, Chief," Mack said weakly. He raised a hand in salute. "Where's the others?"

Tietjen had to work to recall their names: Janelle and Tom and José, who had come to the Store with Mack and Maia. "All okay, I think. Except—" He broke off, remembering Maia's impossibly light, impossibly damaged body in his arms.

"I saw." Mack shook his head. "She went big, Chief. Great gesture. She saved your ass."

Tietjen and another man, a stocky black man, Gillis, Gellman, something like that, grasped the end of the plank and lifted. Mack sank back, wincing.

"She really loved you, you know? You were the one thing she remembered from before that she really loved." Mack's voice became more insistent. "You know that, Chief?"

"I know," Tietjen said.

Mack shook his head. "No you don't. She talked about you. And your kids, and how you helped her build her new house—that's what she called it, her new house, you'd think you'd built her a palace instead of a shack—and the things you did for people on your block. She thought you were fucking God on a plate, man. She loved you."

Tietjen didn't know what to say. Clearly Mack didn't think Tietjen appreciated what he was saying. He turned his face away and lay still while Tietjen and Gellis carried the stretcher out to the pavement where the wounded were gathered. The wound in his thigh was seeping blood through the bandages. Tietjen remembered stitching up Kathy Calvino's leg, and wondered if they'd brought thread, needles, anything useful for after the battle.

"John?" It was Barbara behind him. She murmured in his ear. "Allan's gone. I'll take over here." She squeezed his shoulder and pushed him away. "Hey, Mack," she said.

"Hey, Barbara." The faun's leathery face crumpled and he began to cry. "They got Maia, you know?"

Heedless of the blood and dirt, Barbara sat down beside him on the pavement and put her arms around him. "I know, I know," she said crooning. Tietjen waited for a moment before he went to find Allan Hochman. The high was gone; the deaths had punctured the moment of exhilaration. Tietjen didn't have the words to tell Mack and the others that he knew what Maia had done for him; he did not even know how to tell them how special she was to him. He thought of coffee and a juicebox every morning, and of sitting on the stoop or fixing her lean-to in the evenings. She had waited up for him in the evenings, asked after his kids. His good angel, she had saved his life and gone again.

Tietjen was among the first to reach the Store, sometime after noon. He had taken turns carrying a stretcher the thirty blocks from Grand Central to Seventy-second Street; his arms and back were in knots by the time they reached the building; his bruises felt like knots. He could barely open his hand when he set the stretcher down. The rest of the party straggled in behind, carrying stretchers, supporting the walking wounded.

Sandy Hochman met them at the door, smiling, with her daughter and the Calvino girls and DeeDee behind her.

"It's finished," she said positively.

"It is," he told her gravely. "Sandy." He tried to think of what to say. "Sandy." He tried again. She looked at him, still with the smile fixed on her face. "Sandy."

She turned to the girls. "Go inside and tell Elena they're here," she said. "Go," she insisted, when they stayed clustered around her. "Go now. Go." Not until all five little girls were back inside the building did she ask, her face turned away from him, looking at the door Missy had gone through, "How bad?"

Tietjen wanted a word to replace the bald, cold, ugly one he had to use. "Allan's dead. Sandy, it was quick," he added. But it was not quick for her. She began a dry shaking that turned to tears and silent sobs. He realized that she was trying to keep quiet so the children wouldn't hear. Feeling completely awkward and inadequate, Tietjen put his arm around Sandy's shoulders and stood, waiting, while she wept on his chest. Around them others arrived and went into the Store, carrying, helping, holding. Tietjen stood there, feeling as if his arm were a shell through whose fragile surface Sandy Hochman's grief might break. At last Elena Cruz came and took Sandy back inside.

Mack's stretcher arrived. The faun lay back, eyes closed.

"Couldn't stop the bleeding," Barbara said. She sounded tired, all dried up. "He wouldn't even try. His heart was broken."

Tietjen looked at her.

"Maia. He really loved her, John." When Tietjen opened his mouth to say that he had loved her too, Barbara shook her head impatiently. "She was—" She faltered, trying to find the words. "She was home for him, you know? Since the disaster, since Mack found Maia, she was—*home*. He couldn't live without her. Didn't you notice, wherever he was, he always had to know where Maia was?" Tietjen could not understand why she sounded so angry. He felt stupid and logy and couldn't get what she meant. He had not realized he'd said that aloud until she answered. "Of course you don't. Mack needed her, and she died, and he didn't have the heart to go on living. At least we can bury them together."

In the end they buried all the dead together, in a trench in the ruin of a white-brick apartment building to the east of Madison Avenue. They had dug the trench weeks before, before the war had started, when they had decided to find a place farther from the Store for burying the dead from nearby buildings. Mack and Maia they placed side by side, Maia still in the velvet drapery from Gable's tent. Sandy Hochman did not come, but all of the children were there, gathered around Elena. Except for the people in the infirmary, everyone in the Store was there. Barbara had told Tietjen he had to say something, but he didn't know what to say to them. *I'm sorry. I didn't want anyone to die.* Not quite right.

He stood by the side of the trench, looking out across it to a row of wrecked brownstones on the south side of the block. Past the ruins, across Madison Avenue and down Seventy-second Street, the building that housed the Store was washed in honeyed pink light from the setting sun that blazed over Central Park. He could make out the fence and stakes of the vegetable garden Allan Hochman had helped clear and plant. Razor wire glinted at the edge of the roof, and he remembered standing there, watching Maia make figure eights as she yelled down to him. The boards were coming down from the windows of their building, and the glass shone in the late sunlight too.

Tietjen cleared his throat and began.

"There were ninety-seven of us when we left this morning, including the children and the ones who stayed behind. We lost fifteen—no, sixteen. There are eighty-one of us left. It's a goddamned miracle. I mean that: we had help, and we helped each other, and we won because we wanted each other to live, because we're doing something here, we're building something.

"I don't know if we'll ever know what happened to the city. I don't know if anyone will ever come in and find us. We have to live as if they won't. But I know we can do it, because we did this—" He gestured toward the Store. "And we did *that*—" South, toward Grand Central. "We won it. We had some kind of help I don't even understand, just like there are things about the city now I don't understand. But whatever helped us, it's *for* the city. That means it's for *us*, it wants us to be safe, to build and rebuild."

He looked from face to face to face. A breeze had risen and was fluttering hair, making clothes ripple with small snapping noises. Ketch looked at him impassively; Barbara was almost smiling; Bobby, arm splinted and in a sling, nodded from time to time. The color of the sky and sunset, something about the breeze and the warm, soft air, something perhaps about the exhaustion that he felt in every muscle, called a memory out of nowhere, the exaltation of a spring evening and a faint echo: *I will live this way forever.*

"That's what I wanted to say," he finished. "Everyone who died today was part of the Store and part of our home. Everyone who died today was part of the city, the same way you all are."

One by one the people around the trench's edge nodded or smiled or bowed their heads. Each seemed satisfied. Tietjen stepped back a pace, and the crowd started to turn away, head back to the Store.

"One last thing," Barbara called out. "Tonight, we're having a wake. And a party. John's right: we won this damned thing."

It was, as Ketch said, looking around the room, a pretty piss-poor excuse for a party. There was some food, nothing fancier than what they ate every day. A couple of cases of wine and many cases of beer, brought back to the Store that afternoon by four of the younger men still trying to work off the adrenaline of the morning's battle. There were a couple of guitars, and Bobby brought out a cardboard box and a stick and began drumming happily, one-handed. The kids, even Missy Hochman and Greg Feinberg, chased through the room, giggling at whatever game it was they were playing. Not much of a party, but it didn't matter. A few people began to dance, someone else started to sing. The pent-up emotions of the day were expressed in as many different ways as there were people, in dancing, in drinking, in weeping, in telling tales.

Tietjen walked around talking with people, catching the tale ends of conversations and flirtations and reminiscences.

"Working the crowd?" Barbara teased him when he passed close enough to hear her.

He hadn't thought of it that way. Mostly, he didn't have more than five minutes' worth to say to anyone unless it was about the Store, and tonight was not time for that. Ketch had given up trying to stay at his side and was standing against the wall, a bottle of beer in her hand, talking with two men who had been in her knife-fighting class. Dressed in black tights and a shift that left her arms bare, she looked dark and powerful. She had a cut across her forehead which had been cleaned and dressed. Everyone carried a scar, a cut, a wound of some kind. Tietjen had been startled at the bruising that ran down the length of his left arm where Gable had brought the pole down on it.

"Working the crowd?" Barbara asked again. Startled, Tietjen realized he had been pacing in circles.

"Just too tired to know what I'm doing, I guess."

"Then go to bed." She patted him carefully on the left shoulder. "It's been a long day."

He thought about it and realized she was right. The party would go on without him; he wasn't necessary to it. Barbara waved at him, waved him away toward the stairs, as if it were a big joke. Across the room Ketch was dancing with Gellis. If she saw Tietjen leave she gave no sign. Elena sat cross-legged on the floor, with DeeDee in her lap, telling a story to the girls who circled around her. God's in his heaven, Tietjen thought lightly. As he wove through the crowd people reached out to touch him, pat his shoulder, brush a finger against his hand as if for luck; smiles, muttered good-nights.

He felt light. Despite the aches that made climbing the stairs to his lookout an exhausting chore, despite the memories of the day and the losses, he felt light and young and hopeful, really hopeful, in a way that he could not remember having been—since forever. When he reached the twelfth floor and settled in against the win-dowsill to stare out at the velvety night of the city, it felt like coming home again. Like coming home for the first time.

Now it begins, he thought.

From the park Jit stared up at the building, watching for the Man. He wore the coat the Man had given him and stroked at the fleecy collar with one hand. It was too dark to see in through the unlit win-dows; Jit let himself nestle within the Man's mind, warm in com-plicity. *You won, Jit help,* he thought. *Beat our enemy.* Gable had told the monsters that Jit was their father—Jit wanted to push the thought away with his hands, to make it wither and die like the grass did in winter. Gable was ugly, like the oily smudge of dirt that had marred the shoulder of Jit's coat. He looked at the stain and thought: *Hate you, bad man. You so dead.*

Jit looked through the Man's eyes; he was watching the city, looking out over the Park toward the Hudson and the cold distant sparkle of New Jersey. What the Man felt was a patchwork of long-ings and regrets and triumph: too rich a combination for Jit to un-derstand. The boy stood spread-eagled against the mesh fence staring up at Tietjen's building, wondering when he would see the Man again.

The word came to him: father. Gable was wrong, *Tee-jin* was the father. The word made Jit feel warm, as if he'd wrapped himself in blankets. It made him feel like smiling, and he had a shadowy memory of *father* that was warm and embracing, although he wasn't sure the memory was really his own.

Jit wondered what he could bring to the Man, what gifts. To make him understand how they were connected, tell him the fight was *their* battle together. *I was there with you, even when you did not know it.* How to make the Man love him. How to keep for himself a small corner of the warmth the Man felt for the city, for the old woman and the young one and the people in the house.

Father, he thought again, but, overcome by shyness, he did not send the word into the night.

Jit slid down to sit at the bottom of the mesh fence, staring upward.

Now it begins, Jit heard the thoughts as clearly as if Tietjen had spoken them. *Sweep the city clean, make it thrive. When they come, the outside, when they finally come back, they'll find us rebuilding, keeping the city going. Now we can build. We can make it better, we've got good people here. And maybe, when they come*—for a moment Tietjen's eyes reflected the starlight with a kind of clean, holy anger. *Maybe then we'll find out what struck the city down and created Gable and those things.* That's *what we need to purge from the city. When we find it we can make it pay. Destroy it.*

The Man's rage was a fine, clean thing. It burnt in him as bright and uncivilized as the fires Gable's people had let burn through the night. It rooted him in the stone and glass and brick of the city. Destroy the thing that had broken the city. Someday . . .

Jit felt the Man relax against the sill again, relax into the fullness of his exhaustion, his victory, his triumph, and let the rainwashed cool of the city air fan around him and smiled. And Jit, hidden in the darkness inside the Park wall, pulled away from the man, had taken the Man's rage with him, stung with it, filled with its poison. Jit spat a single word into the night. *Father.* Sour as spoilt milk.

Jit helped you! he railed. *Jit helped you, you don't know, Jit sent the angel, Jit save you. You hate?* he asked. *You hate* me? *You don't know!*

The boy pushed backward from the fence, away from Tietjen and his people, shrinking into the darkness as if the dark could swallow hurt. *Hate me!* He began to grizzle: *Hate* me!

The words sang in Jit's head, echoed, rattled against the pain. He could see nothing of a man above him in an unlighted window. The air was black with hatred. *You hate me!*

Hate you.

In the night air, two thoughts, the same and wholly different, met and twined together: Now it begins.

PART THREE

1

I T was a hot day without any breeze at all. Jit sat under a broad-branched tree, feeling the coarse bark prickling through his shirt, and listened, watching the sun move in and out of the clouds, listening to the Man and his people. They were happy. The happiness made Jit sick. He wanted to slap and pummel and kick until he'd beaten the Man's face out of his own mind. Happy. *You happy now?* he asked the Man. Jit spat at the squirrel that sat nearby, transfixed and silent. The sun moved out from behind the clouds again, and its hot silvery light gleamed on the edges of the squirrel's fur; Jit could see its heart beating. He reached with his mind, not very far at all, and squeezed that furiously beating heart until it burst and stopped and the squirrel lay like a rag in the dust.

Nothing okay, Tee-jin.

But what was he going to do? How was he going to let the Man know how badly he had failed him?

Tell him a story. Tell him stories and dreams, steal away his sleep . . . Jit had lots of stories, lots of dreams, all the stories in the world had come rushing through him when the bad thing happened. Let him hear what happened till he can't go away from it and it put *him* in a little little box, and then he know what Jit can do. Let him hear the stories no one was telling, the ones no one was alive to hear. Make him hurt. Like Jit.

In the wake of the victory things began to return to what Tietjen called normal. One afternoon, as he helped shift furniture in one of the large third-floor apartments that they planned to make into a dormitory, Tietjen began to laugh. The man carrying the other end of the breakfront gingerly lowered it to the ground and looked at him.

"You okay? he asked. The man had come to the Store in the weeks just before the final battle with the monsters; Tietjen had been told his name but couldn't remember it, and didn't know how to ask without seeming rude. He did have a memory of seeing the guy with Ketch's team at Grand Central, swinging at one of the monsters with an aluminum baseball bat. Now the man swiped a trickle of sweat from between his sandy eyebrows and cocked his head, waiting.

"Back to normal," Tietjen gasped between laughs.

"Yuh," the guy prodded. "So?"

Tietjen sat down, still laughing weakly. "What's so normal about this?"

After a moment the man sat down too. "I see your point." He did not laugh, but managed a lopsided grin.

Summer heat had arrived; most days the skies were clearer than Tietjen could ever remember them being, faultlessly blue, without clouds to break the glare of sunlight, without city exhaust and smoke, without rain. Barbara sent a few of the teens scavenging for sun-stop, and no one went out unless they were liberally daubed with the stuff and carrying safe water. On one particularly brutal day Tietjen declared a holiday, told everyone to stay inside in the shade. Bobby Fratelone had rigged a hose from one of the water tanks atop a neighboring building, and had flooded the basement next door, creating a wading pool where adults and kids alike sat. Tietjen had protested at the waste of potable water, but Barbara convinced him the morale boost was worth it.

The aching heat of that day finally settled, and in the early evening a light breeze began to play through the Store. Tietjen took a plate from Elena's kitchen, piled stew and a lump of bread on it, and took it with him to sit in one of the back windows, thinking of work he could accomplish in the evening cool. Downstairs in the alley kids were playing: Greg and the three other boys at one end ricocheting a ball from sidewall to sidewall, the little girls sitting in a circle at the other end. Kathy Calvino sat, as always, on a box, with her sisters on either side. DeeDee sat in front of Missy Hochman, who was braiding the littler girl's hair.

"Tell a story," Tietjen heard DeeDee say. He remembered the

tone: "Tell *that* one." "What's the boy *saying* to the monster?" "Daddy, read it *again*."

"What story?" Missy asked patiently. From where he sat Tietjen could see her fingers gently working tangles out of DeeDee's fine red hair.

"A DeeDee story."

The Calvino girls nodded and made a chattering of indecipherable speech, apparent assent.

"Okay. Then listen." Missy did not look up from her work, but gathered them in, even Tietjen, with the slow, rhythmic tones of a true storyteller. "Once upon a time there was before, when everyone lived with their Moms and Dads—"

"And their brothers," DeeDee interrupted.

When Missy repeated, "And their brothers," Tietjen realized how many times she had told this tale before.

"And their brothers and sisters, and no one got hurt and no one got sick, and all the houses looked like houses—"

"And there wasn't any bad people that tried to hurt you."

"*DeeDee*." Missy sounded exasperated. "I'm telling the story, okay?" The littler girl nodded, then leaned her head on her fist to listen. Tietjen found himself listening too.

Missy continued. "And everything was just the way—" DeeDee murmured something. Missy cocked her head to listen, then nodded. "Everything was just the way it was supposed to be," Missy continued, "even when kids didn't live in houses or apartments. It was okay before, right?" She looked at her audience and one by one Karen and Colleen and Kathy Calvino nodded; DeeDee dropped her head back to look at Missy, and nodded too.

Listening as Missy built the tale, Tietjen realized that it was DeeDee's story, literally, that this *was* her story. She had lived with her mother and her father and her brother Mickey, in a lean-to outside of one of the huge old apartment blocks on the west side, one with a courtyard, heavily guarded so that little girls could not play there. "They never let you inside," she repeated twice at that part of the story, the grief still hot in her voice. "And there was trees in there."

Her Daddy worked in an office building somewhere, doing something. Mama didn't work because Mama was sick, or sort of sick, all the time. DeeDee took care of Mama: that was her special job. After school she went home, no stopping to play, to make sure Mama was okay, to rub her feet or brush her long dark hair because Mama said that made her feel better. Mickey did the shopping because DeeDee was too little, although DeeDee knew she could do a better job than Mickey because she remembered more about what Mama liked than he did. DeeDee was learning to cook, Mama was telling her how, because it made Mama feel dizzy to cook these days, and DeeDee was so smart; Mama said so.

When DeeDee's father came home, Mama would be brave, and would finish the cooking and give them their dinner and ask brightly about Daddy's day at the office, and Mickey's school and DeeDee's school, and Daddy would ask what Mama had done that day and Mama would look very sad and say that she would really try tomorrow, but she'd felt so weak today. . . .

"Daddy din't understand Mama," DeeDee said, twice, coaching Missy. "DeeDee's daddy didn't understand her mommy," Missy repeated, then went on.

The *Day It Happened*—Missy put the words in italics—DeeDee had been on her way home from school. She stopped for a few minutes to look in at the trees through the security grating and the ornamental fence of the Bessborough—that was the apartment block's name. Then she went on home, although Kai Chanadar was playing jacks and wanted her to play too. Mama was sleeping; she had that sweet, powerful smell she sometimes had in the afternoon, a smoky sweet smell that clung to her fingers and hair, and she slept deeply. DeeDee sat down beside her on the mat, waiting for Mama to wake up.

The first thing was earthquakes," Missy Hochman said.

"No! The first thing was the angry monkey-man running up and down the street yelling at everyone."

"DeeDee, there wasn't a monkey yelling at people," Missy said.

"There *was*. I saw him. It was a monkey-man, and he ran up and down the street and called people names, really bad words, and he bit Kai, too, but he didn't get me because I stayed in with Mama. And he was the first thing. Tell about the monkey-man."

With a sigh, Missy told about a monkey-man which had run down the street terrorizing the children, teeth bared, snapping and chattering. Tietjen wondered what that had been: a chimp escaped from the zoo or a pet store? Or some real, awful, thing made by the disaster the same way Gable's people had been. He didn't know.

Missy went on to the earthquakes. "The ground shook up and down and Mama and me got shaked around in the lean-to, but Mama was so asleep she din't wake up even when a piece of the lean-to fell down."

"DeeDee was scared," Missy said.

"I was *very* scared," DeeDee corrected.

"But she stayed with her mommy because her mommy was sleeping, and that was her job."

Listening, Tietjen pictured the child and her mother—drugged senseless, probably—thrown around their shack, buried in their own possessions, their cookstove upsetting and catching fire, the fire extinguished when part of the roof fell in on them. Through it all, DeeDee pulling on her mother's arm and crying "Mama, get up, Mama, please—" What was odd was that those weren't the words Missy Hochman was saying, although her bare-bones telling matched his inward vision. More of the strange in-tunedness which had struck the night they plotted the attack on Grand Central, he thought gratefully. More of the city becoming interpreter, intercessory.

"DeeDee cried, and pulled on her mommy's hands and tried to wake her up, but her mommy wouldn't wake up. Then there was water—"

"She woun't wake up, and there was water that come in the lean-to and got higher and higher and higher, and—"

"Then the water went away again, only there was a lot of mud that got all over DeeDee and her mommy, and—"

The flood that followed the fire and the earthquakes—Jesus, the poor kid had been hit by everything—had receded quickly, but had left a deep pocket of foul-smelling black silt around and in the lean-to, so that DeeDee's mother, still unconscious, had been mostly buried, and DeeDee herself had been coated in the stuff. Still she sat beside her mother (What had the woman been smoking, Tietjen wondered. What would have knocked her so profoundly out for so long?), pulling on her hands, saying, "Mama, you got to wake up now." Hours after the disasters began, DeeDee had heard a noise that scared her. In Missy's telling, that was the whole of it, but for

DeeDee, Tietjen knew, it had been more than frightening. She had heard something so terrifying that, exhausted as she was, frightened as she was, she found a new kind of strength and got to her feet, crouched in the ruin of the lean-to, and pulled on her mother's arm, trying to pull her out of the lean-to, to get somewhere safe.

"DeeDee pulled really hard, but she couldn't do it, and her Mama was asleep and couldn't help her, and finally DeeDee got tired and she fell asleep." Missy added quickly, "But she didn't mean to."

"I didn't mean to," DeeDee repeated softly.

Jesus, didn't mean to: a five-year-old child punishing herself because she'd fainted, hungry and exhausted and scared out of her wits. And when she came to again her mother was dead.

"And DeeDee's hands had got funny, like they are now."

Looking down, Tietjen watched DeeDee raise her hands and look at them, as if for the first time: black pincers, hard-shelled, like lobster claws, suited for grabbing and holding, so that DeeDee would never fail to grab what she needed again. *What a sick fucking joke,* he thought.

When DeeDee's father and brother finally found her the change had already happened, and her mother was already dead. The father had tried for more than a day to get back to his home; Tietjen shied away from imagining the familiar despair and rage the man must have felt. Mickey had run, just run, away from the block and his school and his sister, and only returned a day later to find his father waiting for him, his baby sister asleep, covered in dried mud like a cocoon, his mother dead, the mud filling her mouth. He never told DeeDee or their father where he had been.

"Then her daddy said he'd take care of her and Mickey—" Missy began. Again DeeDee interrupted, muttering low. Missy said, "*No,* her daddy said it *wasn't her fault.* So they found a real house to live in, and DeeDee's daddy went hunting and took Mickey with him so he could learn how to hunt for food, and DeeDee stayed home to watch things."

How small a change this was for the girl from her old life: stay home and watch Mama, stay home and watch the things that her father managed to pull out of stores and the rubble of other people's lives. Probably the father hadn't even meant it when he told DeeDee she was in charge of watching things. Probably it never occurred to him that she would take him seriously, that if anyone had come to take their stuff, DeeDee would have died defending it. Just null sounds, the sort of meaningless noises people make at children.

He had brought them down to Midtown, to one of the fancy old brownstones in the East Fifties, so that his kids should have somewhere nice to live. For DeeDee's father the disaster was a chance to prove himself, a chance to even the score with all the people who had more than he did, a chance (Tietjen thought) to lose the suffocating burden of an addict wife. He and Mickey hunted and foraged, practiced fighting; it was like Adventureland for them. But DeeDee had always been her mother's child; he really didn't know what to do with her, except encourage her offers of help, let her feel she was helping.

For a few weeks, they managed. Sometimes one of the family heard a voice, saw a figure vanish around a corner, a skirl of dust in the street outside their window. DeeDee stayed in the big house all day, wandering from dim room to dim room, barefoot, afraid to walk on the white carpets in her shoes, reluctant to sit on the stiff, uncomfortable chairs in the downstairs rooms. She liked the littler rooms on the upper floors; it was from one of those windows that she saw monsters in the street one day, pointing to the house. She was afraid they would come and try to take the things Daddy had left in her care, but they never did. Daddy, when she told him about the monsters, shook his head and told her there were no such things.

Daddy decided to take DeeDee with him one morning. They were going to find a drugstore, and Daddy wanted her to help carry. That made her feel good: DeeDee didn't like the new house, though she never told Daddy so.

They had gone a few blocks, Daddy walking briskly, Mickey keeping up with him, DeeDee falling behind, her slender legs too short to match their strides, when the first of the monsters came out from behind a crashed car. Then another, and another.

Daddy had raised the gun he carried and waved it at them.

"Give us the baby, mister," one of the monsters had said. DeeDee didn't realize for a moment that *she* was the baby.

"Yeah, mister, give us the little girl. She b'longs with us now," the other monster said. They talked slow and quiet, so that DeeDee wasn't scared of them. Daddy was, though. He believed her now, DeeDee thought, pleased. He knew she wasn't lying.

"Give us the baby, mister." A voice behind them. DeeDee turned and saw five more monsters, each one differently funny-looking. One of these had a chain that she kept sliding through metallic fingers; another had knives, a belt filled with knives, and a single round knifelike tooth that pinned his mouth closed. One looked like a big yellow bird and fixed DeeDee with his cold, round stare, and that did scare her.

"Let us pass," Daddy called. Mickey grabbed DeeDee's arm and pulled her close.

"Fuck off, man. Give us the girl, she belongs with us." That was the woman with the chain. She smiled at DeeDee and DeeDee shrank back against Mickey. "Come on, sweetie-pie. We're your family now," the woman continued.

"Dad," Mickey said waveringly. The monsters behind them had been joined by a few more. The two ahead now were six, each with weapons, each with a scary sort of smile. "Dad, what're we gonna do?"

"Shut up, Mickey." Daddy reached out, grabbed DeeDee tight with fingers that hurt, and pushed her behind him, sandwiched between him and Mickey. Then he pulled Mickey in close.

"Back off. I don't want to hurt anyone," Daddy said. He swept the gun in a half-circle, threatening the monsters.

"But the monsters didn't get scared," Missy said, her tone echoing DeeDee's own incomprehension. "They didn't go away, they just kept coming closer. And one of them hit DeeDee's Daddy."

In fact, the woman with the chain had swung it at Daddy, and he had ducked, but the movement knocked him off balance and he lost the gun for a moment. In the seconds while he regained his weapon two of the monsters—the knife-man and a short, round young man with bad acne who waved razor-fingered hands as if he were trying to hypnotize—got close enough to Daddy to knock him down again. Daddy shot the razor-boy with his gun. "Not shot-him-dead," Missy explained. "Just shot him so he couldn't fight no more. But the other man, with the tooth, knocked DeeDee's Daddy down and they started fighting, rolling around and hitting each other hard, and DeeDee was scared 'cause the other man had lots of knives."

"I was very *very* scared," DeeDee said, almost in a whisper.

Mickey was fighting someone or something behind them, too. DeeDee didn't turn to look. She was watching Daddy roll around with the knife-man, one on top, then the other, round and round, panting and cursing, each one bleeding from little cuts. DeeDee watched the knives in the knife-man's belt, watched until Daddy and the monster rolled back near to her. Then she jumped on the knife-man.

"Don't you hurt my Daddy!" DeeDee screamed, pulling at the monster's arm, hitting his head and shoulders with her funny new hands, kicking at him.

Another monster—the woman with the chain—pulled DeeDee away and held her with an arm across her chest, murmuring, "Hush, kid. They're not your family anymore; we're your family now."

For the first time since she was changed, DeeDee opened her hand—her claw—and bit it savagely into the woman's arm. The woman screeched and fell backward and DeeDee ran forward again, screaming "Daddy, Daddy!" until she got close enough to see the blood, so much of it, and DeeDee knew nothing was going to help. Then she turned around to see where Mickey was: behind them, with an old man bending over him, raising something to hit Mickey. Again DeeDee threw herself on the monster, using her claws to hit and tear, pulling the man away, screaming all the time "Go away, go away, leave us alone!" in a high high voice. The voice of panic, Tietjen thought, like the voice that had driven him back to New York.

The woman DeeDee had clawed called for help; she was bleeding. The old-man monster—his face had ridges running across it, as if his nose couldn't decide where to settle—broke away from DeeDee's attack. Mickey was bleeding, but not like Daddy. Mickey was alive.

DeeDee grabbed him with her claws, grabbed carefully at his collar and waist, trying not to nip her brother's skin, and she pulled. Mickey was heavier than she, he had to help her: push with his feet, slide on his butt, do whatever he could to help her move him away from them.

In his head Tietjen could hear her voice, a tearful, high stream of words: "push-Mickey-push-with-your-feet-help-me-I-can't-pull-you-you're-too-big-please-Mickey-please-Mickey-push-they're-coming-please-pushpush*push*—" But the monsters weren't coming now. They'd turned away, carrying the fat razor-boy and the chain woman and the knife-man.

"We'll be back for you, sweetheart," the chain-woman said, sweetly, as if she was reassuring DeeDee. "Don't you worry."

DeeDee pulled Mickey to a building, pulled him inside, found a door that opened, urged him through it. Then she looked at her brother, not much hurt, bruised and a cut on his arm, and scared. He pulled away from DeeDee and rolled himself into a ball, crying. DeeDee sat down at his side and began to cry too. After a while Mickey rolled over and they cried together, arms wrapped around each other, DeeDee with her claws gingerly held away from her brother's skin. They cried until their stomachs were empty, then sat together shaking, hiccuping, dirty and ragged, very small in a corner of the big room they sat in. After a while they fell asleep.

"When she woke up in the morning," Missy said quietly, "Mickey was gone."

Tietjen started at the matter-of-factness of it. Mickey had vanished overnight, left his five-year-old sister to the mercies of Gable's people. There had been no sign of a struggle—the kid had left on his own. *Jesus.*

"So then DeeDee had to hide out for a long time, and stay away from the monsters and stuff. And then she saw Mr. Tietjen and the people from Here and she went up to them and they took her home and now she lives with us."

DeeDee looked up and backward at Missy, muttered one more comment.

"And she *did* pull Mickey away, and she was brave."

Tietjen leaned his head against the windowsill. *Brave.*

"What are you looking at?" Barbara asked. She had come up behind Tietjen, and startled him so badly he almost lost his plate out the window. "Sorry, but what's up?"

He made a place for her on the windowsill. "Shhh. Listen."

"That's the end," Missy said. "I want to play ball now." She stood up, and Kathy's two sisters stood with her, looking at their sister as if to ask permission. She gabbled something at them, they nodded and followed Missy, with DeeDee following them calling "I want to play ball too!"

Tietjen relaxed against the windowsill. "Jesus, that poor kid. Have you heard her story? I wonder how much of that is true?"

"All of it, I should think," Barbara said.

"But God, it's less than six months since the disaster hit, and already there're legends about it." Tietjen shook his head. "Legends told by children."

"Not legends. Reassurances. When Gordie knocked out his front tooth riding his tricycle, that became his favorite story: How Gordie Lost His Tooth. He wanted to hear it every night, and I couldn't leave any of the gory details out. He wanted the blood, and the stitches, and the crying and the fear and everything in the story. I must have told it a hundred times, I could probably tell it now."

"Why do they do that to themselves," Tietjen wondered, appalled.

"They don't do it because it hurts, John. They do it because it heals. Kids tell themselves stories about the things that scare them until the things lose their power, until it becomes safe."

"When does it become safe? How could it ever be safe?" DeeDee's story felt like a stone in his gut: Tietjen could not understand how the little girl had survived, could play and run around and sing like any normal child. Barbara patted his knee briskly.

"It's safe now, John. Look at what you've done: it's safe now." Barbara rose and took her plate back to the kitchen. Tietjen looked out the window, watched the four little girls playing with the ball, watched Kathy Calvino sitting with her crutch, calling gibberished warnings to her sisters. The boys had come inside to get dinner; soon enough Elena would call the girls in too. A routine, quiet and known. Safe. Was Barbara right? He finished his food and went back to work.

2

HE dreamt of Irene at the end of the world.

Behind her eyes, listening to her thoughts, he understood at last and for the first time her fear, the suspicious terror that other people, their autonomous motives and intentions, had always evoked in her. He knew the fierce love she had for their sons; the mixture of pride and resentment she felt for the work she did; and the reluctant, sad remnants of affection that Irene had for him and their marriage. He came the closest he had in a long time to loving her wholly: even in sleep he grieved as he watched helplessly from behind her eyes, waiting for what would come.

Irene had been shopping, buying socks and underwear for the boys, sorting through plastic packets of boys' underpants until she found one that met her inscrutable criteria. She disliked these trips into the communal world, sharing the same space, the same air with hundreds of strangers. She could smell a mix of perfume, sweat, polish and disinfectant on the air; it made her feel unclean and sick to her stomach. An elderly woman fingering the neat rows of plastic-sealed packages next to her suddenly turned and shouldered past Irene, so that her hip hit the display counter painfully. Reflexively, Irene turned and stared at the woman's awkwardly retreating back, hating her: a clean, holy rage aimed like an arrow at the old woman's shoulders. Irene turned back to the display.

She had moved from underwear back to the socks and was deciding between a soft golden brown that made her think of Chris's hair, and a dark navy that was safe, long-wearing. She was absorbed enough in the choice that, at first, she did not realize that something had happened.

Then it happened again. There was a sizzle and the smell of

ozone, and the greenish fluorescent lights blinked. The floor underneath Irene's feet moved in a slow, easy undulation, rolling from one
wall to the other. The heavy display counters hardly shrugged in the
motion, but farther down the floor Irene could see the rise and fall
of a sea of racks, the hangered contents waving gently with the motion.

New York does not have earthquakes. Tietjen could hear her
thought. At the same time she denied what had happened, she was
quietly putting aside the socks and underwear she had chosen and
was trying to remember where the elevator was. No, not the elevator. If this was an earthquake (*New York does not have earthquakes*)
the elevator would not be safe. The stairs. *Chris and Davy should be
home by now, they'll be downstairs in the after-school room at the
building, someone will take care of them until I get home. I'll call
and let them know I'm all right. But New York does not—*

It started again. The scariest thing was the slowness of it, the
laziness of that rise and fall. This time the peak was higher: Irene
could feel herself slipping, her feet swept out from under her in slow
motion. Across the floor a quick shriek rang out, fast and out of
tempo with the slow dance of counters and racks. She caught herself
as she fell and pulled herself upright. The stairs. Light flickered and
dimmed, and in the twilight the counters and racks churned lumber-
ingly. A voice called for a clerk, lights, help. She heard someone crying.

She was on the sixth floor. (*Why is the children's department up
away from everything else?* she wondered.) Irene held on to two
sides of the display counter and scanned desperately for the emer-
gency-exit signs, which should have been flashing in the dimness but
were not. Six flights of stairs; how long would it take to get down six
flights of stairs? A dark form scuttled by her, the store ID badge
glinting faintly in the traces of light. "Where are the stairs?" Irene
called.

The figure did not stop. The light flickered on for a moment and
Irene could see a young woman stuffing things into a shopping bag,
grabbing whatever she could reach indiscriminately and filling her
pockets, her handbag. No clerk came to stop her; Irene thought she
saw a man in a store blazer retreating toward a far wall. The stairs,
she thought triumphantly. Angrily.

The floor flexed again. There was a crash behind her, but Irene did not stop to look. She clung heavily to the counter for another minute until the world stopped tossing, then began to follow the clerk, slipping into a bent-kneed crouch that was uncomfortable but gave her a feeling of stability. Then, with shocking abruptness, the air crackled with ozone and the heaving of the floor stopped. She had a sudden feeling of peace and stability that was almost uncanny. The lights came back up on the gigantic disarray of the displays and racks. A pair of mannequins, towheaded children, clung to each other on the floor as if for comfort. A woman's voice rang out with uncertain humor: "I suppose next thing, there'll be an earthquake sale!" Someone called angrily for a sales clerk. A very young child began to cry noisily; without even seeing him Irene imagined him, his mouth gaping widely, his face glistening with mucus and tears, probably black or Hispanic, she thought. She felt no pity for the child, just a crushing rush to get *gone*. The stairs.

She worked her way across the floor, wading through a bright sea of fallen blouses in what a downed sign called LATEST LITTLE GIRL COLORS, pushing past islands of disaster, sales clerks clustered around the body of a young man that lay too still. Irene curled her lip, as if the man had committed a crime against decorum. It was dangerous at the best of times to stop and mix with strangers. The exit signs were functional again, glowing a pale green against the off-white wall. The elevators were probably working, but just in case . . . Irene turned toward the stairway.

The door was heavy steel, meant to seal out fire and smoke. When it slammed behind her and she was alone in the starkly lit white stairwell, her relief was mixed with a sudden, passionate desire to go back to the sales floor, be among people again. The air in the stairwell was cool and musty. Irene leaned against the railing for a moment, then started to descend, taking a leisurely pace. She had made it down one flight when the lights went out again.

Someone in the stairwell above her screamed. The stairs tilted again, creaking. Irene clung heavily to a banister made of iron and wood-grained plastic that felt insubstantial and malleable under her hands. Behind her the door to the sixth floor swung open with a clang, steel door and steel wall singing out in protest; even in the dark Irene could see the indistinct shadows of people moving around her, spilling silently into the stairwell. The lights flickered on again, the stark yellow of emergency floodlights this time.

Tietjen in his dreaming felt his own skin prickle as the crowd pressed into the stairwell, more people than he—or Irene—had thought were contained on the sixth floor. Some looked weird—grotesque, somehow, as if something had twisted them. The old woman who had bumped into Irene earlier pushed past her again, arms thrust stiffly out in front of her as if she were warding off dangers. Again Irene glared at her, her rage at all crowds and all strangers spearing through the old woman's shoulders.

There was a cry and the woman pitched forward, a shaft like an arrow centered in her back.

Someone to her left cried and would have stopped, but the press was too insistent, the force of bodies behind them too strong. Irene, pushed past where the old woman lay, thought, *I did that.* She was not proud of it or sorry, just certain. *I did that.*

Then she was carried along in the tide of people around her, down the stairs, so that she barely felt her feet touching the concrete steps. Her anger rose up at the familiar touch, so many shoulders and stomachs and legs and hands, too close, too insinuating. The anger was suffocating; she tried to turn it into concern, to drown the urge to shriek in thinking of her sons. They would be safe in the after-school room in their building. Maybe this thing—what the hell was it? Everyone knew that New York did not have earthquakes—wasn't happening that far uptown. Still, she pushed against the nubbly cloth of the coat in front of her. *I must get home.*

The stairs shook convulsively, tossing the tightly packed bodies together, apart, together again. There was a diminishing scream: someone must have fallen over the banister. Irene shook her head as she pushed forward. Acid rose in her throat and she felt dizzy. "What is happening?" she heard someone cry, and echoed the thought. For the first time it occurred to her that she might actually die, here in the stairwell, in a crowd of people who had probably been buying underpants for their own children, or winter jackets or gloves or tablecloths. Among strangers.

"No!" Irene pushed hard against the coat in front of her, waiting for the body to give way, let her past. She never willingly touched a stranger, but now she was beyond such refinement. She pushed again and felt a hard shove in her own back. "Stop it," she said without turning her head. She pushed again, again felt the hands pushing square in the center of her back. She turned her head to yell at the person behind her, "I'm trying, can't you see I'm trying?"

As she turned she lost her footing.

For a long moment she thought the pressure of bodies against her own would hold her up as she sought desperately to find the concrete stair under her feet again. It eluded her, as if it were deliberately jumping away from her. Irene felt herself slipping, the nubbly coat rough against her cheek as she fell. The hand at her back pushed again.

"Stop it, please help me, stop it, please . . ." Nothing stopped, the pressure did not cease, something was dragging her downward into the concrete stairwell as inexorably as if it were quicksand. "Please," she tried again, grasping at the coat of the stranger in front of her. She had no idea if it was a man or a woman, she hadn't cared, but now she wondered. *I'm going crazy,* she thought. *Who cares?* "Help me," one last try. The words were swallowed up in the nubbly tweed cloth, and she felt herself pitching forward down the stairs with frightening slowness, defying the laws of gravity to fall with terrible grace into nowhere. The hand behind her urged her head forward, down the stairs. Her chin hit the metal runner at the lip of the stair.

"NO!"

The first foot in the small of her back, quickly, almost apologetically. A heel on her hand. Feet stepping over and between her legs, then another foot, this time heavily on her shoulder. The insult of pain was so stunning she hardly felt it. A sharp heel like a nail in the soft flesh of her side. Someone kicked her head.

chris davy boys what am I going to do chris davy they'll be safe at home in the after-school room yes they will someone will give them dinner someone will take care of them until I get home chris davy davy chris a sharp blow near her temple, and the reciprocal pain of the metal runner biting into her neck. *john.* She thought of him like a life preserver. *he'll take care of the boys until I get home o god it hurts I knew it would hurt like this.* Her mouth was filled with blood. The stair heaved and tossed below her, and something— someone—landed heavily on her. *new york does not have earthquakes.* All she could see was feet, legs, strangers. *I knew it I knew they will kill you. O god oghhd.*

Tietjen, safe in his bed, listened as Irene's thoughts grew incoherent, flailing, dim, until at last, fragmented by pain, they died out altogether.

Then he woke up.

He sat up sweating, heart pounding, his breath quick and shallow. Very slowly his eyes focused on the gray shapes that stood indistinct against the darkness. The chest of drawers with a pile of his dirty clothes on top of it. The armchair. The curtained window. On the night table a half-burnt candle, a box of matches, and a pile of books. The foot of his bed and the muffled shape of his own legs and feet under the blanket. His sides still ached from the kicks that Irene had suffered in his dream, and his jaw hurt from clenching. He was safe at the Store, home.

He let out a slow breath. "Jesus." Tietjen made himself breathe slowly, trying to will his pulse to a normal beat. *Inhale* to a slow count of eight *exhale* 1-2-3-4-5-6-7-8 *breathe, breathe slowly.* After a while he felt steady enough to pull the covers back and move so that he was sitting on the edge of his bed. The air in the room felt chilly. Shivering, he reached for the sheet again and pulled it around his shoulders. He couldn't keep still, went into the living room, then out into the hallway, pacing its length, waiting for the fearful pounding in his head to lessen its intensity.

"John?"

McGrath stood in the doorway to her rooms, wary. Looking for Ketch, he realized. Ketch was on watch tonight. McGrath wore a robe over pajamas; her feet were bare. In the faint light from the window her hair was a pale golden glow; it made Tietjen wonder briefly what color it had been before it went white.

"John?" she said again.

"Something wrong, Barbara?" He was surprised at how calm his voice was.

"I thought I heard you yelling. I was just checking—" She sounded awkward, as if she were unsure about intruding too deeply into his nightmares. "Are you all right?"

Tietjen nodded slowly. "Bad dream. I'm sorry if I woke you. Did I wake anyone else?" He began to edge back toward his rooms, but with a gesture that invited her along, if she cared to come. Barbara followed him into his living room.

"I don't think so." She half-sat on the edge of the chest across from his bed. "What was your dream about? Sometimes it helps to tell." She crossed her arms and tilted her head, ready to listen. Tietjen remembered that he once had thought that Barbara and Irene had a common look; with the image of Irene burned into him by the dream, he could not look long at Barbara.

"I dreamt about my wife. What happened to her. It was . . . rough."

McGrath nodded.

"We hurt each other."

"It's hard not to." She did not move, did not even uncross her arms to reach a hand to him, but Tietjen felt an unmade gesture reaching out nonetheless. "When Gordon died I spent a long time regretting, feeling sorry for him; I wasn't exactly the model wife by local standards. Then I decided that that was a kind of presumption—he was a grown-up, who was I to feel sorry for him? I swing back and forth between those two poles. Grief doesn't just go away."

"I wish it would," he snapped. Aware of how stupid that sounded, he added, "There were things I never understood about— I was probably the single worst person in the world for her to have married. She hated this city, hated people. The way she died—"

"You can't know how she died," McGrath objected.

"I *know*," Tietjen said.

For a little while both were quiet. When he looked up, McGrath had dropped her head. All he could see was the nimbus of her hair. "What color was your hair?"

She raised her head and tilted it again, surprised, smiling. "Reddish brown. Dull auburn, you could say. But it's been white since before my fortieth birthday."

Irene's hair had been black. "Just curious," Tietjen said.

The silence again. It was the friendly, companionably awkward quiet that waited for someone to say something.

At last McGrath uncrossed her arms and pushed off the chest. "You should get some sleep. You sure you're going to be all right, John?"

He rose from the bed. "I'll be fine." The sheet slipped off one shoulder, the air was cool on the skin of his chest and back. A little awkwardly Tietjen hiked the blanket back into place as a shawl, and tugged at the waistband of the sweatpants he wore. "I'll be fine," he repeated.

"Right." McGrath smiled, walked over, and touched two fingers briefly to the side of his neck. "If you need anyone, you know where to find me."

He thanked her. She looked as if there was something else to say, then shrugged and turned and left the room.

For a few minutes he sat at the window, staring out at the moon-lit street. Finally he went back to bed, piling the covers up to ward off his chill.

Ketch was asleep beside him when he woke in the morning, the covers thrown off, the dark red T-shirt she wore rucked up to her waist. Back arched, legs bent, arms stretched above head. It looked like the most uncomfortable way to sleep that Tietjen had ever seen. Gingerly he got out of bed, pulled on pants and a singlet, went into the other room to make coffee on the tiny campstove in his kitchen and sit in the window to drink it.

"Hey." Ketch, dark hair rumpled, her eyes slitted against the sunlight, stood in the bedroom door, scratching her hip dozily. Relaxed, without the tough-girl tension in her face, her mouth was soft and sensual. "What time is it?"

Tietjen looked at his watch. "Seven. What time'd you get in?"

She shrugged. "Four-something. Wanna come back to bed?" The smile and the smoky lift of her eyebrow made the casual question less casual.

Tietjen looked out the window. "I ought to get to work," he said. "You go back, though."

Ketch's back stiffened. "Figures," she said quietly. She turned away, heading back to bed.

What did I do? Tietjen wondered. Aloud he said, "Li? What?"

She didn't turn to look at him, just shook her head. "You wouldn't get it. G'wan, now." She dropped back onto the bed with her face turned toward the wall, ostentatiously settling herself for sleep.

"Goddammit, what's going on? What wouldn't I get?" Irene had fought just the same way, by accusing and refusing to explain, hanging him on his own incomprehension. He hated it. "What is it?"

Ketch rolled over, up to sitting. "I get a little tired of being the last resort, okay? It would be nice to be someone you *wanted* to play hooky with, even if you knew you couldn't. I'm, like, what you do when it's too dark out to work and no one else wants to sit and plan with you. Christ, you could take up whittling and not miss me."

He stood there with his mouth open, unable to think of a thing to say. "That's not true," he said at last.

She sighed. "Not exactly true, but true. John, why'd you get involved with me in the first place?"

Because you asked was the first thought he had, but he knew how damning that would be. "I liked you. And you seemed to like me."

"I did. I do. God knows why, though. I've never been involved with anyone as—Christ, I don't know what to call it. Even gang boys let you in closer than you do, John."

Stung, Tietjen tried to throw the accusation back at her. "Li, I never thought you wanted to be that involved with *me*. I thought you liked this because it was—loose."

"Loose is okay. But it's like there's this plate-glass thing runs all around you; I can see in, I can touch you, but I can't get hold of you. I don't even know if I really want to grab hold of you, you know? But I'd just have liked to have the option."

Again he felt angry. What did she want from him? "There's nothing around me; I'm right here, but I'm just me, right? If that isn't enough for you—I'm sorry," he finished lamely.

Ketch stood up, dropped the sheet, pulled the T-shirt over her head in one easy motion. Her stomach was flat, breasts small; her thighs were thick and muscular; she looked powerful, even tossing through a pile of clothes for the shorts and tank suit she had worn the night before.

"Not enough. Fuck this, I don't need it. Look, any time you want to get real, John, you know where to find me."

"Is this because I wasn't going to stay? Li, if it's important to you—"

She shook her head. "It's not about getting laid. It's about being important to you, and I'm not. I can't compete with the Store; I don't *feel* like competing with the Store. I'll come around later and pick up the rest of my stuff." She bent and picked up the ankle-high hiking boots she'd worn last night, slung them over her shoulder by the laces, and walked out.

Tietjen watched her go. She was wrong. He knew it, but he couldn't think of what to say to her. He went to the window and stared out unseeingly, trying to figure it out. Maybe he kept thinking of Irene because of the dream he'd had—his hands clenched when he recalled it—but it felt like Ketch had been using her words, her arguments. They didn't make any more sense to him now then they had years ago. He heard a voice, one of the men calling something below, and remembered that he wanted to start a survey of water tanks in the neighborhood. Tietjen left his apartment and went downstairs.

Jit lay under the ground, in his tunnel, listening. The Man was still angry and scared and confused by the dream Jit had sent, and that was good. Jit had made the dream out of found images, true rememberings that had slowly washed back into him like a lazy tide. He had matched the woman to memories in the Man's own dreams and known that this would be a dream that would hurt. There were other memories and stories Jit could use later. And the Man had fought with the dark woman and she'd left. Jit didn't understand the emotions or the words, but the result—that the man was alone again—was what mattered. *Wait you see what else Jit can do,* he thought, and grinned.

Tietjen didn't avoid Ketch; she didn't avoid him. He had never declared her his consort, and she had never demanded to be treated that way, although her occasional public intimacy had always left him feeling rattled. They behaved now as if nothing had happened, still conferred together, ate together sometimes and apart sometimes. Li was still one of the people with whom he took walks, like in the old days, miles-long hikes south and west, to investigate the damage around town, to bring in new people, find resources. On the walks she was a little quieter than formerly, but seemed determined that nothing would be any different. He was relieved about that.

If anyone wondered about them, Tietjen was not aware of it.

Even now, as the leader of the Store, he found it difficult to believe that anyone would care who he slept with, who he loved.

Barbara seemed to have noticed something, but she said nothing, and he couldn't find a way to open the subject. Tact itself, Barbara was. Whenever he left on one of his walks she'd see him off, joking about packing him a box lunch, her fine features lit with a smile that was the last thing he saw of the Store when he left. Sometimes he thought he saw a shadow on her face—Barbara, the least shadowy, least hidden person he knew—and that was when he wondered if she'd noticed about his split with Ketch. She would probably have something comforting to say, but Tietjen wasn't in the mood for comforting.

At the end of each scouting trip when he returned, Barbara would be waiting to hear about it, nodding, asking good questions, reporting on what had happened in the hours since he had left. He teased her once about being the Mother to the Store, "like we're all playing House, and I'm the Daddy and you're Mother"—but when she frowned at him and changed the subject, Tietjen realized he'd presumed too much on their friendship. Still, sometimes he thought of her that way, to himself: the gracious, thoughtful, clever den mother to all of them. When he thought about it, she really did not resemble Irene at all.

3

DREAMS were not enough. It was time to hurt someone.

Jit had tasted Tee-jin's fear and his sorrow with each dream and story he had sent, and he knew they were working. But the Man didn't stop, didn't run away, didn't face his fear. Did not acknowledge Jit's power. He didn't bleed the way Jit wanted, rich and fast-flowing: the Man bled slowly, little hurts that didn't satisfy.

Jit had sent him more stories after the Irene-woman dream. The best was the story of his babies, little boys crying for their Mommy and Daddy, locked in a tiny room where they had hidden when the bad things started happening. At first Jit had savored the taste of their panic as fingers of smoke combed their hair and tickled them into coughing. He felt Tee-jin's sleeping face crumple up in pain, listening to their baby voices as they got softer and softer, drowsing off to death. He rolled the taste of the Man's guilt and anger and despair when he heard what his babies were waiting for: for him to come and get them, for him to be their Daddy, who was big and could do anything. For him to make them safe. . . . At the end he sent the Man a picture of his babies, tousled and rosy, curled in each other's arms, dead and reproachful, and let the man watch as the skin slowly puckered and sizzled in the flames that finally found them.

It was a good dream for the Man, Jit thought, but he didn't listen too closely to it himself—something about those feelings made Jit uncomfortable. It was not fear he disliked; he knew fear too well, it was familiar and tasted safe to him. But the *wanting*, the waiting for someone to make them safe, the believing made Jit mad. Those babies never lived long enough to know that no one was coming, not the Irene-woman, not Tee-jin, not nobody. Jit had known that for years, forever. No one came, no one stayed. *No one,* he thought at the Man.

The Man cried some nights, in the dark. Jit heard him, listened to the crying until it filled him up warmly like a good stew, tasted Tee-jin's grief on his own tongue. The Man cried, but it wasn't enough. Every morning he went back outside and started talking with the other people, making things, giving orders, living. Crying wasn't enough. Jit wanted the Man to know who hated him.

It was time to hurt someone.

The more things went on track at the Store, the more it seemed to Tietjen that he was falling apart. He dreamed of Irene, and Davy and Chris. He dreamed of his mother dying years before in a cancer hospice, her skin pocked with IV sticks and gummy with adhesive from monitor leads, the unyielding fluorescent glare of the hospice room gradually driving her toward the light that everyone swore would welcome her. . . . In the dream, as in his memories, she railed against him and the doctors and the disease, all of them conspiring to kill her, spitting with rage as the cancer ate away at her: "You never loved me. You never loved me. If you'd loved me you'd have saved me."

He had wakened from that dream in tears, staggered out of bed, and vomited, the tears still running down his face.

All his dreams seemed haunted by death: one night he dreamed of a deer he'd hit while driving down a dark country road at night, felt the meaty impact in his own body, saw the blood that fanned across the windshield, felt the animal's deep wordless terror in the approach of headlights, the sudden blinking out of fear and light and life. . . . He dreamed of death and pain, until he dreaded sleep.

He was always tired. In his waking moments, as he watched the Store deepen its roots, grow and strengthen and reach out to gather in survivors and insure its own survival, Tietjen would drift off into reveries on failure: daydreams of his own bumbling, times when his stupidity, his inability to understand the people around him had let him hurt people, disappoint them. In the middle of a reverie someone would come to him with a question, Beth Voe or Ketch or Bobby Fratelone, and Tietjen would stare at them blankly for a moment, unable to understand why they wanted an answer from him.

What could he possibly say that would help them?

Then after a moment he remembered, pulled his thoughts together, solved the problem or posed a new question, absorbed the data, gave directions. It bothered him that no one seemed to see that he was falling apart. Ketch was cordial but never came close enough to see what was happening. Barbara maybe saw something, but stayed distant, as if she was afraid to ask if he was all right. Bobby and Lo-yi and Beth and all the others saw only the guy who gave them answers and directions. He was passing for whole, passing for able. But he didn't know how long he could do it.

When he could, when there was time, he did what he had always done and went back to the city for help. Waking from nightmares, he climbed up to the twelfth floor each night and sat himself in a window, looking out over the dark shadows of the city, his mind supplying details his eye couldn't see. When the sun came up he was often still there. And he walked, sometimes with the scavenging parties, but more often alone; it was hard for him to keep his eyes to the ground as he should, read signs, look for drugstores and grocers and hardware and book and electronics and clothes stores. He wanted to look up, examining the stonework, drawing strength from the solidity of the city around him, closing his eyes in prayer to the spirit that still, for him, kept New York alive.

And he could hardly tell anyone about that. Barbara might understand. Might. No one else would, even Ketch. No one else in the Store saw what they were building as anything but a lifeboat for an indefinite stay. Over the months he had seen each person in the Store realize that help, if it ever came, was not coming soon, that they had to make the Store work. Elena and Sandy had a school for the children; Barbara's infirmary was stocked and equipped with the best they could steal; the garden Beth and Elena had planted was already showing life. It was all about survival.

Only Tietjen felt he was dying, bit by bit.

Bobby's arm had been pronounced sound again. At least McGrath had examined it, made him bend the arm every which way, consulted two books, and admitted that since they had kept the arm immobilized for four weeks and he showed no discomfort, that was the only way she had to gauge his fitness.

Bobby grunted that he was fine, what was the fuss? But he grinned when Ketch and a few of the others threw a "coming out" party for his arm after Barbara removed the zipcast, and sat drinking beer and listening to the others gossip about the past. Greg Feinberg showed up with a battery-powered boomer and a pile of disks, and Ketch sorted through them, taking half a dozen from the pile and tossing the rest to one side, uncaring of Greg's chagrin.

Tietjen and McGrath watched from a table against the wall as Ketch put music on and began to dance with Gellis. It was gaido, street music with a heavy thudding bass line and high, wailing vocals; Tietjen had never cared much for it. Ketch and Gellis moved together hip to hip, hands upraised and eyes closed, swaying.

He realized Barbara was watching him. "She's good," he said at last. He could not think of what else to say.

Barbara nodded.

Fratelone came over to join them, draped his healed arm across Barbara's shoulders. "Dance?" There was something boyish about him when he asked, shy and daring at the same time; it sat oddly on blockish, undemonstrative Bobby.

Barbara smiled at him. "Sure. John?" she turned back to Tietjen, excusing herself.

"What? Oh, sure." He was a little surprised to hear Barbara say yes; thought it was rather like a teenager asking the chaperone at a prom to dance, and anyway, Bobby would have to teach her the steps.

Only he didn't; she taught *him*, moving with a loose, easy authority that startled Tietjen. Among the other couples moving in the center of the room to the percussive beat, Barbara looked at home, arms raised in a graceful, sensual curve above her head, rib cage swaying in opposition to hips, back and forth. Meanwhile Bobby ducked and hopped, hopelessly separate from the rhythm despite Barbara's best efforts to guide him. Finally, laughing, she steered him off the floor.

Tietjen didn't see what happened, only that one moment Bobby Fratelone was coming toward him, chagrined at his failure, head turned to listen to Barbara's laughing reassurance. The next minute Bobby was on the floor screaming, his left leg bent at a sickening angle. As he moved forward to help, Tietjen could see nothing that

Bobby could have tripped over, nothing that would have hit him, no one except Barbara near enough to have been able to strike or push or pull him down.

"What happened?" he muttered to McGrath as he knelt next to her.

She shook her head. "He just—dropped. Like that. I don't know. Bobby? Bobby, we've got to straighten that leg, sweetheart." Her voice gentle and steely at the same time, McGrath put one hand on Fratelone's thigh, the other on his shin. She motioned to Tietjen to help her and he reached down to grasp the man's shin, feeling the rough, uneven scar tissue on the back of the leg, where he had been flayed by Gable's people. McGrath shook her head. "Hold his shoulders," she murmured. "Okay, sweetheart, this is going to hurt like Holy Fuck-me," she said, deadpan.

The shock of profanity worked. Fratelone gave a ghostly, painful smile. When Barbara grasped the shin and turned the leg to face its proper direction he jerked under Tietjen's hands, but did not cry out, did not pull away. "Holy Fuck-me," he agreed weakly, and fainted.

"Let's take advantage of the faint and get him upstairs," Barbara said to the crowd around them. "Four people—bring him up to the infirmary. I want to get some of the cast on while he's still unconscious."

The party broke up. Ketch and Gellis, holding hands unselfconsciously, paused by Tietjen to ask what happened, but he shook his head, shrugged his shoulders. *Jesus, what a hell of a thing.* What could make a man's leg just break like that, no fall, no blow, nothing.

"Delayed stress, I guess. Maybe the dancing set it off," Barbara told him later that night when he stopped in the infirmary to see how Fratelone was doing. His leg was cased in zipcast and plaster from thigh to heel and he was sleeping. "He insists someone hit him—with a baseball bat, I think he said. I will say, it *looked* like someone had hit him with a baseball bat: lots of surface bruising, abrasion, that kind of stuff. But I think you can have spontaneous bone fractures if there's been earlier damage. I *think.*" Barbara's face settled into an expression Tietjen recognized from the night Kathy Calvino was so sick: a hard cold hatred of her own helplessness. "I set it the

best I could, but God knows what that leg is going to come out looking like, working like. I may have crippled Bobby for life. Dammit,
there has to be some way to get out of New York and get help."

There was no use arguing about it; every couple of weeks a
scouting party would attempt to cross the river to the Bronx, or to
leave the city in some other way: by raft to Brooklyn or New Jersey.
Something always stopped them; they were as sealed *in* as the rest of
the world, apparently, was sealed out.

In the morning Fratelone insisted again that someone had hit
him. "With a bat, Boss. Something like. I don't fall for nothin' less,"
he maintained.

Tietjen, remembering the scene, Bobby, head turned, walking
away from the dancers—no baseball bats, no attackers, no one behind him at all—nodded and agreed that something weird must have
happened.

"Damn bet," Fratelone said.

Then the room was filled with the Store's children, the Calvino
girls in the lead, who had come to sign Bobby's cast. The tough-guy
mask settled more securely over Bobby's ashy features; he was gruff
with the kids, pretending irritation. Tietjen was startled to realize
that all the kids, not just the Calvinos, but the others as well, loved
Bobby.

"No purple on my cast," he was saying. "Purple's some kind of
sissy color. No purple, you kids," he was saying loudly, as one of the
boys wielded a purple marker over his knee.

Tietjen edged toward the door, feeling as though he had somehow invaded Bobby's life and found something he wasn't supposed
to know. *Bobby Fratelone is a sucker for kids.* As Tietjen went out
the door he passed Barbara, shook his head, and muttered, "It's a
zoo in there." She grinned and answered, "I know. Great, isn't it?"

Bobby's accident was the first of the small accidents and catas-
trophes that beset the Store in the next few weeks. Small things,
nearly explainable: a ball bearing rolled under a plank which slipped
out from under one of the carpentry crew and sent him flying across
the room; Elena's arm scalded by boiling water from a cooking pot
("But I'd only started heating it," she wept as Barbara took her upstairs to the infirmary. "It was just getting warm!"); a plague of bat-
tered thumbs and splinters and cuts among the work crews; a
salvage crew that brought back nothing more than poison ivy.

"It's like we broke a mirror or something," Tietjen heard Greg Feinberg saying to Sandy Hochman one afternoon. "Everybody's got bad luck."

Sandy shook her head and said she didn't believe in luck. Not since her husband's death, Tietjen thought. She had changed, a rosy-faced, plump woman with an easy laugh, become gray and spare, tender with her daughter Missy, evenhanded and dutiful with everyone else. Like Barbara without the grace notes, Tietjen thought, and then felt ashamed of the thought. Sandy had been through enough.

They had spent weeks clearing a vacant lot three buildings to the east of the Store of rubble, trash, and bodies—there had been an apartment building there before the disaster, not a beautiful building, Tietjen remembered: a solid square hulk of limestone with its one beauty, a pair of iron and glass doors, hidden by the security grille. Now they were building a fence to keep out scavengers from their garden. Lo-yi and some of the gardening crew were turning the earth over, breaking it up, preparing the soil. Sandy and Greg knelt to one side, making improvised grapestake fencing, nailing slats and pickets to one-by-fours. Tietjen was working in Lo-yi's crew, hoeing up earth until his shoulders ached unmercifully, enjoying the freedom of being just another member of the crew, taking Lo-yi's terse orders with pleasure. The sun had been brutally hot in the middle of the day, but now the air was gentled with a light breeze, and the worst of the day's heat had faded. It was nearly quitting time.

Tietjen paused to wipe his forehead on his T-shirt, which he had stuffed into his back pocket like a rag once the heat got bad. So he was watching as Sandy Hochman leaned around Greg, dug her hands into a bucket of nails, pulled out a handful—

—and screamed, opening her hand to drop the nails, then shaking it as if something dreadful clung there, then cradling the hand in her arm and bowing over it, keening.

Greg turned away just long enough to yell for Tietjen, who had already started over to the fence. The boy was trying to tug Sandy out of her curl, to see what had happened to her hand. She kept rocking and saying, "Hot, hot, hot."

"See if there's anything in that bucket," Tietjen said, thinking perhaps something had crawled into the bucket and bitten Sandy. Beth Voe, who had been putting up the fencing, dropped to her knees beside Sandy and, arm around her shoulder, coaxed the older woman to lean into her side, relax against her, let someone examine her hand.

He expected to see a welt or a bite, maybe even the marks of a snakebite. Instead, there were the stigmata of branding, as if the handful of nails Sandy had grabbed had turned suddenly white hot. As Tietjen looked, the burns began to blister. One of the men picked Sandy up and began to carry her off toward the Store.

"What the hell happened," Tietjen asked Greg as Beth moved out of earshot.

"I don't know," the kid said desperately. "Sandy picked up some nails, and like, she was just about to start work again when she started screaming, like. Saying they were burning her."

"Was the bucket hot?" Tietjen asked. The boy shook his head. "Was there any way the bucket could have gotten hot?" he asked.

Again, Greg shook his head. "I don't know what happened. I thought maybe it was a hornet or something, but you saw what happened to her hand, sir." The word made Tietjen uncomfortably aware that he was supposed to supply the answers.

"Where are the nails she dropped?" Tietjen asked.

Mostly they were scattered, flung down when Sandy felt the pain. But they found a clump of nails, welded together into a bristling lump. Melted. Tietjen and Greg and Lo-yi stared at the clump of nails. How much heat would it take to melt No. 10 flathead nails that way? And why did the bucket and the nails still in it show no sign of heat? They were as cool to the touch as the bucket itself.

"Close-up time, bring your tools!" Lo-yi called to the people who were still there. As he gathered up the hoe he had been using—and Sandy Hochman's hammer and rule—Tietjen felt the others watching him. Resentfully, he thought.

"It's beginning again, dammit." He said it to himself. Something weird was happening. Things that shouldn't happen, the sorts of things that he thought had died with Gable on the floor of Grand Central, were happening. The people of the Store thought everything was normal again. What the hell was this weirdness to break that deal?

When he got back to the Store Barbara was waiting.

"I've treated the hand best I could, and given her antibiotics to keep off infection." It seemed to Tietjen that she, too, looked at him as if he had failed to keep the injury from happening. "What *happened*?"

He told her. As he was telling her, Barbara's mouth straightened into a hard line.

"It's after us again," she muttered angrily.

"What?"

She turned back to him. "Come on, John. Haven't you *known* there was something behind all the things that have happened since the disaster? Some kind of intelligence? We can't get out of Manhattan; no one's come in to help us; all this weird stuff keeps happening, the monsters, and the lions the day we went to Grand Central—"

"The lions were on our side," he protested. Tietjen didn't want to have this argument, certainly not with Barbara. Because if he admitted that something was directing Sandy's accident and Bobby's, and the rash of ill luck that had beset the Store in the last few weeks, he would have to believe that it must be the city itself doing it, and he couldn't believe that. Nothing else, he thought, had that kind of power, and after so many losses he could not bear to believe that the city itself could turn against him. Rather than acknowledge the power or the blind faithlessness with which it seemed to operate, he would refuse to believe there was any logic to the things that had been happening.

"What do you think, it's like the Wicked Witch of the West sending out her weirdness troops to get us? Come on, Barbara . . . This isn't personal, it's chaos, that stuff I talked about months ago. I think it's chaos, and it's left little pockets of weirdness here and there, that we keep stumbling over. Okay?" He needed to convince her, and was relieved when she seemed to *be* convinced. Her shoulders relaxed, and her face lost the stricken look.

"Sandy will be all right," she said at last. "Her hand will. But she's sort of shut down, right now. She won't even see Missy." Tietjen didn't know what to say to her. "Give her time, I guess," Barbara answered herself after a long silence. "I've got kitchen duty with Elena tonight. See you later, John."

•   •   •

After Sandy's accident the spate of injuries seemed to have run its course, but unaccountable accidents and things breaking, or running down, or going haywire, still seemed to haunt the Store. The batteries that supplied power for the lights and the few electric appliances the Store used—a refrigerator in the kitchen and one in Barbara's infirmary—all died one morning, and the backups proved useless. A layer of cement poured over the broken slate floor in the basement of the building next door refused to harden and cure: after six days it remained as soupy as the day it was poured. Every single piece of lumber cut to measure for the new gate to the Store was found to be off in length or width by exactly half an inch, either too much or too little. The ax heads came loose from the handles—one flew across the alley and narrowly missed one of the kids playing handball there. Lo-yi almost fertilized the new garden with rat poison, and insisted later that the label on the bag had read Fertilizer.

But no one was hurt. Just a pocket of bad luck, Tietjen told himself. They'd been so lucky, really.

In the midst of all this it was a relief to go out with the salvage parties. Tietjen joined one that went as far down as Houston Street, where he saw for himself the drowned spires of lower Manhattan. Little Italy and Chinatown and all but the roofs of SoHo were under water; the ground seemed to dip down sharply just after Houston, making a new shoreline. The upper stories of the Puck Building still rose out of the lapping green water. Lulled by the soft slap of the water on the cobblestones at his feet, Tietjen imagined swimming from rooftop to rooftop, diving down through the windows to wander from room to room in the old tenement flats, seeing the lives there undisturbed, pictures in place, furniture ordered and waiting. In fact, when he tried swimming out to a rooftop and then down, into an apartment, it was too dark to make much out; even when he came back with a flashlight, he saw only barnacles clinging to the furniture, and a pair of bloated bodies bobbing along the ceiling, placidly nibbled at by fish. He turned and kicked back up to the surface and did not try again.

Drying in the sun, safe on the shore looking south, he could see the glittering uppermost floors of buildings which had been skyscrapers. The Customs House was under water, he thought sadly. The Stock Exchange. Old City Hall. Beautiful old buildings, all of them, lost underwater while their characterless cousins of the last fifty years survived.

On the trip they found some salvage, picked up a couple of people who cautiously came along "to see what you got up there," and as always on salvage trips, burned bodies they found. What did it say about him, Tietjen wondered, that he had become expert at locating dead bodies by smell? Now, nearly six months since the disaster, the smells were usually subtler, less horrible than in the first weeks, and the bodies more desiccated and less like something human. Still, it was agreed among everyone at the Store that one of their jobs was to dispose of the dead, and any salvage group might stop several times to say a word over dead bodies, then burn them. On this trip they stopped four times. The next day, after a night spent camping in the shattered atrium of a handsome new condo building in Chelsea, the party headed back to the Store. It was late afternoon when they got there; crews were still out, having rested during the fiercest part of the day's heat. Lo-yi was in the garden with half a dozen helpers; the grapestake fence, painted white, shone in the late sun. A woman was sitting on a windowsill washing the window, one of Sandy's crew. Near the roof a makeshift scaffold rocked slightly as three people moved back and forth. Repointing the brick near the roofline, he thought; Gellis and Ketch and Jimmy Weeks, one of Bobby's recruits.

He stood for a moment, drinking in the sight of home and its activity. Barbara was probably in the infirmary, Elena in the kitchen or the basement room that had been turned into a classroom. The woman—no, there were two, in different fifth-floor windows— washing windows made him nervous. Leaning out too far, trusting to the sills to hold; were they secured in any way? Had Barbara permitted this?

He did not see the fall begin. A blur of motion caught his eye; then he heard the screams. For a moment long enough to see that the window washers were still in their windows, looking down, horror-stricken, he did not realize who had fallen or from where.

Near the roof, the scaffold dangled in two useless pieces, snapped in half. Gellis swung from one half, his leg tangled in one of the ropes, holding on with both hands, screaming for help. Jimmy Weeks stood dumbly at the roof's edge for a moment before he began to pull on the rope, trying to raise Gellis up. Ketch had fallen.

Tietjen ran with everyone else, the people in the garden, his own raiding party. He pushed his way through the crowd to where Li lay, broken and somehow still alive. She'd taken the impact feet first; her legs were shattered, bits of bone splintered through the skin. Maybe her back was broken too, he thought. Her eyes were open and she recognized him.

"Ahh, shit," she wept. "Ahh, shit, John."

He was afraid to gather her up in an embrace that might have comforted her, afraid of hurting her further. Instead he lay beside her, stroked her hair from her forehead, murmuring "Shhh, shhhh," as he might have to a sick child.

"Damn, I can't even feel my feet," she said. "I must be pretty fucked up." She smiled and winced and smiled again, pure bravado.

"Shhh, Li. Don't talk. We're going to bring you inside and get you all fixed up—" he began. But it was useless, she knew too much. The look Ketch gave him made it possible for him to go on. Internal injuries, dozens of fractures, probably. Even a hospital might not be able to fix her; what the hell could he and Barbara do?

"Miz McGrath's gonna be deeply pissed," Li said, echoing his thoughts. "Damn, I kinda wish it hurt a little. This is sort of scary, you know?" Her voice was filled with liquid trills, as if she were drowning from the inside out. It took Tietjen a moment to realize that maybe she was.

"Lie still," he said, sick. As he said it he had a flash of Li in his bed, moving beneath him, her dark eyes looking up at him as they did now, asking for something from him. How simple had it been to give her pleasure? It was impossible to help her now.

Her breathing became more liquid. The only other thing she said was "*You* know, John." Then she worked at breathing for a little while longer. Someone had brought a blanket to cover her legs and fend off chill in the relentless afternoon heat; she smiled gratefully but said nothing.

Powerless, horrified, Tietjen lay there stroking her hair and murmuring stupid, comforting noises, past the time when Ketch's liquid breathing had stopped.

"John." It was Barbara, just behind him. "John, get up now and let us take care of her."

Numbly he stood up and let someone take him away. Gellis, rescued from the scaffolding, came forward to explain, but Tietjen waved him away; what the hell did it matter?

"It just melted out from under us," he heard Gellis saying. "Solid as a fucking rock, then gone." Tietjen heard the horror in the other man's voice, and remembered that perhaps he had loved Li too.

"Not your fault," he mumbled, then turned away and blindly made his way into the Store, upstairs to his own room where he could be alone. He did not think of leading, of the Store, of what anyone would think.

He sat on the edge of the bed he and Ketch had shared and sent a thought, a prayer out, not really believing anything would answer. "What the hell do you want from me?"

Of course there was no answer. The silence rang like laughter in his head.

TIETJEN went up to his room that night after dinner and the quick memorial service that Lo-yi and Barbara had staged. He lay on his bed for hours, staring at the ceiling. He was unable to stop the slow replay of Ketch's fall from the scaffolding and the way she had slipped away from him, sliding into death. In memory he traced the tear that had rolled from the inside corner of her eye, down the side of her nose, moistening her lips, cutting through the powdering of grime. He could still feel her broken weight imprinted on the muscles of his arms.

Even in the dark, sounds, voices mostly, filtered in from the hallway, up from the alleyway. Every now and then Tietjen heard footsteps near his doorway, voices speaking low. The second time it happened he realized that McGrath had stationed herself outside his door, turning the well-wishers away. Taking care of everything as usual. Taking care of him. Thank you, Barbara. Now and then Tietjen thought he should go out to the hallway and tell her he was all right, she could go to her own room and get some sleep. But it was comforting to have her there, so much so that he could not make himself send her away.

The apartment was still and hot. He moved slightly to unstick the sheets from his back and legs. Tietjen did not want to sleep and dream of Ketch. Remembering was bad enough. When he closed his eyes he listened for sounds he had not heard in months; the rattle of cars and buses on the avenue, the faint sizzle of the streetlamp outside his window. All he heard was Barbara outside his door, murmuring that he shouldn't be disturbed tonight.

When he drifted to sleep at last, he did not dream of Ketch but of his sons. He knew at once it was not a true dream, as the ones about Irene, and his mother, and about the boys during the disaster had been. In this dream he was walking through the zoo in Central Park, the way he remembered it from his boyhood, bright, safe, well maintained. The zoo was empty of people. Tietjen wandered around, spent some time watching the polar bears and the penguins, before he moved on to the next exhibit. It was an old-fashioned iron cage; on the other side of the bars Chris and Davy stood, staring blankly past Tietjen. He called their names but they didn't respond, just held on to the bars of their cage and ignored him. When he reached for them through the bars the boys shied away. Tietjen looked around him for someone to help, but there was no one. He climbed over the guardrail and reached again into the cage. The boys looked at him anxiously for a moment; it was only when they turned and ran that Tietjen realized the cage had no back wall and that his sons had run away into the Park, into the city, where he would never find them. He was left clutching the bars, watching the boys as they ran, watching long after they had vanished into the green of the Park, trapped behind the bars and unable to run himself.

In the morning he rose and dressed and went downstairs for breakfast at the same time as always. He felt people watching him, but no one said anything. It irritated him, being watched that way. He felt as if they were waiting for him to go crazy. They should know by now, Tietjen thought. After everything they'd been through they should know he wouldn't blow up.

Barbara came and sat down beside him. She smiled matter-of-factly, but Tietjen suspected that she was watching him too. They ate in silence for a few minutes, as long as Tietjen could bear it. Finally he put down his fork and turned to her.

"*What?*" he asked.

A corner of Barbara's mouth turned up. "Nothing particular. How are you doing?"

"I'm not rabid. I wish people would stop looking at me as if I were a bomb about to go off."

Barbara kept her eyes on her plate, where she was tracing patterns in her grits with the tines of her fork. "I don't think 'bomb' is what people are thinking, John. Give us some credit—we're concerned about you."

Sullenly, Tietjen looked down at his own plate. "I'm okay, all right? You don't have to watch me. I'm not going to start screaming or anything."

"Why not? Aside from the therapeutic benefits, it'd let people around you know that you're human."

"Human!" He felt like his head would explode. "I'm just the same as always. I got some sleep, I'm eating something . . . like a normal person."

"John." She put her hand on his forearm firmly. His mother used to hold him just that way, keeping him still until he could think things through. "It's *not* like always. Ketch died yesterday, in your arms. Did you think no one knew that the two of you were involved? Do you think no one cares about your grief? Everyone is watching you—and Marty Gellis—and no one expects you to act like everything's all right. Lighten up, okay? People need to worry a little."

Tietjen looked at the hand on his arm, losing himself for a moment in tracing the veins on the back of it, noting Barbara's long fingers, the dull jade of the ring she wore. In the green of the stone he remembered his dream, his sons running from him while he stood behind bars watching, always watching. Lighten up. "Okay," he said at last.

He wasn't sure what he was promising when he said it, and he suspected that Barbara knew that. Still, she released his arm. After a moment they began to talk about the water tanks on the buildings across the street.

Tietjen moved through the haze of sympathy that surrounded him for a few days, working hard to accept graciously the smiles and pats, the questions and murmured condolences. The first time he and Marty Gellis ate dinner at the same table there was an awkward hush; Tietjen thought the people watching them were waiting to see if their bereavements consumed each other or struck sparks. After a few minutes Tietjen asked Gellis a question, Gellis answered, they spoke for a few minutes between mouthsful. The electricity in the air dissipated quickly then: no sparks at all.

Tietjen worked until he could only stagger upstairs to sleep. When he was working and around other people, he didn't think too much or too long about Ketch's death, or Irene's or Chris's and Davy's, or about Bobby's fractured arm and leg. Once he opened a door to such thoughts, every passing notion or memory led back to death or disaster. When he was overwhelmed this way the only thing Tietjen could do was blink and breathe hard and hope the thoughts would go away. If he looked into the tarry blackness too long, he was afraid he would never escape.

Despite his exhaustion there were still some nights he could not sleep. It was not just missing Ketch; she'd been gone from his room and his bed for a while before her death. But Tietjen was lonely. It seemed to him that the more established the community he had founded became, the further away from it he grew. What was it that was drawing him away? The darkness he knew was still out there, that no one wanted to hear about. Was he the only one who saw the blackness? Was he the only one there who knew that the city was not done with them? When the loneliness got bad Tietjen would climb upstairs to look out at the city, but more and more that was not a hiding place either.

One evening McGrath found him sitting on the stair between the sixth and seventh floors, slumped back so the risers cut into his shoulder blades. The stairwell was bathed in moonlight, which threw Art Deco shadows against the walls; Barbara's hair and skin took on the silvery blue of the light and made her look carved out of marble or silver. She sat down on a lower stair and for a little while they were quiet and the loneliness in Tietjen subsided a bit.

Finally, Barbara murmured, "Why is moonlight supposed to be romantic? It always looks creepy to me."

Tietjen smiled. "Me too. Makes you look like the ice lady."

"I'm not," Barbara said, too quickly and too coldly. Then she leaned back again and said more easily, "You look wrung out."

"In the moonlight?"

She shook her head. "For a while now you've been looking bad, John. It's not just Ketch's death; you've been in trouble for weeks now. What's going on?"

He wanted to say, and believe, that it was nothing. "I don't know. It's nerves, my imagination, something like that. Only a feeling . . ." It sounded so insubstantial Tietjen did not want to go on.

"Feelings count," Barbara prodded dryly. "I'll trade you a feeling. Sometimes I get a sense that I'm being watched." She threw the words out with an elaborate casualness which was not at all casual. "No, not watched. Like someone was eavesdropping." She laughed. "It's a little weird."

It was Tietjen's turn to shake his head. "Not that weird, Barbara. I feel that way sometimes, too. And worse."

"Worse?" She leaned back farther and tilted her head toward him so that her hair drooped over one eye. There was some old film actress, Tietjen remembered; from the black-and-white era, someone famous for the hair that fell in her eyes. Barbara looked unaccountably seductive in that pose; it made him uncomfortable. He shook his head and concentrated on trying to make his thoughts clear.

"I've been having dreams for weeks—since right after we fought the monsters at Grand Central. Dreams about Irene and the kids and my mother, about how each of them died. What's weird is that I know they're true."

Barbara turned. "How horrible." Her face was right side up now, the hair out of her eye. She looked herself, and worried. "But how can you know they're real, John?"

"The same way we knew that Grand Central was where we'd find Gable and his people. That kind of knowing. Irene was trampled to death in a stairwell at Macy's. The boys were in the babysitting room in their building and a fire broke out, and they hid in the bathroom and—just passed out, waiting for Mommy and Daddy to come save them." Tietjen couldn't control his voice, which was shaking and wet. "My mother—how the hell would it know about my mother, she died six years ago. Cancer. She was so brave, we all thought she was so brave . . . and in the end she died hating us. God, the way she hated everyone who was living, the nurses, the doctors. Me. Especially me. And she kept smiling and smiling until there was nothing left of her but the drugs, and the drugs told us everything she'd hidden from us."

The shaking in his voice got too bad for him to continue. Tietjen hung his head and waited for it to stop. Without words, Barbara moved from the step she had been sitting on and sat next to him, gathering him into her arms as unself-consciously as if he had been five years old. "Shhh," she murmured. "How horrible, shhh. It's okay, it's okay." Sweet, meaningless sounds that gave him time to recover. She rocked him, with his head against her shoulder, stroking the hair away from his forehead. Tietjen listened to the strong beat of her heart under his cheek.

"It's not just the dreams," he said at last. "Whatever is watching us *hates*. I don't know if it's me or the Store or—I can't help feeling that all the shit that's been happening, Bobby's leg breaking and Sandy's hand, and Ketch—"

Barbara pushed him away from her. "Don't say they're your fault, John. The Store doesn't need that kind of self-aggrandizing guilt crapping up the works, do you hear?" She looked stern, not angry, but there had been real force in her hands as she held him away from her.

Tietjen sighed. "It's just, they all feel related. Like whatever killed Ketch sent my dreams."

"Look." Barbara settled next to him again, her hand loose around his arm. "Maybe what happened to Ketch was bad luck. Maybe what happened to Bobby and Sandy was back luck or some freak of nature we don't know anything about. Maybe all the shit we've been through in the last six, seven months has loosened up a lot of repressed guilt in you, and that's why the bad dreams. Maybe we only think we're being listened to because this is a big city and we're not used to it being so quiet. Maybe, huh?"

For a few moments her words hung in the air of the stairwell, shimmering in the moonlight. At last Tietjen sighed and put his arm around Barbara, leaning his head against the top of her head. Her curling white hair tickled at his chin and nose, but he didn't move. "Yeah, maybe," he said. "Barbara, of all the things that have happened in the city since I got back, finding you was definitely the best." He kissed the top of her head quickly, then released her and stood up. "It's going to be another hot day tomorrow. We should try to sleep."

Barbara nodded, but did not rise. "You go ahead down. I'll follow in a couple. I want to enjoy the moonlight."

"You're sure?"

"Yes, I'm sure. You afraid I'm going to run into trouble between here and the second floor?"

Tietjen smiled. "You're too tough for trouble. I'll see you in the morning." He turned and went down the stairs, feeling her eyes on him as he went, a comfortable sense of being watched.

• • •

Through the Old Woman's eyes, Jit watched the Man go downstairs. The woman was filled with an excitement Jit did not understand, something about the cuddling and the words that had been spoken. What Jit understood from the words was that the Man had begun to acknowledge Jit's power. The Old Woman had tried to turn Tee-jin away from it, but the Man knew.

Jit lay under a tree near the old zoo on the east side of the Park. He was curled up on a pile of blankets, a circle of candles burning around him. He liked the Man's pain, he wanted more of it. When he left the Old Woman he began to surf the currents of the night, collecting dreams, searching out hopes and fears, looking for new ways to hurt the Man. There was a dark rainbow of feeling in the night air, but in the end he came back to the Old Woman. Tee-jin liked her. If he hurt her that would hurt the Man. But she had given Jit the coat; he did not want to kill her. And there was something about her dreams—she dreamt often of the Man, and when she woke she was always uneasy. Afraid the Man would find out.

Jit reached out to her again. She had left the stairs and gone to her own room to go to bed. In the dark she took off her clothes and wiped a wet cloth across her back and neck, down around her breasts, the length of her thighs; Jit could feel the relief of breeze against her damp skin. Then she lay down on her bed and closed her eyes, remembering over and over the embrace in the stairwell, the Man's words, his kiss on her head where she still felt it. As if she had been hit, Jit thought. But there was no pain. He stayed with her into sleep and when she was quiet he whispered a name to her sleeping mind: Tee-jin.

Her breathing sped up. He said again, "Tee-jin." Then, remembering the name she used for the Man: "John. John." She took a sharp inward breath and Jit felt a spread of warmth across her chest that had nothing to do with the sultry weather. Her nipples tightened—Jit's own contracted and he stirred uncomfortably on his pile of blankets—and she crossed one arm over her chest.

Jit suggested nothing more, waiting to see what would happen. The mother-woman provided a cascade of images and sensations. Sitting at Tietjen's side and watching the play of light across his face, or the way he held a clipboard; imagining his hands stroking her breasts or cupping her face. Working outside in the sun, constantly aware of Tietjen, just feet away: of the sheen of sweat on his back and his smell on the hot breeze; of his voice as he spoke to her, making endless plans for the Store, waiting for her patient, reasoned replies. She moved restlessly on her bed, her body shaping itself to Tietjen's phantom one.

Jit wriggled, himself. He did not like the sensations, did not like the old woman's power to stir him this way. It was too much like the feelings he had stolen from Tietjen and the dark woman that had torn through him and left him aching. Jit did not want that again.

Give it to the Man.

Jit almost laughed, there in the candlelit darkness, by himself. Let Tee-jin feel the mother-woman's feelings that were like and unlike the feelings the dark woman had had.

Slowly Jit reached with his mind and joined them, Tietjen and the mother-woman, like forcing people to join hands, his own hand clasped around to make sure the joining worked. Always before he had taken dreams and memories and transplanted them into Tietjen's sleeping mind. But this time Jit wanted not just the dream-matter but the mother-woman's sensations and feelings, wanted the Man to feel the woman's aching and to share the anger and fear that lay just below the surface of the dream itself. Jit bound the dreamers together, smiling as he did so, and waited to see how the man was hurt.

Tietjen slept, wondering what the dream would be tonight. The talk with Barbara had taken the edge off his fear and made it easier to dare the dreams. When he did dream, it was vivid and erotic. It was as if he were inside someone else's body, a woman's body, and the man who was making love to her was himself. The hands that caressed her breasts were his own; the taste of the skin her lips brushed was his own; the lips that grazed her collarbone and traced their way down over her belly were his. But he felt her responses, felt his breasts—her breasts—swell and yearn toward him, felt the aching between her legs, felt himself, as her, wanting the man who was caressing her.

In the dream Tietjen was outside himself, in love with himself. Even in his dreams about Irene, where he had finally understood her affection and rage, and her impatience with him, Tietjen had never felt, or understood, the kind of sweetness or pain of the way this woman loved him. He remembered with her memories the sight of him working outside in the hot sun, or teaching one of the people in the Store, or listening, late at night by the light of kerosene lamps, in the planning meetings for the Store. He remembered wanting to trace the shape of his mouth with her fingers, forgiving him when he ran out of patience or was clumsy with people in the Store, loving him when his pleasure and excitement in what they were accomplishing shone, to her eyes, like a lamp. Aching for his pain: for Ketch, for Maia, for his own paralyzing self-doubt. She believed he was lovable. She loved him.

He knew all this the same way he knew her body, what it was to welcome him inside her, reaching to pull him closer and deeper. Too caught up in the heat and sweep of sensations to care, Tietjen followed her into orgasm.

But the dream did not end there. Her belly ached afterward, and her face was turned away from the man above her. Tietjen felt tears running down his—her—cheeks. Of relief and pleasure and joy.

Of fear.

Fear? Curiously Tietjen began to tease the fear out, but it resisted him and he was distracted by the image of his own dark hair brushing her collarbone, the weight of his head cradled on her breast, the freckled tan of her arm across the dark brown of his tanned shoulder. Again he felt the welling up of love for him, and the tang of fear that accompanied it. *My skin is so old,* he heard her thinking. She looked at her fingers as they twined through his dark hair—it felt different to her fingers than to Tietjen's own. Her wedding ring glinted in the moonlight, recalling the memory of the man she had married long ago, another lanky, dark-haired man. A ring with a green stone on her forefinger, which her husband had put there, wrestling it on over the knuckle as both of them laughed.

Looking at the ring, trying to remember where he had seen it, Tietjen drifted out of the dream and back to consciousness. He felt groggy and heavy, aware that the sheets were soaked with sweat, but too exhausted to do anything about it. Whose body had he occupied in his dream, he wondered. Whose ring was that he had seen on his—her—hand before waking?

He slept without remembering.

5

TIETJEN woke feeling marvelous. He didn't know why; the weather was still miserably hot and humid and his muscles ached from the work of the day before. He did not remember dreaming. He just felt good. Sitting on the edge of his bed, he looked at the piles of paper and dirty clothes, the rumpled mess of bedclothes, the stack of unwashed cups by the door. He'd been letting things go, he thought. Time to clean up. Maybe it was Barbara's pep talk from the night before.

He stripped the bed, gathered the clothes and sheets together by the door, sorted through the papers. Finally he left with the laundry under one arm and dishes to return to the dining room balanced on his clipboard. In the basement Tietjen dropped the clothes in the room they had made over as the laundry—a utility room with a floor drain, slop sink, and sufficient space to string clotheslines—and signed himself up for a shift on laundry duty later in the day. Then he went upstairs to the dining room. Elena and one of her helpers were already working on breakfast: dry cereal, canned fruit, coffee. Tietjen said good morning, took his dishes out into the alley where the washing water was, and began to wash them and the other waiting dishes.

"You don't got to do that," Elena said from the doorway. She was looking at him a little sideways, not suspiciously but curiously.

Tietjen shook his head. "You let me get away with too much, Elena. It's only a couple of dishes."

She shrugged and went back inside. Tietjen felt a little ashamed as he washed the last couple of plates. He didn't remember the last time he'd washed a dish or hung up laundry or swept a floor. No one complained, but the others let him get away with behaving like the

Boss and leaving the scutwork to other people. He'd have to talk with Barbara about it.

It was early; people were only beginning to wake and come down for breakfast, and Tietjen didn't see Barbara among them. He wasn't hungry yet, and he was filled with energy. He wanted work. As he headed back down to the laundry room, he wondered again: why do I feel so good? It was like—he tried to remember when he had last felt this kind of elation and physical energy and *bounce*. In college, maybe. Or when I first met Irene. It felt like the morning-after-the-first-night buzz of a new relationship.

Wrestling with his sheets, Tietjen realized that the last time he'd done laundry was with a machine. They had taken the washing machines and dryers out of the room and moved in two big tubs. Tietjen sloshed clean waste water into one of them, dropped in a dollop of detergent, and began to stir his sheets around in the tub. He didn't really know what he was doing, and felt clumsy and stupid, in a cheerful, adventurous way. As he worked he looked at the blotches of mold on the baseboards of the ugly green walls. "Bleach," he thought. "Maybe I can find some when I'm done here." He was trying to wring water out of a sheet, six or seven inches at a time, without letting the squeezed part drop on the floor or fall back into the sink, when he heard a chuckle behind him.

"If I hadn't seen it, I would never believe it," Barbara said. "Here, you're making a mess of it." She took the sheet from him, then offered him back a corner. "Stand over the floor drain. Okay, now: open the sheet, fold it once—that's it. Now, twist." Between the two of them they had the sheet wrung and hanging on the line in a few moments. "Whatever possessed you to do laundry at this hour of the morning? It's not as if you have an aptitude for it," she added. She was smiling, but Tietjen thought she look tired.

"I woke up feeling good this morning, and I realized I've been getting away with not doing my share around here." Tietjen washed the second sheet in the tub energetically.

Barbara snorted. "Are you trying to persuade me that you don't work hard enough?"

"I'm saying it finally dawned on me that I don't do a lot of the routine junk like the laundry and cooking and—"

"John, you *clearly* don't know how to do wash—"

"And I couldn't be taught? I feel like I'm being given preferential treatment. I'm surprised no one here has wrung my neck for it."

The second sheet came out of the sink, was wrung and hung to dry between them. Tietjen had to step around the corner of the sheet to see Barbara's face. She was reaching up, smoothing out fine wrinkles in the sheet as she listened.

"Look, can you honestly tell me you haven't let me get away with not doing kitchen duty, or laundry duty, or cleaning the toilets, because—"He broke off, distracted. He flushed suddenly and wasn't sure why. Something about Barbara or the way she looked. Something.

"Because?" she repeated. She turned to face him. After a second she stepped back and raised her hand to her cheek. "What?" she asked. "Have I got a smudge on my nose?" She brushed at her nose, smiling uneasily. The jade ring on her ring finger caught the light.

"Have you always worn that ring?" he asked.

Barbara nodded. "Gordon gave it to me. It was his grandmother's. Why?"

Memories filled Tietjen like tides. Every touch, every sensation of the night's dream came back to him and he felt drowned in it. He turned away from Barbara, hoping she wouldn't see what the memories were doing to him.

"John? You okay?" Barbara put her hand on his shoulder to turn him back to her; her hand was only inches from his face. He remembered clearly how that hand touched him in the night. He kept his body turned away from her, embarrassed by his erection. "I had a dream with your ring in it last night," he said, as lightly as he could, and pulled away, went around the corner of the sheet again. This time it was Tietjen who reached up to smooth away a wrinkle, buying time, willing the memories to go away.

"A dream?" She sounded doubtful, a little shaky herself.

Tietjen made himself laugh. "Yeah. I don't remember anything else, just that there was someone wearing that ring." He pulled the clothesline low enough so that he could smile at her over it. Barbara's answering smile was wary; he imagined her lips tracing the skin along his ribs. He let go of the clothesline and it snapped up a few inches, hiding his face. "Ooops," he muttered. If he didn't look at her he could get the feelings under control, he thought.

He spoke more loudly than necessary. "Anyway, can you really tell me that you don't give me special treatment because—" He stopped. He had been talking about special treatment because he was the Boss; maybe that wasn't it at all.

"Because why?" Barbara asked. She stepped around to his side of the sheet and faced him. "No one asks you to sew or cook or wash because no one thinks you'd be any good at it, and you're very good at a lot of other things. That's the reason." She stepped closer, and Tietjen was suddenly aware of how small she was, slight and fine-boned and delicate; there were freckles between her breasts.

"It's not anything else?" Leave it alone, he thought. Leave it alone. But the question hung between them like something tangible.

She began to sound irritated. "Like *what* else?"

Tietjen took a step back. "It was just a dream," he heard himself murmur. He thought it was a non sequitur, but it wasn't to Barbara. She looked as if he'd struck her.

"What?"

"Nothing. I was thinking about your ring again. It was nothing."

"What the hell was the dream, John?"

Tietjen still couldn't look at her. He felt like a kid caught with a dirty magazine, like he had double vision, seeing her as Barbara, as always, and knowing her as the woman in the dream.

"God, Barbara, look, whatever I was dreaming about last night, I hope you don't think I think of you—I'd never—the last thing I want is to—" He was making it worse, he could see by her look.

"*I* had a dream last night, too," she said coldly. "It was *my* dream. I—I don't know how you know about it, but if that's what this is about . . . If you're down here snickering at me, if it grosses you out, that's your tough luck. *I'm* not going to apologize: it was just a dream."

Tietjen felt like he'd back into another nightmare, one of those where he walked in halfway and didn't know his lines. He wasn't sure what they were arguing about. "I—it wasn't—I wasn't laughing at the anything. I didn't mean—did I hurt you? I'm sorry, but Jesus, Barbara, that wasn't what—" He heard himself go on, not saying what he meant, too confused to be sure what she wanted.

She turned and left the laundry room.

Tietjen sank to his haunches with his head against the cool damp of a hanging sheet, trying to figure out what had happened. The marvelous feeling of that morning, the feeling of pleasure and possibility, of being loved, had dissipated. He had had a dream that—that Barbara was in love with him? Something. And Barbara had had the same dream, and was angry. Why? Because of a dream? Because he knew something about her that she didn't want known, he thought. Because now he could hurt her. Already had.

He was frightened. He had to talk with Barbara, get this all straightened out. They needed her, the Store couldn't do without her. Just imagining it—the Store without Barbara—made him feel cold and panicky.

He couldn't do without her.

He thought of Irene and Ketch, of his sons and Allan Hochman and Maia. "No." The word wrenched out of him. I've lost enough, I've lost too damned much. I'll find her and figure out what's going on and we'll get it sorted out, he promised himself. I can't lose Barbara. He got to his feet and smoothed the sheets absently, waiting until he felt centered enough to go upstairs.

Barbara was not in the dining room, but Sandy Hochman was, with a list of questions about the plumbing. Tietjen let himself sit down long enough to have a cup of coffee—which turned into two cups and some breakfast—as Sandy, then Lo-yi, then Elena brought questions to him. He sat and answered for over an hour.

The first flush of fear that he would lose McGrath had faded. Irene and Ketch and Maia had all died; Barbara was in the Store and safe. There was time, he thought, and finished his coffee. He needed to think a little more about what had happened in the laundry room, not go to her half-cocked as he used to with Irene.

"John?" It was Sandy Hochman again. "We've isolated the problem in the D line; Paulo thinks he can fix it with the Super's plumbing tools, but do you want to take a look first?"

Tietjen rose and said sure. A sewage problem was potentially disastrous but far easier to face and fix. He would talk to Barbara later, when they had both had time to cool down.

Something woke Jit in the cool tunnel where he slept most mornings, something strong enough to reach out to him. For a moment he was scared; his heart beat as fast as a squirrel's and there was a buzzing in his ears. Gable back? he thought. Can't be no Gable back. Jit had seen Gable's broken body himself, had spat into the gaping mouth and thrown back at the dead man all claim of kinship. Gable was dead, but something had woken Jit now, something strong.

Jit rolled up to sitting and blinked to let his eyes get accustomed to the dark of the tunnel. With his mind Jit swept the city, coming last to the place where the Man and his people were. There were no new voices, no one with power like Gable's. Maybe the strong voice that woke him had been Jit's own, in a dream. He touched the Man, found him confused, with the memory of the Old Woman's dream sighing through him. Then Jit touched the Old Woman.

At once he knew that this was what he had heard, her anger and sorrow distilled into one roar of pain. Through her eyes he saw her room, the neatly tucked corner of the bed she sat on, the piece of flowered sheet she kneaded as she thought. She was angry at the Man, she was angry at herself. *If I could* die, Jit heard her thoughts. *If I could die and just never have to see him again.* At first, Jit did not understand the anger. The Man knew something about the Old Woman. Something about the dream he had given to Tee-jin the night before had given him power over the Old Woman. At least she thought so.

Jit began to understand. The Old Woman had loved the Man. The Man must have pushed her away. Jit knew that feeling. Now she hated the Man. And loved him. And hated herself. The Old Woman's feelings were like a storm, blowing everywhere at once in every direction. Jit pushed her rage; it burned hotter in response. "Idiot. Stupid cruel emotionless self-involved idiot," she muttered.

The anger felt like a line between the two of them, Jit and the Old Woman, as if it tied them together and made them one. Cautiously, Jit reached deeper, pushed the anger again, felt the knot strengthen. He pushed the shame and the knot strengthened. And he swept the love away, imagined a door for the Old Woman and put the love there, where it would not interfere with him. Then he tried something else.

"Bastard," he said aloud. "Bastard!" she whispered.

Then Jit mimed tearing something, tearing hard enough to kill. The Old Woman took the sheet she had been twisting between her hand and tore it. Jit wiped his brow; the Old Woman wiped hers. Jit pushed the anger again and she shook with it. Jit smiled; the Old Woman smiled too, with tears coursing down her face.

He had a weapon.

Jit hesitated; he hated the Man, but the Old Woman had been nice, had spoken gently to him, had given Jit a coat. Her voice had been funny, gentle, sad and curious; with the anger pushing everything else out of the way, all that was gone. But Jit hated the Man, and now she did too, and it was so good to share that. To have a weapon.

For hours Jit sat in his tunnel, sharing his anger, honing his weapon.

Tietjen did not see Barbara for the rest of the day. He wondered if she was avoiding him, but that seemed so un-Barbara-like. More likely their tasks just took them in different directions. He stopped late for dinner and wandered into the dining room when most people were finishing up. As he took his plate, Beth Voe stopped him to ask where Barbara was.

"I haven't seen her since this morning," he said.

There was a breeze stirring: Beth pushed a strand of hair out of her mouth. "She was going to come plot out the winter garden with me today. It's not like Barbara not to show up." She shook her head and walked away.

Bobby Fratelone had come downstairs for dinner. He was still on crutches, and his broken leg appeared to have set badly. Tietjen ate with him and Bobby worried loudly about the state of their fighters now that he was not training them.

"Hey, where's Miz McGrath?" Bobby asked at the end of the meal.

Tietjen shook his head. "I don't know. We had an—argument—this morning, and I haven't seen her since."

Fratelone looked Tietjen up and down. "You be nice to that lady, Boss. She's the best thing we got here. And she's crazy about you, so just be nice, okay?"

Tietjen nodded. Be nice. That sounded simple enough. He pushed himself away from the table. Time to find Barbara and be nice.

It wasn't simple. She wasn't where she would normally be at this time of day—in the dining room, in the kitchen, taking advantage of the relative cool of the early evening to work in the garden. Tietjen checked there. She was not in the infirmary, not in the laundry room. Most of the people he asked said they had not seen her that day; a few said they had, but could not remember where.

That left her room. Tietjen climbed the stairs slowly. What to say? And what would he do if she was not in her room—where else could she be? As he went down the hall to her room Tietjen began to feel light-headed and scared. "Don't be an idiot, John." he said aloud, and knocked on the door.

No answer.

He knocked again. Again, no answer. Gingerly, Tietjen tried the door; it was not locked. "Barbara?" He stepped inside, looked around. No one there. Her bed was neatly made, the few clothes folded on a chair. Something fluttered under the bed, scraps of fabric stirring in the breeze.

Again downstairs, Tietjen started asking everyone he could find about McGrath. Finally someone knew something.

"She said she was going for a walk. She said she needed to clear her head, now that it was cool enough to go outside again." The woman looked unconcerned. "Sure, she looked okay. Just said she was going out for a bit."

Un-Barbara-like, Tietjen thought. But the whole damned day had been un-Barbara-like. Maybe the kindest thing he could do was to wait for her, let her set the pace. He owed Barbara kindness.

He checked again in an hour. Nothing. An hour after that, the watch said, Yes, McGrath had come in. "I told her you'd been looking for her. She said she needed to clean up first. I guess she'll be up in her room."

Tietjen nodded and went back to his room, wondering if he should go to her or let her alone. What he really wanted, he realized, was to ask Barbara for advice. "There's this woman," he wanted to say. "And I handled it badly, you know what a jerk I can be, and what do I do now?" Only he couldn't do that. It was dark now, hot and humid. The breeze that stirred the trees to whispering did not cool the air. There was a film of sweat on his cheekbones and forehead. Until the thing with Barbara was settled, he couldn't sleep, so he sat in candlelight knitting a singlet, the way Barbara had taught him.

"You wanted to see me?" Barbara was framed by light from the hall lamp, a silhouette with her voice, her halo of white hair.

"All day," Tietjen said. "Come in, Barbara. I want to apologize—"

"Why, John?" Her voice was sweet. Tietjen wished he could see her face better. "There's nothing to apologize for, is there?"

"Plenty, I think. I was stupid and dense and insensitive—"

She laughed, a brittle, silvery laugh. "You're always stupid and dense and insensitive, John. Is there something else you want to apologize for?" Something was wrong, more wrong than the words or even the unpleasant coquetry of Barbara's tone. She moved farther into the room, and the wan candlelight washed over her. Barbara swaggered, one hand on her hip in a parody of seductiveness; the other hand floated up and down along the placket of her sleeveless blouse, toying with buttons, gliding on the sweat that Tietjen saw beading at the top of her breasts. He was unable to look away from her hand, and memories of the damned dream from the night before came back again, overwhelmingly. He should look away, Tietjen thought. Barbara wouldn't want him staring at her chest like a horny teenager.

"Staring at my breasts, John?" she asked, still too sweetly. "Mustn't do that. Someone might think I was attractive. Someone might think I was capable of sexual feelings. Besides, you don't want to stare at my breasts, John. They're *old*."

Tietjen remembered the dream, the weight of her small breasts, the pale freckled skin, their responsiveness. Horrified, he realized he was aroused. He looked away. "Barbara, what's going on?" he asked. "I wanted to apologize for this morning; I hurt you, I know, and I'd sooner cut off my arm—"

"Than deal with it," she finished. She sounded delighted, as if she had supplied the missing word in a trivia game. "Sooner lose a leg than let someone close enough to know that they mattered. Sooner lose Ketch and ignore the little bump that made in your life than to figure out how she was important to you and to tell her." Barbara opened a button on her blouse, revealing the lacy top of her bra. Tietjen looked away again.

"You'd sooner cut off my leg than tell me directly, *Oh no, thanks, you're too old for me, Barbara.* Telling me directly would be too messy. Can't take responsibility for that. God, John, you're such a coward. I even thought that was lovable for a while, d'you believe it?"

Tietjen felt like he was caught in a black hole, falling forever toward the event horizon, unable to move, listening to McGrath pour out a depth of rage and hurt he had never suspected. Not for him—for God's sake, it had nothing to do with him. He cleared his throat. "Barbara? Barbara, what do you want? What can I do?"

She smiled. "You can't do a damned thing, John. That's the point. Love comes to you and you push it away, you stick something in between it and you—between you and Irene, or Ketch, or your damned kids. Then you get romantic and remorseful about it, but you don't stop hiding. I just don't feel like being romanticized. You hurt me. I want you to rub that into your skin and die a little bit every time you think about me, because you made me feel like shit, old plain dependable Barbara shit. Because you couldn't love me." She did not say it as a complaint but a statement of unassailable fact.

"If anyone—any goddamned one staggered in off the street and volunteered to help with this place, you loved them a little—not enough to remember their names, or what had happened to them, but you loved them a little. It's the people who want more you can't deal with." Barbara's voice got higher, more strident; the sexy drawl was gone. "If a kid walked in from Central Park tonight and wanted you to take him in, you'd call him a city-killer and push him away. You're worse than Gable, you're worse than anything, you push anyone away—"

Tietjen stood up and grabbed Barbara's shoulders. He shook her. "Barbara, what are you talking about?"

A light, something he had thought was reflected candlelight, went out in her eyes. She looked at him blankly for a moment. "Too tired to make sense," she said lightly. "Or too senile." She pulled out of his grasp and turned away, toward the door. "Don't worry, John. I won't bother you anymore. I'm gone."

And she was gone, moving quickly out the door with a quiet, Barbara-like movement. Tietjen felt as if she had taken the air in the room with her. When he realized he had been holding his breath he began gulping in air, making himself dizzy with it. Nothing made any sense. He sank back on the bed and let the guilt and horror wash through him, because she was right: it was his fault, had been his fault his whole life. He'd never had a relationship he hadn't run from, ever. Taking the blame, accepting the blame, made him feel perversely good, as if he were doing something right, really playing the hero at last.

That made him stop. He might almost have heard Barbara's voice, asking dryly if he wasn't taking himself too seriously. Life as an opera, and himself as the tenor. That was no better. What, then? He sat up on the bed, staring at the flickering light cast on the far wall, thinking.

Barbara was right. He had hurt her, and he hated that and wanted to fix it, and knew that there might not be any chance of it: the hurt might run too deep. He wanted, with a deep, childish wanting, to take it back, be allowed a second chance. He hated the unreasonableness of a universe in which time wouldn't roll back and allow him to do it all over again. He went back and forth between anger and guilt for a long while until finally, lulled by the candles' flicker in the dark, Tietjen dozed off.

When he woke it was still dark, and he wasn't sure that he wasn't dreaming. The candles were guttering out; the light they cast was dark gold and did not cut the darkness but simply drew pictures on top of it. For a few minutes Tietjen thought that the face he saw on the wall was a trick of light. Then he closed and opened his eyes and the face was still there, a narrow, pale face with dark eyes, a shock of dark hair, sharp-set bones. He had seen the face before, but could not remember where.

Then he did remember. The kid he and Barbara had talked to in the street one night. Scrawny and shy; Barbara had given him her coat. Tietjen blinked. The face still flickered against the wall, watching him, as if it was waiting for him to speak. What time is it? Tietjen wondered. Must be late; I'm dreaming.

Then the face on the wall spoke. The voice was a boy's, husky but with cracks in it. The way he spoke—it was not like any New York accent Tietjen knew, or maybe it was a combination of all of them, lowspeak and street talk, East Side and West.

"Tee-jin, Tee-jin," he taunted. "Old woman she mine now." The face smiled.

Tietjen sat upright. "What?"

"You push her. She come to me. She hate you. Pushed away. Like me—"

"Like you?" Tietjen prompted.

"Old woman she mine," the voice repeated. "I keep her."

"Where's Barbara?"

"Stupid Man," the voice said. "She come to me. She be mine now. Unless . . ." It took a sly tone. "Unless you want get her. I give her you come, Stupid Man."

"Where are you?" Tietjen asked.

"You want her, Jit help you find her."

Jit?" It was the boy's name, Tietjen remembered. The boy with the coat. "We gave you a coat, right?"

The voice changed. "God, John, you're such a coward." It was Barbara's voice and intonation, the words she'd used earlier that night. Tietjen went cold at the sound. "I even thought that was lovable for a while, d'you believe it?" The voice changed again, to the husky boy-voice. "You want her, you find Jit, Stupid Man."

"Where?" Tietjen asked.

The head shook disapprovingly. "You know where. Like with Gable's people—"

"You're at Grand Central?" Tietjen asked.

"You're not getting the point, John." Barbara's voice again, calm and reasonable. It was still the kid's face that Tietjen saw. "How did we know to look at Grand Central? What told us the monsters would be there?"

Tietjen remembered. Sitting in a room, dimly lit, talking; each one of them had known some part of the puzzle, and when the pieces were fit together it worked—more than that, they had all known absolutely that the answer was . . . the answer. "I'll know?" It was unsatisfactory, too slim a reed to hang Barbara's life on.

"You know," the boy's voice agreed.

The face watched Tietjen somberly for a few moments without speaking. Then, slowly, it began to fade into the guttering candlelight. The image was almost gone, no more than a whitish smear, when he heard Barbara's voice again. "Get some rest, John. You're going to need it."

6

ARBARA was gone. Tietjen woke completely out of a sound sleep knowing that, and knowing it was up to him to get her back. It was still dark out, but the moon shone on the face of the building across the street, and his room seemed filled with light. He pulled on shoes and, after a little thought, put a penlight and his pocketknife in his back pocket. Then, walking gingerly, he left his room.

The Store was asleep. Tietjen moved through silent halls lit with the thin, buttery glow of camping lanterns. The air was hot and unmoving, even with dawn several hours away. No one stepped out of their rooms to see what the matter was. Downstairs in the lobby, the sentries at the front door straightened in their chairs and patted the pistols that lay across their laps, but both of them nodded Tietjen unquestioningly through the door. That made him frown: they should have asked anyone leaving the building at three A.M. what his business was. Barbara would have asked, Tietjen thought. Barbara would have stopped him.

Outside the Store there was a soft breeze blowing. The street was as silent as the Store had been; only the rattle and whisper of dried leaves and paper tumbling across pavement made a noise. Tietjen stood for a moment, waiting. Then, with a sense of rightness, he turned toward the Park. At the corner he turned north, up Fifth Avenue. What Barbara had said was true: he knew now, bit by bit, where he had to go. It was coming to him, the pull as strong as the panicked call back into the city he had followed months before. This time, however, there was a loosening in his chest as he relaxed and followed the tug of his internal compass. He was scared: he had no idea what he would find when he reached the end of his walk. He was also relieved to be doing something—anything, after what suddenly seemed to him to be months of inactivity. I missed this, he thought, and realized that "this" was the wordless pull that led him through the streets.

At Seventy-ninth Street Tietjen stopped and looked into the silvery darkness of Central Park. He had not gone back into the Park since the day he had crossed it, coming back to the city. In the dark it looked like a web of silver and black shadow; moonlight shone dully off the Metropolitan Museum up Fifth Avenue ahead of him. Tietjen wondered what had happened to the curator who'd gone crazy and had tried to capture him there. He and Barbara had sent an armed party back to explore, but they had found the museum deserted, without a trace of the curator or his prisoners. Remembering Barbara with her hands tied behind her, calmly explaining to him how they would escape, made Tietjen grin in the dark. He held that image in his mind as he crossed Fifth Avenue and braced himself to walk into Central Park.

It was better than he had expected: the prickly wrongness he remembered no longer hung over the Park like a mist. Still, something, perhaps only the silvery moonlight on the branches and leaves over his head, made Tietjen think of the word *enchantment*. He was in an enchanted wood, a place where magic lived. Not the evil he remembered or the good magic of fairy tales; the Park breathed a kind of power that was heady and frightening because it was for itself and not for good or bad.

On the path under the trees the moonlight didn't penetrate; he made his way through the shadows more by feel and instinct than by sight, although when he looked ahead the mass of Belvedere Castle shone with moonlight, and the moon reflected across the surface of Belvedere Lake, stirring like ribbons in the breeze. Not only was the Castle still standing, but the graffiti that Tietjen recalled had covered every spare inch of the Castle was gone—what he saw was plain gray stone lit by the moon.

He was so busy looking at the Castle that he didn't see the man walking toward him until they were almost nose to nose. Tietjen jumped aside and the man continued on without stopping. Tietjen drew a breath and looked after the man, and realized that he wasn't a man at all but a shadow, man-sized and shaped, moving intently down the path toward the East Side. After all these months, the weirdness could still creep up on him, Tietjen thought. His hands trembled, and he jammed them into his pockets. In the moonlight he was not sure which was more frightening to him: the shadow-man's insubstantiality, its determination, or the thought that he himself might be just that determined and just that insubstantial.

When he looked west again he saw two more shadow-men coming toward him. It took nerve and concentration to stand there and watch them come, but Tietjen did not duck aside this time. He stood his ground and let them walk *through* him; the sensation was strange, hollow-feeling and cold, but not frightening. He turned to watch the shadow-men melt into the darkness under the trees, their shadow forms fraying into grayness at the edges, the grayness spreading inward until the men blinked out against the black of the tree line. He stood watching, and only knew by the sudden sensation of hollowness and the sight of another dark silhouette trudging eastward that another shadow had walked through him. When he turned back to the west there were dozens of them on the path, walking toward him. For a few moments he just stood there, letting them move through him, wondering what it felt like to them, where they were going. They were going nowhere: as they reached the eastern edge of the field the shadow-men dissolved, fraying into the darkness until there was nothing left. Looking eastward, Tietjen felt more of them walk through him: the hair on his arms and legs stood up and there was a taste of metal on his tongue. He had the idea that if enough of them walked through him he would build up an electric charge that would keep him rooted where he stood.

Tietjen turned west and took a step, then another. The shadow-men kept walking through him, two and three abreast now. As he followed the curving path around the lake toward the charred shell of the Delacorte Theater (had it burned down in his lifetime? Tietjen could not remember) Tietjen began to feel the weight of the phantoms press against him, as if he were walking into a stiff breeze. When he looked at the shadow-men rather than through them, he began to see features: beaky noses, jutting chins, hollow eyes. Comic-book likenesses, at first nearly identical, then more and more individual.

Then one of them jostled him in passing. Tietjen was turned clear around by the impact, not hard but unexpected, and watched the black phantom march purposefully along the path to the trees on the far side of the lake. As he stood watching, another one bumped into him, and then another. Tietjen turned and saw a crowd of half-solid shadow-men bearing down on him like a stream of people through a rush-hour doorway. He began to move forward again, threading himself through the crowd, bumped and jostled again and again, as the shadow-men grew more solid and took on faces of their own, the sorts of faces he might have seen on any day on his way to work, carved out of something as dark and unreflective as night.

Dodging through the crowd, he finally rounded the shell of the old amphitheater and followed the slope downhill to the access road. The crowd began to thin around him, but the shadow-men who came toward him seemed more and more solid. More than that, at last they seemed to see him. One gestured to him, pointing back toward the east; another shook its head, dark eyes that were simply another shade of black against the blackness of its face, meeting Tietjen's. Finally, one stopped in front of him and grabbed his arm, gesturing frantically.

"What?" Tietjen asked. *I'm talking to shadows, dammit, and Barbara is waiting.* "What do you want?"

The shadow-man kept pulling on his arm, his hand sweeping urgently eastward. His face was as real as Tietjen's own now, frightened and angry. Tietjen turned to look behind him at the shadow-men who were dissolving at the edge of the horizon, come to life just to frighten him, their lives measured in the time it took for them to stride from clearing's edge to clearing's edge. What would happen to them if he turned back west; would they live? At least until the sunrise?

"I can't," Tietjen said. "Someone is waiting for me, I'm sorry. I can't stay."

The shadow-man grasped Tietjen's arm with both hands now, pulling so hard he had to brace himself to keep from being dragged down the path. Looking east, he saw another figure fade into dark. "I'm sorry," he said again. "I have to go on. What if you—what if you just stayed here? Don't walk east? Would you live?" The figure stepped away from Tietjen, dropped its arms and turned east, hopelessly. "Wait," he said. He put his hand on the shadow's shoulder, felt it sink into lush darkness for a moment before resting on solid warmth. "Don't go. Stay and see."

The shadow-man did not turn to look at him. It shook its head sadly, pulled away from Tietjen, and started walking. Tietjen turned back toward the West Side and walked a few paces, but couldn't keep from looking back again. The sparse crowd of black figures behind him rose and fell like an uneasy sea swell; as each reached the edge of the trees, the shadow-men simply faded into the moonlit air. Tietjen thought he saw the one who had stopped him disappear that way, and felt bitter and angry.

"Why give something life if you're just going to take it away? Did you think they would stop me? Did you want to choose between their lives and Barbara's? What are you doing?" He spoke the words aloud, but there was no answer.

Tietjen crossed the access road and found the thickly grown path to Eighty-first Street. He was alone again, as suddenly as that. As he walked, the compass pull reasserted itself, as certain as if someone had taken him by the hand: he was going to the Museum of Natural History. It was an old friend, home ground: Tietjen could envision the enormous whale, the elephants and lions, the immense barosaurus skeleton in the lobby. Chris had loved the elephants—African and Asian—and Davy the dinosaurs. That was a sweet thought: he could imagine his boys' voices, their pleasure as they darted through the museum halls. The warmth of the memory leached out of him when the images changed. Tietjen imagined the elephants rioting, the barosaurus smashing him into a wall with one careless sweep of its skeletal tail. He sagged against the Park wall, weak as water.

"Weak as water?" Now he heard Barbara's voice—imagined it, but it was a true imagining, full of her humor and ginger. "Water isn't weak, you idiot. Think what you saw of SoHo and Wall Street. Water levels *cities*." He felt a tide of longing for Barbara, his good companion. With her voice he imagined her, not as he had seen her last, but as he knew her day to day, neat and practical and funny and lovable. He felt a twist of shame that he had hurt her—then discarded that as self-pitying.

Tietjen straightened and looked up at the museum again. His compass said that Barbara was in there, guarded by the dinosaurs and elephants and stuffed lions, and the pale, frightening boy who held her. It was time to go in and get her. For Barbara he would be as strong as water.

•   •   •

Tietjen could not even guess what weapons the boy had or how powerful he was; his only hope was that logic was *his* weapon. So he began to reason out an approach to the museum. From where he stood it looked as if the planetarium on the north side had been smashed in; a crater extended out into the driveway, as if, fittingly enough, the building had been hit by a meteor. What was left of the glass and steel seemed to be thickly covered in ivy. A steady breeze stirred the leaves; he could hear the rustling from across the street, but Tietjen barely felt the air move. Now that he stood outside the Park again it was hot.

No entry through the north way. There was an entrance on the south side, on Seventy-seventh Street, and the main entrance on the east side, with the statue of Teddy Roosevelt looking out over Central Park West and the Park itself. He was pretty sure the west-side staff entrances had been sealed years before, when the green there had become a shantytown. For some reason—the mysterious inner compass again—Tietjen was nervous about walking around to Seventy-seventh Street.

So he would have to enter through one of the main doors on the east. Probably the boy would expect him there; maybe the kid had planted his unease about the southern entrance. What if he fought the pull? He tried an experiment. "I'll go down to the south door," he said aloud. He took a few steps toward Seventy-seventh Street. Immediately, he was filled with a terror that had him lead footed and shaky. In the warm breeze he was suddenly icy cold, and he kept shuddering, whole-body tremors that made it difficult to stand. It was like the sensations he had had when he went toward the East River, but worse. Behind the feeling, just palpable, was a sense of rage. Someone was very angry that he'd tried to disregard his clear instructions. Tietjen stopped, and the terror subsided at once. The boy hadn't hurt him—and he could, that was obvious. He simply wanted Tietjen to go a certain somewhere, where Barbara was.

He started toward the doors on Central Park West.

Crossing Central Park, Tietjen had moved briskly. Now he approached the museum slowly. A few minutes before he had been chilled and trembling; now his neck was sticky with sweat, and sweat rimed his nose and cheekbones; it felt too hot to move any faster. The air felt thick. Despite the moonlight, the front entrance and stairs were in shadow. As Tietjen walked closer he realized that the statue of Roosevelt, astride a horse and flanked by Indian guides, lay on its side. Vines had overgrown the steps and twined around the granite horse's legs. They covered the stairs and the statue and most of the ornamental stonework of the museum. When he got to the steps he realized it was not ivy, but some kind of dense leafless thorny vine. In places the growth looked deliberate and ornamental, as if a gardener had labored hard to produce the effect. Tietjen tried stepping over or around the thorns, but found all he could do was to step on them, beat them back with his feet. The vine grew steadily, fast enough so Tietjen could see it happening: he watched the vine cover Roosevelt's statue completely in the time it took him to climb from the street to the doors. By noon the whole museum would be impenetrably covered with the black, thorny vines, which seemed to root into the granite of the steps. Trapped inside by the thorns: he wiped sweat from his hairline and the back of his neck. One of the revolving doors stood open.

Maybe it was stupid to use the open door, but his internal voice was urging him through it, promising that Barbara would be safe at the end of the journey. The boy had brought him to the museum without killing him, so either there were limits to what he could do which Tietjen needed to understand, or the kid would not hurt him until he had had his say. Against logic, even against fear, the internal compass was a powerful force. Logic and fear trembled like heat mirages, insubstantial and unpersuasive in the dark.

Tietjen rubbed the sweat off the bridge of his nose and stepped through the door.

It was cool inside. At first Tietjen thought it was the cool that massive old buildings have. Then he realized it was so cold inside the museum that his breath plumed before him in the dark. The temperature outside had been in the high eighties, Tietjen thought. Inside it felt like low forties at best. He took a couple of steps into the lobby, letting his eyes adjust. The barosaurus still reared above the skeleton of an attacking allosaurus, protecting its young. He could not dismiss his imagining, of that tail whipping around to slam him against the wall: Tietjen hugged the walls tightly, out of range, he hoped. Once he was on the far side of the lobby the cold lessened a little, although Tietjen kept rubbing his arms fitfully against the chill. There were lights scattered around the lobby which gave off a dull orange light, just enough to throw shadows. Votive candles, Tietjen guessed, judging from the flickering. Then he realized they were battery-powered emergency lights. Surely they had not been shining since the day of the disasters, back in February?

Ahead were the African mammals, with a herd of elephants, some stuffed and posed, some holographic, standing on a plinth at the center of the hall. Tietjen half-expected the exhibits to come alive at any moment, but apart from the noiseless trumpeting of the holographic elephants, nothing moved. Were they running on batteries, or the kid's goodwill, he wondered. He moved past the lions, the kudus, out of the hall and into a narrow gallery which was almost pitch dark. He heard nothing but the clicks of his shoes on the floor, faintly echoed. He followed the gallery into another hall filled with old-fashioned displays of warriors, hunters, gatherers in grass skirts. The few painted faces he could see in the darkness stared back at him. He moved as fast as he could without stumbling, hating the feeling of those blank, unwatchful eyes staring at him.

At the end of that hall Tietjen turned right. Immediately he recognized where he was: in one of the South or Central American exhibits. The dull orange emergency lights shone on priapic stone fonts and wooden carvings. Tietjen's inner compass told him he was near, almost there. He scanned the room from side to side, searching for something; he almost overlooked it when he found it. To his right there was an immense Olmec head, taller than Tietjen, its red stone cheeks glistening faintly in the orange light, its eyes watching Tietjen impassively, its smile close-lipped and enigmatic. At its base there was a bundle of clothes, including the coat Barbara had given the kid. Tietjen bent and touched the cloth, then went on.

Twenty yards away he found Barbara, curled fetally against the cold, soundly asleep at the foot of a huge Aztec sun stone. Tietjen looked around, wary of a trap, then bent over her, shook her arm, called her name. She did not move. Fearful, Tietjen tried to find a pulse on her neck and could not—but felt the moist warmth of her breath on his wrist.

"Barbara? Come on, we've got to go now. Come on, sweetie, wake up." She did not stir. He tried again, shaking her harder. "Come on, Barbara. This isn't a good place to be right now. Come on, honey."

She did not waken. Tietjen's sense of urgency was growing steadily stronger; he wanted to be outside, out of the cold and the orange light. It would be close to dawn now. They could go home. . . .

Awkwardly, Tietjen pulled Barbara's arm around his neck and took her in his arms. She was lighter than he expected. He settled her quickly in his arms and started back toward the door.

"Don' go . . ."

Tietjen almost dropped Barbara; his legs wobbled with the shock of the low, rumbling voice that echoed in the hall. Loud, like the voice of God. He looked around but could not see anyone else. He went forward again.

The Olmec head smiled a serene, close-lipped smile before it spoke again; the stone lips moved slowly to shape the words. The voice rumbled. "Don' go, Tee-jin. Leave old woman here . . . she mine now. Jit *like* to have her."

The smile broadened. "Tee-jin don't have her now. She like Jit best." The head displayed blunt round teeth in a huge, open-mouthed laugh that echoed like a bell in the room. The laugh undid Tietjen: something in the undertones of it was more frightening than the stone head it came from. The laugh rolled through the room with a malevolent rumble, a hungry demonic sound—the tones in it made Tietjen want to howl, to drop down on the floor and roll around in misery.

Instead he ran, Barbara still clutched to his chest, back the way he'd come, turning a corner and running through the dimly lit hall with the glowering African warriors. The rumbling laughter pursued him, and he thought he heard footsteps as well, though he couldn't be sure in the echoing hall. There was a long, narrow hallway off to the left; he dodged in there, dropped Barbara's feet to the floor so that he was dragging her, and felt along the wall for doors. The first he came to was unlocked. He shoved it open, put McGrath down as carefully as he could, and turned around to lock the door. Then he pulled a heavy table up against the door.

Tietjen expected the room to be entirely dark, but as his eyes got accustomed, he saw that there were windows on the far side of the room, and a little predawn light spilling in around the edges of the blinds. He nearly tripped over McGrath on his way across the room, but when he opened the blinds there was just enough fading moon-light to see by. The room was cold, filled with stale, damp air; he was shivering. He pulled his collar closer, and went back to Barbara, who lay still unconscious, dressed only in a lightweight shirt and denim skirt, summer wear for the summer that was happening outside the museum. He had nothing to cover her with. In the thin light Tietjen thought that Barbara's lips were blue, that he saw her shivering. He turned to watch the door, and slid backward toward the wall until he was sitting beside her.

She lay still as a rock, no shivering. Tentatively, Tietjen stroked her hair back from her forehead, which was cool and dry. The white hair looked greenish in the dimness. After a moment, he put one hand under Barbara's ear and lifted her head to pillow it on his thigh. Sitting like that, with Barbara curled beside him and his hand in her hair, Tietjen sat watching the door of the room. It seemed impossible to rest with his mind racing, wondering what to do next, but exhaustion won; he fell asleep still wondering.

Barbara was still unconscious when he woke. His body ached in a hundred different directions, protesting the cold, the damp, the position, and the hardness of the floor. Tietjen cradled Barbara's head in his hand again and moved it off his thigh, settling her gently on the floor before he let himself move. Standing up hurt like hell. The room was no warmer, but the greenish moonlight had changed to the pale watery light of morning.

It seemed impossible to be too gentle with Barbara, too careful. Each time he looked at her, feelings welled up: guilt and pain and fear and love. He wondered if she would ever believe the last. He wondered if she would ever forgive him. If they ever got out of this room and back to the Store again.

"John."

His back was to her; the hairs on the nape of his neck straightened at the sound of her voice. Then a knot he had not known was there untied itself in his stomach, and he turned to face her.

Barbara had tucked her shirt neatly into the waistband of her skirt and smoothed the wrinkles out of the fabric. As he watched, she ran her hand through her hair and patted it back to its accustomed shape. "Where the hell are we?"

"The Museum of Natural History. I got you away from him and brought you in here—"

"Thank you, John." She sounded formally polite. Angry with him? He hadn't apologized yet, he realized.

"Come here." She held out a hand to him. And smiled. Something was wrong. "John?" she asked. A wounded edge to her voice. "What's wrong?" There was something wolfish in her smile, he thought. Something peculiar and un-Barbara-like about the way she watched him. "Hey, I won't bite you. Unless you want me to." The smile broadened. Tietjen wanted to recoil and fought the impulse, afraid to hurt her. If it was Barbara.

"How are you doing?" he asked haltingly.

"I'm fine. Don't I look okay?" She held her right hand out to him, palm up. "What's the matter, John, are you scared of me?"

Yes.

"No," he said. "Are you warm enough?"

"Come warm me up." She reached her other hand to him, her arms open in a broad embrace. Her expression became hungrily sexual. Tietjen managed not to recoil, but he did not move toward her. Her smile slipped. "Don't you owe me that much? A little warmth?" Her hands clawed up, and she ran her thumbs over her fingertips as if she were sharpening talons. "You made me feel like shit, John. Did you know that? Was it so grotesque to you that I wanted you? Am I supposed to be dead from the neck down because I'm twenty years older than you are?"

"I never said that," he blurted out, stung.

"You didn't have to." Her manner was again flirtatious, airy. "It was quite clear. Poor John, you've got a face like a billboard sometimes: *dis*may, *dis*gust, *dis*tress." On each *dis* she took a step closer, poked her chin at him as if she could knock him down with it. "I thought it was me that disgusted you at first," she said slowly. "Then I realized: you can't handle anyone caring about you. *Dis*may, *dis*gust, *dis*tress. So you pushed me away, and you, you poor bastard, don't even know what you're missing." She smiled seductively, licked her lips and caught the lower one between her teeth in a parody of a courtesan's gesture.

From her left eye one tear launched and lazily slid down her cheek.

Tietjen took a step toward Barbara. Her smiled ripened. Her hand came up and her fingers combed the hair back from her forehead, a kind of gesture he had never seen McGrath make, like something from an old video.

"Jesus," Tietjen murmured. Whose gesture was it? It was not Barbara smiling; the gestures and the words were not hers. All that he saw of her was in the expression of her left eye, the one the tear had fallen from, as if everything that was Barbara was trapped inside her, being run by someone else. By the kid, Jit, Tietjen thought. But why? How?

Barbara's body took an awkward step, moving like something out of an old horror movie, with the stiff, hanging gait of Frankenstein's monster. "Come on, John," Barbara's voice said. "Live a little. It'll be better than my dreams. . . ." With one hand she toyed with the buttons on her shirt; the other rubbed open-palmed along her thigh. The whole thing was a parody of an old porn seduction. What was horrifying about it, what made Tietjen frightened and achingly sick, was that *it was not Barbara*. Barbara was trapped inside somewhere, acting under force. God knew where Jit had found the fantasies she was acting out—whether they were her own or someone else's. If they were Barbara's fantasies—no one should be stripped this way and exposed against her will to even the most sympathetic audience. If the fantasy was someone else's, no one should be forced to be a vessel, a vehicle for another person's dreams.

Another tear dropped from Barbara's eye. Tietjen thought he saw entreaty there, anger and despair. Barbara's body stepped closer; the right hand came up and wrapped loosely around the nape of his neck; the left hand stroked her own breast, then moved to run across Tietjen's chest.

"Come on, John. You know what I want, don't you? You're not afraid to give me what I want, are you?" Tietjen took a step backward. Her smile broadened and another tear welled in her eye.

Tietjen's hand closed into a fist. With all the strength he had, he hit her.

1

THE Man took the Old Woman and carried her away. Jit scrambled to his feet atop the big stone head, howling. The Man did not stop and that only made Jit angrier. Tee-jin was gone, running into the black hallway while Jit stood on the stone head, screaming. "Jit get her," he screamed after. "Old Woman awake, Jit get her again."

His voice echoed, grew smaller, weaker, as it bounced down the halls. Jit's rage changed, for a moment he simply hated the walls and floors and stone of this place. With all Jit's power it still felt dangerous—too many walls, too many places to be cornered. The memory of being caught teased at him: "Whose little boy are you?" Panic fluttered in Jit's stomach. "I Jit!" he yelled loudly. His name made a hard echo through the hall. "Jit kill Gable! Jit do *things*." That felt better. But he had to think.

The Man had run away. Jit made a face of disgust: the Man he had seen in his head, in the Old Woman's dreams, had been big, powerful. Wise. The man who had crept through Jit's shadow men in the Park, who had groped his way to the Old Woman, was *small*. The shadow-men had not stopped Tee-jin; he had found the Old Woman . . . but the keeping-going, the finding had been *small*. Jit had wanted to see the Man's power. Disappointment stung him, and Jit wanted to show Tee-jin how nothing he was, making him cry before Jit's power.

The big stone head grinned at Jit in the thin orange light. Jit wanted to be gone from this place. He reached out for Tee-jin's voice, and the Old Woman's; they were somewhere inside, in the dark. Outside, the sun was coming up; Jit felt the sun reaching to him. The Man wanted to leave too. Jit imagined the Man on the big steps of this place, running away. Saw him looking up, scared. *Scared as big as the Park,* Jit thought. *Scared as big as the city.* What would scare the Man that big? Gable had, but Jit did not want Gable or Gable's people. Something else. Fierce. Cold as stone. Jit remembered the stone lions he had sent to help Tee-jin and his people in the battle with Gable. He could bring the lions again. And other things, ugly stone men with wings, bears and snakes and elephants. All the stone animals in the city, come not to help Tee-jin this time, but to make him scared. They would bow to Jit, show Tee-jin Jit's power. Jit reached out through the city, reaching for stone, for iron and brass. He felt the creatures rising up, turning toward the museum. Then, as he reached, Jit found something new. Close to his own old home, the tunnel in the park, they were carved from stone, huge and beautiful and terrifying, but broken, buried deep in the earth. Jit would make them whole and strong. Tee-jin would be afraid.

Jit smiled, slid down from the stone head, and crouched in the darkness working.

McGrath stirred in Tietjen's arms. He had hit her, then caught her as she fell, and sat holding her, wondering who would wake up with him, Barbara or her dreadful parody. His hand stung like hell, and he thought he saw a bruise purpling along her jaw.

Barbara moved again. "He's gone," she said. Her eyes were closed and her head was tilted to one side, but her voice sounded normal.

"He's left the museum?"

"No." Her voice was sharp. "He's gone from *me.* Thank you." Barbara opened her eyes and turned to look at him; she touched her jaw lightly with one finger. Her tone was matter-of-fact. "Thanks, John. It was—pretty unbearable being trapped in here, watching what I was doing. I couldn't stop, couldn't change a damned thing. He went rattling around in my head like someone pawing through my underwear drawer." Her carefully neutral tone failed her. "He probably knows everything I know. All about the Store, and our defenses, and—"

Tietjen touched her hand. "Barbara, do you think anyone who can move into your head and take over needs to worry about the defenses at the Store? Go easy. It wasn't your fault."

"Wasn't it? If I hadn't been so angry, maybe he couldn't have got into my head. Shit, John." Barbara's voice trembled. "You have no idea how horrible it was."

Tietjen thought of the dreams he'd had. Irene dying, the boys dying, his mother cursing him with her last breath. "You're right," he lied. "But it wasn't your fault. That I do know. Look, can you walk?"

Barbara cleared her throat and smiled. "He messed with my mind, not my legs."

"Okay. He hasn't come after us, and it's been a few hours. Let's get out of here now, before he comes up with a new idea."

"Okay," Barbara said, but reluctantly. "I don't want—I'm afraid—Jesus, John. I don't think I could bear it if he took me over again."

"I won't let him," Tietjen said. He was conscious of how stupid a promise that was, but Barbara seemed comforted by it. He had another thought. "Barbara, when he had you, was there—did you find out anything about *him*?"

"When the abyss was looking into me, was I able to look into the abyss?" Barbara stood up and paced back and forth a few times. The room they were in appeared to be a laboratory or workshop with benches, sinks and cupboards lining the walls; Barbara paced among high metal lab stools, her mouth twisted in concentration. "He hates *you*," she said. "I don't know why, exactly. And he's like—this is difficult to explain. It's as if he'd poured every thought and memory and idea that everyone he ever met had into his head, but he doesn't know how to make sense of them. He picks ideas that he likes and plays with them. The thorns outside are from Sleeping Beauty."

"What?"

"Someone, some memory someone had of the story Sleeping Beauty; the castle gets overgrown with thorns, and the prince has to cut his way in with his sword in order to kiss the sleeping princess. Talk about literal thinking." Barbara closed her eyes.

"I need a sword?" Tietjen asked.

"It wouldn't hurt. Though, come to think of it, you've already got into the castle and rescued the sleeper. It's not my favorite fairy tale."

Tietjen stood up and shook the stiffness out of his legs. "It's my favorite, *now.*" He smiled. "We're going to grab a sword and get the hell out of here and go home. Then we'll figure out what to do about the damned kid." He held out his hand to Barbara, tucked her arm through his own, and started bravely out into the hallway.

There was nothing there. No one. The light from the room behind them mingled with the sullen orange glow of the emergency lights. Ahead, Tietjen saw the cases of the African tribal exhibits. There were spears, and something that looked like a machete. Nothing else. The biting cold was gone, the halls were warm and humid. The elephant holograms in the African hall had shut off, leaving only a few sad-looking stuffed elephants at the center of the room. In the main lobby, sunlight poured through the lacy vines that covered the windows, making pools of light on the floor that were almost too bright to look at. Tietjen and Barbara threaded their way through the dappled light to the doorway, which stood open. It was completely blocked by the thick thorn vines.

"Sword?" Barbara asked.

"Damn, I forgot."

They began to search the lobby, finding nothing more useful than a pair of scissors at the information desk. "Wait," he told Barbara. Tietjen went back to the hall with the tribal displays. He had a feeling of cringing sacrilege as he kicked off one shoe and hammered at the glass of one of the display windows until it broke. He took a spear, machetes, another spear, a knife. "Sorry," he said to the plaster mannequin that stared at him. "Emergency." He went back to the lobby.

Even with both of them using machetes, it took a long time to hack through the vines; his shoulders began to ache and he could feel a new blister starting at the join of his palm and thumb. Barbara cut at the vines with small, savage chops, stopping only to push her white hair off her face. When they had made a hole in the latticework of vines large enough to climb through, they crawled as fast as they could, both of them haunted by the idea of being impaled on the fast-growing thorns. The vines grew as they pushed through them, grasping at them with the appearance of intent, but they got out, they got free, and stood in the middle of Central Park West, looking up at the museum and its veil of thorns.

Tietjen had his arm around Barbara's shoulder, his face thrown up to the midday sunlight. He felt her stiffen beside him. "Look," she whispered. He followed her gaze: the street at the south end of the museum was a clutter of stone. At first it looked like a huge mass of fallen rocks or construction debris. Then Tietjen realized there were shapes: lions, birds, gargoyles, griffins, most of them stone, a few made of metal, many of them cracked or damaged. All of them waiting.

"They helped us before," Barbara said quickly.

"Not this time. When we fought Gable, the kid was on our side. This time they're *his*. Barbara," Tietjen turned away from the sight of the stone creatures. "I want you to get back to the Store."

"Like hell," she said warmly. "Like bloody hell."

"Exactly," he said. "I don't have time to argue with you. Be a good soldier and get the hell out of here."

"No fucking way."

"Barbara—" he broke off. The ground under his feet shook. "Jesus, what now?"

He looked south and saw dinosaurs. There were three of them, made of stone, lumbering up the avenue. The smaller stone creatures parted to make way for their coming. Two of the dinosaurs were unfinished: their feet were clubbed in blocks of uncarved stone. All three were detailed with rich swoops of stone, serrated eye ridges, flared and chiseled jaws, dragonish and ornate like Victorian decorations grown huge. Across the gray stone of the dinosaurs ran cracks, as if they had been broken up and reassembled.

"Sweet Jesus," Tietjen said again. "What does he want?" He looked back at Barbara. "Go," he said again.

"Like hell," she said grimly.

The dinosaurs began to charge.

They couldn't run fast: Tietjen and Barbara were able to move back into the shelter of the vines before the dinosaurs were on them. But the monsters stood in a ring around the steps, holding the two humans there in the tangle of vines that grew more close and confining with each moment. The air was thick with steamy dust that sent Barbara into a coughing fit. *They're breathing,* Tietjen thought. *None of this can be happening.* Barbara coughed again, shuddering with spasms. The vines danced around her as she shook, and she backed into a close canopy of thorns. One scratched her deeply along her temple; the smell of blood seemed to madden one of the dinosaurs—the one that looked like a stegosaurus designed by William Morris. It brought its head down and began cropping angrily at the vines on the steps, breaking off pieces and chewing them between huge, flat stone teeth, pulling up another mouthful, exposing the steps and part of the Roosevelt statue. Another few mouthfuls and Barbara would be out of the thorns' shelter completely.

Barbara stood up, away from the vines, and struck at the stegosaurus with the machete she still held. The iron made a grating sound against the gray stone of the dinosaur's fluted nostrils and the machete blade snapped in two. The stegosaurus dropped back, shaking its head; Tietjen saw a few faint marks where the machete had scratched the stone.

The apatosaurus came closer, weaving its head back and forth on its long arched neck; its breath left a film of stone dust on Tietjen and the vines around him. This close, he could see the fissures that ran across its neck, small holes where whatever had repaired the statues had lost chunks of stone. Old stone, dry and brittle. Once cut, some stone becomes more brittle, more easily broken. I know stone, Tietjen thought. If it broke once, it will break again. I need a hammer, a chisel. He looked over at McGrath, shrunk back against the stairs as far as she could get. The stegosaurus was eating vines again, tearing at Barbara's cage of thorns, sniffing at her like a dog at a rabbit; the vines did not grow back. This time Barbara didn't try to strike at the dinosaur. She lay back on the stairs, eyes closed. Behind the first two dinosaurs, a third watched: a tyrannosaurus with the same elaborate style of carving, but less finished, as if someone had stopped halfway through.

"Stone, stone, stone," Tietjen hummed under his breath. "If it broke once, it will break again. Stone, stone, stone." He feinted to the left, as if he might leave the dense shelter of the vines. The long-necked dinosaur darted after him, moving clumsily so that its head scraped along the stairs striking sparks. The cloud of stone dust thickened and Tietjen sank back under the vines, trying not to cough. The apatosaurus took a dainty mouthful of vine and pulled, rearing back, until the stairs below Tietjen were laid bare.

"Fight stone with stone," he called out to Barbara. She didn't answer, but opened her eyes to look at him, one eyebrow raised. "I'm going to try something."

"What?" Barbara cried out. Her eyes were fearful. "Don't do anything, John. Stay there, we can wait them out."

"The hell we can. Sooner or later we're going to need food and water, and anyway, we can't stay on these steps too long or we won't be able to get out of the vines. It'll be okay. I know stone, okay? These guys don't have a chance." The bravado distracted him from how frightened he was. Gingerly—the vines had very nearly overgrown his hiding space—he slid out from their shelter and crouched on the uncovered stairs. The apatosaurus reared its head back like a snake. Tietjen kept his weight on the balls of his feet, rocking from side to side, watching the small stone head follow his movements. Can I do this? he wondered, calculating. And tried it.

Tietjen dodged right, toward Barbara, watching the head swoop down toward him. Then he threw himself left and down, hitting the stairs and rolling, shrugging off the pain as a stair edge bit his shoulder. The apatosaurus, caught off balance, furiously threw itself back in the direction Tietjen had gone, moving so hard that its head again hit the stairs. There was a huge grating noise, stone against stone, and the dinosaur's head snapped off of its neck.

But the thing didn't stop. Without its head it couldn't see Tietjen, who had started moving up the steps again, away from the street, but it kept moving, shambling toward the steps. One of its stone legs had not been finished, and the thing stumbled, trying to move the clubby block of stone up onto the stairs. It fell, headless neck swinging wildly, long tail lashing out. Tietjen stayed frozen where he was, praying that the thing would not hit him or land on Barbara. The apatosaurus's neck snapped twice; without that counterweight the long tail overbalanced the body, and the whole massive stone form teetered and fell on its side, motionless.

For a moment everything was silent. The sun glistened on flecks of mica in the dinosaur's broken head. The other dinosaurs—and the stone creatures in the distance—stood stone still, watching Tietjen.

"Barbara, it's time to move," Tietjen said very quietly. "Come on, honey, let's go." He put his hand out toward her very slowly, watching the other dinosaurs all the while. From the corner of his eye he saw her move, trying to get through the thorny vines.

"Shit. John, I'm stuck." Her voice was as quiet as his. "I need the knife."

He drew it very slowly from the back pocket he'd put it in. They were too far apart to hand it to her. "I'm going to throw it, okay?" She didn't like it; he could see from her face. "Sorry, Barbara. I don't want to distract your playmate up there." He took the knife by the blade and pitched it to her underhand. It landed within a foot of her hand—then the stegosaurus dropped its head and charged at him, and he dodged out of the way, farther up the stairs. Barbara was sawing at the thorns, and the motion drew the dinosaur's attention again. It turned ponderously back to her, shaking its head, the ornate plates on its spine rippling, clacking against each other. Again it lowered its head, snorting; dust plumed from its nostrils.

Barbara wasn't free yet; he had to do something. Tietjen grabbed a stone—the jaw of the apatosaurus, broken at his feet—twirled with it in his arms and let it fly toward the stega. The stone hit its side with a clack; half a dozen plates broke off the dinosaur's spine, and it lumbered backward. Barbara broke free of the vines and clambered over them, up the stairs.

"I need a hand," Tietjen called, and she darted down the stairs again, to his side. "Grab there," he said, pointing at one end of a segment of the apatosaurus's neck. Barbara bent, and the two of them struggled to lift the thing.

"I can't," she sputtered. "I can't."

"We have to," he said. "Come on."

Tietjen closed his eyes and focused on drawing strength from the ground under him. A lifetime ago he had breathed in the air of the city, filtered through the breath and sweat and dreams of millions of other people, and believed that that air was his strength. Now he closed his eyes and felt the rock of the city, the concrete beneath him, felt himself rooted into bedrock, and drew on that strength until he felt it flood him. "Come on," he said again, and heaved.

The stone came up in his hands, balanced against Barbara's bracing arms. He turned and swung the long narrow stone, heaving it once, twice, a third time before he let it sail in an arc toward the stegosaurus. It landed on the dinosaur's eye ridge, shattering the head.

"My God," Barbara breathed. "What did you do?"

Tietjen shook his head. "I don't know, exactly. I asked for help, and I got it."

The stegosaurus stood, frozen. Behind it, the third dinosaur, the tyrannosaurus, watched, its head bobbing slightly. Farther back, the ranks of stone animals watched too, unmoving, waiting to see what would happen next.

Tietjen moved his feet, just to see if he could. The connection, the rootedness into stone had seemed so real. The sun overhead cast strange shadows—of the thorn vines, of the dinosaurs. Tietjen's own shadow seemed too large and broad to be his.

"John?" Barbara stood beside him. "Is it over?"

"Wait," he said. The last dinosaur still waited for him, and the animals, and he had to make them stop. For a few moments before he had been a part of the stone; maybe he could use that. His back hurt, and his legs, and he didn't want to fight any more. "Wait for a second. I need to try something."

Tietjen planted his feet firmly on the granite of the steps, imagining roots that shot down through the blocks of stone, through the sidewalk and subway tunnels and into the bedrock that underlay the city. As he made the connection he imagined flowing through it, not drawing from it this time but sending out a message, a command. *Stop. Be what you are. Be stone, washed by rain, worn by sun and breeze, smoothed by human hands. Be what you are. Be stone, worn and broken, glittering in the hot sun. Be stone. Like me.* When he opened his eyes there was stillness, and Tietjen knew that he had been heard.

"What did you do?" Barbara asked again.

"I asked them to stop," he said quietly. "This isn't their fight. I told them to be stone."

Barbara blinked. "Is that all? You couldn't have said so an hour ago?"

He shook his head. "An hour ago I didn't know I was stone too."

They sat down together, close but not touching each other, grimy with sweat and stone dust. Tietjen felt tired with the kind of pitiless melting exhaustion that felt eternal, as if he had always been this tired and would always be this tired. "So now what?"

Barbara shook her head. "I don't know." Her face was paper-white and there were deep gray patches under her eyes. "John, can't we just go home? I don't want to fight any more. If I have to, I will, but—" Her voice went high and much softer. "I don't want him taking me again. I couldn't bear that again, it's like being trapped at the bottom of a well, doing things—" A quick sidelong look at Tietjen. "It's like being crazy and knowing you're crazy, not being able to help it. I couldn't. I'm sorry, John."

He wondered if she would let him put his arm around her and hold her. Tentatively he reached out and took her hand. She did not flinch or pull away. "I wouldn't ask it of you, Barbara. It's me he wants."

"How do you know?"

"How do I know anything? How did I talk to the stone? I don't think I can beat him, Barbara. But it's me he wants, and I can give him that. Jesus, look what he did to the city, what he did to the monsters, what he tried to do to you. I wanted to lead a fucking crusade to make New York well again, and it looks like all I did was to get some people killed, almost get you killed. He didn't want you, or Ketch, or Bobby, it was always me. I don't know why, but I can stop it now. I'm going to. You go home."

He turned his head and called out: "Okay. I'll come. Just stop, after that. Just stop." He tried to get to his feet but Barbara held him down, both arms around his shoulders.

"*No*. Even if he could hear you—what good would it do? He gets you and he . . . does whatever he does with you. Then you're gone and what's left? Who else is going to motivate people at the Store? When he decides to come after the rest of us, we won't even have you there. Allan's dead, Bobby's no damned use, and don't gloss over that, Bobby's out of it and you know it. You can't leave us."

"It's me he wants. He won't fight the rest of you. It'll be the end of it. If we keep fighting there'll never be an end. I know it." He put his own arms around her shoulders and drew her close so that her head rested on his shoulder. He let himself feel the pressure and shape of her body against his own, her breasts, the muscles in her shoulders and arms, the sweat that rimed her skin and mingled with his. He felt a stab of desire and familiarity, as if they had been lovers for years and her body was territory known and beloved. She held him tightly, trying to keep him with her. After a few minutes the desire passed, and there was only the need to comfort and say goodbye. Tietjen began to talk to her as to a child, as he would have spoken to one of his sons. "It's up to me, Barbara. It's my job. You keep things running, keep rebuilding. You don't need me. You'd *like* to have me," he teased gently. "But you don't have to have me there. You were the one who knew how to get things done."

She would not be teased or soothed. "Please, John. Let's just go, maybe he'll forget it. He's only a kid."

"He's a kid who steals minds and destroys cities. I'm not going to sit around talking when I know what will work." He reached up and took Barbara's hand from his neck, rocked back onto his heels and stood up.

She looked away, turned back to him, rose less steadily to her feet, and fingered her bruised chin. "The only way to stop you would be to sock *you* in the jaw, I guess."

Tietjen nodded sadly. "Barbara." For a moment he looked down at her, memorizing her: white hair curling wildly, blue eyes fearful and desperate, her mouth pressed thin with fatigue and too many emotions, closed to keep crying shut away. "Barbara." He said her name as if it were a charm. "You've been my friend and companion and advisor, I don't even know how to say what you've been. I will always love you."

She looked down, embarrassed "I love you too. But that's not the point right now. John, don't do this," she added, dry hopelessness in her voice.

He didn't answer, only leaned forward and kissed McGrath very gently on the mouth. Then he stood up and helped her to her feet. "Go home now."

McGrath shook her head. "I'll wait, thanks." She settled back down on the steps, arms crossed as if she were holding something in, or together.

Tietjen turned and started down the stairs. He felt tired and a little giddy, light. He stepped through the stone rubble of the dinosaurs, heading for the lions and unicorns and gargoyles at the end of the block. He expected to be afraid but he just felt tired and empty, as if he had cried so much he had washed all feeling away.

The stone creatures were densely crowded together; it was hard to move through them. Sandstone, granite, brownstone forms bristled around him. He almost missed the boy's narrow, hawk-boned face among them. The kid sat astride a lion, leaning forward to watch Tietjen come. The long, unpleasantly pale face was tipped to one side, and the boy smiled, a satisfied, savage, weirdly innocent smile.

Go ahead, you monster. Take me and then stop it. Take me and have done with it.

Tietjen took a step forward, spread his hands and said, "Well? I'm here."

The boy smiled wider and said something, the words so garbled that Tietjen had no hope of understanding them. He only wished the kid would do it, kill him or hurt him or whatever he needed to do. Do it, before his own courage failed him. *Come on, kid,* he thought.

The boy smiled. The world was swallowed whole.

8

IT was not death, then. Not what he had expected. It was not nothingness, exactly: he still thought, still remembered. He knew that his favorite color was green, that he liked the smell of coffee wafting on cold winter air, could imagine the jounce and balance of riding the subway late at night. *I'm still here,* he thought.

There was nothing to see, not blackness or grayness—as if seeing didn't apply here. Yet he remembered seeing. He conjured up the image of his old block at sunset. Sitting on the stoop with Maia, drinking coffee from china cups—the cups were hers, she said they were easier to hold with her damaged hands—and watching children play on the sidewalk. The gold and pink of the fading sun lit the bare branches of a ginkgo tree and cast patches of light on the white brick of the upper stories of the school building across the street. There had been the smell of cooking from shanties along the block, and he and Maia had watched parents trying to gather in their children for supper. Maia, her wiry gray hair moving in the breeze, had laughed at the children, her dark, seamed face alight with amusement as she told him all the ways those children had of outwitting their parents. When he asked how she knew kids so well, Maia laughed again and said, "That'd be tellin', now, wouldn't it?"

And she had wings.

Tietjen tried to rearrange the memory to fit the truth: Maia had got her wings in the disaster; on the fall day he was remembering, she had been as normal as himself. Knowing that did not change the image: he remembered Maia with her delicate leathery wings, as if they had become too much a part of her to be left behind by memory.

Tietjen loved the memory. It warmed him and he wanted to stay there—certainly it was better than the nothing. If this was what sur-render to Jit was like—forever sitting with Maia, drinking coffee in autumn sunset—he was all for it. For a brief moment he remem-bered something else: the sight of Maia's body, broken and crumpled on the marble floor at Grand Central, her delicate wings torn, her face a bloody mask.

"Now, John, you don't want to be thinking like that," her voice remonstrated. "Come back into the sunlight." And he did, smiling at Maia, relaxing against the stone of the stairway he sat on.

A flock of kids ran past them down the street, the last of them a tall, skinny kid with milk-white skin who stopped, reeled around, pointed at Tietjen and said "No!" As he watched, the kid grew, like something out of a nightmare, until he was as tall as the brown-stones, his long-fingered white hand reaching out for Maia, gather-ing her up. She kept smiling, kept talking as she was lifted away, waving her teacup and sloshing coffee onto her clawed hands. The boy's hand held her as delicately as a butterfly at first. Then he closed his fingers, mangling her wings. Maia screamed. The hand closed on her legs; Tietjen could hear bones snapping.

"John!" she screamed.

Tietjen was on his feet, grabbing at the boy's monstrous arm, screaming himself: "Stop it! Stop it." The boy smiled his weird sav-age smile and closed his hand completely. Maia's arms and head dangled limply; a trickle of blood ran darkly down the kid's arm.

"Gone," the boy said. Tietjen wanted to close his eyes but after a long, horrible moment, the memory faded into grayness again.

He was in Irene's head, with her on the day the city fell. His hands—her hands—sorted through boys' socks, searching for a cer-tain feel that meant softness as well as long wear. She—he—frowned at the elderly woman who pushed past her to get to the girls' dresses, hating the old woman for pushing her, daring to touch her. Hating her for wearing an old, too-worn coat in a color Irene liked. Hating her for being old, which frightened Irene. He felt how tired Irene was, how much energy it took to be angry all the time, how much she needed the anger to keep herself safe. As she chose socks and looked through the piles of sweaters, Tietjen felt how much she loved and hated their sons, who reminded her with every breath how dangerous living was. She loved them with every breath she took—and knew that if anything happened to them it would destroy her. She could keep them in, away from danger—except when they were with their father—

The thought wasn't finished; the flood of anger at Tietjen stalled abruptly when the floor rippled under Irene's feet. Her stomach lurched with terror. She would die. No one would help her, no one would take care of her. Rage broke through again: *no one would take care of her.*

Irene used the rage to push herself through the crowd, hating all of them—not one of them cared about her, none of *them* would take care of her—pushing her way to the stairs and into the crowd that was making its way down, slowly. Tietjen, remembering it all, understood at last how he had failed Irene; the fact that no one, probably, could have taken care of her enough, didn't matter. *I should have taken care of you,* he thought now. *I will take care of you now.* It was his memory, after all. He could change it.

He imagined himself as the old woman to Irene's left. "You go first, dear." She waved Irene ahead of her. Irene looked at the woman with distrust, but moved ahead in the line. "Here, watch your step, miss," he said, speaking for a big maintenance man who took Irene's arm to steady her, then took his hand away at once. He smiled at her, and Irene twitched her lip at him in a sketch of a smile. "You just stick with us, we'll get you down safe," another man said, a thin man with a weedy mustache. The knot in Irene's stomach loosed slightly.

Then there was a tremendous clang and the stairs shook, rippled like the floor, almost tossing Irene over the banister. Tietjen's many hands reached out to steady her. The noise came again, the word NO said so loud it was almost unintelligible. *Tee-jin can't help!* The stairs shook again, and Irene lost her footing, started to slip down under the feet of the crowd.

The hell you say, Tietjen thought. First as one person, then another, he reached for Irene and tugged, pulling her back to her feet. It worked again. But we're five stories up—if the kid doesn't keep adding stories on. We could keep this battle up forever. Already he was tired. Tietjen settled in the body of the maintenance worker again, one hand on Irene's shoulder to steady her. Then he thought *down* again, as he had done with the dinosaurs and the stone lions; felt himself draw strength from the concrete, the steel, the foundation and bedrock beneath it, and give that strength to the stairs, holding them still while Irene and the people around her made it down to the street. He held them that way until he saw her out on the street, surrounded by the people who had helped her get down, smiling at them bewilderedly. Then Tietjen released the power, and the building began to buck and waver. Abruptly the memory ceased.

Tietjen was sightless again, with words ringing in his mind: *No good! She dead! They all dead!*

And Tietjen saw again: Ketch dying on the pavement before the Store; Allan Hochman's bloody body carried back from Grand Central; Mack, fur matted with blood, dying before he could reach the Store. And Chris and Davy, pressed against a door in the after-school room, crying, waiting for Daddy to come. They had died of smoke and suffocation, their cheeks pink with carbon-monoxide poisoning. Chris had taken Davy in his lap and told him stories of how Daddy would come, because Daddy wasn't afraid of anything, Daddy walked in Central Park where the knives were. But Daddy hadn't come, maybe because they were bad boys, because they weren't brave enough, because they didn't want to walk in the Park or play with the street children that lived near his house. Daddy hadn't come.

They all dead, Jit said again, with relish. *Man can't fix it.*

Tietjen was sick. The kid was right: he could not fix it, could not be where he had not been. It was all very well to imagine saving Irene, but he hadn't saved her. He couldn't save his sons. Or Ketch, or Allan or Mack or Maia.

But I saved Barbara, he remembered. Like a tonic, he imagined her tart voice: "You couldn't help them, but you can help other people—if you don't roll up in a ball and die. Snap out of it, John."

Tietjen imagined his sons curled by the door, and he opened the door and gathered them up and carried them out to the fresh air, away from fire and terror and loneliness, all the while telling them, "You're the best boys, you're brave and wonderful, and nothing terrible will happen to you because I love you and nothing you could ever do could change that—"

And the kid's voice, Jit's voice, broke up Tietjen's words and shattered the memory of his sons, and Tietjen was back in the nothing again, alone, unable to stop his mind spinning. "You lie! Tee-jin lie! Man lie!" The high voice echoed over itself like half-a-dozen voices all at once, garbled and furious, until they felt like physical blows. Had he had a body, Tietjen would have been crouched down, arms around his head, trying to ward off the beating: "You lie! You lie! You lie!"

How do I lie? What did I do to you? Tietjen wondered, through the cacophony. "Why are you so angry?" he thought at the boy. "What did I do?"

The boy's voice boomed out, "Tee-jin lie!" His voice was huge, as if he had again grown enormous. "Tee-jin lie!" Lied how, Tietjen wondered wildly. In the middle of his bewilderment something felt familiar, a tone or something, as if he had played this scene before. Then he realized what it was, and felt stupid that he hadn't known before: Jit sounded like one of his own kids, furious over some huge betrayal which had been the result of a moment's thoughtlessness, the different points of view of child and adult. Is that what this is about? Tietjen wondered. Have I hurt his feelings?

"I'm sorry that I made you angry," he said at last. He kept the boy's image in mind, but pretended he was talking to Davy, whose feelings had been as easily bruised as a ripe peach. "I didn't mean to, and so I don't exactly know what it is I did."

The boy roared. "Don't lie! Tee-jin hate Jit so Jit hate Tee-jin. Don't lie, *Man!*" And he filled Tietjen with the image of that autumn day on his street, filled him so there was no room for anything but the sight of Maia's crushed body in the fading golden light, and of Jit, four stories tall, standing over him. The boy laughed, his long face twisted as though he were crying, and he bent to sweep one hand along the crowded sidewalk, pushing people like dolls until they lay crumpled against cars and stairways, crushing the shanties that leaned against brownstones. "Don't lie!" He reached for Tietjen.

At the moment the long fingers touched him, Tietjen was shocked by memories, none of them his: of the floods and earthquakes and fires and explosions, the bleak gray dawn of the morning after the disaster, of Rockefeller Center and the Public Library collapsed in on themselves, of the dead everywhere, of Gable and his monsters. A holocaust of stone and flesh, and nothing to stop it, no one to stop it. Jit's hand closed around Tietjen, squeezing the memories into him, while he turned to swipe backhanded at the houses on the street, knocking out windows that rained glass onto the people below. Tietjen felt everything, more than anyone should feel:

their terror, the terror of the city as it fell, the rage of the survivors, the ones who left. And one thing more, almost impossible to catch among the operatic emotions that flooded him.

Tietjen stopped struggling. Remembered that what was happening was all memory and fantasy, real and unreal. What he had sensed, under everything else, was the boy's fear. Jit was afraid.

"Stop now," Tietjen said firmly. He used the voice he had used when Chris threw a tantrum or Davy got overexcited. "Stop it." He drew on that old voice, and the new strength he had, the city in him speaking to the city in the boy, stone calling to stone. "Stop now, Jit." If the boy could change these dreams and memories, so could Tietjen. He thought himself as big as Jit, then larger, adult size to the boy's adolescent slightness. Tietjen put his hand on Jit's shoulder firmly. "Stop now. It's time to stop."

The kid turned to Tietjen, but thrashed wildly, hands balled into fists, feet kicking, doing damage to the streetscape, not to Tietjen. "Stop hurting people. I'm the one you want to hurt."

"*Jit kill you!*" the boy answered, striking more viciously.

Tietjen grabbed his hands and held them down. The boy struggled. Tietjen pulled him closer, until he was pinned against Tietjen's chest. The image of the street around them was broken up by pictures of Irene, dead, Chris and Davy, dead, Ketch and Mack and Maia, all dead. Anything to hurt Tietjen. He shook them off.

"You won't kill me, and I won't let you hurt anyone else," he said quietly. "Tell me what I did, Jit."

The boy kept struggling, making a high, keening noise through his nose, like an animal in a frenzy of panic. Tietjen held on to the image of holding the boy, centering himself, calling on the stone he had discovered in himself, calling to the stone he could feel in Jit. He had never been this kind of calm before.

Jit's words, when they came, were almost lost in the whining. "It was a accident." No broken lowspeak; the heartbroken sound of a very small child fearing the most awful consequences in the world. "Accident," he said again.

"Of course it was," Tietjen said quietly. *What?* What would he say to Davy? "Whatever it was, you wouldn't have done it on purpose, Jit. I know that. Tell me what happened and we can fix it."

Again the city all around them, quakes and fires and broken stone, death and fear. This time Tietjen saw Jit sleeping, curled up in a tunnel, light filtered through a grating, patterning his face and the pile of grimy blankets draped over him. He turned in his sleep, rolled from one side to the next as if he were dreaming. Then, he sat up, head back and eyes closed, hands at his side . . . and after a moment sank back again. In that moment Tietjen saw something flow from the boy, a flash of darkness, something indefinable. And he understood at last what the boy had done, and felt sick with horror.

The kid was trembling in his arms. Mindlessly, Tietjen began to stroke his shoulder, murmuring, "It wasn't your fault, it was an accident." All the time he was thinking, *I can't forgive this. No one could forgive this.* The boy's trembling turned to struggling again. Tietjen held on to him. *Tell me what it is and we can fix it,* he had said. And he had tried to fix it, and the boy had tried to hurt him. What wasn't he understanding?

"Jit, why are you so angry with me? Did you"—he thought of how to say it—"did you have that terrible dream that hurt the city because you were angry with me?"

The boy stilled in his arms, looked at Tietjen with tearless venom. One more memory played: himself, sitting in one of the windows at the Store on a dark night, looking out over the city. It was—it felt familiar, but it took Tietjen a few moments to remember. It was the night of the day they had won their fight with Gable's people. It was the night he had believed that all their battles were over. He felt the breeze again, saw the velvety blackness of the city, clusters of shadow hinting at size and mass; glitter of distant windows in the moonlight; a festive awning of stars, their light uncontested by the city. Remembered his own memories that night. Then remembered Jit's: *Gable had been wrong: Tietjen was the father.*

Tietjen saw it all: Jit had helped to win the battle with Gable, had given them gifts. Jit had loved *him. Now it begins,* he had thought. And he had filled himself with anger, with rage as fiery and feral as anything that Jit had ever felt—at the thing that had hurt the city. At Jit.

Tietjen wanted to laugh, it was so horrible. So much death and pain and fear—because he had cared so much for the city, and the boy had cared so much for him. What a sick, sad joke.

Jit broke away from Tietjen's grasp. "Tee-jin lied," he said again. "Tee-jin lying right now."

He was right, Tietjen thought hopelessly. He had lied, without knowing it. How could he forgive the boy for laying waste to New York? For killing Ketch? For creating the monsters who had killed Maia. For making Barbara his tool, stripping her of herself and using her to speak his outrage. You don't forgive things like that.

But Barbara had forgiven *him.* Or at least loved him enough to see past her hurt. And this kid, who was almost man-sized but thought and felt like a kid Davy's age—he was all hurts, all loneliness. I can't forgive him, Tietjen thought. Maybe that's not what he needs.

Quietly he spoke. "It's all right. You didn't know, and I understand that now. I'm sorry I hurt you; I hope you can forgive me. But it's over now, Jit. It's okay." He took the boy in his arms again and rocked slightly, feeling the motion comfort himself as much as the boy. Tietjen breathed deeply. "It's okay. Nothing you could do would keep me from loving you—not now that I know you. It's okay." He said the words over and over until they were nonsense on his tongue, and kept saying them still. The boy stopped moving, stopped trembling, seemed at last to have fallen deeply asleep, and still Tietjen repeated the words, listening to the truth of them that became clearer with each repetition.

The streetscape, the images of the blasted city, everything faded until there was only Tietjen and Jit, rocking together, silent and unseeing.

It was hot. Tietjen moved and felt his muscles work, not the gliding, frictionless motion of nowhere but the movement of reality. Something hot trickled down the back of his neck. He could smell his own sweat, and see the redness of sunlight through his eyelids. He opened his eyes.

He was standing among the stone animals. He could not tell how long he had been there—the sun was still high in the sky. A few feet away the boy lay on his side, curled up as if against the cold. Tietjen reached a hand out to feel the pale skin which was sweaty and cool. Shock, he thought distantly. Shock.

He turned and looked north. Barbara was standing there, watching. He waved at her. Waved again, when she was slow to move toward him.

"Are you okay?" she called when she got a little closer.

"Okay," he called. "You?"

She made a face at him; he wanted to laugh. "I'm peachy. Fine as frog hair. Wasn't he there?"

"What do you mean?"

"Wasn't the boy there?" she asked again. She was almost abreast of him, and followed his glance. Then she started, as if she'd suddenly seen a snake. "Jesus. What happened to him?"

Tietjen ignored the question for a moment. "How long have I been here?"

She blinked. "You've been standing there for about twenty minutes. I was afraid he'd—I don't know. Frozen you in place, or sucked your brains out or something. I couldn't walk away, but I was getting—nervous."

Tietjen put an arm out and around her shoulders. "I'm sorry." He knelt at Jit's side and felt the boy's skin. Still sweaty and cool. Pensively, Tietjen took off his shirt and draped it around the boy.

Barbara frowned. "That's sweet. What the hell happened? What's going on?"

"He tried to hurt me, but I was a little tough to swallow, I guess." Tietjen smiled. "I want to go home. Are you hungry? I'm hungry." From Central Park he thought he heard birdsong, and there was something else, a faint ringing he knew he should recognize.

Barbara looked at him, her mouth gaping theatrically. "You're a little tough to swallow? I guess so. You want to go home?"

Tietjen nodded. "I do. Don't you?"

"Ye-e-es. And what about him?"

Tietjen pulled the boy into his arms, awkwardly, and tried to stand. It had been easier in his head, but then, things usually are. "We bring him." The ringing came from the west, faintly. From over the Hudson, he realized. There are boats on the Hudson, going downriver. He's let us loose again; we're free.

"We bring this boy back to the Store?"

"To the Store."

"After what he's done?" Barbara asked.

Tietjen shook his head and shifted the kid's weight in his arms. "You don't know the half of it," he said. "Come on, let's go home."

It was time for the World to come back. Time to go home. They started back across the Park, empty of shadows.

ACKNOWLEDGMENTS

This book was a very long time in coming together, and many people helped it on its way: the Cambridge Science Fiction Workshop; the Clarion Writers Workshop, 1981; Elaine Rado, Steve Popkes, Melissa Ann Singer, M. Lucie Chin, Connor Cochran, Duncan Eagleson, Laura J. Mixon, Claire Eddy, Kij Johnson, Donald Keller, Shira Daemon, Patty Fuller, Stephanie Smith, Margaret Bishop, Barbara Krasner, Jane Brown, and Danny Caccavo, all of whom have read, suggested, raged, soothed, and otherwise been friends and critics when either or both were needed. Gratitude also to my online correspondents and my coworkers at Acclaim Comics, who encouraged me through the last stages of Terminal Book.

I got much needed assistance from the Maps Office of the New York City Parks Department, including (slightly bemused) help with Central Park tunnel maps; from the Library of the American Museum of Natural History with data on Benjamin Waterhouse Hawkins and his stone dinosaurs; from Sage Walker, who told me cool stuff about dead bodies and amputations; and from the staff of the Bookstore Cafe at Barnes and Noble's branch at 82nd and Broadway, who let me sit and finish the book when home and children became too distracting. Enormous gratitude goes also to my excellent—and very patient—editor, Patrick Nielsen Hayden, and his equally excellent wife, Teresa, without whom, etc., and to my friends and former coworkers at Tor, a place where people truly love puttin' out books.